THE SLAYING GAME

THE JOLVIX EPISODES

FAITH GARDNER

MIRROR
HOUSE
·PRESS·

Dedicated to my enemies,
may they Rest In Peace.

CHAPTER 1

THE GAME

One day, I'll make a perfect ghost.

I've spent my life learning how to haunt.

How to skulk crowded streets, to step into the shadows on instinct.

How to comb my hair and choose outfits in a way to render myself forgettable.

When I was young, I used to hate how unremarkable I am—a hair color that can't decide if it's blond or brown, eyes that could look blue, gray, or green depending on the light, no freckles, dimples, or cleft chin to distinguish me. But I've learned over time that's my strength.

I'm no leading player, I'm a supporting actor people see a hundred times in different roles with an uncanny wave of déjà vu but never learn their name.

Madison La Rosa has no idea what's coming.

I'm watching her through her back window right now.

She's on the only rat race she's ever known—her treadmill—ponytail swishing in rhythm as she watches her big-screen TV, a cooking show with meals far too caloric than she likely ever consumes.

Every now and then, she wipes the sweat from her forehead with the edge of her pink bedazzled workout shirt.

For all those Broadway dreams, she ended up a McHousewife in a McMansion outside of Fresno.

She looks older than her twenty-seven years when I zoom in to examine her face. It's expressionless.

Her husband is out of town most weeks so she spends her evenings alone, scrolling her phone while the TV blares in the background and she drains a bottle of wine. I've seen her cry, late nights up in her bedroom when her curtains are open and her husband isn't home.

I wish you could see it—you deserve to see such a sight, after what she did to you.

The delivery truck just pulled up to Madison's house, right on cue.

Madison must be a shopaholic because that truck rolls up every night and it's always the same: *ding-dong*, Madison flicks the blinds to peer out the window, waits until the driver pulls his truck back into the street, then flounces out to retrieve her package from her heart-shaped doormat.

Tonight, though, when the driver goes whistling back to his truck, I emerge from behind the oak tree to cross their expansive lawn.

I crouch on her porch beside the mailbox.

As soon as I see her shape in the opaque window on her front door and the doorknob turns, I spring to my feet and lunge like a hungry wildcat, push her back inside.

She splats backward on her wood floor with a yelp, recoiling, eyes shining with terror.

I close the door behind us and lock it with a *snick*.

I point the gun down at her like someone in a movie.

It feels good to imagine I'm a leading player for a change.

"Don't scream," I say. "Do what I say and I won't shoot you."

She's panting, putting a hand over her own mouth as if she doesn't trust herself to follow directions. Her eyes are so wide they look like they could pop right out of her head.

I give her a second to calm down while I stand here near the hat rack and look around.

The place is spotless, which isn't shocking since I've seen the maid service that comes Tuesdays and Fridays. Furniture so forgettable and colorless it looks staged.

The living room's got picture windows that I've been looking through for the past month, but the space looks different now that I've stepped inside it.

Real for the first time.

Warm, cozy, upscale—though the deer head above the fireplace isn't really to my taste.

"Get up," I tell Madison.

She scrambles to her feet, manicured hands visibly shaking.

She doesn't recognize my voice. Of course she doesn't.

I was never a talker and she was never one to listen.

I dig the gun under her chin and gesture for her to start up the carpeted stairs, which she does, slowly, rigidly, turning as if she's made of glass to glance behind me after every step.

"What is that on your face?" she whispers.

"Eyes ahead," I say.

She snaps her attention forward and we pause at the landing, the hallway lined with wedding photos and nothing else, confirming what I've suspected: this here's a woman who peaked at twenty-three.

I point the gun toward her bedroom, where the blinds are drawn and the lights are off. A king-sized bed, a vanity, a dresser. She leads the way there, sobbing, "Please don't hurt me."

"I'm not going to hurt you," I tell her.

And I'm not lying.

I tell her to turn around and I duct-tape her wrists behind her, duct-tape her feet together at the ankles, too.

"What do you want?" she asks. "Money? I—I can get you money, whatever you want. Take whatever you want, I won't tell anyone."

"Take a seat on the bed," I tell her.

Her gaze is locked on the gun. "What are you going to do to me?" she whispers.

"I'm not going to do anything," I tell her. "You're in control."

"But—I'm—" she sputters. "I don't understand."

With my right hand, I keep the gun on her. With my left hand, I open my backpack and pull out the VixSpex— a black, shiny virtual reality headset with a special attachment on the side where a gun fits. I hold it up. She squints at it.

"What—what *is* that?" she asks, a wave of curiosity

watering down her fear for just a second, until she notices the weapon attached. "Wait, is that a gun?"

I take a nice deep breath, savoring this moment, memorizing it for future replay.

Stepping forward, I slide the headset on her skull as Madison gasps.

A grin spreads behind my plastic mask, warm and slow as honey dripping.

"It's playtime," I say.

CHAPTER 2

LEELA

A shattered storefront window, four missing cats, and a trail of blood leading all the way down the block—this is not how anyone wants to start a workday.

The Berkeley street I work on is usually peaceful this early in the morning, ash trees and shadows, no traffic, maybe a few pedestrians, a bicyclist or two. Right now it's a gut-wrenching crime scene. I take off my sunglasses and squint at the horrific mess that spans a quarter of a city block.

"Jesus fucking Christ," I say.

"It was like this when I got here," my co-worker Esmerelda says in a quivering voice, shaking her thick head of curls. "I looked around the corners but I didn't see nothing, I—I don't know what to do."

I hold my purse tight, pulse racing as I take in the devastation. Someone could have been seriously injured. What if we'd been open? What if I'd been training volunteers? Horrific hypotheticals firework in my brain. I step closer to Esmerelda, glass crunching under the soles of my boots.

"I'm just thinking of the kitties, you know?" Esmerelda wipes her eyes with her talon nails. I'm in awe of how she gets anything done in life with nails like that. "I don't want anything to happen to them. Should I go look for them?"

"Right now, no, let's wait for the cops," I say. "Did café staff see anything?"

Esmerelda shakes her head. "They're around the corner."

"And they didn't hear a cinder block exploding a plate glass window next door?"

"You know how loud they listen to their music."

"Any other witnesses?"

"I don't think so. Meditation place is across the street, but they're not open mornings. Neither is Dry."

For the most part, this block's a ghost town of shuttered commercial buildings. It's an industrial neighborhood in Berkeley between downtown and the marina. The most exciting thing around here, besides our cat café/shelter of course, is a sober bar called "Dry."

I squint at the sidewalk, where blood's puddled on the ground in front of the open window, bright red, still wet. My stomach does a nasty somersault. If someone hurt our cats, I swear to God. "Man, I hope that's human blood."

Esmerelda gasps like I stuck her with a tiny knife.

"I'm sure it's human," I assure her. I follow the trail a few steps. Down the sidewalk, there's a rainy splatter that peters to a drizzle at the corner and then disappears completely, right where the loading zone is.

"I wonder if they jumped in a car there," I say. "Oh! Cops."

A cruiser pulls up and Esmerelda stands closer to me. "You seem so calm. I'm about to flip out."

"I'm just good at faking it." I wave down the two police officers taking their sweet time as they strut up the side-walk. "Hi there. Leela Crowe, Volunteer Coordinator at Feline Better. Thanks for arriving so quickly. From what I've gathered, the suspect hurled a cinder block through the window about—" I take a quick peek at my phone. "—ten, fifteen minutes ago. Four cats that reside in the Meow Meow Lounge are missing. There's this trail of blood—" I point to the ground. "—leading up there, to the corner, where it stops in the loading zone. Unfortunately, doesn't seem like there were any witnesses. Our café staff are around the corner and don't have visibility into the cat shelter. They didn't hear anything either, according to our Operations Manager Esmerelda Hernandez here. Nothing was taken. The motive's unclear."

Both cops are female, thirtysomething I'd guess. One has pocked skin and big doe eyes, the other has glowing skin and beady pug eyes, and both share identically jaded Mona Lisa expressions. Doe Eyes pulls out a pad and starts asking questions and taking notes. Her partner paces the sidewalk, following the blood, and then disappears behind the corner.

After we give our statements, they do a search through the neighborhood. We step over the window shards and inside the Meow Meow Lounge, where broken glass glitters like crushed ice on the cat beds, cat toys, cat dishes, litter boxes. That's going to be hell to clean up later. No sign of anyone, no cats left inside. Luckily most of the cats sleep in the back rooms and are all oblivious to this mess. The cops ask about employees or volunteers who might have done this, but I shake my head.

"We're a non-profit cat café and cat rescue org. It's not like we make a lot of enemies."

"It could be personal," Doe Eyes says, pointing at Esmerelda and me with her pen. "Anyone who might be targeting you?"

"I'm a happily married woman of twenty-five years," Esmerelda says, as if that answers the question.

That old familiar *oh shit* feeling creeps in. I hadn't even entertained the idea that this could be someone after me specifically. I've been living a boring, low-profile life for a solid year now. There are no fresh vendettas out there with my name on them.

There is no such thing as the Leela Curse. Bad things happen to everyone. I whisper these things internally, my private mantra.

"I don't think it's personal," I tell the cops.

"Could be completely random," Doe Eyes says.

Her partner nods. "We've had a few car break-ins in this neighborhood; nothing taken, just windows smashed."

"We'll be following up with you soon," Doe Eyes promises.

"This place looks like a lot of fun," her partner tells us, smiling at the cat paintings on the walls. To Esmerelda, she says, "Love the shirt."

"I made it myself," Esmerelda sniffles.

Esmerelda's wearing one of her favorite airbrushed

creations featuring Jesus surrounded by lambs but instead of lambs, it's kittens. She's not wearing it ironically either.

The cops thank us and head out. When they're gone, Esmerelda and I turn to each other.

"Mugsy needs his medication," she finally says. "And Ethel's ear drops—"

I'm not a hugger, but if there's a hugger in need, I can make the sacrifice. I put my arms around Esmerelda and she hugs me back, shuddering with emotion. She's probably eight inches shorter than me and she smells like cheap hairspray. I pat her back awkwardly. Is that what people do when they embrace? I forget.

"It's going to be okay," I say. "The cats in the other rooms are all fine. We'll call and get the window fixed and the blood cleaned up."

"The kitties ..."

"They're probably hiding somewhere nearby. I'll take a few walks today, see what I can find." I pull away from her. "Your mascara's smeared on that side."

Esmerelda wipes under her eyes and makes it worse.

"I need coffee," I say. "All this and I haven't even had caffeine yet today."

"The new volunteers are coming for orientation at one," she reminds me.

"Damn," I mutter, taking out my phone. Imagine a set of bright-eyed cat lovers showing up to this shitshow. "I'll have to move it to next week."

Across the street, a local news van pulls up with a crane on it and everything. Look at that—sharks smelled the blood in the water. I sigh. Guess I'm not getting my coffee for a while.

Hands on hips, I wait for the reporter to emerge from the van and think through the outcomes of media coverage. After about five seconds, I decide that it will work solely in our favor. The audience will eat this up like buttered popcorn—a vandalized cat shelter, missing cats, suspect at large.

My prediction? This will be the best fundraising month this organization's ever seen.

CHAPTER 3

A little over twenty-four hours later and I've proven myself right.

"Leela," my boss Daisy says as she refreshes the donation page on her computer for the hundredth time this afternoon. "This is *incredible*. Almost two thousand dollars in a *single day*."

Daisy has an earnestness paired with a soothing voice and a manner of speaking that reminds me of charity commercials. *For the price of a cup of coffee a day, you could save a kitten's life ...*

A room away, the Mr. Window people are replacing the storefront. We found the four missing cats yesterday and paid a crew to power wash the blood off the sidewalk this morning. By evening, no one will ever be able to tell we had a smash job. Good as new, with two thousand extra bucks in our account and two dozen people calling and wanting to adopt our cats. It's been a day and a half.

"Thanks," I say from the desk behind her. This is how

we work—back-to-back in a closet-sized room crowded with cat pictures all over the walls.

Daisy acts so surprised about the news clip, but as executive director of Feline Better, she was the one who hired me. She knows my resume. I guess she's only seen me recruiting our "Feline Support Specialists" and instructing people on how to scoop litter boxes. Until yesterday, I almost forgot I had it in me too. But truth is, I know a lot more about public relations than I do about coordinating volunteers at a cat shelter. For two years, I worked in PR for Jolvix's Virtual Reality sector. Before that, it was at the suicide prevention nonprofit Keep Going in DC.

Feline Better specializes in "hard to place" cats—seniors, kitties with health or behavioral issues, cats who've been abandoned, neglected, or mistreated. The space is divided up into two sections. There's the Meow Meow Lounge out front, where our most adoptable cats hang out on display, facing the street. Then there's the back, where we have ten rooms with glass doors for other cats fitted with cat furniture, cat toys, food, and litter boxes. This is where the cats get restoration and relaxation and the nurturing environment they need before moving to the Meow Meow Lounge. This back area's where our two offices are as well.

When I first got this job last year, it was an absolute dream. I made the leap from corporate hell and even though I make less than a third of what I did before, it's well worth it. You can't put a price on sanity. I'd take a day with a busted window, spilled blood, and escaped animals over a day of whatever PR disaster is going down at Jolvix, hands down.

"Just fabulous," Daisy is murmuring, watching the news clip of me that she shared on social media. "Did you have media training?"

"I *led* media trainings," I say as I work on the volunteer calendar on my computer and attempt to tune out the sound of my own voice.

"You are so articulate. And telegenic."

"Thanks."

The phone rings—it's been ringing a lot more since yesterday. A couple reporters, a few people interested in large-scale donations, and lots of folks asking about volunteering after seeing us in the news.

"Feline Better, Daisy speaking." Pause. "May I ask who's calling?" Pause. "Sure, hold on one second."

I hear her chair swivel. Daisy taps me on the shoulder. I turn around and she has the phone in hand. Daisy's always dressed like she's cosplaying a 1960s fashionista—flower power dress, white lipstick, big fake eyelashes. I do admire that she puts that much effort into how she looks when she works mainly with cats.

"For you," she whispers.

"Who is it?" I whisper back.

"Someone named Teddy."

She might as well have kicked me in the stomach with her go-go boot. Ugh. Of all people, of all days. I shake my head.

"You know what?" Daisy says into the phone. "She stepped out. Can I take a message?" She widens her eyes at me. "You say you want her cell number?"

"No!" I whisper-scream.

"I'm sorry, I can't give that out," Daisy says. "Just give me a message and she'll be calling you back, okay?"

She hangs up with a click.

"She will not be calling him back," I say.

She laughs at my comment and then adds, "Just FYI, no personal calls on the business line."

"Oh," I say, a little startled by her sudden turn in tone, that reminder of the hierarchy that divides us. "Right, sure."

"Who's Teddy?" she asks, brighter. "Business or pleasure?"

The correct answer is probably *both*, but I go with, "Neither."

Even the thought of him makes me feel like I'm about to break out in hives. I check the time.

"I think I'm going to head out." I slip on my beloved black faux fur milly coat. "We're all good on the training next week."

"Full day of appointments tomorrow," she reminds me.

"Yep. I'll be in early."

"Have a good night."

"You too. Don't stay too late. Need me to do anything for the kitties?"

"Can you check on Gus, make sure he ate his food?"

"Will do, boss."

CHAPTER 4

Me to video cameras: moth to flames. But I wasn't born this way. I was made.

I've never been able to shake the sense the world is watching. As a child, strangers complimented my appearance—my startlingly black hair that contrasts with my pale skin, my almond-shaped green eyes. I can't tell you how many times I've been described as "striking." It's a horrible thing to say, pretty privilege problem, but I became bored with these compliments by the time I hit grade school. I worked my ass off to be brainy instead. I read every book I could get my hands on and won the spelling bee and ran for student council. But nobody ever seemed to give a shit about the mind behind the face—first and foremost, my mother, my maker.

My mother, who will not answer to "mom" but only to her name "Shasta" and no that's not her real name, has constructed an entire identity around how she looks. This is a woman who has weekly blowouts, facials, and eyeliner tattooed on her eyelids because she can't stand looking at herself without makeup. A woman whose bills go unpaid but whose clothes are designer. A woman who got me a talent agent before I was old enough to walk. A woman whose lip fillers last longer than her wealthy boyfriends.

Thirty some odd years ago, prom queen Esther Dillard of Frankenmuth, Michigan packed up her suitcase decoupaged with pictures of Marilyn Monroe, boarded a bus to Hollywood on her eighteenth birthday, and never looked back. She changed her name to Shasta Crowe. She bleached her hair and teeth and got a nose job with wait-ressing tips. She went to audition after audition and didn't get any roles, so she worked as an extra.

On one of those projects, she met some bigshot on set —a mystery man who my mom insists is a famous actor and director—and he flirted with her and made glittering promises about helping her land a speaking part. Instead, he got her pregnant and paid her off when she signed an NDA.

Romantic, right? I was probably conceived on a casting couch. To this day, Shasta won't tell me who my father is. It used to bug me, but I stopped caring long ago.

After Shasta landed the unexpected role of single mom —finally, a leading role!—she pivoted her spotlight hunger to me. And oh, what a hot, blinding force that was. My childhood was peppered with getting pulled out of class for auditions and the occasional commercial. Mostly, as a child, it was just a drag, like how I'd imagine sick people feel about constant doctor appointments. "The camera loves you!" people said. But underneath all my people-pleasing and following orders, I suspected that the camera was a hunk of plastic that didn't love me and that the people behind it were exactly the same.

But Shasta wanted it so badly for me and she was always at her happiest when we were doing the audition thing. I tried to smile and go along with it and tell myself I liked it. Being born and raised in Hollywood, I wasn't the only kid I knew with a stage mom. But I always felt different than the other child actor types I sat in rooms with, waiting for casting directors to come out and say our names. And it was both the best and hardest thing I ever did when I confessed I wasn't going to pursue acting anymore as soon as I got my acceptance letter from UC Berkeley. Most parents would be delighted, right? To know that their daughter got a 4.2 GPA and was accepted to one of the finest public universities in the country. Well, Shasta Crowe is not most parents.

"You're throwing everything we worked for down the drain!" Shasta cried. We were at brunch and she was three peach bellinis deep. "Berkeley? Do they even have a Theater department?"

"I don't know. I'm majoring in English."

"Why does anyone need to major in English? You speak it just fine!"

"I don't want to be an actor," I told her. "I don't want to spend my life in rooms waiting to be told no."

"God dammit, Leela," she said, fanning herself with a drink menu. "What a waste."

Shasta cries at the drop of a wide-brimmed hat. Good thing she tattoos her makeup on because it would have been running down her face. But that day was the mark of

18

the beginning of my life, my real life, the one I wrote for myself.

Fast forward ten years and Shasta remains a rhinestone's throw from obsession when it comes to me. She's downsized her celebrity dreams, but she still has an alert set up for my name and whenever I'm mentioned anywhere online, she calls me. Which is why tonight, after I come home early from work at Feline Better, I get a video call from her. There's no mention of the cat café disaster, just pure joy in her expression. Shasta is a walking, talking exclamation point. I can see the reflection of the ring light behind her as she sits on the flowered sofa in her pink living room.

"The clip! I saw it! Did you see it?" She pauses, reads my face. "You haven't seen it?"

"I saw it," I say, dropping my purse on the floor and collapsing in my black velvet armchair. My cat Nosferatu jumps on my lap and I run fingers through his shiny black fur.

"Oh it was so nice to see you on screen again. My sweet girl."

I'm neither sweet nor a girl but I can't help the smile I crack at Shasta's gushy attention. "You're such a mom."

"You looked so gorgeous! Is that a new jacket?"

"Thanks. And no, same old jacket."

"Oh, we're pouting, are we? Why the poutfest?"

"I'm not pouting. This is just what my face looks like."

"Well, I'm so proud of you." Shasta shows me her arm, a close-up shot of her cockatoo. It has white feathers and beady eyes. The bird's name is Sugarkins and I've been told Sugarkins is my brother but I refuse to entertain this delusion. Shasta waves her hand on the arm where Sugarkins sits. "Sugarkins is proud, too."

The bird opens and closes its black claw. I don't return the wave.

"Did you see I shared the clip?" she goes on.

"No, not yet."

"I shared it as soon as it went up! It got a lot of likes."

"Cool."

"Did they catch who did it?"

"No."

"Don't you have cameras?"

"Not on the side where it happened. The cameras are where the café entrance is."

"Sounds like time you all upped your security!"

She's trying to be helpful. It comes from a good place. But Shasta loves to offer obvious solutions to problems she has no actual grasp of and it gets on my nerves. I change the subject and listen to her ramble on about a makeup line called TITE she's now selling and her new boyfriend Huey who's fifteen years younger than she is who works at the bird food store in Malibu. When it veers into TMI territory, as most conversations about her love life do, I tell her I need to get going. That frozen dinner's not going to make itself.

"I wish you had someone," she says, not taking the hint that I'm trying to wrap up the conversation. "You know? You deserve that."

"Mmm-hmm."

"It's time you stopped living in the past."

"Okay."

"You should download one of those dating apps. Soul Mate—you ever hear of that one?"

Never in a million years.

"Maybe," I say vaguely, taking off my boots and throwing them in a corner. "Listen, I've got to—"

"Huey has a nephew—"

"Please stop. Shasta, seriously, I need to eat or I'm going to pass out."

"Okay, okay. Have a good night, babydoll. Talk soon."

"Mmm-hmm."

The silence in my apartment is so delectable I close my eyes to savor it. Nosferatu purrs in my lap. As I pet him, I can't help but notice the disturbing parallels between my mother and me. She with her bird, me with my cat, she in her all-pink living room, me in my all-black living room. With an ache, I wonder if I'm doomed to end up alone like she is. Because while Shasta might have an everlasting parade of potential men, she's always, at the heart of it, alone.

My phone rings with an unknown number. I ignore it and go to my freezer where I have twenty of the same frozen meal—chicken, veggies, and rice—and throw one in the microwave. Watch it spin in the bright light. Next door, my neighbors are laughing through the wall. Ha ha ha, our lives are so great. I put on a heavy metal record to drown it out.

While I'm eating, my phone rings again with an unknown number. The sight of UNKNOWN there lighting up my screen gives me goosebumps. Yesterday morning's unexplained cinder block through the window has kept me on edge these past couple of days, though I've tried to ignore it. I stop chewing and finally decide to answer it.

"Hello?"

A long silence, long enough to seize me up.

"Hello?" I repeat.

"I didn't expect you to pick up," he finally says.

I put my fork down. That playful, soft voice—I would know Teddy anywhere. "How did you get my cell number?"

"Oh, it was easy. Just hired a private detective through Tasky. Took twenty-seven seconds." He clears his throat. "So what are you up to?"

"What am I up to," I repeat.

Unbelievable. Last time I saw this man, it was almost a year ago and he was following me out of the Jolvix building as I toted my box of belongings out the door for the last time. "I trusted you!" he screamed, as if trust isn't a bridge built both ways.

"Are you drunk?" I finally ask.

"Am—what? No. Are you?"

"Of course not."

"Why would you ask me that?"

"Because I'm trying to figure out why you're calling me all of a sudden when I thought you and I weren't really talking anymore." I sip my water. "I thought maybe this was a drink-and-dial situation."

"What are you listening to? Sounds like music you'd sacrifice goats to."

I get up and turn down the record player. "Teddy, why the fuck are you calling me?"

The silence is so long I wonder if I lost him.

"Hello?" I ask.

"Do you know what day it is?"

"Monday?" I glance at the phone. Monday, May 17. An invisible hand closes over my heart and squeezes tight. "Oh Teddy."

"I thought no matter where we were, what we were up to, we promised that we'd reach out to each other." His voice sounds strained. "Did you forget?"

I can't say the words, *I forgot,* even if they're true. A hot shame pours over me.

"Wow, Leela," he says.

I squeeze my eyes shut. "It's been a wild of couple days at work, okay?"

"Wild at the—what—kitten store? I'm sure, very high stress."

I both want to reach through the phone to give the asshole a hug and I want to hit him over the head with a shoe.

"Look … I'm sorry." I push the meal away and look at my left hand, at the place where once upon a time I wore a black diamond ring. That black diamond ring now lives in a box in my underwear drawer, too precious to ever see the light of day. "You want to—I don't know. Meet up soon?"

"If you think you can stand to see me," he says.

"Don't be a big baby. I just offered to see you, I wouldn't offer if I didn't want to."

"Five years," he says.

I shake my head and swallow a lump of pain big enough to choke me. "I'm sorry, Teddy."

"It feels like he was just right here. Doesn't it?"

"Yeah," I say, even though it's a lie. The pain's always fresh, but somehow the memory of Jack has lost its definition. Sometimes I find myself staring out a window trying to remember the exact sound of his laugh. When I think of that girl I was when Jack was alive—she's dead too. She's just as dead as Jack is.

It's guilt that makes me vaguely offer to meet up with Teddy for coffee sometime. But there's one more strange and selfish reason that I'll only admit to myself in the faintest of whispers: as much as Teddy drives me insane, sometimes when I see him, when I squint my eyes and look at his face, I can imagine what it would be like if Jack was still alive.

CHAPTER 5

Jack Lindmark had hungry blue eyes and an intense smile that came and went as quick as a flash of lightning.

The first time I met him I was a junior at UC Berkeley. I was late to my film noir seminar and squeezed into a desk next to him. He didn't seem to notice me—he was so engrossed in *The Big Sleep* that he took notes on a pad of paper with the dedication of a stenographer. But I sure as hell noticed him. I couldn't stop looking at his profile, his quiff hairstyle, his square framed glasses, the tattoo on his forearm of a skull on a stack of books. Immediately, even in that dim room, I wanted to peel back his layers and know what was inside of him.

Jack didn't look my way when the lights came on and class discussion started, though I kept hoping he might notice me there next to him in my lace tights and miniskirt. Even when I leaned over and whisper-asked if he had a pen I could borrow, he just shook his head without a glance. It wasn't until I raised my hand and opened my big fat mouth and started ranting about how the plot of the movie made no sense that his gaze finally stuck on me.

His hand shot up in the air.

"Hey, can I speak to her point?" Jack said. Our professor nodded and Jack went on. "It's true that the plot makes no sense. There's no clean ending. We still don't know who killed the chauffeur. I was reading that the Hollywood scriptwriters adapting the book—which included Faulkner, by the way—those writers called up Raymond Chandler himself to explain the ending and he couldn't do it. But ... who cares?" Jack looked straight at me, from less than two feet away, deadpan. "Seriously, who cares if the plot doesn't make sense? It's a movie about an investigation, not an outcome."

"Because plots matter," I said, getting heated at his pushback. "It's not satisfying to watch a movie about a mystery and have the denouement unresolved."

I threw that hundred-dollar word in there just to make my intelligence abundantly clear. I folded my arms to show him I came to class ready for debate.

"To each their own," Jack said, shrugging. "It's one of my favorite movies. The chemistry between Bogart and Bacall is pure magic."

I wanted to get the last word in, but the professor moved on to other people's opinions. I sat there the rest of the class going over what I'd said, wondering if I was too much. I've lived a lot of my life that way: speaking out like an unapologetic bitch and then spending hours replaying my bitch moments in my head uncertain whether I went too far.

It was a night class. After it was over I left the

building and went out front to the bike rack. I was bent down fiddling with the lock when suddenly I heard this voice behind me saying, "It's an interesting rabbit hole of film history when you start picking apart the *why* of the plot not making sense. Because a lot of it actually had to do with cuts they had to make to please production codes at the time, the Hayes code, you know the Hayes code?"

I turned my head. Jack was there, talking nonchalantly, picking up the class discussion from an hour ago and rolling with it as if no time had passed.

"Plus the filmmakers were working to capitalize on Bacall and Bogart's screen time together, since they were still riding the coattails of *To Have and Have Not*," he went on.

Ah. I saw it now. Underneath his careful hairstyle and bad-boy tattoos, he was nothing but an earnest nerd. I shot him a half-smile. "Class is over, bro."

"I know. I just think the plot holes are interesting when you contextualize them."

I stood up, pulling my bike out of the rack. "You're cute."

"I'm getting cuter every minute." He waited a beat. "That's a line from the movie."

What a dork.

"Yeah, I remember. I was there. Hey, walk me home."

"But you have a bike—"

"Walk me home," I said again.

There was nothing flirty about Jack. He had no game. But I saw a flicker cross his eyes, a little sexy squint as he sized me up. His eyes lingered good and long on the sight of my lips, the gloss I'd just put on. I wanted to smear it all over him.

He cleared his throat. "Sure," he said. "I'll walk you home."

Even though it was seventy degrees out in September, I got a shiver. We walked under the streetlamps and the ginkgo trees that cast skeleton-shadows across the plaza. He filled in his life details: he was from Los Gatos, which was just a couple hours south. He was an Interdisciplinary Studies major focusing on the intersection of twentieth century film and literature. Useless. Cute. He wanted to get his PhD and write books and teach. I could imagine him as a head-in-the-clouds professor someday with his shirt buttoned wrong. As we exchanged small talk, I had this déjà vu feeling, eerie but good, like I was starring in my own movie. I could feel how important this was—this was a scene that would never get cut. It was essential to the plot of my life. This was the night I met Jack Lindmark.

A week later we were lying in bed.

A month later we swapped *I love you*s.

A year later he slipped his black diamond ring on my finger.

A year after that he was dead.

CHAPTER 6

Friday night, I'm sitting in an Irish pub that smells like piss, questioning my life choices.

I sip my bitters and soda water and glance at my phone yet again, noting that Eve is almost ten minutes late. Ten minutes is all I'll do in life. Make me wait more than that and I'm gone—especially if I'm here doing your ass a favor. Right at ten minutes, I hear a voice calling, "Leela!" and see her there at the bar, a short little volcano of a woman with an explosion of wild red hair. She's carrying a frothing pint of beer and coming over to join me.

"You're such a vixen," she says loudly as she comes to the table. "My God. I hope people think we're dating."

Eve Alexopoulos is an acquaintance, a journalist I met when we were positioned against one another in a livestreamed debate at a tech conference stupidly called "What the Tech?" a little over a year ago. Eve played attack dog against Jolvix and I was there to play defense. It got heated. We ripped each other to shreds. The video clip was passed around in media stories about Jolvix and enjoyed its viral moment.

Anyone who watched the clip would think we hate each other's guts, but as soon as it was over, Eve and I were shaking hands and exchanging compliments backstage. And ever since, Eve has been pestering me to meet up with her. I really hope I didn't just walk into some excuse for a date. I can't read Eve, exactly. She's playful but I can't tell if she's flirty. She's been cryptic about why she wants to see me.

Eve slides into her seat and thunks her purse on the table. It's big enough to be an overnight bag. "What are you drinking?"

"Bitters and soda water."

"Don't have too much fun now."

"That's never a worry with me."

"So what happened over at Jolvix?" she asks with a wry smile, holding her pint glass up to her lips. I'd be a liar if I said that beer didn't look delicious. I've come to accept I'll wish I could have a drink every single day of my life. But three years sober now, I'm used to telling my id to shut up.

I heave a sigh and shake my head. "A lot," is all I say.

A raucous group in a dark corner near the pool table all laugh at once like a pack of human monkeys. They look to be three beers deep already. Eve and I share a mutual eyeroll and resume our conversation.

"A lot of what?" Eve asks.

Eve's charming, she is. She's droll and sharp and she's not bad to look at, either–wide bright eyes and wild red hair. If we'd met in another context, I could see us maybe making out or even being friends. But we're not friends. She's a writer with an agenda.

"I was just ready to get out," I say. "You know how PR work is. I burned out. I wanted to wear jeans and frown when I felt like it and not live my life in a perpetual state of urgency."

"Oh, I get that. I do. You and me both. Can't tell you how glad I am to be done with *Said* and being a slave to the news cycle."

I take a sip of my drink. "Did you write news? I thought you just had your column."

"I did at the end," she says. "Still. Fucking deadlines. Fucking metrics."

She emits an enormous burp, one so loud the pool players across the room applaud. I can't help but laugh.

"Excuse me," Eve says, sounding annoyed.

"So what are you working on now?" I ask, flipping the conversation around on her, wanting to get to the reason we're here.

"My book."

"Right. When's that coming out?"

"Well, it was slated to come out at the end of next year, but the publisher's pushing it back. My draft is due by the end of the summer. That's why I'm up here. I live up here now—did you know that?"

"Weren't you in LA?" I ask.

"I was. Now I'm up here."

"In Berkeley?"

"Cupertino."

"Isn't that like … I don't know. Some weird geographical form of Stockholm Syndrome? Moving into the belly of the beast that abused you?"

I've only met Eve in person once, at the debate. We didn't have a lot of schmoozing time. But as someone who worked PR at Jolvix, I know her story well. She bought a Sunray, a solar-powered car powered by Jolvix technology. An internet troll who she'd written about in a column ended up virtually hijacking her car and almost killing her. I thanked my lucky stars that I worked in the VR division and not the AI navigation division because that story was everywhere and Jolvix stock tanked for months afterward. That PR team probably had a collective aneurysm. Eve popped up on every news network to retell her horror story and fan the flames of public fear about automation in cars. I realize Eve lived through an experience so traumatizing I'll never understand it, but I also see a strange, vengeful delight in her eyes every time she talks about it. It's the event that defines her. She's obsessed. And now she moved to Cupertino, what—to be closer to the Jolvix campus?

Eve leans into the table and whispers, "I'm going to take those motherfuckers down."

"Good luck with that," I say, raising my eyebrows.

"Come on," Eve says, pulling back and smacking the table. "Cut the pokerface. You know you want to see me do it."

"No comment."

"A little birdie told me that there was some *friction* when you left."

"What else did your little birdie tell you?"

"That it had something to do with your boss."

I wonder who her source is. Someone in the office, obviously. Probably that dingbat Cher who was always hovering around Teddy's office.

"Your little birdie's full of shit." I pull my phone out, which is buzzing in my pocket. There's a notification that I have a message in the social media app Peeps. Who cares. I put my phone back and aim my attention at Eve again. "He was only part of the reason why I left. And no, I know you and everyone else is wondering—I wasn't fucking my boss."

"I saw that footage of what's-her-face clocking you in that restaurant."

Near the end of my tenure at Jolvix, a little over a year ago now, I was having lunch with Teddy when his then-fiancé—a state senator's daughter, Genesis McBride—"caught" us. She went on a tirade (that someone filmed) calling me a whore and then she punched me in the face. Her engagement ring cut my cheek open, which is why I have this fun star-shaped scar now. The cherry on top of the shit sundae is the fact the video went viral. Half a million views, fuck my life. The only satisfying thing to come out of that was seeing State Senator Tiger McBride's favorability rating tank for a little while. And my mom's delight about me going viral, despite the reason.

"I should have sued her," I muse.

"You should have. You'd be rolling in it."

The parade of *should haves* pass through my mind. This is just one of many things to haunt me on sleepless nights.

"So is that why you left?" Eve asks.

"Because of Genesis? Hell no."

Eve puts her hands on the table, makes them into fists. "Then why?"

I jiggle my leg under the table and consider how good it would feel to tell someone about the bullshit I put up with when I worked there. "Tell me more about your book," I say, pivoting the conversation again. "I thought you were writing a memoir."

"Ostensibly, yes. Publisher's Marketplace announced it as a memoir. I've been referring to it that way in interviews. But between us? And seriously, Leela, this has to stay between us." She leans in and lowers her voice. I can smell her: beer and fruity lip gloss. "I'm writing a book about Jolvix, about the horror stories involving their products and employees. You know, the unceasing reckless endangerment that company has been involved in over the years."

Bold. Jolvix is a litigious monster. If they even had a whiff of this book, they would find a way to snuff it out. My heartbeat picks up speed and I can't help but smile as I shake my head.

"See? You get it, don't you? You're all about it." Eve sits back and drinks her beer, looking victorious.

"They will destroy you."

"Come and get me, motherfuckers. After the shit I've been through? Bring it on."

"What … cases are you specifically writing about?" I ask.

"Well, let's see. We've got rogue companion bots, we've got the Maxines, we've got an unsolved murder and stolen equipment involving one of their archivists, we've got that guy who used his Jolvix clients in his deepfake scam, we've got the kids' self-driving cars—"

I close my eyes and shake my head. "Oh God."

"I could go on and on," Eve says. "And then my story, of course."

"What is your end goal?" I ask. "With the book?"

Eve shrugs. "The same goal I always have: to tell the truth."

I cross my arms. The pool players have left and we have this whole dark back room to ourselves. Up front, the place is sparkling with conversation and bumping with music.

"Tell me why you left Jolvix," Eve says. "I feel like you've got a story for me. I think I can take a guess as to what it is."

"What is it, then?"

"Something having to do with the killer VixSpex."

I don't answer her and try not to react, but I can't help the jolt of shock. How the hell does she know?

"You left immediately after that whole thing blew up," Eve says, as if she can read my mind. "Am I wrong?"

I sip my drink. "Look, I signed an NDA."

"I'll make you an anonymous source."

"It'll get tracked to me anyway."

"So it *was* the killer VixSpex."

"There isn't a story there," I tell her. "It was just a stupid move on Jolvix's part and it drove me to the edge." I get up. "Want to play pool?"

Eve takes a deep breath in. I can tell she's full of fire and wants to keep on this, but I don't. My fire died a long time ago. My Jolvix life is behind me now. I just want to live a quiet existence where I don't have to think about ulcer-inducing crap like killer VR goggles.

"Sure, we'll play a game of pool," Eve says, getting up. "I'll kick your ass, too."

"We'll see about that," I say as we head to the table.

Eve starts racking the balls and I chalk my stick. After she sets it up, she steps back and tells me, "I'm not done bothering you about this, you know. I live in the area now. And I'm relentless."

"You can break," I say, nodding toward the game.

"Nah," she says with a smile. "I want you to break."

I'll bet she does.

An hour and a long walk home later, I'm back in my apartment, greeted by a very dissatisfied cat who expects his dinner at 5:30 every evening on the dot.

"I'm sorry, bud," I say, heading straight for the wet food. "I know, I know."

While my furry beast devours his chicken and gravy, I plunk into my chair in the living room and look at my phone. I open Peeps to read the message I was notified about earlier, which is a disappointment: Shasta texted me a picture of Huey's nephew, who looks about fifteen years old. I don't dignify that with a response. I check my other inbox to clear out the spam and freeze when I see not spam at all but the name of a sender on a message from over a week ago—Madison La Rosa.

Dear Leela,

I'm so sorry about how I treated you in high school.

> I should never have locked you in that closet and made you miss the audition for Macbeth.
>
> I'm sorry. I hope you can forgive me.
>
> It's been a real pleasure,
>
> Madison

I stare at this message long and hard, as if it's a mirage, as if it might disappear.

"What the fuck?" I mutter.

High school is ancient history. I've grown up, been chewed up and spit back out again since then. I've been burned down and rebuilt since then. It was over ten years ago that I had this rivalry with Madison and I give zero shits about it at this point, even if the sound of her name still makes me itchy. And yes, she did that to me, that jealous prima donna. But I got her back aplenty. I keyed her car. When she got the part of Lady Macbeth and I didn't *because she locked me in a fucking closet*, I put pepper in her eyeshadow and hot sauce in her lipstick.

Why is she so suddenly sorry? Did she find God or something?

Madison's profile picture makes me flinch. That smile —she was always smiling, even when she was calling me a cunt. Her hair's blonder now. I click through some of the other photos. Wedding pictures. Honeymoon. Brunches. Running a 5K. Yep, she remained about as unremarkable as one would expect. The only thing she was ever good at as far as I could tell was acting and sabotage. I click to her wall to see recent posts, trying to figure out why she would reach out to me. All I see are a flood of posts from other people.

I'm so shocked to hear the news

I can't believe you're gone

Heaven gained another angel to sit at God's table

Madison, miss you and love you

I just don't understand, Maddy. We had just talked, you seemed fine, why?

My hand flies to my mouth. Holy shit.

Is Madison dead?

My skin wants to turn inside out. I was hungry, but now I just feel sick. I plug her name into a search engine and gasp when the obituary pops up in recent results.

Dead. She's fucking *dead*.

I look at the date of her death and compare it to the message in my inbox—same date. Scrolling through the messages on her wall again, no one says it, of course, but it reads like it was suicide. People are angry, people don't understand, and finally, someone posts a suicide prevention number and urges people to share it with loved ones.

Fuck.

I turn my phone off and lie my head back, eyes burning. It's crushing. I wish I had never checked that fucking spam inbox. I should have known, what the hell good ever comes from spam? I wish I had never seen that message she sent, I wish I had never known she died. Suicide. The word makes me hurt. The word itself is a black hole I cannot, will not let my mind fall down. There Madison was, struggling, at her rock bottom, and she was ... thinking about me? About *high school*? On her last day on earth? Was I the only person who got a message from her?

Was she trying to right her wrongs at the last minute? Did she leave a note? What method did she use? A gun, a noose?

A combination of alcohol and pills and a plastic bag tied over her head?

I want a drink so badly I could break a window. Instead, I clip my mini punching bag to the ceiling and I pummel it until my fists are pink and limbs are noodles and sweat runs down my face, beating that invisible destructive force back, beating it like it's a person, beating it like it's an entity that can ever be beaten.

CHAPTER 7

I haven't stayed in touch with many people from high school unless you count the occasional thumbs-upping of online photos "staying in touch." The only person I talk to semi-regularly is Ricky Rodriguez, who's still in Hollywood living in a ground floor unit in his mom's apartment building. Post-production might be his career, but gossip is his passion. Half the reason he went into an editing career was the proximity to celebrity so he can feel like he has the inside scoop. He's the shortest man I know but he's also a hottie and he knows it—glorious pompadour, perfect line of five o'clock shadow, a daring sense of fashion.

"I know why you're calling," he says in a singsongy voice when he picks up my video call. *"Ding dong, the witch is dead ..."*

Ricky was in crew in theater, usually painting sets. He and I were best friends during Madison's mission to destroy me. In fact, he convinced me to key her car for

revenge—always playing the part of the little adorable devil on my shoulder.

I put my sunglasses on and continue my stroll down the street, shade from the ash trees overhead speckling the sidewalk. "So you know," I say.

"Mmm-hmm," Ricky says.

"I'm in shock. I just saw last night."

"Oh, I've *heard* things."

"From who?"

"Maya, who heard it from Stefan."

Maya, who played every frumpy mom character in every high school play. Stefan, who was Madison's jock stepbrother. It doesn't matter. These people don't matter now. But I'm impressed that Ricky's got this level of intel —the man should start his own tabloid.

I spot an empty bus bench and plop down on it, eyeing the advertisement on the bus shelter asking voters to continue the Berkeley-wide ban on bots. Berkeley's led the national movement to keep robots out of police forces and city jobs, and after living in Cupertino and working at the Jolvix campus, I get it. It's part of the draw of Berkeley living, honestly. KEEP BERKELEY HUMAN, the flier says.

"Okay, so spill," I say to Ricky. "What happened?"

"What is there to say? She killed herself. Did you know she was living in *Fresno* and was married to a truck driver? I'd off myself too."

"Can we not joke about suicide?" I say, annoyed. "This hits close to home, Ricky."

"Shit," he says softly. "I'm sorry. I wasn't thinking."

"Details? I have five minutes before I have to get back to work."

All the fun has drained out of Ricky's expression and his eyes are shining with pity. God, I hate that pity-shine people get in their eyes when they remember Jack. "All I know is that she'd been spending a lot of time alone—she was isolated, I guess the move was pretty recent. But you know Madison. Are we surprised? I mean, we weren't even close to her and we knew how unhinged she was."

"How did it happen?"

"A gun."

"She blew her brains out?"

"I assume." He clears his throat. "Leelee, I know it's juicy, but why do you have that look on your face?"

"What look?"

"Like you're ... having *feelings*."

"Because I am."

"You didn't even like her. May I remind you, you hated her. Life's too short to mourn people you hate."

"She sent me a message right before she died," I tell him. "Saying how sorry she was."

His jaw drops. "What did it say?"

I describe it to him, paraphrasing, though I've probably read it enough times now that I have it memorized.

"I didn't get an apology," he says indignantly. "Remember how she used to call me Lil Dicky?"

Ricky's such an adorable narcissist. The compass of conversation always points back to him in the end.

"Oh mercy, I can hear bossypants is here and I can tell he's on a rampage," he whispers. "I've got to get back to work. Talk soon? I'm having dinner with Shasta tomorrow night, by the way."

"Give her a hug for me," I say. "Tell her to stop sending me photos of what's-his-face."

We hang up. I'm left staring at the air until a bus pulls up thinking I need a ride, but I wave it away apologetically and get up to walk back to work.

Ricky's information was scant. I don't know what I was looking for. But now I can't shake this horrid image of Madison with a gun to her head.

CHAPTER 8

The thought of Madison is relentless, a *drip-drip-drip* in the back of my mind as I cosplay a normal person and work my job this week. I lead a volunteer training cracking jokes that make our newbies laugh. I pet kitties and refill food bowls and work on updating the website's mission statement page. But she's there with me, this apologetic ghost whispering in my ear every now and then and giving me a chill in the full light of day. When I'm off work eating my frozen dinner and petting Nosferatu, I keep circling back to reread the message, to scan her obituary, to scour her Peeps page for any other information.

What am I expecting? She's dead. Door shut. Story over. I don't get why this is so personal, why it chokes me up. Then again, who am I kidding. It's bringing Jack right back up to the surface. It's blowing the cobwebs off that pain and making it fresh again.

Twice this weekend I find myself lingering outside a liquor store drooling at the neon glow of the OPEN sign with a bone-deep thirst. I can imagine the quieting burn of bourbon down my throat—that hushed, peaceful moment that follows and forces my brain to shut the fuck up for once. I go for a run. I hit the punching bag. Finally, I make myself attend a meeting even though I'm a loner who hates meetings. But it helps the itch pass, to sit with other itchy people a while.

Over the next week, my preoccupation with Madison's death fades a little bit as the novelty of the news wears off and real life drags on. Work has picked up—nothing like a cinder block through a front window to drum up interest in an organization. I have three dozen potential volunteers on the waiting list, which is a first. People have been walking in all week to inquire about it after local media coverage.

"Are you one of the cat ladies?" a short man with side-swept black hair asks as I open up shop this morning.

He startled me. I try not to let on, but on a quiet street this early in the morning, a man popping out of nowhere is enough to spike my blood pressure.

"Yeah ... but we're not open yet," I say. "Is this about adopting, or volunteering?"

"Neither," the man says.

The guy has a youthful look about him—round face, dewy skin—but intense bags under his eyes that make him look aged. He could be twenty or fifty, I can't tell.

"I work at Berkeley Jiu Jitsu across the street?" he says. "My name's Kelvin."

"Oh." I relax a little, give him a friendly smile. "Hey, I'm Leela. Nice to meet you."

"Did they ever figure out who broke your window?"

I shake my head.

"We had one of our windows broken a few weeks ago," he says. "We never found who did it, either. It happened in the back, near the dumpster."

"Sucks," I say. "Did they steal anything?"

"No. Just smashed the window and ran." He tosses his hair. "But I wanted to let you know we have cameras on the corner. It caught some of the break-in at your place. Should I ... do you want to see it?"

"Sure, that would be great," I say, surprised. I flip out my wallet, grab a business card and hand him one. "Would you be able to email it to me?"

"Yeah, definitely. The footage is grainy—our cameras aren't the best quality. But I don't know, maybe you'll see something there?"

"Thanks." I give him a wave and push the door open. "Have a good one."

Three furballs rub against my leg as soon as I step inside.

"Morning, kitties," I sing.

A few cats hop off their perches to come meow at me. I stoop to pet them and when I stand up, I can see Kelvin still standing there outside. He's staring into the spotless new display window with an eerily faraway expression, moving his lips. Goosebumps prickle my skin and I hold my breath until I realize he's staring at one of the cats in the cat tower.

At least, I think he is.

With an uneasy feeling in the pit of my stomach, I make my way to the back, flipping lights on in the office. I collapse into my office chair and drop my purse on the desk and hold my hand out into the air to confirm that yes, I'm shaking like someone who's had ten cups of coffee rather than zero. For a couple of minutes, I sit with my head in my hands and attempt to collect myself.

"Keep it together, Leela," I whisper.

I check my inbox and right at the top there's an email from asskickinkelvin with a file attached. The man moves quickly.

The footage is worse than grainy, choppy and black-and-white and low-res. I blow it up and watch the thirty-second clip about five times. A dark car—could be blue, black, gray, who knows. All I can tell from what I'm seeing is that it's a sedan, no idea what the model could be or how old it is. The car glides into view at a sharky pace and stops in the middle of the street. A slouched man with a hoodie over his head hurries out of the driver's side, opens his back door, and grabs a cinder block. You can tell he's struggling with how heavy it is. He goes to the window, swings it a couple times to get momentum, and lets go. As the window glass explodes, the guy falls down like a bumbling idiot and then gets up, holding his arm and turning this way and that. Even without much detail, there's obvious panic in his frantic movements.

"Oh, you hurt yourself, you fucking dumbass?" I ask the screen. "What the hell is wrong with you?"

At least that explains the blood. The guy then runs back to his car and speeds away.

I watch the footage again and it only makes me more irritated. Why? Why would someone do that? I'm muttering curse words when Daisy comes in looking like the little flower she is, holding a teapot with a cord wrapped around her arm like a bracelet.

"I got this for our office!" she says, smiling with pastel-pink lips. "It's electric."

"Cool, fun," I say as brightly as I can muster, which isn't too bright.

"What's wrong?" Daisy asks.

"Just watching footage that the martial arts guy sent of the incident."

Daisy continues staring at me, shedding her peacoat and hanging it on a wall hook shaped like a cat claw.

"The cinder block through the window?" I remind her.

"Oh—oh, right." She sits on her chair and finger-combs her pigtails. "Martial arts guy?"

"Catty corner to us."

"Can I see the footage?"

I show the short clip to Daisy, who just shakes her head. "I don't get it."

"Neither do I." I swivel my chair, contemplating the many cats on the wall. Cats in knitted hats. Cats in messes of unraveled toilet paper. A cat on an unidentified person's head. I love cats but sometimes I feel almost claustrophobic here—*clawstrophobic*? Everywhere I look, there are thousands of photogenic cats ready to pounce on me. "Is there any reason anyone would target us?"

"We're a cat shelter," Daisy says, turning to her computer.

No shit, Daisy. Daisy's one of those uncurious people who, in a worse mood, I might call boring. We work in silence most of the day. Sometimes she shows me a funny meme that I expel a *ha ha* at. Her style's the most exciting

dream on me, the audition parade, but theater was different. Theater was mine.

I would have appreciated a trigger warning on the second picture she ever posted, because it's Madison dressed as Lady Macbeth in a medieval velvet dress with bell sleeves. She's undeniably gorgeous, the kind of gorgeous I just want to wreck, hair twisted in a crown of braids atop her head, regal look in her round doll eyes. Really, she ended up being the perfect Lady Macbeth, right? In retrospect maybe the cold-hearted girl willing to lock someone in a closet to eliminate the competition is the proper choice for the part. *Look like the innocent flower/ But be the serpent under't.*

I don't dwell often, but being locked in that closet was one of the most terrifying things that ever happened to me.

Auditions were at three, right after the last bell dinged. The theater kids were gathered outside walking around in circles and mumbling their monologues aloud like a bunch of loveable nutjobs. Madison spotted me and waved me over to her with a smile. I should have been suspicious. Madison and I were like mirror images in some ways—both dark-haired, both drama queens, both juniors, and that made us resent each other. I had no idea she was that dangerous though, so like a stupid little mouse, I came right over to the serpent and said, "What's up?"

"How are you feeling about the audition?" she asked, concern shining in her dull blue eyes. My eyes were much brighter, a screaming green that demanded to be seen.

Hear what I'm saying? Even her eye color made me competitive.

"Pretty good." I kept my arms crossed, suspicious of her kindness. "You?"

"Same." She softened her voice. "Hey, can we talk somewhere privately real quick?"

Behind her, Brett—our theater teacher with the haircut of a poodle and the attitude of a drill sergeant— was clapping her hands and opening the back doors for students to file inside.

"Can it wait until after the audition?" I asked.

"It'll just take a minute." She walked down the hall past the band room and beckoned me toward a door I'd never seen open before. "I have an inside scoop about the play I *really* think you're going to want to hear before you audition today."

Reluctantly, I followed her. But a little teeny part of me was maybe not reluctant. A part of me thought, hey, maybe Madison's a considerate person underneath all the glares and the shit-talking she does. Maybe we could end up being friends. I followed her inside the small room with nothing inside it except for a hole in the tiled flooring that exposed the concrete underneath. It looked like it used to be a bathroom. We stepped inside together and then she put her finger in the air.

"Hold up a sec," she said, stepping back out.

I can remember exactly how her face looked, the sunlight in her hair, the shine of her toothy grin and the mean squint of her eyes. It was the last thing I saw before she closed the door in one cruel, swift second. The door with no knob on the inside. The door that locked from the outside. A pitch-black cell, a daytime midnight except for a single slit of light on the floor.

If I had my backpack on me, my phone on me, the prank maybe wouldn't have been so bad. I could have texted Ricky or someone else to come let me out. But both Madison and I had just gotten out of the sixth period advanced theater class and my backpack was still at my seat inside. She must have known that, must have seen my backpack still sitting in my usual back row seat. She saw it sitting there the whole hour and a half that the auditions dragged on and when she got up to leave and when everyone filed out of the classroom. She might have passed the closet one more time on her way to the parking lot before she drove away and left me there. Overnight.

Yes, I was there all fucking night.

It was cold, all tile and cement. My teeth chattered for hours, short sleeves in a meat locker, my sweatshirt abandoned with my backpack. The emotions ran the gamut. I started with disbelief, which melted into rage, which morphed into despair, and devolved eventually into a frozen, tearful terror that I would never get out. I lost my voice from screaming for hours, no one hearing me. I banged on the metal door until my fists throbbed. That tiny slit of light faded and faded until I couldn't make it out anymore and there was nothing but darkness. Finally, I let sleep take me—a sweet respite, a kind dose of death to rescue me from the nightmare of life for just a little while.

Like a prisoner in solitary confinement, I woke up in a puddle of my own cold piss. The razor-thin line of light was beginning to appear under the door again, signaling morning. I began another round of screaming and beating my fists on the door. After a short miserable eternity, a janitor opened the door gasping and whispering *Christ almighty* and I got up on wobbly legs. It was zero period, the hour before school, and I slunk down the hall shrinking from the sunshine like a vampire. I slipped into the theater building where another janitor was vacuuming the floor and grabbed my backpack from the back row and I walked out to my car in the parking lot and I drove home. When I walked through our apartment door, Shasta was on the phone to LAPD reporting me missing, her face puffy from crying.

It became this big deal, as it should have been. The school investigated the incident. Shasta threatened a lawsuit against Madison's parents. But the problem was, there were no witnesses at all, it was my word against Madison's. I guess Madison La Rosa deserved the best actress award she won at school that year because she swore up and down that I was lying and that she was never anywhere near the closet and the school administration believed her. In fact, most of the other students believed her—they couldn't fathom she was capable of doing something that cutthroat. Ricky was on my side. Shasta too. Some of the theater kids told me they believed me, making sure to do so privately, because now everyone feared Madison like the Lady MacBeth she was.

It's smothering to remember this. If I close my eyes, even here and now over ten years later, the black wall of my eyelids brings me back to that chilly concrete closet, that roomy coffin I was locked in. The dizzy panic of trying to breathe in nothing but my own expired air. A place with no doorknob, no escape. When I think of death, I think of that room.

And now Madison's in that room, isn't she?

Now Madison's there and she's never getting out.

"Leela? How's that handbook going?"

Daisy's chipper voice cuts through the deathly silence like the tweet of a bird. I turn around and see my flower-powered supervisor swiveled my way and looking over my shoulder at the picture of Madison. Daisy's got a perky, knowing smile on her lips. This right here is the in-person equivalent of a "friendly reminder" email—an easygoing, fun way to reproach someone for their shitty behavior. How dare I stray from the dire task of adding cat puns to the handbook.

"Going well," I say, closing the tab I had open. Good-bye, Madison. I click back on the handbook and as I refocus my attention to my tedious task, I can feel Daisy's watchful gaze lingering a good ten seconds to make sure I'm following the oh-so-important job at hand before she goes back to her computer.

Working for Teddy was its own pain in the ass and there was nothing I wanted more when I worked at Jolvix than to flee that dystopian nightmare job, but there are flashes when I miss it. Or not *it*, exactly.

When I miss him, I guess.

CHAPTER 10

THE GAME

The game is sacred. Ritualistic.

Slipping on this costume, the black pants, the black sweatshirt, the black shoes, the hug of the rubber mask on my face, the Bettie Page wig.

It's a travesty of imitation.

I look nothing like you, Leela.

But it's my own private joke with the universe—and hopefully one day, when I reveal myself, a private joke with you.

Lotus Windsong: a human sponge with a name like a gift shop that sells crystals and dreamcatchers. I heard you saying that once. It was hilarious, even if Jack didn't laugh.

Lotus was a sponge.

A sponge for attention, a sponge for drugs and alcohol, a sponge for anyone to do her work for her, write her papers, wash her dishes, pay her bills.

I would go further.

I would call her a human black hole.

That tangled hair. Those look-at-me eyes. The halter tops she wore without a bra and those long broomstick skirts that waved back and forth with her *va-va-voom* strut.

You'd be happy to know that she's quite unremarkable now.

She lives in Oakland and works at a law office and wears button-up shirts and pencil skirts.

Her hair is bobbed and coiled and she's plump and pale.

She's the kind of person you would meet and then forget her face by the time you've stepped past her.

I know her kind because I am her kind.

I follow her as she drives away from her office tonight in her sleek electric car.

Careful. I'm careful. I make sure to keep space between us.

I did the same last night though it wasn't right.

She ended up driving to someone else's house up in the hills. I turned around and went home and peeled off my costume.

But tonight she drives straight home through traffic, a straight line down Telegraph Avenue from the downtown skyscrapers to a stretch of fusion restaurants and wine bars.

Her apartment's on a side street, a flesh-colored ground floor unit with a maple tree out front. It's in a hip neighborhood and even that unexceptional apartment must cost a pretty fortune.

The weather swelters and colors the evening in lazy

.dges. The sun blazes extra orange, some salsa music wafts in the breeze.

I crank my AC and study her front window for a sign of life behind the blinds and wait for the sun to go all the way down.

I can see her balcony from here and grin when Lotus opens the sliding glass door.

Yes. That's it.

Let's make tonight's entrance an easy one, let's make it a sneak attack.

I didn't like what I had to do with Madison.

Front doors are risky.

I kill time while the sun sets by looking you up on my phone and going through your pictures again.

You don't post often. Just an occasional selfie or cute shots of cats at your shelter.

I watch the news clip again, zooming in on your face, and—it's embarrassing to admit this—kissing the screen.

Will we laugh about that later, together?

Is that something you'll love about me one day?

Will you come to appreciate all the sacrifices I've made for you, how much of my life I've carved out for you without you even knowing?

It's terrible what happened to Feline Better.

Unfair. Unjust.

If they find who did it I'll smite them, Leela.

You'd like that, wouldn't you?

"You know, we're just glad the kitties are okay," you laugh in the interview, keeping your hair back with your hand as a gust of wind blows it.

Your bright and sunny smile—even through the

phone, it's an electricity that seems to link your lips to mine and I have to smile with you.

Over the years I've come to realize that the rareness of your smiles is what makes them so precious.

You readily smile in pictures and interviews but the truth is you don't smile often otherwise, Leela.

I hope it's not my fault.

I want to right my wrongs.

That's what I'm here for.

Once the sun is good and gone, I hurry out of my car and up the sidewalk.

The streetlamps flicker overhead as I sprint across the street and dash through some bushes and behind her balcony where I can't be seen.

I wait a few minutes for the street to still, for the last gasp of dogwalkers and power walkers to pass.

And then I make my move.

I emerge from my crouch, grasp the bars of the balcony and jump over it.

The sliding glass door is open, but the screen door is closed.

I pull it gently and it doesn't open. It's locked.

But there's a hole in it near the bottom corner and I poke a gloved finger through it, pull it to rip it open. It takes a few seconds for me to rip a hole wide enough to step through.

My boots hit her tile floor and I survey the place in a split second.

The painting of a dolphin above her sofa that looks like the work of an amateur.

The dancing feather duster and robo-vacuum.

The scent of sauteed garlic in the air, some kind of contraption on her counter that makes a whirring sound that I'm guessing is cooking her dinner.

Next to it, there's a cutting board with a mess of vegetable remains on it.

On her living room side table, a machine that looks like a Maxine is blinking red.

It occurs to me a woman with this many devices might already know I'm in her apartment.

She might be in her bedroom with the door locked, calling the police.

I clench my jaw, my pulse a jackhammer.

But then I step toward the dim hall and hear a heavenly sound—water dripping, a shower.

Couldn't be more perfect.

Quick as a blink, I go to the pulsing machine, unplug it, and turn it off.

I put it in her freezer for the time being. Just in case, so it can't record anything.

I peek my head into the two bedrooms in the hall.

One has no art on the walls, a double bed with a coverless duvet, a television. Guest room.

The other room has an unmade king-sized bed with a satin blue comforter and a hideous rainbow sea of clothes all over her floor.

The dripping water noise stops; I hear the plastic crackle of a shower curtain opening.

I dash for her walk-in closet.

It's disgusting in here, filled with strewn clothes that might be dirty or clean, who knows.

I'm grateful for the darkness as I close the door behind

me, leaving it open with a sliver wide enough that I can watch Lotus as she comes inside her room.

She's naked. I flinch at the sight of her bare skin and then can't help myself from looking, from drinking in the sight of her.

So that's what she looks like under her costume.

I've wondered.

After all, I'm only human.

I forget to breathe, distracted, and I imagine things I could do to her.

But I won't. I'm not that kind of monster.

In fact, when I spring to attack here, I will do her the kindness of letting her get dressed before I watch her murder herself.

I take the gun out of the holster under my sweatshirt, slip my finger onto the trigger, and push the door open when Lotus's back is to me.

But she hears the noise, senses it, and whips around.

Her eyes go so wide they're mostly whites, her face contorts and she immediately cowers, covers her breasts.

"Oh my God, oh my God, oh my God!" she shrieks.

I step over a pile of clothes. "You need to be quiet right now if you don't want me to shoot you."

I wondered if she would know my voice—if she paid any attention she *would* know my voice—but there's no recognition in her stare. She's tearful and whimpering, cornered like an animal that just realized it was prey.

"Please," she begs.

"Don't talk," I say, louder.

I step next to her now, point the gun at her head.

"You can get dressed," I tell her. "Don't say anything. Put on clothes."

"Why do you look like that," she whispers, getting up.

She flinches when she glances at my face, as if looking into a blinding light.

Stooping cautiously, she grabs a bathrobe from the ground and slips it on.

Shivering. Pale, in shock. Unable to meet my eyes. Her face contorted in pain.

I wish you could see her suffering, Leela.

Justice is such a magnificent sight.

"What do you want," Lotus whispers, her hair dripping on her shoulders, her teeth chattering.

With the gun still pointed to her head, I reach my other hand behind me and unzip my bag.

I pull the VixSpex out of my backpack and dangle it in front of Lotus's face.

Her expression doesn't change. There's something far away in her slate-gray eyes, something resigned in her terror, as if she's looking down a tunnel and sees the end already.

I tap the headset to startle her back to the present and am tickled with the warmest feeling, the moment mounting into something majestic, something permanent, something that can never be undone.

I will never forget the terror-shine of Lotus's eyes as long as I live.

"It's playtime," I say.

CHAPTER 11

LEELA

I love life most when I forget myself.

A depressing statement. But back in the days when I would drink myself into a state of blissful obliteration, that's why I did it. To forget me. When I go on a run around the city streets, my soles pounding the pavement, I forget me. In a darkened theater, or tangled with a stranger in a bed, or gaping at a piece of art—I forget me, I forget me, I forget me.

I'm contemplating this on the BART train on my ride back from the city. I strolled around the MOMA and ogled paintings and forgot my existence. Right now, I am in the Transbay tube, my ears popping from being a hundred and thirty-five feet under the San Francisco Bay. When I first moved to Berkeley to go to school, this terrified me. Every time I rode the train to and from the city I imagined an earthquake, a shooter, a fire happening while we were under a little piece of ocean and it was a crushing waking nightmare. But I guess the upside of having my soul shattered and becoming a jaded hag halfway through my twenties is that my own death doesn't faze me anymore. Bring it on, grim reaper. In the window, there's nothing but black, me reflected in a dark mirror, so I look away.

The train's packed and I'm lucky to have a seat. A man in a surgical mask sitting at a seat across from me has been eyeing me without blinking this entire ride. I pretend to ignore him. An invisible spider crawls up the back of my neck, the sense that I'm always being watched, the paranoia that the cinder block incident resurrected. But isn't that just some backwards-ass narcissism? To walk the world thinking I'm important enough that anyone's after me? Across the train, another guy's smiling at me, this one in a leather jacket and black jeans. They're not all after me, I tell myself. They're just horny.

When the train emerges from the underworld into Oakland, orange city lights sparkling like little fires through the dirty windows, I check my phone. No notifications. But in a sick reflex, I find myself going to my Peeps inbox to read the message from Madison again. I do it probably four or five times a day at this point, rereading rereading rereading as if there's a clue. Mourning a woman I hated who I hadn't thought of in years. The fucking internet, I swear. There's another message now though in that inbox, one that makes my throat tighten when I see the sender's name.

Lotus Windsong.

Lotus Windsong. I haven't thought of her in years. A woman with the name of a souvenir shop. A woman with zero boundaries. Those four syllables are packed with a lot of dusty pain.

"What the fuck?" I whisper, opening the message.

> Dear Leela,

> I am so sorry.

> It was wrong of me what I did to Jack.

> I knew he was with you and went for him anyway.

> I wish I could take it back.

> Please forgive me.

> It's been a real pleasure,

> Lotus

I swallow. There's a certain inkling I've gotten only a few times in life, that precious moment before discovering everything is terrible and nothing will ever be the same. I had it the night Jack died, when I saw the horrid shape of him in the dark but hadn't yet flipped the light switch on. I had it when I came to visit Michael in the hospital back in DC, the second before I opened the door. And now.

The message is fresh, just two hours old. My heart's galloping, the panic a drug speeding everything up. I answer it this time.

> Lotus? Are you okay? Can you answer me?

My chest feels like someone's sitting on it. There's feedback in my ears. *Lotus Windsong.* I stare at that name until it goes blurry, as if I can make it disappear. When the train stops at Macarthur in Oakland, I spring to my feet and rush out the door even though it isn't my station. I need air. Fresh air. I wait near the BART map catching my breath for a minute as people pass by laughing, listening to music, chatting, and then find a bench to collapse on. The man in the surgical mask passes by me, asking, "Are you okay?"

"Fine," I snap back. "I'm fine."

Once he's gone and most of the train's passengers have vanished down the escalator and it's just me on this platform and the city lights and a spilt-ink sky with some weakling stars, I'm finally brave enough to open my phone again. Her name there in Helvetica, *Lotus Windsong*. She hasn't answered my message. There are no new posts on her profile, just a zillion happy birthday messages posted last month in August. The fist that has had a hold on me relaxes, just a little. Maybe it's a coincidence. This has to be a coincidence.

Lotus?

Nothing. Silently screaming into the void. Refreshing, refreshing, refreshing until my finger gets tired and the next train comes.

I take a deep breath and get back on, return my phone to my pocket. But that inkling's still there—that doom cloud, that suspicion that something's very wrong and I have no real sense of what it is.

CHAPTER 12

Esmerelda is one of those people who thinks her dreams are interesting enough that she's compelled to recount them in full detail to the people she works with. It's been five forever-feeling minutes of this as we dangle feather toys in front of the cats in the Meow Meow Lounge.

"Oh! And then I forgot to tell you this part!" Esmerelda says, putting a hand on my arm. "One of the guys was Geoff, you know, who works at the sandwich place?"

I stoop to give the stocky orange cat Tiggie a back rub. He pushes himself into my hand, half-closes his eyes, and purrs. "Geoff, huh?"

"Yeah, and then that guy in the movie … you know the one with the spaceship? He was, like, their *leader*."

We're approaching agony here. As Esmerelda tells me about the imaginary bad guys who were chasing her through the streets of New York City and throwing donuts at her, I nod and smile and wonder what it would feel like to have that amount of oblivious self-importance to think other people would care to hear this. Mean, I know, but thank God I'm allowed to be mean in my head.

"Wild!" I say, inching toward the glass door that leads to our offices. "Another day awaits. You ready?"

Esmerelda follows me through the door and we split off into our offices. I shed my jacket, hang my purse, plop into my chair, and let out a giant sigh. Elbows on my desk, I rub my temples.

Unlike Esmerelda, I did not enjoy a healthy amount of REM sleep last night. I kept waking up with a jerk and reaching for my phone to check Peeps for any word from Lotus. Kept checking her profile to make sure she wasn't dead. Then I lay on my back staring at the shifting tree-shadows on my ceiling and wondering if it was all a coincidence. Or maybe some zeitgeist thing? Maybe there's a sudden culture shift of introspection, of people contacting those they'd wronged? But in my heart—that relentless tic I could feel throbbing in the dark—I knew that there was something wrong. And I still know it now, this morning.

Daisy comes in humming like a happy little bee. "Hello hello hello!" she sings. Then seeing me, her face falls. "You okay?"

"Fine," I say, flashing her a smile. "Just didn't sleep well."

She opens her computer. "Drink too much last night?"

The accusation is like an arrow. I raise my eyebrows. "I don't drink."

"That's what I thought," she says, sliding into her chair. "Just making sure."

Making sure? Excusé moi? Who does she think she is, my sponsor? Most of the time I'm glad to be the supervised and not the supervisor, relieved to be rid of that level of responsibility, but what the hell, Daisy? I'm a grown-ass woman who led an entire team in my previous position. I don't need to be scrutinized like I'm a teenager on my first job.

I turn to my computer and bite the side of my tongue. In my screen, I can see the reflection of Daisy's computer; Daisy's reflection in her own computer screen is reflected in my screen, and she's looking at me. It's dizzying, like a house of mirrors. I shift my screen an inch so I don't see her. I open the handbook again and try to ignore the tiny coal of rage that interaction stoked. Apparently telling Daisy I was a recovering alcoholic was a mistake, because now she's scrutinizing me for signs of relapse. But it's fine. Moving on. Reworking sentences to include more cat puns and questioning my life choices.

A while later, Daisy takes a coffee break. When I told Daisy I was in recovery, by the way, she answered with, "Good for you! I've never been addicted to anything. Unless you count vanilla lattes!" and laughed. Someday I would like my own office where my negative vibes can thrive. I open a new tab to check on Lotus. Still no response to my messages. But I freeze up when I see there's one new post on the top of her page timestamped just twenty-three minutes ago from someone named Pansy Windsong.

> I'm in shock. Absolutely gutted. My sister died last night. Please pray for my family.

No.
Not this.

Anything but fucking *this*.

It's like there's a trap door underneath me and I'm suddenly falling through the floor. I stare in utter disbelief, scrolling through the comments. There are fifteen already. Everyone offering their condolences, their useless condolences. Like offering someone a jarful of air.

What happened? one comment asks.

She took her own life, her sister responds. *I'm so angry right now. I don't understand. She left a note. I didn't even know she owned a gun. I can't stop crying.*

A gun. Just like Madison. The word fires in my mind —*gun, gun, gun, gun, gun.*

The sound of a trigger so close to the ear. A boom loud enough to shatter a human being. Blood, a glistening red puddle on a floor. Chunks of skull and hair, brain-spatter on a white wall. Instead of a head, it's meat, just meat.

I think I'm going to be sick.

I close my computer, spring to my feet and grab my purse. Daisy's coming in with her vanilla latte and bright eyes framed with thick false eyelashes and sunshine in her hair. "Everything okay?"

"Emergency," I manage.

"Family emergency?"

"Not family," I say, putting my jacket on with shaking hands. "Acquaintance."

"An acquaintance emergency?" Daisy repeats. "Okie dokie."

I can't tell if she's sarcastic. Maybe her sunny disposition is all sarcasm that continually goes over my head, wouldn't that be a plot twist? I don't have time to analyze it, I murmur an apology and head out of the office, out of the front doors, into the blinding light of the cloudless day. I put on my sunglasses and step into the shade, pulling out my phone. Holy mother, it's exactly the nightmare scenario I feared. Lotus is dead. Madison, then Lotus, and where does it end?

A real pleasure.

I need to talk to Teddy.

Two women have died suspiciously, suicide by gunshot, and I don't know, I don't know, I don't know, but this lead-bellied spidey sense is saying this has to do with the VixSpex and Teddy is the only person on earth who knows as much as I do about that disaster. I could call the police. But what would I say? That I got two apologies from two women in two separate jurisdictions who happened to kill themselves? And, worst case scenario, if this *did* have anything to do with VixSpex, I couldn't tell the police anything. I signed an airtight NDA. Jolvix would ruin me.

No, it's got to be Teddy. And I don't even have his number. I could hire a private detective through Tasky like he did to track my cell number, but only creeps do that shit. Instead, I open an app and hail a self-driving taxi. Destination: the Jolvix campus in Cupertino. Ground zero.

"Good morning," the taxi says as I slide into the passenger seat. The car pulls away from the curb and continues driving. "How are you today?"

"Horrible."

Taxi doesn't care. "What kind of music would you like to listen to?"

"Doom metal. A playlist."

The music fills the car and quiets my brain for a little while. For just a tiny blissful period of time, I close my eyes and disappear. When I open my eyes again we're on the freeway. I can't help but think about Eve and everything she went through. I can't even imagine being stuck in a car like this at the mercy of some faraway deranged dude. Fucking Jolvix. Eve is right to go after them. They're responsible for a good portion of twenty-first century misery. I think about the VixSpex, an invisible wrench tightening my stomach. I think of two women I know dead. Women I had beef with. Women who I guess were my enemies, if I have such a thing as enemies. I think of the curse I've suspected for years now. I always tell myself I'm being silly, I'm imagining things. There's no such thing as curses. But what if I'm wrong?

What if there's an intangible dark magic out there with my name on it?

CHAPTER 13

The first time I saw Teddy I thought he was Jack, I really did. My first thought when he walked through the doorway of his parents' house was, where the hell did Jack's glasses and tattoos go? And why's he dressed like a fucking golfer?

"Hey-o!" Teddy boomed, doing a finger-gun thing at me. "This the female I keep hearing so much about?"

The female. I'll never forget that. What a dumbass.

Jack walked in behind him and said, kind of apologetically, "Leela, this is my brother."

"I gathered," I said as Jack came behind me and slipped his arms around me, the warmth a gush that made me smile.

"You crazy lovebirds," Teddy said, opening the fridge. "When's the wedding anyway?"

I twisted the black diamond ring around my finger and turned to widen my eyes at Jack.

"Um, we're thinking the year after we graduate," Jack said.

Teddy, who was guzzling juice from the carton like a thirteen-year-old, almost spewed orange. He turned around. "Are you serious?"

Jack and I nodded in shy unison. We were one thing, one beautiful thing.

"You're *engaged* already?" Teddy said.

He looked like a man who'd been slapped. Now that he was closer, I saw the minutiae that distinguished Jack and Teddy from one another. Teddy's hair was carefully coiffed, gelled. He had a scar that ran through his left eyebrow, a white slice through the middle of it. His posture was so much better than Jack's that he stood a couple inches taller. While Jack had a permanent creased-browed look of deep daydreams, Teddy had a wide-eyed look of here-now wonder. Jack had professor energy while Teddy had CEO energy. They'd been stamped by the same cookie cutter but were decorated wildly differently.

"Well congratu-fuckin-lations!" Teddy shouted after a stunned moment. "Where's the Dom Perignon? Let's celebrate!"

"Shhh," Jack said. "I haven't told Mom and Dad yet."

"Oh shiiiiiiit," Teddy said in a stage whisper. He pantomimed zipping his lips. "All right. Okay. Well, I'm honored. First to know. Best man? You know it. I'm going to throw you a bachelor party for the *ages*. Vegas. You know it has to be in Vegas." He wiggled his eyebrows and that was the first but definitely not the last time I wondered if I hated Teddy Lindmark. He was like the Florida of people: an embarrassment yet oddly compelling, someone who would be fun enough to wrestle an alligator after snorting bath salts but also vote Republican.

Teddy's not that different now. I just tolerate him because we share so much misery. Losing Jack five years ago was a glue that kept Teddy and me together. We've been through so unspeakably much. And even though he's somewhat of a buffoon, when I hit rock bottom three years ago, he was the one who reached his hand to help me out. He went into recovery six months before I did. So we share that misery too.

"What are you doing out there anyway?" he asked me in a video call three years back. He was sitting at a country club café, the douche. "You're alone in the DC snake pit. You're working at a suicide prevention org, which is probably the worst possible choice for a job you could possibly make."

"I want to help people," I said weakly.

I was calling him from my bathroom floor, in my pajamas. There was vomit in my hair and a bruise on my thigh the size of a shoe that I didn't remember getting. As I said, rock bottom.

"Help yourself first," he said. "Christ, after everything … seriously, Leels, give it a break. It can't be healthy working an org like that."

I didn't give him the satisfaction of telling him my therapist said the exact same thing.

"You look like shit, by the way," he added.

"You look like shit too," I told him. "You're wearing newsboy hats now? Who are you?"

"Look, I'm serious," Teddy said. "Come work at Jolvix

with me. I'm hiring a PR head and I'm sure it pays better than what you're making at a nonprofit."

"It's not about money."

He lowered his voice. "There's a rehab center here, one of the best in the country. Everything's outpatient. They'll dry you out. I'll pay for it."

"Teddy, no."

"It's what Jack would want," he said.

I sighed. My head was throbbing, but honestly, I was grateful because it was distracting me from the screaming ache of the hole where my heart used to be. And I knew he was right. I knew Jack would hate to see me this way, drinking every night until the blackout erased me. A slow suicide of my own.

"Okay," I said.

And that was it.

The next day, I was on a plane to San Jose.

CHAPTER 14

And here I am again, three years and a lifetime later: back at the Jolvix campus—or as I like to call it, manchild heaven.

Bowling alleys, arcades, restaurants, an honest-to-God ice cream truck that drives around doling out free sundaes. It's a well-known secret that a hefty percentage of employees live here, sleeping in the Bliss Bay "relaxation stations" that are essentially bare-bones studio apartments available round the clock for employees to sleep or bang each other in. It's what Jolvix wants ultimately, isn't it? To own their employees. To provide such luxury and convenience no one has any reason to leave. Jolvix sure puts the "cult" in work culture and now that I'm back here, I'm reminded of how grateful I am to not work here anymore.

I'm in the Welcome Dome, an all-glass cylindrical building where visitors check in for guest passes. I've been told by the receptionist to wait. I chew my cheek, hands shoved in my jacket pockets, watching some suits play badminton in the grass outside while some smilers in athleticwear stroll up a bricked path with steamy coffee cups in hand. It's always like a damn commercial here. Once I watched a woman lose her marbles at a work party in the Happy Days Pavilion, calling everyone fuckfaces and getting dragged out screaming and kicking by security guards. I related. I think of her often with deep respect.

"What in hell?" a voice says from behind me.

It's Teddy, walking through the automatic glass doors. He's wearing a sharkskin suit with no tie and loafers with no socks. His hair's a few inches long and styled in a side part with just one little string of hair falling across his forehead that I know he did on purpose just to look fashionably careless. Narcissus had nothing on Teddy's love of reflective surfaces. He's got his hands on his hips and a suspicious squint in his blue eyes.

"Good morning, kind sir," I say.

"What in hell?" he repeats as he comes up to me.

"Can we talk?"

Teddy shoots a glance at his smart watch. "I've got meetings all day, why didn't you call first?"

"I just—I needed to talk to you. In person."

He continues staring at me like I'm a bomb ready to explode. Behind him, a marquee flashes with a looping computer animation showing a skeletal robot hand throwing confetti that spells out *Jolvix: Tomorrow Today*.

"Please, Teddy, I need you," I say, hating how my voice catches in my throat. Hating that it's true and that it spilled out of me like that, without warning, my pathetic need announcing itself out loud before I even realized it was there.

"Okay," he says slowly. "Sure. Can we just—I have an eleven o'clock I can't miss. Can you wait in my office until it's done?"

"Yeah."

He leans over and sniffs me.

"What are you doing?" I ask, shoving him away.

"Just checking in."

"I'm not drunk," I say, teeth grit.

"Okay," he says, hands up. "You passed the smell test. Literally. You have a visitor's pass?"

"They're waiting on you," I tell him, pointing at the reception desk.

"Get her a pass, please, stat," Teddy barks to the receptionist, clapping. "I have to jet here."

As we exit the automatic doors into the fresh air and I slip the visitor pass lanyard around my neck, Teddy says, "I can't wait until they replace those receptionists with bots."

"God, you're rude," I say.

He shrugs and pulls out a tin from his front pocket. "Efficiency over politeness. Mint?"

I take one without thanking him and we head further into campus.

"So you still saving the kittens or whatever?" he asks.

"I don't save kittens. I work as a volunteer coordinator."

"Yeah, I know. At the, uh—" He snaps his fingers. "What's the org called again?"

"Feline Better."

"Feline Better," he chuckles.

"Don't pretend it's funny."

"It *is* funny," he says. "It's hilarious."

"You've always had the sense of humor of a Laffy Taffy wrapper."

"And you've always had the warmth of an Eastern European circus trainer."

My brow furrows. "What is that even supposed to mean?"

"I don't know, all kinds of weird stuff comes out of this mouth sometimes." He waves a hand. "Suffice to say, I like the idea of you saving kittens."

"Except I *don't save kittens*."

"You and your big heart."

My annoyance ratchets up and I get that itch on my neck that only Teddy gives me. "Do you even hear a word I say, or are you just stuck in a lifelong one-man show I've been invited to now and then?"

"I like that. What a fun way to think about my life."

Sometimes Teddy's immaturity has the positive effect of chucking any notion of my own imposter syndrome right out the window.

"Come on, Leels. Just trying to goad you. You know it's one of my favorite things."

"Yeah, yeah," I mutter.

We walk, in step, into the sunshine. It's a route I know so well, a meandering pebble path I walked nearly every day for two years from the campus entrance to the Virtual Reality sector. A footbridge, a whispering creek, a stretch of lawn sculptures that look like giant gold turds but are apparently worth a lot of money and we're here.

We're here again.

This mirror-box building with a fountain out front. When we get closer to the fountain, the water disappears. It's just a hologram. Cute, right? A holographic fountain outside the Virtual Reality building. A couple boulders nestled in the oak trees out front are not boulders at all but speakers playing classical music.

I hate it here.

When I get upstairs, it's like I never left. It's like I blinked and it's a year ago, same faces through what people here call "privacy walls" that are actually just Plexiglas cubicles. Same nature sounds piped through the speakers, birds tweeting and rivers rushing, to make people forget they're spending most of their wild, precious lives staring at screens figuring out how to get other people to stare at screens. Past the cubicle farm, an open workspace is configured with rainbow-colored furniture and yoga balls. My old office was the corner office which appears to now be some kind of padded-walled game room where a lone man in VR goggles swings maniacally at some invisible enemy.

"What happened to my office?" I ask as Teddy and I round the corridor to the executive suite.

"Oh, it's the Fun Room now," he says breezily, opening the door with his fingerprint and heading in. "Employees are required to spend an hour a week in the Fun Room."

Might not be the stupidest thing I've ever heard, but it's up there.

"Who's your new PR head?" I ask from the doorway.

"There is no new PR head. Broke up the role and outsourced it."

There's some sweet little satisfaction to know I'm irreplaceable.

"What about the rest of the team?"

"They got absorbed by comms."

I hesitate in the doorway, déjà vu washing over me in a hot-flashy wave as I glance to my right. On the far back wall of the dark, empty conference room across the hall, I spot the killer VixSpex gleaming from its spot behind a case of supposedly unbreakable glass. It's a black VR headset with an attachment on the side where a custom handgun slides in. The attachment is fixed with a magnetic sensor that can pull the trigger. Goosebumps prickle my arms. The sight of it always makes me a little bit sick. Today that sickness comes with just a touch of relief, too. I don't know what I expected, but they're here. They're still here.

Still, I'm not breathing easy. I step into Teddy's office, a spread of white marble with a gleam that always reminds me of a hospital. Same white leather couch I used to lay on afternoon after afternoon strategizing and brainstorming—usually with a cold cloth on my head waiting for the Xanax to kick in because every day was a clusterfuck from hell.

"Hi, hello, how are you, nice to see you, Teddy, thanks for taking me on such short notice," Teddy says in a mock-amiable voice as he slips his man-purse over his shoulder.

"Oh thank you, my liege," I say fake-breathlessly as I sit on the sofa with a squeak. "For deigning to come down from your castle to speak to a mere peasant like me."

"I see. A minute ago it was 'I need you, Teddy' and now we're insulting."

I'm about to tell him to shut up, but he's on his way out the door.

"We can have lunch when I get back. Don't get into any trouble. If you see Evan, can you remind him that I need an updated copy of the Q1 reports?"

I would remind him that I no longer work here, but Teddy's already gone like a human tornado. Takes a moment of silence for my consciousness to fully catch up with the scene at hand. I am back in Teddy Lindmark's office, back at Jolvix, and I can't even fully articulate why. I lie my head back and kick my boots up, stretching out on the squeaky leather.

Closing my eyes, the memory of my first day of work out here replays like a movie.

How overwhelming the campus seemed, how futuristic and surreal. I wasn't a shell of myself, I was worse than that. I was finally *without* my shell. I was the raw, pink, frail creature that lives inside it. Shaky and sweating with withdrawal and trying to hide it all under a pantsuit and a sheen of heavy makeup. If wearing sunglasses inside was socially acceptable, I would have been rocking shades indoors. God. I peered at myself in a compact mirror as I headed in for my first day at Jolvix. How was I going to pull this off? This surviving and pretending to be normal thing?

"Teddy?" I asked, pushing the door open to his office. "Knock knock."

Knock knock? I sounded grossly chipper. His office was empty and I had this horrible feeling that I was perhaps a world-class idiot for coming here and thinking Teddy Fucking Lindmark was going to pull me out of my half-dug grave. What if he didn't mean it? What if he'd forgotten all about his offer, bought me a plane ticket and then breezed on with his, I don't know, yacht-sailing, wine-tasting life? Or—worst of all—what if he took one look at my sunken face and skeletal figure and quivering hands and decided I was a mess that wasn't worth the time?

All these fears were soon displaced when Teddy's face popped up from behind his desk. He had the look of a terrified child.

"Teddy?"

"Close the door," he hissed.

I did as he said, glancing back over my shoulder. The executive suites, like all offices in the building, were a hundred percent glass. Because that was what Jolvix was about—*transparency*. I can't ever say that without wanting to bust up laughing and spew whatever I'm drinking, it's so ridiculous, but that is a thing the company says. What they don't add is that transparency everywhere equals privacy nowhere. This explained why Teddy was hiding behind his desk, I guess.

"Teddy, what the hell are you doing?" I asked, still trying to sound friendly and cheerful to convey my appreciation for him bringing me out here and taking a chance on me. But this was beyond weird.

I came and crouched next to him. He was tucked, cross-legged, under his desk where his chair belonged. His tie was loosened.

"Listen, I'm kind of having a difficult day," he said.

"Are you high?"

I asked it facetiously and was so disappointed when he gave me a *so sue me!* grimace.

"Are you kidding me right now?" I said, that carefully arranged smile melting off my face. "I come all the way out here to dry out and you're fucking high on my first day of work?"

"I'm not high like that," he said. "It was supposed to help the creative juices flow. You know, a microdose?" He pulled my sleeve to bring me closer to him. "But I've never been good at math, you know that, so I dosed a little wrong and … turned out it wasn't that micro."

"Oh, so you're tripping balls right now," I said.

"Lil bit, yes."

I stood up, tapping my fingers on his desk as I considered this and exchanged a little silent word with the universe. Okay. What was this, some kind of poetic justice? There was nothing poetic or just about trusting this man to straighten me out.

"I like that sound," he said after a half-minute of me drumming my fingers. "Can you keep doing that?"

I stopped and shook my head at the glass doorway, which read CHIEF OPERATING OFFICER OF VIRTUAL REALITY, but backwards. Perhaps that's all any of this was. I lived in a backwards world where up was down and in was out. Somewhere, in the right world, Jack was alive and we were married and I wasn't a drunk and life still stood a chance at being beautiful.

"Teddy, I don't even know what to say to you right now," I said.

"You can't call me that," he hissed.

"Call you what?" I asked, utterly confused. "Your name?"

"'Teddy.'"

"That's … your name."

"No. I go by Ted. I'm a grown man now."

"Are you joking? I can't tell if you're fucking with me."

"I'm serious."

I paced around his desk and studied him. "Grown men don't hide under their desks."

"I would argue that under some circumstances, they do."

I crossed my arms in front of my chest. "Seriously, Teddy, would you please come out?"

"You can still call me Teddy in private," he said, standing up and brushing the, I don't know, invisible microscopic demons off his shirt. "But in public, you need to call me Ted."

His hair was fluffed on one side. Even though I didn't want to, I stepped forward and brushed it into place with my fingers.

"I don't care what they call you here, or how big and important you think you are now," I said. "You're not going to be pulling my strings and I'll call you whatever I want to call you."

"I'm not ordering you," he said, fluffing his hair back the way it was.

Fine, he wanted it that way, he could have it that way. I gave up, stepping back.

"I'm *asking* you, friend to friend," he said.

In the quiet, there was a ghost between us, an

unspeakable history, an invisible connecting wire of pain. Finally, I nodded. "You got it."

"Thank you for coming to my Ted talk," he said with utter seriousness.

I rolled my eyes. A child's brain, a man's looks, a grandpa's sense of humor—Teddy Lindmark, in a nutshell. Oh, excuse me … Ted.

"You going to be okay?" I asked him.

"Are you?"

"I will if you will."

"Deal," he said.

Really, even after finding the man cowering behind his twenty-thousand dollar desk from accidentally macro-dosing instead of microdosing, I knew there wasn't anyone I would have trusted the shattered pieces of my life with more than Teddy. Because he knew. He tightrope-walked over the same void that I did. And who can you trust more to help you out of the mess than the person who wallowed in the same mess themselves?

CHAPTER 15

But all that was three years ago.

I recall it like a hazy dream, startling awake again to the crisis of the present moment.

Teddy tries to take me to *stro* for lunch, the douchey campus bistro, probably because he's too cheap to buy me lunch. But I insist we go off campus because we can't take the risk of anyone overhearing this conversation. As Teddy and I sit in the back of a Jolvix "chariot," AKA a fancy self-driving golf cart shuttle, he murmurs in my ear, "Is this about the thing?"

"It is."

"Because, look, part of your NDA includes you not talking about it with anyone, including me. In fact, you can't even talk about not talking about it."

In the front seat, the self-driving golf cart emits a whistling song. Above the mini rearview mirror, there's a camera pointed straight toward the back seat at Teddy and me, blinking red with its accusing light.

"Let's just wait until we're somewhere else," I whisper.

"If it is about the thing that I definitely don't know about and that you're not even supposed to be pretending to know about, I mean it, I don't want to go there."

"Two women who hated my guts died within a month of one another right after sending me eerily identical apology notes," I tell him, and then whisper slowly, with emphasis, "*Shot through the head.*"

Teddy's expression doesn't change, but even in the merry California sunshine, he visibly pales and holds up a hand to stop me from saying more.

"Let's just wait until we're somewhere else," he says.

"Told you so."

"There it is," he mutters. "Leela Crowe's favorite three words in the whole entire world."

I don't argue with him, enjoying the silence and how, for just one sweet long minute, the skyscraping redwoods dapple my vision with shadows and sunlight. But as I turn to Teddy, his scowling profile in sunglasses that probably cost more than a used car, I can tell he's already bothered. As he should be. My gaze lingers on him for an extra second because it's at times like these—times Teddy gets bothered, heated, or rattled in some way—that he most resembles Jack.

We get a corner table at a fancy taco restaurant. I wouldn't have gone for a place that has a sommelier, white tablecloths, and salad forks, but I'm not going to argue with tacos. We order a couple sparkling waters splashed with bitters and lean in.

"Two people you know were murdered," he says.

"I don't know. I don't know what they were," I say, trying to not let fear raise my pitch. I fold my hands on the table and dive into the news of Madison and Lotus's deaths, the notes they sent me, both dead by so-called suicide, guns to their heads. The unmistakably eerie coincidence of these two nearly identical deaths happening one right after the other.

"Suicide," Teddy says, letting out a sigh of relief and sitting back. He clutches his chest. "Okay, there. Jesus, *suicides*. That's great news. Not great, you know, but ... you know, less terrible."

My throat goes dry, even when I down half my soda. "Less terrible *how?*"

"Because they're not fucking murders, Leela," Teddy whispers to me, like I'm an idiot.

"And if they were, *Teddy*, don't you think they'd look like fucking suicides?" I sit back and shake my head at the venom in my voice. I take a moment to look at a stained easel that is passing itself off as a piece of art on the wall to calm my ass down.

"Look, it sucks," Teddy says, reaching out to touch my hand and then, seeing the fire in my eyes, thinking better of it and pulling his hand back to his lap. "I know it's—it's triggering."

"Please tell me you're not making a sick pun about guns right now."

"That was completely unintentional, I swear. I'm an asshole but I'm not that big of an asshole."

A woman comes with a basket of chips and Teddy and I both correct our posture and beam smiles and thank yous at her before sinking back into our miserable stances and hushed conversation.

"If I were you, I'd be freaked out, too," Teddy says,

munching a chip. "But hey, who knows. What if it's, you know, a copycat?"

"A copycat suicide," I repeat.

"Sure."

It's so stupid it doesn't even seem worth a response, but I entertain the possibility for a second anyway. "The two women didn't know each other, though."

"How do you know?"

"They have zero mutual friends on Peeps. Madison lived in Fresno and Lotus lived in Oakland. I'm the middle of the Venn diagram here."

"Okay well … it's weird, but why is your first thought to come to me and act like it's got something to do with the thing?"

"They both said the same things in their notes," I tell him. "They mentioned it had been a 'real pleasure.'"

"So?"

"It's the fucking slogan, man!" I say. "'VixSpex: A Real Pleasure.'"

"It's also just a common thing people say," Teddy says.

"Don't act purposefully stupid," I say. "That's way too much coincidence."

I watch a waiter carrying a tray of margaritas to a group of laughing older women, the kind of well-dressed women who probably own Pomeranians and host fundraising events and get neck lifts. Honestly, they remind me a little of Teddy and Jack's mom. I let a long sigh out of my clenched throat.

"How's your mom?" I ask him.

"She's fine. Cancer-free for a year now."

"That's great."

"She's all into this horse therapy now. Trying to convince me I need to buy a horse and it'll fix all my problems." He checks his phone. "How's your mom?"

"Also fine. Super into her cockatoo."

"Those are those, uh—half poodle dogs, right?"

"No. Cocka*too*, a bird. Kind of like a white parrot."

"Mmm." Teddy folds his napkin on his lap. "I could never trust a pet that's going to outlive me."

The tacos come and we go on like this as we eat—a meandering, not unpleasant small talk, but one that has a tension underlying it, a thing neither of us know how to talk about or what to say. It occurs to me after five or ten minutes of this that maybe what I came out here for wasn't to sell Teddy on some farfetched conspiracy theory possibly involving the murder goggles. It was just to be near someone who understood my pain without me having to explain it. I can tell that he's turning the thought of these suicides over in his head like a polished stone in his hand. That he's bothered by them, too, and that he feels the absolute fucking unfairness of having this many suicides touch my life for no apparent reason. He won't say this, of course. But then again, he's Teddy. He doesn't have to.

"Look, Leels, I'm so sorry about everything," he says as he slips his coat back on and he and I head outside. "I'd be a wreck if I were in your shoes. But there's not anything there. I promise. The thing—there is no thing, remember? Never was."

"Okay, can you just not lie for, like, one second?"

"There never was," he whispers with raised eyebrows.

"There fucking *is*," I say, annoyed. "I just saw it hanging on the wall of the conference room."

He shakes his head and leans over to whisper in my ear, so close I get a shiver. "That's not it."

I pull back, giving him a look. "What?"

"When Barnett retired, he took it," he whispers. He points accusingly at me. "You did not hear that. But the headset hanging in the office? Fake now."

"Dammit," I say, pushing Teddy. My pulse goes through the roof and all I can think is, it's out there. It's out there somewhere. "When did Barnett retire?"

"Didn't you see the news?"

"I didn't see the news. I don't read tech news. I don't have to anymore, thank Jesus, my life is cats now."

"So one could say you left the news for the mews." He bats the air like he's waving away a stink, as if his own joke was so inappropriate and bad it even offended him. "He retired a few months back. Look, I repeat, Barnett has it now. It's probably hyper-sealed in some diamond-walled survivalist chamber, safer than it would be it were still here."

"Why does it even have to exist?" I say.

"Because rich boys like their toys," he says, patting my arm.

I'm burning with confused rage. "I hate the world."

"Oh, stop it." He gives me a side hug. "It's not worth hating or loving." He shrugs and offers me a mint. "It's just the world."

Wind runs its invisible fingers through the trees and stirs Teddy's hair, musses it up without him knowing. He looks better that way; I don't know, more human.

"How's Genesis," I say flatly as I summon a taxi on my phone.

He scoffs. "I don't know, ask her."

I slip my phone back into my pocket. "I see. Back on the prowl again."

He watches me for a beat. "What about you?"

"I'm a nun, Teddy."

He gives me a half-smile. "I'm sure."

I hate it when he looks at me like that. I see Jack when he looks at me like that. I shouldn't have asked about Genesis.

The self-driving taxi drives me home. Lucky self-driving taxi, lucky AI. I'm just a tangled mess of emotions. What I wouldn't give to get rid of them. On top of everything Teddy does to me, there's this throbbing worry now that is repeating itself like an uninvited heartbeat: *Barnett, Barnett, Barnett.*

Barnett Briggs. Former CEO of VR at Jolvix. The babyfaced gargoyle essentially invented the VixSpex—or at least, he took credit for it. He's certainly responsible for the fucking murder goggles, the special VixSpex headset that could kill a player by shooting a bullet into their brain when they lose a game. He hung it on the wall of our office as a "novelty"—sort of like a hunter puts a severed animal head on the wall. Barnett wasn't just an idiot genius and a worthless millionaire, he was also a sleazy toad. The most positive thing I can say about my time working with him is that he wasn't around very much.

My head is swimming as the car glides through stop-and-start traffic. If Barnett has the murder goggles, then

… who knows. What if he sold it? Gave it to someone? What if someone in his life has access to it?

Or—and I don't know if this is worse, I really don't— what if the headset has nothing to do with this and I'm simply losing my mind seeing patterns in every tragedy that touches me? What if the fact I'm the connection between so many people dying is just the fact I exist and every person in the world who exists knows people who die? It's not because of me. Correlation, causation, etc. I'm not the center of any universe except the ones of my own creation.

My phone buzzes with a message. It's from a number with a San Jose area code.

> Don't fall down the rabbit hole, Leela.

> Sometimes things just happen.

> (This is Teddy, by the way.)

Shaking my head, I start typing, *Fuck you, man. The only reason you want me to drop this is because you're afraid it has something to do with the murder goggles too and you're worried about your own ass. I saw it in your eyes.* But that's too much. So I erase it. I don't answer his text, but I program his number into my phone.

And then, as if lit by a new flame, I text Eve.

> Hey, maybe we could meet up again soon to talk.

CHAPTER 16

Lotus Windsong. Madison La Rosa. Faded nemeses I happily would have never thought of again. Now I'm forever chained to them by their deathbed apologies.

Over the coming week, like a scrambling digital rodent, I scour the internet for any crumbs of information I can find on them. Madison's is just sad, mostly her smart watch posting how many miles she ran on her treadmill. Sometimes there was an automatic "check-in" from a smoothie bar she visited. On anniversaries and Valentine's and birthdays, she posts about how much she "wuvs her sweet hubby bear." I would barf, but rest in peace. Lotus's virtual footprint is faint. Not much on Peeps. She seems to have interacted on professional networks more than personal. She posts facts about litigation laws. Not the future I saw for Ms. Can't Keep Her Tits in her Shirt, but again, rest in peace.

This past week I admit I've started to unravel. As in greasy hair, skipping meals, didn't open my curtains for three or four days, staring into space thinking about dead people, et cetera. Just yesterday, I got a "Friendly reminder: You've got mental health days to use!" email from Daisy—while she was not three feet away from me, I might add. Passive aggression in the twenty-first century, man. What a trip.

Next week I'm supposed to meet Eve and the stress is mounting. I don't know what I'm going to say to her, but I'm sure whatever it is will be too much. Teddy would kill me if he knew I was going to talk to a reporter writing a book on Jolvix. Hell, Jolvix might *actually* kill me—I've heard the stories. It's like dealing with the mafia, only way worse because they're fucking tech geniuses. The nerd mafia. But this inkling I have about the murder headset being a part of this story—those three words, *a real pleasure*—I can't kick it. I've got to spill to someone who will believe me, someone who gets it. And soon, or I'm going to lose it.

There's the truth about VixSpex raised up like my own personal zombie, and then there are these identical "suicides." Together, they're driving me to the brink. I feel sick with the shit I know and sick from the shit I don't. I can't win. I'm always sick.

Ricky drives up from LA to spend the weekend with me and I've never needed the company more.

"You look amazing," he tells me when he hugs me in the doorway, tight enough to take my breath away. Behind him, there are two oversized suitcases decoupaged with Marilyn Monroe.

"I do not," I tell him. "You're such a liar. Are those my mom's suitcases?"

He pulls away. "They are! She let me borrow them

indefinitely. She's downsizing, did she tell you? Huey's moving in."

As I process this stunner, Ricky wheels the suitcases large enough for a month-long trip to Spain into my apartment. I press my fingers against my lips and use my toe to gently keep Nosferatu inside before shutting the door.

"She didn't tell you?" Ricky says, collapsing on my velvet loveseat with a skull blanket tastefully draped along the back. "Not surprised. She thought you'd get judgy."

"Why does she think that? It's her life." I take a seat across from him in my favorite chair. Nosferatu recognizes the cue and jumps right up into my lap. "I mean, it's a completely stupid decision and I don't understand how she can make the same mistake ten thousand times, but it's her life."

"As previously noted, *judgy.*"

Oh, this feels so good, to have him here. To be near enough to him that I get to smell his stinky cologne and get infected by his gorgeous half-moon grin. Besides Ricky being my best friend since freshman year of high school, there for every play, crush and breakup, passing drama, and reason I was grounded, the two of us have something we called the NQA policy—anytime one of us requests it, the other will fly out No Questions Asked. Ricky lost his mom six months before I lost Jack. Grief is a quiet understanding we share.

"So how are we?" asks Ricky, shedding his suede coat and folding it perfectly in half, then laying it beside him.

"We're holding ourselves together," I say. "You know. As we do."

Ricky's eyes are a rich, warm brown, almost amber, and have this mischievous slant to them. He also has shapely eyebrows he pays careful attention to and he raises one of those at me right now. "The whole dead enemy parade has shaken you, hasn't it?"

"Wouldn't it shake you?"

"Yes. Though I'm such an asshole I'd probably enjoy it more than you are."

"You say that, but if they were really *actually* dying, you'd be weirded out, too."

"It's only two people," he reminds me. "I mean, how long's your shitlist?"

"Oh, Ricky," I say, fighting a bitter laugh. "You know me."

He smiles, showing off his dimples. "Well, I'm just glad I stayed on your good side all these years."

"Watch yourself," I say, pointing a black fingernail at him.

He cackles.

See, this was why I invited him here. It's like the air's lighter now. The idea that people I've hated are somehow being targeted is suddenly worthy of dark jokes. It's just me and my best friend, my bro from another ho, the guy I can sit in a room with for hours after years and years and still find infinite things to whisper and squeal and argue about.

We go out for sushi and make a spontaneous stop at a karaoke night. Let me tell you, it takes a lot of guts to do karaoke as a sober person in comparison to the days when I used to stumble onstage with my fifth whiskey sour in hand. But it's exhilarating and when the crowd swells for my off-key rendition of "War Pigs," for a moment, I remember how good it feels to have strangers' eyes on me. How much I loved that blinding light, the thrill of a rapt audience, pretending to be someone else, getting to forget myself.

"You're such a ham," Ricky says when I get back to our high-top table. He stands up and hugs me. "Seriously. The stage still adores you."

"I don't know," I laugh, sipping my soda. "You going to sing something?"

"Um, there isn't enough Klonopin in the world."

As infectious and gregarious as Ricky is, as loud as he can be at a restaurant, he has debilitating stage fright. This was why, in high school, he was always painting sets or sewing costumes while I was vying for the leading role. Behind Ricky, a drag queen with glittery lips and a red wig the size of Texas sits at the bar staring at me, just staring at me like she's trying to burn a hole through me with her eyes. And suddenly, I get a shiver and dislike the attention I just brought on myself. Why do I do this? What's up with my fraught relationship with the limelight —flying toward it like a dumbass moth, then hating the burn of it and flapping away?

"This person is just staring at me," I mutter to Ricky. "Behind you. My twelve noon. Drag queen."

"Oh?" Ricky turns around. "Yeah, that's this thing people do sometimes when they want to jump your bones."

"You want to head out?" I ask.

Ricky looks surprised. He adjusts his collar. "Really? Already?"

"I could use the fresh air," I say, slipping my jacket on.

That's an understatement. I'm suddenly finding the air in here smothering, the proximity to so many cheering, smiling, yelling half-sauced people oppressive.

Ricky chugs his vodka soda and we head out into the night. Berkeley is alive right now, the downtown streets filled with laughing college students, a juggler performing in the square, a guy riding back and forth on the sidewalk with a bicycle and a blown-out speaker playing hip hop. Two blocks up, there's the west-facing mouth of campus. Years ago Jack and I used to go downtown Friday and Saturday nights. We'd get dolled up and go out to dinner and it felt so *fancy* at the time, like I was still a kid cosplaying an adult, scanning wine menus and pretending like I knew what any of it meant. It was nothing to Jack. His dad worked at Jolvix and was swimming in it, his mom was born with a trust fund in her pocket. But me? I felt like a queen.

"You okay?" Ricky asks, putting his hand on my arm. I suddenly come back to present and realize I'm hesitating at the crosswalk, lost in space.

"I'm fine," I say. "Just remembering when Jack and I used to come down here."

Ricky takes my hand and we cross the street. He says nothing. I know he's waiting to see if there's more—like when your best friend's holding your hair while you vomit.

"We just passed the five-year anniversary," I say.

Ricky squeezes my hand. "Oh, Leelee. I'm sorry."

"I forgot all about it. That's the craziest part, Ricky, I just—I forgot."

We pass by a tea shop, a pizza joint, and stop in front of a vintage shop with headless mannequins in fashionable dresses. Without discussing, we head inside together.

"That's … I mean, that's good, in a way, right?" Ricky says lowly as we start browsing the round racks near the front. "Shows you're moving on."

"Teddy had to call and remind me."

"Mmm, how is Tedward?"

"Oh, you know. His usual obnoxious self."

"You see a lot of him?"

There's implication behind Ricky's tone and I glare at him to show I'm not having it. "I do not."

"Mmmm, kay." Ricky picks up a striped blazer and shows it to me. "Eh?"

"You'd look like a candy cane."

He puts it back. "Your mom's trying to pawn some nephew of Huey's on me. Would that be weird? Double dating with your mom?"

"Ugh. She was trying to pawn the same guy on me."

"Man must be desperate. I'll take him."

"Please do. I guess he must swing both ways?"

"All the best people do."

We bump fists like a couple of dorks. I file through the rack saying silent *no*'s to every item of clothing—ugly, ugly, ugly. I stop to consider a glittery halter top. Not because I want to wear it, Lord no, but because it reminds me of someone and the smile melts from my face.

"Ricky?" I ask.

"Mmm?"

I look up, over the rack, over a pair of rainbow clogs that no creature on earth's surface should ever wear.

"Would it be weird if we went to Lotus's memorial service tomorrow?"

He stops what he's doing—trying on a scarf and making duckface at a nearby mirror—to turn to me. "Is this the real reason you invited me up here?"

I swallow and offer a sheepish smile. "Maybe subconsciously."

Ricky steps closer and says, lower, so the shoppers clicking through the racks can't hear us, "You want to go to a memorial service for a dead woman who once tried to fuck your fiancé?"

I nod.

He breathes in deeply, puts a hand on his chest. It's as if I just told him he won a prestigious award. "I would love nothing more."

Ricky doesn't ask why I'm going, what I hope to get out of such a thing. Which is good because I have no idea. All I know is this: Lotus Windsong is dead the same way Madison La Rosa is dead and I want answers.

CHAPTER 17

The memorial service is held at a steepled church in the Oakland Hills. Parking sucks and we end up having to walk uphill and by the time we get to where the crowd is milling outside the church garden, Ricky and I are panting. We stop near the entrance to get in a short line where a woman is handing out pamphlets and leis.

"Damn, I'm going to be sore tomorrow," I say.

"Could be worse," he says, pointing to the table where a teardrop-shaped urn gleams in the sun, right next to a picture of Lotus's smiling face.

"Thank you, Ricky," I say sarcastically.

Flower petals lead the path from the front garden into the church. We take our seats in the back pew. There are probably fifty people here. A handful are suit types who stick tightly together and I imagine that's her work crew. The rest of the crowd here look like new agers, which doesn't surprise me. The name Lotus Windsong tells a story. Multiple people are rocking tie-dye and a man with a braided white beard plays the flute near the podium. Up front, a slideshow of Lotus plays onscreen and I try not to focus on it—on the tangled-haired, smiling child; the teenager hugging a llama; the girl I knew in college with that wicked smile and wild, sun-streaked hair.

JOYOUS JUBILEE FOR OUR BELOVED FLOWER LOTUS, says the pamphlet in my hand. It's printed on bumpy paper that apparently can be planted in the ground to sprout wildflowers. I run my hand along it and realize I haven't been to something like this since Jack's funeral. Unfortunately, I was so blotto drunk I barely remember anything but puking in a tulip bed on my way out. The memory fills me with hot shame.

"Maybe we shouldn't have come," I whisper to Ricky.

Right as I say it, bongos bang along with the flute and a couple guitars join in. A microphone announces itself with a shriek of feedback and it takes me a moment to locate where it's coming from, but then I can see a woman in a kaftan dancing through the center aisle, twirling with a smile on her face. She's coming from the front of the church, where the organ and stained-glass windows are, toward the back of the room where we sit.

"We're going to begin this service with a collective interpretive dance," she says. "All rise for Lotus!"

"What?" whispers Ricky, turning to me with panic in his eyes.

"I told you we shouldn't have come!" I whisper back.

"We're here because you said we *should* come," he whispers back sharply.

We have fast become the only people not standing in the room and so, alas, Ricky and I rise up and glance longingly at the shut back doors. The whole room erupts into a dance to the new-age music, everyone moving from their seats and milling about the room. Ricky and I stay in our spot, waving our arms, wiggling minimally to the music, waiting for it to be over.

"Come!" an elderly woman in a long purple dress says, reaching her arms out to me.

And suddenly we're swept up in this ridiculous dance fever that has come over the room, not because we want to, but because we must—it's like clinging to a rock in a rushing river. The people pull us in and we're moving around the room now, down the side aisles while people I have never met sing and chant and clap and dance. Every time I twirl and catch a glimpse of Ricky he looks like he's in agony. I also catch a glimpse of the clique in suits who move through the crowd as stiffly as a gaggle of Franken-stein movie-monsters. Finally, after an eternity in inter-pretive dance hell, the bongo playing gets wilder and wilder and then stops and everyone mills back to their seats.

"This is what Lotus would have wanted," the woman with the microphone says. "This is what my flower child would have wanted. I know she grew up and I know she got her fancy job and gadget-filled apartment—" She pauses here to nod at the people in suits. "—but under-neath all that, she will always be my flower child." The woman's up front now, near the podium, beaming a grin at the room. "Today, we're not going to talk about death, because death isn't *real*. What is real is a *soul migration*. And today we're going to celebrate that soul, celebrate it, even if we weren't ready for it to migrate yet." Her voice catches at the end.

Her grief's so familiar. I wasn't ready for Jack's soul to migrate yet, either.

I have to disassociate right now, tune the woman out, go to a safe room inside my brain I reserve for emergencies or else the emotions will overwhelm me. I'm not here anymore and I can't hear the eulogy a mother is giving her youngest child. I'm teleporting to a different time and place.

CHAPTER 18

If I had to pinpoint the apex, the climax, the biggest spike on the happiness graph of my life, it would be senior year at UC Berkeley. Spring break. After a mean and rainy winter that spun Jack into a seasonal affective depression, the sun was out again and Jack's perpetual frown melted. Blossoms snowed pink on the Berkeley streets. Jack was accepted into UC Berkeley's PhD program and we celebrated in the city, a film festival, tapas, and ended up in a vintage shop in the Haight looking for wedding outfits— only half-seriously, because we hadn't even decided on a date yet. We ended up picking out the worst things we could find in the vintage shop for the other and trying them on. The moment we came out of the dressing room doors and saw each other we started laughing so hard Jack almost peed his pleather pants.

Wiping tears away, I showed off the orange fake fur ballgown. "I look like a muppet!"

"Do you see how tight this is?" Jack turned, displaying

the back of his pants. "I'm going to need to have it surgically removed."

"Look at that shiny, juicy man booty," I said, wiggling my eyebrows.

Jack turned around and pulled me into him, kissing my neck and making me squeal. "Come here, you crazy muppet."

Take a picture, Leela. That was it. That was your apex.

I didn't realize it was the apex though; I thought I was at the foot of the mountain. Life was supposed to begin after graduation. Now that we knew we were staying for Jack's PhD, a beautiful future was materializing. I could picture it, Jack going to school, me getting a job, our little funky cottage on a quiet Berkeley street. There's something unequivocally gorgeous about potential and that's the true allure of youth—being in a place where the future is unwritten and could contain anything. The world is infinite. Soon infinity will snap like a thread and all those dreams will be dust, but shhh, let the young dream a little while.

We could live a dozen futures in a single discussion.

"How about a destination wedding, kitten?" Jack said one afternoon. *Kitten.* His nickname for me, because of my cat eyes. His head laid on my lap as we lazed on the lawn outside the co-op he lived in. "Maui. Mexico. Ceremony on the beach."

I ran my hand over his short, buzzed hair, giving myself the best kind of chill. "Or something unique. A botanical garden. A zoo!"

"An Elvis wedding in Vegas."

"I wonder if anyone's ever been married in a hot air balloon?"

Jack and I spent all of spring break together. Though I've strung the memories with fairy lights, the truth is even though it was our apex, there were still dark moments. Jack had mood swings that made him irritable. He told me I drank too much and called me a bad influence and he was right. He found out I was snorting my roommate's Adderall again and we had a fight about trust. I choose not to dwell on those times.

But those times are where Lotus lives in my memories. That afternoon, with Jack's head in my lap, was the first time I saw Lotus—intimidated immediately by the way she swung her hips, her cute crocheted top with unabashed jiggling sideboob. Both animalistic attraction and jealousy awoke in me as she peered at us through her aviator sunglasses, chewing gum.

"Hi Jack," she said in her wittle baby voice, waving her fingers.

He turned his head and squinted. "Hey Lotus." He pointed at my chin. "My fiancée, Leela."

"Fiancée?!" she said, her jaw dropping. "Locking that shit in already?"

"Damn straight," Jack answered.

Lotus strode away, flagging down some guy on the front steps to see if he had any rolling papers. She came off as rude, not even addressing me, and it didn't go by unnoticed that she referred to Jack and my relationship as "that shit." I saw through her. I saw trouble.

Jack's co-op called itself Hearst Castle as a kind of joke —the decrepit mid-century brick building was anything but a castle. It was the kind of place with tattered prayer flags and hammocks on the porch. Friends came and went all day long and the skunk smell was ubiquitous. In the backyard, a rusted refrigerator and a dwindling garden box occupied the overgrown grass. But there was also a magic to the house, which was why Jack loved it there. There was Micah, a daydreaming painter who would stand outside throwing paint at an easel for hours at a time. JJ, a bearded, yeti-looking stoner who was as elusive as Bigfoot himself. Wes was an opera singer who took too much acid and had a nervous breakdown and had to move out. Roy welded, Zach played jazz, the list went on and on. And now there was Lotus who ... I didn't know what the fuck she did. She made beaded necklaces and called it "art."

Fast forward a month. One bright morning at the end of April, I was shocked to see Jack waiting for me at the bottom steps of the English building after my first class of the day. He never did that; his class was on the other side of campus. He had this look on his face, pale and stricken, like he'd just seen someone hit by a train.

"Hey," he said. "Can we talk?"

Those three words. Please, not those three words. Whatever was coming, I felt the world skidding to a stop on its axis.

"Sure," I said, swallowing.

He led me to a stretch of grass and we plunked ourselves under the shade of an oak tree. My heart was pounding.

"What?" I asked.

"Listen, something happened last night," Jack said, not

looking me in the eyes. Not once looking me in the eyes. Bad, bad, bad. "And I need to tell you about it because it's eating me alive."

"What?" I asked, my voice sharp, readying myself for pain.

"You know that girl Lotus who moved in?"

I could have thrown up. "Yes?"

"We—she kissed me last night."

The sting was almost numbing. "She kissed you."

"Yeah. It wasn't—it wasn't anything." He pulled a white clover from the ground and contemplated it deeply instead of giving me the eye contact I deserved. "I'm sorry, Leela."

"If it wasn't anything then why are you sorry?" I asked, sprinkling a little sugar in my tone. "Should I be worried? Was there tongue?"

"A little."

"She shoved her tongue in your mouth," I clarified, smearing a smile on my face, a piece of tape to keep me from falling apart.

He nodded. He still hadn't looked at me once. Meanwhile, I'd been searing him with my gaze like a laser beam.

"And did you return the favor?" I asked.

"Just for—just for a minute."

"A *minute*?"

"Or something."

"You put your tongue in her mouth for sixty seconds?"

"I wasn't counting."

Okay, now I wasn't smiling. My hands shook. The

betrayal was a hot, nauseating force traveling from limb to limb.

"I'm sorry, kitten," he said, finally, *finally* looking me in the eyes. "It was an accident."

But I cut him off. "Walk me through it," I said. "Walk me through this lil oopsie-daisy."

I couldn't keep the venom out of my voice.

Jack started at the beginning—a bottle of wine, a hash-dipped joint, and Lotus on the back porch last night. How they got to talking about marriage and monogamy and Lotus was telling him that humans weren't meant to be monogamous. Then she reached over and started kissing him from out of nowhere. And he was "so wasted" he just "automatically" started kissing her back and then "realized what was happening" and pulled away from her and stumbled up to bed.

A volcano simmered within as I listened to this story, this story that just didn't make sense to me. There was context missing. Description. Dialogue. I needed to know what kind of signals he was giving her, how close he let them sit during this conversation, their body language, how, how could this happen? Instead of screaming like I wanted to, I just started bawling. Jack started crying too and that pissed me off because who was he to get sad about my getting sad when he was the reason I was sad in the first place?

With me, despair and rage are twin sisters. When one awakens, the other stirs, too. After the river of tears dried I said not a word to Jack, but got up off the grass and power walked all the way to Hearst Castle. I stomped inside where Jack's housemates were slouched in the living room on various pieces of mismatched furniture, passing some kind of digital bong thing back and forth. I must have blown in like a storm because the room's laughter and conversation immediately quieted. Lotus was sitting on the end of one of the battered couches, twirling her hair around her finger, slanty-eyed stoned but not guilty seeming whatsoever.

"You parasitic bitch," I said, my voice quivering. "Touch Jack again and I will murder you."

Her jaw dropped and everyone's eyes widened. I liked that I commanded their fear like this, the power I held like a spotlight. I jabbed my finger in the air with each word for emphasis, repeating. "*I will murder you.*"

"Leela," someone said, trying to lure me back to the land of reason.

But I spun on my heel and left Hearst Castle.

I ignored Lotus after that. Ghosted her even when she was in plain sight, would never grace her with a stare. I erased her. Jack and I never spoke of her. But this was the first thread pulled. This was what started the unraveling.

This is why a tiny, horrid part of me secretly smiles knowing she's dead.

CHAPTER 19

I come to, emerging from my memory chamber and refocusing my mind back on the here-now of the funeral, because Ricky is nudging me.

"You're up first," he hisses in my ear.

What? All I see are the backs of heads in pews in front of us. The flute is playing again and I have no idea what Ricky's talking about until there's a tap on my shoulder and the kaftan woman with the microphone is in the aisle right next to me. She nods and hands me the microphone.

"What?" I say, staring at the mic in confusion.

"Say a nice word about Lotus," Ricky whispers.

"Oh."

I hold the microphone to my lips and breathe in. The kaftan woman folds her hands in front of her and watches me expectantly, with shining eyes. One by one, heads turn, waiting for me to say something. Even the flute stops playing, an enormous, suffocating silence filling the room.

"Well," I say into the microphone.

Funny story: Lotus tried to fuck my fiancée once, and now they're both dead!

Ricky's expression is pure fear, his irises islands in a sea of white. It doesn't rattle me. The smothering pause of fifty waiting people doesn't rattle me, either. I worked in PR. The truth is clay; I can work it into anything I want.

"I knew Lotus in college," I say in my soothing publicity voice, coaxing a half-smile to my lips. "A true character. A girl who, you know, shimmied to the bang of her own bongo."

A few titters of agreement from the audience.

"She was a girl who wasn't constrained by anyone or anything. A girl who saw something she wanted and went for it, rules be damned." I clear my throat. "Rest in peace."

The woman in the aisle nods at me and gestures for me to pass the mic to Ricky, who stammers loud enough for the mic to pick it up, "No, no, I'm a plus one. I don't know Lotus! Never met her actually, just knew *of* Lotus. She sounded … yeah."

Awkward, man.

Quickly, Ricky passes the mic to a man at the end of the next row. Ricky's olive skin has seared to a humiliated pink. I pat his knee and he gives me a dirty look as if this shit is my fault. Which I guess it is.

It takes a long time for fifty people to say something nice about a dead person. Finally, the service concludes with everyone getting into a circle around the perimeter of the room, clasping hands, and singing "Circle of Life." It's one of the more excruciating things I've ever had to do.

After the service, Ricky and I stop to conspire on the

steps as everyone heads out into the garden where the reception is.

"That was ... I don't know if I can ever forgive you for that," he whispers.

"I know. I'm sorry."

"Besides the whole thing being icky hippie BS, I resent expending *sorrow* for that woman."

"You and me both."

He looks bothered, stopping to loosen his tie next to a rose bush. "And it's hot. I am sweaty. You know how much I hate sweating."

I rest along the brick wall, next to him, as the slow parade of people in black passes by us. "It also makes me think, though, that I was too harsh on her."

"Oh come on. You didn't *do* anything. Remember how I tried to get you to get back at her—the fake kidnapping idea? Scare the shit out of her and leave her somewhere bound and gagged?"

"Mmm," I say, remembering now. I glance at Ricky. "That's messed up, man."

"Don't look at me like I'm the monster. At the time I believe you considered it."

Joked about it. I had the heart but never the stomach for revenge. As a breeze moves through my hair, what I think about is how much time I wasted hating Lotus Windsong. How much energy that took from me, to hate her. How possibly misguided my hate was and how I never felt an ounce of that for my own fiancé who—I realize right now with a deep pain in my throat—was most responsible for what happened.

I clear my throat a couple times to swallow the pain,

scanning the crowd. Everyone is talking and shaking hands as they meander to the back rose garden. "I think we should mingle."

"Ew, why?"

"Because I want to, I don't know—see if we can find out anything about what happened to her."

"Sure," Ricky says. "I'll just go over the vegetable tray and break the ice with a stranger by asking if they know any gory details about why Lotus blew her brains out."

"Come on," I tell him, linking my arm in his. "You're the king of gossip. Some tea *will* be spilled."

"Bestie," Ricky says sweetly as we walk across the grass, the smell of blooming roses carried by the breeze.

Ugh, he only uses that tone when he's about to condescend some advice my way.

"Have you considered that maybe, just maybe, Madison, Lotus, it's a coincidence?" He takes a comb out of his front pocket and tames his front cowlick as we walk. "I mean, I'm here to do whatever. NQA. But …"

"NQA means no questions asked," I remind him sharply.

"Fair," he says, slipping his comb back into his pocket.

Ricky and I split up to mingle. After some initial somber introductions to a couple of red-eyed, cried-puffy cousins, I zero in immediately on Lotus's work friends. Family's going to wear love goggles that distort everything. Too much emotion there. But co-workers? They will dish. I grab a coffee and approach the suits. There are four of them, a woman and three men, talking quietly in a half-circle.

"Hey," I say. "You all worked with Lotus, huh?"

Nods all around.

"Associates," a woman says.

I gesture to the crowd, the church, everything. "I'm so stunned she's gone."

"I just saw her, hours before she ..." a man says, then shakes his head and drinks his steaming coffee instead of finishing his sentence.

I blow on my cup, a waxed paper cup with little butterfly wings for a handle that reminds me of AA meetings. "Did she seem ... I mean, was she ..."

"She seemed fine," the woman says. "I don't understand it."

"Do you know ... was it *her* weapon?" I ask.

"I would never have thought she'd own a gun. Total lib," says a red-faced man who won't stop smelling the roses.

A man puts his hand in the air, as if he needs permission to speak even though he's the tallest one here. "If I may? I heard the gun was 3D-printed. Those things are everywhere."

"Thanks, *Albert*," the woman hisses sarcastically.

I'm missing some context in the relationship here. But this is interesting. A 3D-printed gun—untraceable.

"Why wasn't her death investigated?" I ask.

The question seems to knife the air, kill the conversation. The suits are squinting at me like I'm a bright light.

"You know," I go on. "Just to rule out homicide."

"She left a note, man," says the ruddy-cheeked rose-smeller.

"Wait a darn second ... you mean *murder*?" Albert says.

"Albert, would you please just *stop*?" the woman snaps.

"Why would you ask that?" the man with the coffee says, almost angrily.

Realizing I've gone too far, I backpedal with an apology. Then, as the group stares at me accusingly, I make a beeline for the shady area where Ricky's got a plastic smile on his face as the elderly woman in the purple dress talks to him, her hand on his arm.

"Let's go," I mouth to him.

I grab a brownie on my way out.

"I found out some things," I tell Ricky as we walk downhill toward the sketchy shoulder where he parked his car.

"I'm pretty sure I just got solicited by a septuagenarian," he says.

"3D-printed gun," I say. "Untraceable. What about Madison? Do you know? Did Maya slash Stefan tell you? Was Madison's 3D-printed?"

Ricky and I stop at the car and he turns to me, an eyebrow raised, his hair getting messy in the roadside wind.

"It was," he says with some surprise.

3D-printed guns, the only kind that work in the novelty killer VixSpex. Those three words: *a real pleasure.*

"Too many coincidences, Ricky," I say.

He rests his elbow on the roof of his car and leans his chin in his hand, thinking. His car is a teal smart car, barely big enough for two people. I'm surprised his luggage fit in it on his drive up.

"Okay so why not go to the police?" he asks. "If you *really* think this is murder, you know?"

I have my answer queued and ready for this, because

I've been turning that question over in my mind for weeks now. "Number one, I doubt they would believe me. I mean, yes, it's farfetched. I sound insane. Number two, different police, different jurisdictions. I'd have to contact the FBI. The NDA I signed with Jolvix would be violated if I *really* talked to the FBI about what I think. And the FBI and Jolvix are like this." I cross my fingers. "You can't tell one without the other finding out. Number three?" I lean on the car next to Ricky, staring at a lizard as it scales up a rocky hillside. "I don't want to get investigated, Ricky. If it's my enemies dying, who do you think's going to top the suspect list? I don't want to get investigated and have it bring up all kinds of bullshit."

"Fair," Ricky says.

There's an edge to his voice, as if he'd like to say more. But he just squeezes my shoulder and the two of us fold up our bodies to fit back inside his toy car and he drives us back down the mountain.

CHAPTER 20

A few days later I sit sipping a root beer in a beer stein at Dry, waiting for Eve. A dry bar is like a sugar-free donut, a cauliflower pizza crust. None of these are first choices. But here we are.

Outside on the patio, bees hover around lavender bushes sprouting in the surrounding flowering garden and the sunset tilts its lazy orange gaze right at me and I can't help but think how much nicer this would be if I was drinking a cocktail, that warmth blooming in my belly, if I were the kind of woman who could just have one cocktail and enjoy an hour of relaxation. But I've accepted that my thirst is infinite and one drink will never be enough for me. I don't have enough until I've lost count and lost consciousness. While root beer in a beer stein is sad, my actions have proven it's certainly what I deserve.

I didn't drink until my senior year in high school. Shasta won't touch the stuff—her dad died of cirrhosis when she was a teenager. She called it poison. But one night I was at a party with theater kids celebrating closing night of *Our Town* and I took a red cup someone handed me of something sweet and burning. The more I drank, the less I cared about the fact that Madison La Rosa was there giving me the stinkeye from across the backyard bonfire. The less I cared about the string of blocked number calls I got on my cell from a heavy breather. It didn't matter anymore that every Saturday was eaten up by going to tedious auditions, living out someone else's dream. I forgot myself and it was beautiful. I went home and vomited on Shasta's pink leather couch and she cried rivers and told me I was breaking her heart.

Then there was college, a four-year bender. My tolerance improved, my liver suffered. I learned all the tricks—drinking water for every drink, hydration packets, ibuprofen before bed. I started mixing it with other shit, dabbling in a pill here, a line there. Drinking nudged itself earlier in the day, mimosas with brunch, beer with lunch. I was highly functional. Always made it to class, got great grades. Jack was the only one who ever seemed to notice how much I "partied." That's what I called it then. I partied so hard I hardly remember the night he killed himself. The haze that paints that entire period of my life is a heavy dread I have to live with.

After Jack died, I got a comms job at Keep Going and decided to start over in DC. I wanted to do something meaningful. Something that pushed back on the Great Nothing that swallowed my almost-husband. I had this whole idea that I was going to get myself together, become one of those women who enjoys salads for lunch and who heads to the gym when work is done. Instead, I drank. I drank from the time I got up and poured whiskey in my coffee to the time I went to bed with an empty bottle on my night table. I carried a flask to work in my purse on days I had to go into the office. There were bottles lining every windowsill in my house. My entire existence was an unending cycle of psychic pain and drinking to kill the psychic pain. When I think about these things, the root beer tastes so much sweeter.

Alcohol was involved in almost every regret I've ever had.

Speaking of regret, I'm a little uncertain now if meeting Eve is the best idea. But I don't know who else I can talk to at this point who will understand, besides Teddy, who's so good at lying he gets high off the smell of his own bullshit. If I don't spill it all to someone soon, I'm going to implode.

"What joyless hell is this?" Eve asks, coming out to the patio with a glass soda bottle in hand. Her wild copper hair's stirring in the breeze as she slips into a seat across from me at the picnic table. "No alcohol in this bar? Seriously?"

I shrug.

"Next time I'll make sure to stop by the liquor store first, get a little hooch for my purse." She winks at me. She's one of the only people in the world who might be cute enough to get away with winking. "So what have you got for me?"

"Look, can we talk today off the record?" I ask.

She twists the cap off the top of her bottle, suppressing a victorious little red-lipsticked smile.

"I mean completely off the record," I clarify. "Like, no

anonymous source whatever. None of this is going in your book. First I want to talk to you, as a … friend."

"Oh, we're friends now?" Eve asks, sipping her soda. "We going to wear friendship bracelets and have slumber parties and braid each other's hair and shit?"

"Seriously," I say, leaning into the table. "I want to talk to someone I can trust, someone who will believe me. There's some freaky stuff going on and I need to unload."

"Unload on me, baby," she says.

The way Eve talks to me sometimes, I can't tell if she's flirting or if this is just how she is.

"I can trust you," I emphasize.

"Of course. This goes both ways, Leela. I told you about my book and that is some top-secret intel."

I take a sip from my stein.

"Is that like two liters of soda in there?" she asks.

"One."

"Jesus. Diabetes, here we come."

I don't laugh. The words I want to say feel stuck in my throat. I've never said them out loud, but I need to. "The reason I left Jolvix was because of the novelty killer VixSpex Barnett Briggs made."

"I knew it!" Eve says, slapping the table. "That day we first met, after the livestream debate? When we talked backstage I could tell how spooked you were. So I called it, the killer VixSpex is what drove you away. Tell me more."

I wait for a frowning barback to finish grabbing a couple empties from a nearby table and go back inside before continuing. "That headset was a PR nightmare from the get-go. Like, every media outlet was covering it, the story was such fearporn. Killer goggles made as a—what did Barnett call it? A futuristic work of art?"

"A nightmare toy," Eve says. "He said he hung it there as a reminder of what territory VR had yet to conquer." She sips her soda. "I prepped before that debate, remember."

"You've got a good memory."

"I sure do. It's why I'm so good at holding grudges."

"I guess the two go hand in hand." I drum my fingers on the table while Eve waits patiently for me to continue. "What people don't know—what me and my boss Teddy bent over backwards to cover up—is that the headset went missing for five days and we never figured out what happened to it."

"Missing?" Eve repeats, eyes widening.

"It happened the week before that debate we did. One day they were on the wall of the conference room at Jolvix's VR headquarters, the next they were gone."

"The gun that was in the attachment too?"

"Whole thing."

"And you covered this up why exactly?"

"Because Teddy and I had just spent months defending the fucking things and assuring the public they were nothing but novelty items. Do you know what that would have looked like, what bumbling idiots the entire VR sector would have looked like?"

Eve's face flickers with thoughts, her brown eyes reading the air. She's visibly processing this and I can see she has *opinions* but she's trying to remain in journalism mode. "And then—what happened, how'd you find them?"

"They just showed up again."

"Showed up where, how?"

"In a cardboard box in Teddy's office after a long weekend."

"This is Jolvix, for Christ's sake. You don't have cameras?"

"We do, but not in the executive suite, which includes that conference room."

"Mmm," Eve says, putting her elbows on the table and folding her hands. "Wouldn't want anything that goes on back there to leak."

I scoff. "Transparency's for the peasants."

"Executives don't worry about security though?"

"I mean, pretty much every other square foot of the building has surveillance every second of the day."

"But like, a shooter comes in there or something?"

"Every room's got panic buttons." I wave my hand. "Listen, the missing VR headset's mysterious disappearance and reappearance, that's only half the story. That happened a year and some change ago. But in the past couple of months, two people I know died. Both suicides by gunshot wound. And I know, I *know* they're related."

Eve sips her soda and shoots me a skeptical look. "Related how?"

Twilight seems to have nudged the sunshine out of the sky. Some automatic lights blink on. They're strung above us in a zig zag. I get a shiver.

"Well, that's lovely," Eve says with surprise.

"It is."

She leans in, already bored of the beauty. "So how are they related? They both Jolvix people?"

"No, no—they're not related to Jolvix. They're both people I've known personally."

Eve's face is frozen in bewilderment.

"It sounds crazy," I say, desperation fluttering in me like a caged bird. God, I wanted this to make sense. I don't want this to just be my own narcissistic paranoia, the world being out to get me again. "But if you could understand it from my perspective—the similarities between the deaths, the fact I got these bizarre apologies from both of them, the phrasing they used in the messages, the fact they both used 3D-printed guns." My mouth suddenly feels so dry. I take a sip of soda, looking for the right words, and then sit back and realize there aren't any. There just aren't any.

My least favorite thing in life is when I'm too stumped to explain myself.

"I'm trying to hear you out here," Eve says. "I'm not getting it."

"Oh!" I snap my fingers. "You want to hear something else? The headset hanging in the office now? It's fake."

"Huh?"

"Barnett Briggs secretly took them when he retired."

"I feel dizzy from this merry-go-round of details you're feeding me right now, Leela." Eve rubs her temples. "Give me a sec to get all this straight. So the killer VixSpex went missing on your watch. You quit soon after. A year later, two people you know died of—" She raises finger quotes in the air. "'Suicide.' But these two people, they're unrelated to Jolvix. And Barnett Briggs left with the headset. Is that public?"

"Very much not public. My ass could get sued for telling you that."

"Okay, I'm just—I'm trying to wrap my head around this."

A silence widens the air between us. I feel like she's drifting away from me and I've got to lure her back to shore.

"Listen, you ever just have a gut feeling?" I ask. "Somewhere deep inside yourself, you just know?"

Eve nods.

"I know," I say. "I *know* these two deaths are related to me and I think they're related to the goggles, too."

"And you're telling me this why?"

"Because I'm wondering if maybe you could look into it. You know, you're a journalist. You know how to … find things out."

"You want me to look into the deaths of these people for you." She says it flatly, almost like she's insulted. But then, with a shrug, she says, "Sure."

"Really?"

"I mean, I can't promise anything, but I can poke around."

I'm not a hugger but I could hug her right now. I really could. A hit of relief relaxes me. "Thank you so much. Just —anything you can find that links these two people, besides me, anything you can find out about their deaths—"

"But if I do this for you, you're going to give me some information." Eve pulls a tube of lipstick from her purse and reddens her lips again. "On background, of course."

Well, that shatters it. I shake my head. "I can't talk

about the VixSpex, even as an anonymous source. The NDA—"

"Yeah, yeah, I know. I'm not talking about that. I'm looking for more general details about the campus, the company. Maybe you can guide me into some directions I can sniff out myself. It won't be anything they can trace back to you."

I let this idea spin its shiny wheels. Here are the fears that jerk through my mind in brief, wordless horror-futures: me in handcuffs for endangering the public by having the VixSpex stolen and covering it up; my life ruined by Jolvix, sued and bankrupted into oblivion; but the one that scares me the most for some reason is the image of these things happening to Teddy.

There are many accounts publicly available of people's lives being annihilated by Jolvix. A woman who used to work in my sector went on a social media tirade about work conditions and ended up sued for defamation and financially wrecked. The ex-executive in AI who was quoted in an article warning about the ethics of companion bots never worked in Silicon Valley again. Come on, Jolvix has an entire sector dedicated to "Legal Protection"—an enormous building with its own cafeteria and hundreds of full-time employees and lawyers on retainers. Then there are the rumors that have floated around for years. You know, critics of Jolvix who stood a little too close to open windows or drove on slippery bridges. Come to think about it, I'm surprised Eve isn't worried about herself. Though she already thwarted death by Jolvix once. Someone else might have been shook to their core by surviving such a nightmare, but with her, it only seems to have blessed her with an illusion of invincibility.

"I'm not going to fuck you over," she says, softer. "Okay?"

I want to believe her so badly. More than anything, I need an ally right now, one who gets what we're dealing with. If I can believe Eve's word, the only information she's going to use from me won't be specific enough to link back to me personally or even to the VR sector. It's on background. I should be fine.

"Okay," I say.

The triumphant glow in Eve's eyes reveals, for just a blink, how badly she values my cooperation. "Now on your thing," Eve says. "Barnett Briggs having the headset now—that's the most interesting lead to follow."

"Yeah, I think so too," I agree. "For all I know, he sold it or duplicated it or … who knows, gave it away as a gift to his pool boy."

"But don't you know Briggs? Didn't you work with him?"

I nod.

"So … why don't you just ask him?" She slips her coat back on. "I can't ask him anyway." She whispers. "'Cause I don't know about where the killer VixSpex really is, remember?"

Thinking of the pride I'd have to swallow to kiss that man's ass for information is enough to make me want to barf up my root beer. But Eve is right. There's nowhere else for me to start untangling this. I have to figure out where the killer VixSpex are.

I have to go see Barnett Briggs.

CHAPTER 21

THE GAME

The Game killed Lotus Windsong three weeks ago. That's the simple fact.

All I did was hold a gun to her head and make her put the VixSpex on.

I watched as she sobbed and tried to blindly run around her bedroom in the headset, her hands bound behind her, stumbling like a person in darkness.

It was like trying to watch an animal whose time was up in a slaughterhouse, a mouse plopped in a snake cage— the panic of prey suddenly realizing they are prey.

Then I turned, left the room, and waited.

While I waited, I glanced at the pictures in her hallway —ziplining in a jungle, riding an elephant, jumping from a waterfall.

She lived adventurously and was about to die the same way.

Once I heard the pop like a single kernel in a popcorn maker, I ducked inside the room again and winced at the sight: Lotus slumped like a pile of laundry on the floor near the foot of her bed, her bathrobe half-open, the contents of her brain polka-dotting her bedspread behind her.

It was an ugly sight, the vision itself a scar in my mind I will have to bear.

I knelt and untied the tape from her hands and peeled the flesh-speckled headset from her face and took my gloved hand to hers, gently putting her fingertips on the gun to decorate it with her prints before letting it slip to the floor in her limp hand.

I didn't kill Lotus.

It was the game—or her inability to win it—that killed her.

Since that evening, a bothered worm has been writhing in my stomach.

I don't like the devices that surrounded me in her apartment, the fact I had to move the Maxine to the freezer, afraid it would record what it heard.

I had watched Lotus for weeks entering her house, scouted the best place and time of day to make my move, but I hadn't expected all the gadgetry awaiting me once I got in there.

I've gone over it and over it in my mind.

I had planned it all and rehearsed it and even brought a stun gun in case I ran into an unexpected third party— and yet if there's one hidden camera, one listening device, this could all be over for me.

Not just for me, but for *us*.

When I was a child, my mother called me a *dimwit*.

It was one of her many disgusting nicknames for me, all uttered as sickeningly sweet as southern iced tea.

Even when I would hide out of reach from her, it seems her words would find me.

Or her shoes. She liked to kick me with her high heels while I crouched under the table.

"Try harder, dimwit," she told me in a soprano drawl as she sipped from her bottle. "You know, the only thing you're good at is hiding. So keep hiding, little rodent. Hide yourself, scatter, *scatter*, like a roach in a wall."

My skin still remembers the stinging jab of the toe of her shoe.

She's gone now, but that's what I'm left with—the memory of the pain she inflicted. The nauseating smell of peach schnapps and vomit. And the important lesson that I was to spend my life in hiding, the human equivalent of an open secret.

This round of the game, I have to be smarter.

Much smarter.

Hunt like a predator but hide like prey.

I already knew Genesis McBride was going to be an even bigger challenge.

Madison was the easiest, alone in that house most of the time waiting like a dog for her husband to come home.

She was also the farthest distance away and hardest to trace back to me.

Lotus was riskier, being in an apartment building in a popular, urban neighborhood.

But Genesis McBride lives in a gated community with security guards and surveillance.

Not only that, but she's engaged again and doesn't live alone.

She has a rotating cast of house cleaners, personal trainers, dog walkers, masseuses cycling through her house.

And then there's the fact she's the daughter of a California state senator—always threatened by the gaze of the public eye.

The risk of trying to surprise her in her home is too great.

Early on Wednesday mornings, Genesis drives to a park and goes on a long jog through the hills of East San Jose.

She takes the same trail every time, one that meanders through meadows exploding with grass and clover, shaded with hulking oaks.

The view is spectacular as the trail continues, Silicon Valley spread out on the land below like a glowing computer board with the bay smudged blue behind it.

What a wonderful place to die.

I got here early today.

Picked a hunched tree to crouch behind, one perched on the edge of an embankment.

Brought fruit snacks, duct tape, and a stun gun—along with the obvious.

It's unfortunate that I have to take extreme measures today.

I feel like some common killer on a true crime show, but I'm just playing a part.

That's all it is: playing.

Mask and costume and all.

Birds twitter in the trees, the sun shifts its gaze, the

day is still and then, in a flurry of pattering footsteps, she's here.

Genesis comes around the bend.

It happens too fast.

In a blink, I recognize her cotton candy running shoes and matching baseball cap.

A pink bullseye in motion.

I stumble to my feet and chase her for about ten feet.

Luckily she's got earbuds in and doesn't seem to sense me until it's too late for her.

The adrenaline feels like too much, like I could burst out of my own skin, and I lunge at her like an animal.

I tackle her to the ground, pebbles scattering, dust kicked up from the trail.

She turns to me with horror shining in her gray-blue eyes and as she finds her voice to begin to shout I press the stun gun into the back of her waist and press it for three seconds.

One Mississippi.

Two Mississippi.

Three Mississippi.

There.

I let go.

The silver duct tape screams as I pull it and snap a piece off, applying it to her open gasping fish mouth before she can yell.

Genesis's eyes are rolled back in her head, all I can see are bloodshot whites like a woman possessed, which is I guess a little better than seeing the terror gleaming in her eyes.

I hope you know I'm not a psychopath, Leela.

I'm terrified too, doing this in the open light of day where I could conceivably get caught by a hiker on the trail.

That should make you even more grateful when you find out someday—to know I'm not a monster but someone with a heart, with feelings, who risked this all for you.

Because I love you.

I love you like the moon loves the earth.

Genesis spasms, gags, thrashes, as I pull her by the cotton candy pink running shoes into the bushes, down the embankment where we can't be seen.

Once we're down in the shadows, once we're low enough that no one can see us and the dust settles, Genesis begins coming to, moaning, shaking her head and trying to sit up.

"I need you to calm down," I whisper.

But she doesn't listen.

She starts trying to get up again and I have to push her down with both my hands on her shoulders.

She's strong, kicking me in the chest, so I take my stun gun out and push it to her stomach, looking away and catching my breath as I push the button.

"You're making me do this," I tell her.

One Mississippi.

Two Mississippi.

Three Mississippi.

Four.

She flops like a fish out of water for a few seconds, dust clouding around her again, then goes limp.

I put the stun gun back into my holster and trade it for the gun.

I hover over her as she lies in the dirt and hold the nose up to Genesis's sweaty temple.

"Don't make me shoot you," I say in a high, sweet voice.

Genesis squeezes her eyes shut and begins screaming.

With the duct tape on her mouth, she sounds like a psychotic muppet, inhuman and muffled, almost comical, as she claws at the tape with her French manicured fingernails.

I take my gloved hand and pull her fingers away.

This is not going according to plan.

Part of me wants to abort mission, run.

I can't believe what a fight she's putting up after two long kisses from the stun gun and now a revolver pressed against her head.

She's either the stupidest or the bravest person I've ever met.

I almost admire her for it, but I conjure up the image of her pulling your hair and smacking you on the face publicly in that horrible viral video.

I wasn't close enough to you then to know how you felt about it all, Leela, and you said not a word about it on social media—but I'm sure it was mortifying.

Unforgivable.

To be accused of such horrid lies and physically attacked in the limelight.

I click the gun's safety, a gentle warning.

Click.

Genesis's fingertips slacken and stop pulling at the

tape. She squeezes her eyes shut. Tears roll down the sides of her face.

I wish you could see her, Leela, I really wish you could.

Lying here crumpled up, a mess, her elbows scraped and bleeding. Though, on second thought, that might be a problem.

I scan her body, her dirt-streaked *McBride for State Senate* T-shirt, her leggings … the tear on the knee.

The story of the struggle is written on her clothes.

She opens her eyes, heaving with breath, every inhalation and exhalation hissing through her nose.

She moves like she's going to sit up and I have to say, "Stay, *stay*," and press the gun harder against the softness of her skull to still her.

I have the sinking feeling this one here could get us in trouble, Leela.

I don't even have time for her to open her phone so I can pen you an apology right now.

The good news is, fingerprints and facial recognition to unlock a phone still works when the person is dead.

I'll write the apology to you after the game is over.

Aren't I resourceful, Leela?

Isn't this genius?

No one else would go to these lengths for you.

They always say true love means you'd be willing to die for someone, but that's not quite it; true love is being willing to kill for someone.

I reach carefully into my backpack for the headset, jiggle it in front of Genesis's face.

"It's playtime."

CHAPTER 22

LEELA

Barnett Briggs lives in a kiss-the-sky Italian villa with a three-sixty view of the green yawn of sloping foothills, the twinkling silver valley scattered like broken glass, and the hazy San Francisco Bay. It's disgusting. No one needs this. No one needs ten thousand feet of living space, nine bedrooms, and sixteen bathrooms unless you're a commune of people with no bladder control. How do I know so much about this ugly toad's house? I looked it up online last night just to glimpse the price tag because I'm a nosy shrew and that information is public. Let's just say I calculated that, on my current salary, I would have to work for two hundred and ten years to afford the mortgage on this place. Sometimes life in Silicon Valley makes me wistful for simpler times—like when guillotines were popular.

The man has three garages, a tennis court, his own private vineyard, a wine cellar, an infinity pool, a home theater, and a fountain with a naked cherub spitting water out of it. I expected this from the virtual open house I instigated with my research last night. What I did not expect was the greeting by a Jolvix companion bot at the foot of the driveway who has a cheese plate and a glass of wine like I've arrived at some luxury bed and breakfast.

"Um, hello," I say as I climb out of the self-driving taxi.

I'm always polite to bots. They'll be ruling us someday, so might as well stay in their good graces as much as possible.

"Greetings. You are Leela Crowe?" the bot asks. She's a woman with blond hair and tanning-bed-orange skin and if I didn't notice the silver in her pupils, I would honestly never be able to tell she isn't human. I get goosebumps here in this uncanny valley I've found myself in as I gaze at her extra-long, studying her features.

I've never been this close to a companion bot before. One would think I'd have rubbed elbows with a few on the Jolvix campus, since they're made by Jolvix. But Jolvix doesn't allow or employ companion bots on their campus. Which makes one wonder, doesn't it? When the inventor so distances itself from the invented. Companion bots are still extremely expensive and there's kind of a stigma around owning them, since so many of them have just ended up in the hands of perverts or people who abuse them because they can. Then there's the ethical and legal aspect of them, big political topic these days. And lastly, there are the news stories you read—that cruise ship disaster, the Grayson family murders, and those two bots who ran away from their owners and have somehow escaped being found for a year now even though there have been spottings of them all over the Pacific northwest.

"Greetings. You are Leela Crowe?" repeats the bot—or woman; I'm just going to think of her as a woman because it's too weird to think of her as a machine.

"Yeah, sorry," I tell her. "I'm Leela Crowe."

"May I see a form of government-issued ID?"

"Um, sure."

I fight the urge to roll my eyes as I reach into my purse and pull out my California ID. Sending a bot out to greet me with wine and cheese and carding me as if I'm buying a bottle of Jack Daniels—come on, man. She studies the license, probably scanning it like a computer or something, then hands it back.

"Would you like some vintage pinot noir grown here at Barnett's private vineyard as I lead the way to his estate?" the bot asks.

"I don't drink, but thanks," I say.

As if the vintage pinot is nothing but tap water, the bot nods and pours it on the ground near her feet. Looks like a purple puddle of blood there.

"Crackers, cheese, or grapes?" she asks.

"No thanks."

I half expect her to throw them on the ground, too, but instead she turns, puts a finger into the keypad, and an ornate iron gate swings opens. The bot walks up a set of stone steps on the side and I follow her, admiring the human-like jiggle of her ass in her pencil skirt and then shuddering when I realize that Barnett probably screws her. He is *exactly* the type who would have a robot fetish.

"Do you have a name?" I ask.

"Twelve. We go by numbers here."

Of course. Like prisoners. How cute.

I can't believe someone lives here. The front yard alone is like an entire gorgeous European park. The grounds are majestic, luscious lawns and sculpted hedges surrounded by redwoods and stone paths. I saw the pictures during last night's snooping session, but being here in person, it's so much more stunning. A bot who looks exactly like Twelve, same sailor blouse and tight skirt and everything, is driving a golf cart with gardening tools across the sparkling, just-watered lawn and waves a queenly wave at us.

"Hello, Twenty-One!" Twelve says.

Twenty-One? Oh my God, how many of these identical lady bots does Barnett have? I expected weird, because Barnett is Barnett, but this all goes far beyond. I think of Eve. She would have a field day seeing how this ex-CEO of Jolvix VR lives.

Twenty-One grins. "Hello, Twelve!"

"We have a visitor!"

"We do!"

"An exciting day!"

"Indeed!"

Twenty-One revs her engine and speeds the cart away.

"We do not often get visitors," Twelve tells me as we head toward the villa.

"Oh?"

"Barnett does business down the hill," she says.

"I see. Does he ... live alone?"

"No," Twelve says, turning to me with a plastic smile. "There are thirty-one of us here."

She proceeds to tell me about the history of the estate —the original Italian owner who built a wine-tasting app, how the vineyard in the back is bioengineered and Barnett owns the patent to the grapes, the custom-built infinity hot tub. I nod but all I can think is, excuse me, *thirty-one?* Am I understanding correctly that thirty-one *robots* live on this estate with Barnett? This is so creepy I'm tempted to text Ricky about it because I can hardly stand the fact I'm experiencing this freakshow alone, but when we pass the spitting cherub fountain and get to the front steps, Twelve stops and holds out her uncreased palms.

"I do have to ask you for your phone or electronic devices before allowing you to enter Barnett's estate. I hope you will understand."

"May I ask why?" I ask, pulling my phone out.

"Barnett is very strict about privacy."

I'll bet. Wouldn't that be fun if a few pictures leaked to the media about the entrepreneur who lives with a congregation of bots? This is all so extremely Barnett— weird in a way that makes your stomach turn. After all, he is a man who thought it was a fun idea to invent a murder weapon and hang it on the wall of his conference room.

"You want to search me for wires, too?" I joke, pulling my jacket open.

Twelve just stares at me. "I am not computing."

It would drive me insane living with this many people without a sense of humor. "Never mind."

She pushes open the grand front door. It's utterly ridiculous, something you might see on a castle. An entire tree probably died for it. Inside Barnett's house, the ridiculousness continues with its high oak ceilings, terra cotta floors, stained glass windows and spiral staircase.

Twelve shows it off and rattles off its history like a museum docent. The imported tilework from Italy. The leather sofa set that once belonged to an ex-president. Meanwhile people are starving, but you know, cool crystal chandelier in your bathroom, bro.

I twiddle my thumbs for a good half hour, walking circles around the living room without my phone to distract me. I worked with Barnett long enough to know this is how he does things: even if he's ready, he makes people wait, always. It's a power play. It tricks people into thinking he's important so that they'll settle for less.

Finally, after enough time to watch two feather dusters float all the way around the room, he comes out. It takes real effort for me to nudge a smile to my lips when I see him there with his arms open. It takes even more effort to walk toward the thing which repels me so and allow it to wrap its arms around me.

CHAPTER 23

"Leela Crowe! The whip-smart pinup girl," he says, holding me so long I'm scared he's getting a boner.

I pull back and give him a playful punch on the arm. "Hey, Barnett. Cool place."

This is me trying to anchor us in the friend zone, undo the absolute yuck that was that hug. I expected the man to come onto me, as he does with anything human; then again, as seen today, even being human is apparently too high a bar for him. The man is a serial sexual harasser, so much so that he doesn't see it as harassment. He thinks you should take a grope as a compliment, consider yourself lucky to be privy to his dirty jokes. With entitlement this out of control, the world is his for the taking. Even someone as ugly as him.

The man is a human Christmas ham. Bald, round-bellied, bespectacled, he gleams pink and sweaty under the lights. He has a condition that makes no hair grow on his body—no eyebrows, no lashes—and it gives him this odd appearance of a middle-aged man who is also, somehow, a newborn baby. He wears Hawaiian shirts and flip flops everywhere he goes, even back at Jolvix, as if he might fly off to an island paradise at a moment's notice.

"Isn't it *sumptuous*?" he asks. "Did you get a little taste of my pinot?"

The way he talks, too, it's like ninety-five percent double entendre, uttered with the most flamboyant flirtation.

"No thanks. I don't drink."

"I had no idea." A lipless, reptilian smile spreads on his lips. "Well, I'm sorry to have played the temptress."

"Don't worry, there's no temptation whatsoever," I say, meeting his flat stare. Two can play the double entendre game.

"How about we sit by the pool?" he asks. "Have a chat?"

"Sounds good! Thanks for having me here."

Barnett leads us through a short hallway, a game room with a pool table, and an enclosed sunroom. The verbal vomit of small talk commences. He pretends to give a shit about me and my life, feigns interest in the "kitty place" where I work. I'm actually surprised and sadly a little impressed with his restraint that he didn't make a pussy joke. We exchange a few unfunny jabs about life back at the office we left as we step out into the sunshine. Barnett's backyard is just as absurd as the front with its gleaming blue pool and infinity hot tub, outdoor bar, and covered patio. An expansive semi-circle of lawn, mowed with perfect lines. But what I can't keep my eyes off of are the four bots lying in the sunshine on lawn chairs ... naked.

"They're solar-powered," Barnett says, as I look at

them and then look away, aiming my gaze at the pool instead. He gestures toward a glass table and chairs. "This is how they recharge. Removing their clothes before recharge speeds the process up. It's for efficiency, of course." Yeah, buddy. Sure. He sits in his chair, folding his hands on the table, his many rings clacking on the glass. "You can look at them, Leela. They're alluring, aren't they?"

Please get me out of here.

Reluctantly, I take my seat. Finally, I manage, "This is a trip, Barnett."

"I live a good life," he says, his forehead crinkling up. Had he eyebrows, he'd be raising them now.

"How's retirement?"

"How does it look? I'm the king."

"Mmm. You don't get the itch to come back to Jolvix?"

He scoffs. "Never again. I have no tolerance for corporate nonsense anymore."

"I hear you. So what are you up to these days? Any new dystopian nightmares in the making?"

I probably shouldn't have said that. Barnett's the type of cream puff who surrounds himself with sycophants and yes people. On the rare occasion I had to work directly with him, I was always respectful even though he didn't deserve it. Firing people was a sneeze to him.

A shadow passes over his face and he takes off his glasses, shines them with the edge of his shirt. "You here to snoop out what I'm working on, Leela?" he asks. "Did Jolvix send you here as a little mole?"

"I don't work for Jolvix anymore," I remind him.

"What are you here for then?" he asks, a little barb in

his voice. "Looking for Uncle Barnett to lend you some money?"

"I'm actually here to talk to you about the VixSpex. You know, the one hanging in the Jolvix office." I lean my elbows on the table. "Or … the one you have here at your house?"

"I don't know what on *earth* you're talking about," he says, automatically, lightly, in a tone that could or could not be joking.

"Look." I squeeze my hands together tight. "I'm asking because there have been some … freaky things going on."

"I love freaky things," he says, leaning in, imitating my stance—elbows on the table, hands clasped. "What kinds of freaky things, Leela?"

Seriously, the way this man looks at me makes me feel disgusting, like I'm not fully clothed. I pull my hands back to my lap and meet his eyes evenly, as if I'm staring at nothing, nothing at all. "People are dying."

"Okay, not *that* kind of freaky." He leans back in his chair and swivels it so he can survey his naked sunbathing robots and then swivels back. "Dying how and why are you trying to bring the Spex into this?"

"Because there have been two quote-unquote suicides back-to-back, both connected to me, that look incredibly suspicious."

"They're connected to you."

"Yes. People I've known." I shake my head. "Look, I'm not going to pretend this makes a ton of sense, it's—it's a gut feeling I have."

"The media's fearmongering hot takes really got to you?" he says, a grin spreading. "You played such a formidable defensive game, but I heard you quit because of the Spex. Is that true? You didn't quit because of a toy on a wall, did you? I figured it was the workplace romance with Ted."

It's as if the manbaby reached into my throat and stole my next breath. I need a moment to recover and I can feel the heat in my cheeks.

"Nothing romantic ever happened between me and Teddy."

"*Teddy*," he repeats, with flourish.

"We go way back."

"I know. He's filled me in."

The delight on Barnett's face—he looks like a pig who just spotted his trough. The idea of Teddy and Barnett discussing me makes my skin crawl. I can only imagine what things were said behind closed doors. On one hand, Teddy saw Barnett for the utter creep he was when it came to the personnel files riddled with red flags and the harassment claims quietly settled by transferring the victims to other sectors. On the other, Barnett was the person who pioneered the VixSpex and is revered in tech circles as a genius businessman. Teddy was able to both hate and respect him at the same time. As for me, I know that men like Barnett built their careers and products by stealing other people's ideas, giving no one proper credit but themselves, all the while surfing the sweet wave of nepotism. Barnett came from a filthy rich family. Teddy's dad is Jolvix royalty after working there forty years. They don't even know what it's like to earn anything.

"I'm asking you for a favor," I say as sweetly as I can. "For my sanity, Barnett. For me. A personal favor."

One talent I've always possessed is knowing just how to sprinkle sugar in my voice so I can feed people anything I want. I'm good at sensing other people. At reading their pauses, at knowing when to back off or when to keep going. I can tell I'm cracking him open right now. The idea of him having a favor to grant me is appealing to him. He leans back, folds his hands on his round belly, those beady eyes beaming at me like I'm a trophy.

"I just want to see it," I say. "I know the headset hanging in the office now isn't real. I know you have the real one. I want to see it, up close." I swallow and up the emotion, fully getting into the part here. I let a little quiver slip into my voice. "I just want to rule out any possibility in my mind that these weird deaths have anything to do with the Spex. Like, I know it's crazy. My mind's going to crazy places and I just—I figured, you're a nice guy. You and I always worked well together, didn't we? You'd let me just see it so I know I'm not losing it, so I know these deaths have nothing to do with the headset."

He plays with his rings on his fingers, twisting the gems one by one. He's considering this as slowly as he can. Reveling in it. The sun is out in full force and the sweat drips down his bald head in rivulets. "If I show it to you, what are you going to do for me?"

"What do you want?" I ask innocently, but my belly flip-flops. If he propositions me, I'm going to jet out of here as fast as my boots will carry me, Spex or no Spex.

"Let's see," he says, swiveling in his chair like a little boy in dad's office. "Well, it's embarrassing to admit, but—well, I've always had an itty-bitty crush on you, Leela."

Flip-flop, flip-flop, my stomach does gymnastics. Not this. Anything but this.

"Oh," I say weakly, expelling a nervous laugh.

"My smart-as-a-whip pinup girl," he says, licking his lips as his chair slows to a stop. "You know what I'd like? What would be a lot of fun for me?" He leans back, folding his arms behind his head. "I want to see you kiss one of my bots."

His words circle through my head multiple times, so outrageous they fail to make sense at first. Finally, I manage, "Excuse me?"

"What?" he laughs. "Is that gauche of me to ask?"

"Um, I wouldn't call it gauche. I would call it gross." I stiffen, watching him with such a wave of revulsion it's almost violent. I want to hit him with a stick or push him into the pool.

"I've been called worse."

He keeps his squint aimed at me and, in the silence, I realize he's serious. He seriously wants me to kiss one of his bots. What is wrong with him? How vile is he? But at the same time, I'm scratching at my brain-walls trying to figure out how else I'm going to see the Spex, how I'm going to put this theory to rest unless I see it in person and know for sure that it isn't in someone else's hands.

"I can't believe what you're asking me," I say.

"I can't believe the same. You come here and want to play with my toys, well, you've got to pay."

He says it playfully, but he's a madman. For a split second I wonder if he's the puppetmaster, the killer. If I'm right and the killer headset is involved and he's the one doing all this to torture me. Hell, he could be sending a bot out to do his dirty work for him. I glance at the sunbathing bots and get goosebumps. It wouldn't be like kissing a person. It would be like, I don't know, kissing a refrigerator. When I think about it that way, it's not that bad.

"One kiss?" I say.

I can't believe I'm saying it. He's rubbing his hands together with glee.

"A good one," he says, then barks, "Twenty-Two! Come here."

One of the sunbathers gets up, walking over with an expressionless face. The mortification I'm experiencing is akin to an out-of-body experience. I stand up as she comes over.

"Leela's going to kiss you," he tells the bot.

"Okay," the bot says, face a blank wall.

There's this moment that hangs in the air right now, my out-of-body experience continuing, something that's probably a little like how someone feels with their toes curled over the edge of a building right before the big jump. The dreadful pull of a single exit.

The robot woman is one of the creepiest machines I've ever seen. The creepy part about her is how ordinary she looks, how her skin that isn't really skin looks like skin, how attracted I feel to her not-real naked body and how much I hate myself for being attracted to a machine. I hold my breath, close my eyes, and plant my lips on hers. I'm shocked at how cold her lips are—it really is like kissing a refrigerator. Or a morgue-chilled corpse. I could throw up. I let my lips linger long enough to hopefully satisfy the perverted hog, then pull away. Beholding his gleaming grin, the excited way he rubs his palms on his cargo shorts, I know I've hit a new low. And this time I don't even have booze to blame it on. I wipe my mouth with the back of my hand and let the regret wash over me.

Barnett heaves a wistful sigh. "I'm going to remember that sight for the rest of my life."

"Now show me the Spex," I say, folding my arms over my chest.

"Come with us, Twenty-Two," Barnett says, getting up and clapping his hands.

As I follow Barnett into his house and a naked robot follows us, I decide two things: one, Barnett could definitely be a serial killer. And two, should I get out of here alive, I'm going to spill all about this to Eve and tell her she's welcome to use me as a source in her book to talk about the freakshow that is Casa de Briggs. I might even go on the record. We step inside and walk down a set of creaky stairs and I'm buzzing with hatred. My ears are ringing with hatred. The humiliation, the shock, the fear, the mess of it all just mixes and becomes one glowing hatred for him.

My inner alarms grow to a piercing crescendo when we reach the bottom of the stairs and I see we're in a dark painted basement, a gaming room ... a perfect place for a man to murder me with no one but a naked bot around to hear me scream.

And there, in a glass case so polished it's nearly invisible, is the shiny black VixSpex with a shiny black gun fixed to it.

CHAPTER 24

I stand, arms akimbo. "That's really them?"

"Don't they just command your attention?" he asks, stepping closer and admiring them through the glass. "It's the perfect statement piece for my gaming room."

I have so many questions. I glance around, do a three-sixty spin to take in the posh gaming room—the hugest leather sectional I've ever seen in my life, probably big enough that this asshole and all thirty-one of his electronic girlfriends can fit on it. A bar with a keg attached. Collectible posters in frames lining the walls and a VR room that looks like a mix between a sound booth and a padded cell.

"I have so many questions," I say. "Why did you leave a fake in the Jolvix conference room? Or has it always been fake?"

"Sit, Leela." His leather sectional makes farty noises as we sit on it. I leave a good six feet of space between us. "No, I had a dummy headset made when I retired, took the real one home with me. I wanted to leave a little something behind for you all to remember me by." He smiles. "Gone, but never forgotten. Gone, but still feared."

I study him, envisioning him as a boy. Sometimes I try to humanize people this way—imagine them as helpless children or feeble old men. I can imagine he was bullied and picked on. I can imagine what that does to a person's character—creates vengeful monsters, people who crave power like a thirsty animal craves water. This man is a bundle of blind insecurities wrapped in a sweaty, pink veneer.

Or maybe he's just an asshole.

"I see," I say.

"I've done a lot in my short time on this planet," he says, admiring the headset on the wall with the same affection some people look at their children. "But I can say, doubtlessly, that the killer VixSpex is my finest work. The world isn't ready for it yet. Someday, though, it will be. The stakes of game-playing will be raised."

"I believe the game's already existed for centuries, Barnett," I tell him. "Ever heard of Russian roulette?"

"That's rudimentary compared to this," he scoffs. "Russian roulette requires no skill. It's pure chance whether or not the bullet's in the chamber when you pull the trigger."

"I see," I say. "I assume you've played the VixSpex yourself then?"

"With the weapon attached? Of course not. I'm not an idiot."

Of course. Just like Jolvix not using their own bots. The people closest to these technological Frankenstein's monsters are the ones who know to steer clear of them.

"Has *any* person played it with a weapon attached?" I ask.

"No."

I'm stunned by this admission.

"So how do you even know if it works?" I ask, sitting up. "What if it's bullshit?"

"Oh, I know it works." He stands up, heaving to his feet with a guttural grunt. "You want to see it work?"

"No," I say automatically, my heart picking up speed.

In a flash, I imagine him forcing it on my head. I imagine the real world going black and my only hope being the dark unending game that lives inside the headset.

"Come here, Twenty-Two," he commands, snapping his fingers.

It shows how far into the bizarro we've wandered that I had totally forgotten a naked robot has been standing in the doorway listening to our conversation.

"Barnett," I say, standing up. "You really don't need—"

"Come on!" He unlocks the glass case with a push of a fingerprint. "You want proof that this is the real deal, right?"

"I mean—"

"Put this on, Twenty-Two," he says, dangling the VixSpex on a single pinky like a policeman collecting evidence. Barnett winks at me as the naked robot walks over expressionlessly and puts the headset on. "I love doing this. It's so much fun."

"Barnett," I say louder. "Really. Stop."

He adjusts the fit of it on the robot's face, tightening the strap, touching the gun to ensure it's clipped in place.

He clicks a button on and there's a tiny electronic whine like a machine warming up. Barnett stands back and gestures for him and I to take our seats for a little intimate homicidal theater. Reluctantly, I sit back down. The truth is, I want to know it works. If I do, I can leave here today knowing that the killer VixSpex likely had nothing to do with Madison and Lotus's deaths. Their suicides could be suicides and their similarities could be coincidences. Wouldn't that be a relief, to finally put this conspiracy theory filling up my brainspace to bed?

The bot puts her hands in front of her and takes a step.

"It's beginning," he says. "The game."

This is beyond revolting, it's unthinkable. I'm getting the sick sweats like I'm about to witness a murder but I keep reminding myself she's like a refrigerator, she's like a refrigerator, she's like a refrigerator.

"What is the game?" I whisper.

"You're a victim," he says. "Running from a slasher clad in black. It's called 'The Slaying Game.'"

"And how do you win?"

"You don't."

All this man needs is an extra-large buttered popcorn and a cherry soda. As the bot ducks down, shielding her head from some invisible terror, the joy in his face is one of the most heinous things I've ever seen. She stands to her feet. She fumbles around the room like a person in the dark, crouched, her hands feeling the air.

"What do you mean you don't win?" I ask.

"It's not a game designed for the player to win," he says.

"So there's no hope for her?" I ask, my voice getting louder.

"Well, I designed the game with one glitch, but none of my bots have ever found it."

I nod for a second and then stop as it registers, as I fully get what he's actually saying. "Wait. What glitch?"

He gestures for me to get closer to him, like he's going to tell me a secret. This is when I learn that, on top of being stunningly unattractive, he also has halitosis.

"There's a trap door," he whispers. "If she can find it—"

The bot stumbles, falling to a crawl. In less than the time it takes me to blink, the gun on the side of her head goes off with a shocking pop and she slumps on the floor, twitching, moving her legs like she's still running. Moving her lips like she's talking, no sound coming out. I gasp, hand flying to my mouth. The sight of the naked woman on the floor—dead, dying, damaged, I don't know what you call this—is grotesque. An inhumane horror. And the fact we're watching her from a fucking leather sofa like an audience makes the entire experience so much worse.

"Didn't even last a minute," Barnett says sadly. He heaves himself to his feet with great effort and stoops to peel the VixSpex from her head. The bot turns her head from side to side, opening her mouth and closing it like a person who can't take a breath. There's a large black hole on the side of her head, a peek of wires and hardware behind her now-peeling human-like face. Barnett gets up again and dangles the VixSpex in front of my face. I flinch. "Believe me now, Leela?"

"Yes," I whisper.

"You'll of course keep this between us," he says. "And

do keep in mind that, in addition to everything I know about you from our mutual time at Jolvix, I have footage of you kissing a naked bot that I'll bet you wouldn't want the world to see."

I gulp and nod. God, of course. Of course he did that—I'm sure there are cameras in every square inch of this nightmarish estate. I'm dizzy. I can't even think right now —the walls seem to be inching in toward me. There's not enough oxygen in here for me to get a breath. I thank Barnett for his hospitality and leave so quickly my boots nearly burn rubber on his staircase.

"May I get you something to drink?" one of the robots asks me as I pass through the kitchen—this one fully clothed, still functional. I can't meet her eye though, having just watched one of her identical sisters shot through the head.

"Just my phone," I manage.

"Of course."

I wait an eternal minute for her to fetch it. Outside, I hurry down the front stairs, pausing only to vomit in his cherub fountain before breaking into a full-speed sprint all the way off his property, never once looking back.

CHAPTER 25

Ever since my early morning jaunt to the South Bay to watch a madman murder a robot earlier this week, my sleep has been horrible. I toss and turn all night, plagued by visions of dead women and dead robots. Getting up a hundred times to check every lock, every window, to peek through the blinds at the empty streets. Twice this week I slept through my alarm, including this morning. Last night was the worst yet; I dreamt of Jack, with a plastic bag over his head, chasing me through Barnett's estate. Michael was there too. I haven't thought of Michael in ages and with a cramp, I miss him.

No time for breakfast. Barely time to brush my hair. I hurry into a self-driving taxi that whizzes me to work and settle into my chair at the office, my nightmares still swirling in my head. I'm so nauseated from it all I remember what it's like to be hung over.

"You okay?" Daisy asks. "You look a little pale."

"Yeah! Great," I lie, my back to her as I open the handbook file on my computer. "You?"

"I'm well! Training starts today?"

"It does. At two."

"Sure you're ready and rearin' to go?"

"Always," I say, in a chipper tone, but I can see my own annoyance in the reflection on my screen. I'm getting a little sick of her vague criticism disguised as concern. I bury myself in my duties, though. Handbook, here we come.

If a kitty swipes at you, we ask our volunteers to *paws* before reapproaching. Please keep in mind that some of the cats here have experienced a *hiss*-story of neglect and abuse!

Good Lord, this is stupid. I erase it and stare at a blank screen again.

Seeing Barnett on Saturday should have put my worries to an end. Barnett has the VixSpex. As much as I think he's a lecherous garbage person, I doubt he's running around seeking revenge on my enemies. I just don't think the man is capable of that level of effort and I don't see a motive. Which means that Madison and Lotus both died by suicide. Which means I should relax and not feel like I'm one clenched muscle.

Everything's fine. Everything's great.

I work through lunch, focusing on the handbook. Somehow, I'm able to mostly ignore Daisy's off-key humming, an escaped cat that Esmerelda chases through the halls, and three missed calls from Teddy on my cell. Proudly, I tell Daisy I got the handbook edited in time for the new volunteers and I go into the bathroom to change into a Feline Better shirt. It's a rainbow tie-dyed shirt with a giant black paw print on it and I hate it. Training sessions and photo ops are the only times in life I will stoop to wear it. I pull my hair into a ponytail and put some lipstick on and practice smiling in the mirror and then go out to meet my new volunteer team.

My job as Volunteer Coordinator means I get to recruit and train the lovely people who will take time out of their busy lives to care for our cats. For a few hours a week, these lovely people feed them, play with them, change their litter boxes, and make everyone's lives a little easier. There's so much joy in this part of my job that it warms my cold, dead heart. It's as if this job is the antidote to the poison of working at Jolvix. Witnessing the humility of giving up one's time to come here and show a little kindness to helpless animals is the polar opposite of the braggadocio of a capital-hungry tech company.

Training sessions involve a tour of our facility and an overview of rules and duties. Along with committed volunteers, we have "shadows"—anyone from the community can come in and see what's expected from the role before deciding whether they want to volunteer. I have four volunteers today and two shadows. Immediately, when I turn the corner to meet my new team, the sight of one of these shadows makes me want to scream.

It's Teddy.

"What the hell—" I immediately say and then, seeing the eager faces of the volunteers, I transform my voice into that of a happy camp counselor and segue the word into, "—hello everyone!"

They're all wearing nametags. Teddy's reads CAN WE

TALK? Classic Teddy. No respect for boundaries. I don't give him my phone number, he tracks down a private detective on Tasky to find me. I won't pick up my phone, he shows up at my work to demand my immediate attention. Utterly disrespectful. My mouth moves with a spiel about how grateful we are for our volunteers and how fun this is going to be but my mind is screaming *what the hell what the hell what the hell.* My eyes are fixed on the elderly faces of our four volunteers and the sullen-looking shadow girl with three rings through her lip. I'm not looking at Teddy. I'm not. Not noticing him there towering behind everyone else, dark hair slicked to the side, his screaming blue gaze.

To ignore something is to pay it a special attention. I've long known this. There are so many things I've done, that I've experienced, that I ignore. But that doesn't mean it isn't there. It doesn't mean I don't notice it. I've just given it its own special box inside me and put away the key.

"We keep anywhere from six to twelve cats in the Meow Meow Lounge," I say as the volunteers and I walk the perimeter of the room. "And as you can see, there's no shortage of toys to play with."

Silence. Nods. Is it me or is this group awkwardly quiet? I've been thrown off my game. I clear my throat. I'm not noticing Teddy as he picks up a cat toy and dangles it in front of Puff Puff perched atop a cat tree.

"The art on the walls," I continue, gesturing toward the many paintings that are replicas of everything from the Birth of Venus to Whistler's Mother, only featuring cats, "was donated by a local studio."

"I love it," says Edna, a woman with short purple hair.

"Mona Lisa," Teddy says to everyone. "More like *Meow*-na Lisa, am I right?"

Everyone in the group laughs and Teddy beams.

"Is that your real name?" asks Marilyn, the one with the giant glasses. She's pointing at his nametag.

"You can call me Ted," he tells them.

Everyone smiles at Good Ol' Ted. With jokes that stupid, he should have rewritten our handbook. The loathing I feel for him right now, bringing his general existence into my place of work, must be turning my face red. I fan myself with my notebook and continue the tour, introducing everyone to the cats.

This space has been sacred to me. I know it sounds weird, but it has. Feline Better was a place I became someone else. The Leela at Jolvix was all about pretending, spinning, lying. The Leela who worked at Keep Going was a soggy self-obliterating mess. The Leela in college had starry eyes for Jack and the Leela before that had a starry-eyed mother who carted her around like a talking doll. After I quit Jolvix, I did a lot of soul searching. What I found when I looked inward, when I *really* looked inward, was terrifying. I didn't have a soul. When no one was watching me, when I finally stood still, I looked in the mirror and I saw absolutely nothing. Was that who I was, underneath life's various performances? Was that all I was?

In a search to find myself, I traveled backward. Soul-searched in reverse motion. I blasted all the way back to the earliest me I could remember: the little pigtailed girl who loved cats. Who drew them and collected them in stuffed animal form. In tragic irony, Shasta was allergic and I could never have one of my own. But I was obsessed. That little girl was unscarred, unbroken. A happy child who liked simple things. So when I saw the job at Feline Better, I thought, I want that. I just want to take care of cats. To be a fresh Leela, a better Leela, one who didn't fuck everything up and get fucked up by everything.

In short, this is my simple, unsullied place and Teddy's here sullying it.

"And now we're moving to the back area, which is, unfortunately, for our registered volunteers only," I say once we've concluded in the Meow Meow Lounge and stand in front of the glass doors with the STAFF ONLY sign. I direct my next line at the lip-ringed teenager with her arms crossed. I'm guessing this "volunteer" experience isn't really a volunteer experience and her parents made her do this. "But if either of you are interested in volunteering, please shoot me an email!"

"Can we talk?" Teddy blurts.

"Sir," I say through my teeth. "I can take questions when I'm done with the training session."

"And when will that be, *madam*?"

"At three-thirty."

"I'll wait then."

"You may wait in the café."

"May I?"

This odd conversation has caused my volunteers to exchange looks with each other. I'm so angry right now I'm sweating. I haven't even been able to meet his gaze the entire session, but as I open the door for the volunteers and wave to the shadow girl with the shitty attitude, I briefly make the mistake of full-on eye contact with Teddy and what I see there hitches my breath.

Around the startling blue of his irises, it's red. He's been drinking heavily. No, crying. I open my mouth to ask him if he's okay but then decide, fuck him and his feelings. If he's here crashing my job uninvited, clearly he has no regard for mine.

I say that but even having him out of the room makes no difference. The entire rest of the training session, all I'm thinking about is Teddy and the redness of his eyes. While I'm showing my four volunteers the art of putting on and taking off a flea collar, I'm thinking about how the last time I saw the man cry was the night Jack died. I've seen his eyes shine with emotion many times. But actually cry? Just that once.

I finish up the training. I thank our volunteers and tell them I'll be emailing them their handbooks and the volunteer calendar. Then I grab my purse and exit the shelter, rounding the corner to the café.

The café is an entirely different world than the shelter. Due to health regulations, the two parts of the building are fully enclosed from one another. Only the cat apartments near the back of the Meow Meow Lounge are visible from an indoor window in the café's interior. The café itself is also aesthetically unrecognizable. It's painted black as a dungeon except for abstract cat art on the walls and their stereo's volume is heavy metal permanently cranked to eleven. I would probably fit in much better on this side of the wall, if we're being honest. Teddy slouches in a corner looking miserable and expensive. He's the only person in here wearing a suit.

"What?" I say in greeting.

"Whatever happened to 'hello?'"

"Amiable greetings are a ship that sailed when you invaded my workplace today."

"Your website said 'shadows' were welcome at any training."

"You're a shadow, all right."

"Nice shirt. Tie dye's really your shade."

"Shut up."

"Leela, seriously. Can we be serious?"

I stand with my arms crossed. I'm not sure if we can. I'm not sure what we are. He holds his hands out to me from his seat. Wrinkling my brow, I tiptoe closer. He takes my hands in his. What is he doing? Touching me? Tenderly? What on earth? He pulls me closer to him so I have to lean down to hear what he's going to say. I can smell him—spice, earth, soap.

"Genesis is dead," he says in my ear.

CHAPTER 26

I shrug off his grip, studying him, my knee-jerk reaction assuming he's messing with me. But of course he's not. Teddy's an ass, but not the kind of ass who drives a hundred miles just to pull my leg by telling me his ex-fiancée is dead. I'm shocked, fingers flying to my mouth.

He points a thumb at the door. "Can we—"

"Yeah, yes, of course."

Once we're outside, the throb of music nothing but a memory pumping through the window, I turn to Teddy. All the rage I had for him evaporates—it's like that with him. Our weather is volatile but fleeting.

"Genesis is dead?" I ask.

He nods.

I reach out tentatively, put my hand on his arm. "Oh my God, are you okay?"

"I'm all right, you know, I'm—in shock. Can we ... is there someplace we can go?"

I consider taking him to my apartment. But then

Teddy would be in my apartment. Instead, I blow out a sigh. "There's a sad dry bar across the street."

"Sad dry bar?"

"No alcohol."

"Perfect."

Ten minutes later, Teddy and I are sitting on the patio of Dry, two steins of root beer in front of us. Despite his red eyes, he's smiling at the sunny patio, the butterflies and bees hovering over the blooming plants.

"I don't know what you're talking about, this place is awesome," he says. He's not being sarcastic, either. He takes a sip. "You see they brew the root beer here themselves?"

"Genesis is dead," I repeat, centering us back on the tragedy that brings us together today.

"I'm sorry," he says, his smile faltering. He puts his hands on the table side by side. "I—I didn't know who to talk to. I tried to call, but—"

"You should have texted and said it was an emergency. I'd pick up."

"Would you?" Teddy looks at me, no smile now, his face looking so different without it.

"Yes, Teddy. I'm here for you."

He rolls his eyes. "Oh, give me a break."

"Begrudgingly," I add. "Begrudgingly here for you." Quieter, I ask, "So what happened? How did she die?"

"They don't know. Her body was found off a trail up in the East San Jose hills yesterday. Looked like a suicide. Shot through the head, with a 3D-printed gun."

My mouth drops open and I can't speak for a good, long second. I can't even move.

"You didn't get—you didn't get one of those messages you were telling me about, did you?" he asks.

"No," I finally manage. "Nothing. I haven't gotten anything on Peeps in days, maybe a week, I ..." I slump in my chair, my powers of articulation lost.

Somehow, when Teddy said Genesis was dead, I didn't think of this. I assumed, knowing Genesis, she died the way she lived: pharmaceutical overdose, maybe a botched plastic surgery. That it could be related to Madison and Lotus's deaths hadn't even crossed my mind yet.

"I haven't gotten anything on Peeps in days," I repeat, fishing through my purse to grab my phone. With shaking hands, I open the app. It's *frozen*. It's frozen on my feed and everything is now six days old. When I try to open it again, it tells me I have to update it, so I do. And that screw that's been there in my stomach for weeks now, it tightens a little bit further.

"Pretty sure it's being investigated as a homicide, though." Teddy clears his throat twice as if he's got a lump in there. "Or suspicious or something. Because I just got a visit from police this morning, asking questions."

"Like what?"

"Oh, you know. Where was I Saturday morning at seven, those kinds of questions. Remember those questions?"

The last part of his statement makes me flinch, but I glide over it.

"You're being *investigated*?" I ask, my voice climbing.

"Shhh, shut up, keep your voice down," he whisper-screams at me. He shoots a glance over his shoulder to make sure we're truly alone out here and then says, softer,

"I don't know. I immediately said I needed to talk to a lawyer and shut the whole thing down."

"You needed to talk to a *lawyer*? Why?"

"Honestly, I froze up, I panicked. I was shocked and—I don't know."

"Now you look guilty, though."

He sighs, long and loud.

"Well, why wouldn't you just answer the questions? Where *were* you on Saturday morning?" I ask.

"In bed. Sleeping. Cuddling my dog." Ugh, I forgot Teddy's a dog person. Of course he's a dog person. "I mean, come on. Saturday morning, I was sleeping in!"

"Do you have proof?"

"Proof? That I was sleeping?"

"Maybe … someone else was there with you?"

"Ohhh. No, *Leela*."

I don't get his tone, quite honestly. Bitter? Playful? I think both Teddy and I are experiencing our own individual versions of shock and are an emotional melee.

"I'm scared," he says.

We exchange a lengthy look and I do see it there, the fear shimmering in his eyes. And I wonder if his eyes are red not because he was mourning Genesis, but because he's just worried about himself. I shake my head, waiting for the right retort to come to my lips.

"I'm sorry," I say, knowing full well *sorry*'s no help.

"I'm in the process of suing her," he says.

"For what?"

"She never gave back the engagement ring I bought her."

I make a sound like someone who smelled something foul.

"What?" he says. "It's worth over half a million dollars."

"That is *so* tacky."

"Is it? Or is it tacky to keep a guy's engagement ring after cheating on him with a professional golfer with no hairline?" He runs his hands through his own hair, as if to comfort himself that he still has it.

I shake my head. "You're both unbelievably tacky."

"*She* wanted to get those Infinities. At least I dodged that bullet." He takes another sip of his root beer, smacking his lips. "You know Infinities?"

"Are you talking about those Jolvix implants?"

"Yes, those cute lil implants in your ring fingers that can track your partner's every move. Of course, Gen said that's not why she wanted them. She wanted something that really meant 'forever,'" he says mockingly, as if forever is a lie. Which I guess it is. "Plus you can program them with these physically triggered messages, you know, hold your breath for ten seconds and that means you love the person and *beep beep* you get a message on your phone."

I'm usually pretty good at controlling my facial expressions, but right now is not one of those times. Imagining Genesis and Teddy together, planning a cute lil dystopian future with his 'n hers implants ... puke.

"Yes, Leela, I can see by the look of repulsion in your emerald eyes that you agree that was a bad idea," he says to me. "So I suggested—delicately, of course, as everything is when you're dating a woman you thought was a bomb-shell but who was actually a ticking time bomb—that we go with a classic diamond ring. I spent a nice chunk of savings on it."

"And now you want it back."

"Is that so wrong?"

"It is. But in light of the absolute clusterfuck that is everything else, I'll let it slide for right now. Where's the ring?"

"Don't know. Cops asked if I have it."

"When's the last time you saw Genesis?" I ask, fixing my gaze on him intensely, trying my best to read him and determine if there's a lie he's burying somewhere. I've always been pretty good at reading Teddy—at least I think so. Unlike Jack, who had a stoic face and who I had to scrutinize and make wild guesses to understand; that was part of what attracted to me to Jack, the challenge of him. Teddy's a golden retriever, his happiness and misery both obvious on his face at all times.

"Months ago. Maybe a year ago. A long time. What's with the questions, you want to join team SJPD?" His brow furrows. "Where were you on Saturday morning, Ms. Crowe?"

"In San Jose," I tell him.

"In …" He chokes on the word and recovers. "Are you kidding me?" He puts his elbows on the table and leans in. "Why were *you* in San Jose?"

"Visiting someone."

"Who?"

"Barnett Briggs."

"*Barnett* Barnett?" he says, nearly shrieking. "Why?"

I shake my head. There's just too much to tell, I don't even know where to begin. "I'll get into it later."

His lip curls in disgust. "Please tell me you're not, like ... he's so disgusting."

The comment zaps me like a stun gun. I glare at him. "The fact you would even think ..."

My phone buzzes in my pocket and I pick it up. It's Daisy.

> Leela, sorry to have missed you! I didn't know you were leaving early today. Friendly reminder: we expect salaried employees to work full eight-hour days. Please take some time to review our time off policies again. ☺

"'Friendly reminder' my ass," I murmur.

The Peeps app reopens on the screen. Now that it's updated, it's lighting up with notifications.

Please, please, don't let me see Genesis's name there in my inbox.

"Everything okay?" Teddy asks.

"It's fine, hold on. Checking something."

I hold my breath as I click on the inbox.

There's one message. Just one. A vise tightens its grip on me, seeing that tiny gold flag signaling it's unread.

It's from Genesis.

The subject says, *I'm so sorry.*

CHAPTER 27

Fuck, *fuck*, FUCK.

I can't bring myself to click on it. I drop my phone on the table in front of me and put my head in my hands. A burning wave crashes over my face and I fight the vicious throb of tears. It's about as useless as trying to stop a volcano.

"What? What happened?" Teddy asks.

"There's a message from Genesis," I say into my hands.

"What does it say?"

I shake my head. Maybe I can stay here forever—just hide in my tear-damp hands, the world nothing but red-orange light coming through my fingers.

"Leels, what? What does it say?"

"I don't know. I don't know, but it's just like the others."

"You don't know? What? Can I see it? Let me see it."

I press my palms into my eyelids until I see psychedelic patterns and then pull them away. Take a deep breath and push the sobs back inside. When I face

Teddy again, his hangdog expression is covered in kaleidoscopic patterns. They fade. I wipe under my eyes carefully to erase the smeared eyeliner.

"Okay," I say, as calmly as I can. "Let's—let's read it."

Teddy comes to my side of the picnic table and sits right next to me. I am aware of every inch of where his body touches mine. Our thighs. Our arms. With a trembling hand, I wake up my phone and press a button to open the message.

> Dear Leela,
>
> I hope you can forgive me for attacking you in that humiliating video.
>
> It was wrong of me.
>
> You don't deserve that.
>
> You deserve only the best.
>
> You're a special sort of beautiful, Leela.
>
> You shine like a lone lighthouse on a dark sea.
>
> Never forget that.
>
> It's been a real pleasure,
>
> Genesis

That's it, the whole message.

"What *is* this?" Teddy says. "Genesis didn't write this. She has the spelling of a fifth grader and uses emojis after every sentence."

"*You shine like a lone lighthouse on a dark sea,*" I murmur.

Where have I heard that line? I swear I've heard that line before.

"This is—this is someone else," Teddy says, pushing the phone back to me. "This isn't her." He turns to me, and asks, softly, "What the fuck is going on?"

I shake my head. "I don't know." I'm numb, a head full of bees. "I should talk to the police."

"You know, it doesn't look super great for you, going to San Jose on the day she was killed," he says.

"Please," I say. "I'm not worried about that."

But the thought does flash through my mind: who would be the prime suspect in a string of murders of my enemies? He's right. I'm going to get pulled into this, investigated. I really, really don't want that.

"I've had this feeling that these deaths have something to do with the VixSpex," I say.

"*Why* though? I'm not getting it."

"*It's been a real pleasure.*"

"People say that though. It's not just a slogan, it's a cliché."

"I have a gut feeling, okay? That's why I was at Barnett's," I tell him. "I wanted to see it myself."

"And did you?"

"Oh did I ever." I shake my head. "I'll tell you all about that dystopian nightmare one day, but yes, I saw it."

I can tell he wants to say something but isn't, keeping his lips tight.

"I'm sorry, after what you told me about the headset—I had to go see it for myself," I say. "I didn't tell him where I heard it from that he had it."

"You're really spinning out with this VixSpex obsession," he says. "I get that the deaths seem related, I'm just trying to understand where you think the VixSpex fit into it."

Teddy and I have a long history of staring at each other and it never gets uncomfortable, that locking of our gazes. It's like a whole world lives in that quiet space between our eyes. But sometimes it does get too comfortable. Just like the warmth of his body bleeding into mine.

"Can you go back to where you were sitting?" I ask as politely as I can.

"Why? You feel tempted when I'm this close?"

"Shut up."

Teddy takes his place on the other side of the table again. When he's gloomy like this, when his cheer is gone, I can see the wrinkles already beginning to form on his face despite the fact he's not even thirty. Losing a twin; hard living, snorting, and drinking; being the boss at a company where shit hits the fan all day long ... it'll wear on a man.

"Do you keep going back to the VixSpex because of what you said on the WTT livestream?" he asks.

I squint at him, trying to decipher what he means.

"The 'What the Tech?!' conference," he says. "The debate you had with whatsherface who was kidnapped and trapped in the Sunray?"

With Eve. Right. The two of us there on the livestream and what was it I said? Teddy chewed me out for it. It was at the beginning of the end of my stint at Jolvix, I was so over defending them.

"Eve asked about people being able to replicate the VixSpex, about there being a potential for copies, copycats," Teddy says. "And then you blurted out something about Jolvix products being more advanced than anything a person could replicate. You said, 'If someone really thinks they can make or find a copy of this, go ahead. Use it to smite my enemies and I'll love you for it.'"

A shockwave. God, he's right. I said that. Well, not *that* exactly. He's paraphrasing. It was such a dumb thing to say, I was exhausted, I was worn paper-thin, I was tired of keeping up a cheerful appearance while the Jolvix world forever burned around me. And it was live. It's why I hate having to do anything live, you can't take it back.

"Yeah," Teddy says, leaning in. "'Member that?"

All I can muster, all I can manage, is to shake my head. It's crazy. This is *crazy*. To think that someone heard that and they're knocking off my enemies one by one … impossible. Yet here we are. A shiver slithers from my tailbone to the nape of my neck.

"I don't think I've ever seen Leela Crowe too stunned to speak," Teddy says.

I dive my head back into my hands, as if I can just hide here forever. But after a minute I emerge and all I have is questions.

"Who would do this?" I ask. "And how? How would they *know* who to kill? They would have to know me. Know me *well*. Well enough to know my high school history, my college history, and Genesis, too."

"Who knows you that well?"

"Just Ricky," I say. "And … it's not Ricky."

"Who's *Ricky*?"

"My best friend. You've met him once, you were just too wasted to remember."

"What about that guy you dated in DC?" Teddy asks. "Mike or whatever."

"Michael."

Saying his name aloud awakens a special little pain.

"Michael would not do this." I play with a leaf that has fallen on the table. It's a Japanese maple leaf, a dainty spring-colored star. "The only other person I can think of … is you."

I look up at Teddy, raise my eyebrows. Study his face for reaction. All I see there though, in his unflinching stare, is fear-tainted sadness. A deep well of fear-tainted sadness that mirrors my own.

Finally, he responds, "I can't even believe you would say that."

"I'm sorry," I say, reaching my hand across the table. I do it so instinctively and before I know it, his warm hand is on mine. It feels so good I pull it away.

"It's okay," he says.

"I don't know what to do," I say. "I can't keep going like this, but I also don't want to get dragged into an investigation. I mean, Teddy, if somehow the VixSpex *were* copied —which is possible, we know that's possible, that's why we freaked the fuck out when it went missing for five days—we'd be implicated, right?"

"I'd be fired. If there were no criminal charges like reckless endangerment or manslaughter, we'd get slapped with major civil suits." He lowers his voice. "Our lives would be over, Leela."

"When does it end though?" I ask.

"How many enemies do you have, for Christ's sake?" he asks. "How long's your shitlist? Who else is on it?"

I chew on the answer but after a good minute, I can't think of anyone else who has wronged me the way those three people wronged me. Locking me in a closet, kissing my fiancé, punching me in the face in a video that went viral ... it doesn't get worse than that.

"I don't know," I finally answer. "I can't think of anyone else."

Teddy and I settle into a long silence, a breeze stirring the plants around us. As he studies the air, I can't tell what's inside him. It's so rare to feel him that unreachable and it compels me to him, makes me wish I could peer inside his head and see what movies he's watching.

"You okay?" I ask.

He snickers. "No. I'm not okay. My ex-fiancé was fucking murdered and now I'm apparently a fucking suspect. I mean, come on, Leels. Am I okay?"

"Yeah. Dumb question."

"I haven't wanted a drink this bad since I quit," he says, clenching and unclenching his fists.

"Don't do it."

"If everything's going to hell, then I might as well just burn it all down first, you know?"

"Don't."

He takes in a deep breath, his chest puffing out, and lets it out slowly. Closes his eyes and opens them again. "You were in San Jose the morning Genesis was killed."

I open my mouth to defend myself, thinking he's going to accuse me of something.

"Be my alibi." He nods at me, encouragingly. "It's perfect. You were near me. I live two freeway exits away. You met Barnett where?"

"I was dropped off outside his house."

"That's right near the regional park. We can say I met you there. We went hiking."

"I cannot believe you're asking this of me."

"Really?" he says, eyebrows raised. "Have you forgotten what I did for you back then?"

"Because you were actually *with* me that night," I shoot back, a zombie anger rising up in me. "You weren't lying, you were telling the truth."

"Please," he begs.

Those stupid blue eyes. I bite my tongue so hard I think I might bite right through it. I don't know what to say, how to answer, but it doesn't matter. Because a deafening crash followed by screaming startles both of us and we jump from our seats, searching for the source of the sound. It's not on the patio—still empty and blissful out here. But now we hear wailing and rubber burning on the road, a car revving its engine and disappearing.

Teddy and I get up and dash through the back door into the bar, following the noise. Inside, the scene is chaos —a woman lying down on the floor, blood everywhere, a man standing over her crying, the bartender on her cell phone calling the police. The large front window of Dry is shattered. The front tables and chairs are tipped over. There's a blizzard of glass all around the woman on the ground, who is conscious, but her blood-streaked profile is wrenched in pain. As Teddy and I approach, the injured woman turns toward us. Her temple and cheek are pink and glistening as raw meat. There's a river of blood oozing down her face and I can see a large shard of glass poking out of her closed eyelid.

I gasp, wincing.

"Help," she cries.

"It's okay, honey," the man crouching next to her says, his voice shaky. "Don't touch it. Just be still. It's okay. We're waiting for the ambulance. You'll be okay."

And lying next to her, a single cinder block.

CHAPTER 28

Teddy and I, well, we have a history with alibis.

The memories of the night Jack died are so pain-soaked I keep them out of mind as much as possible. If one surfaces, I get busy: go on a run, beat on my punching bag, call Shasta, hug my cat, scrub my floors, anything, anything to shove it out of eyesight. The worst part of the memories I have are how blurry they are, nothing but jagged fragments surrounded by blank space.

I was sloppy-wasted that night—the night my almost-husband died. The day started out golden and sunny. I do remember that part. I remember waking up in bed with Jack in his house. I made us tea with the electric kettle he kept in his room and we laughed about stupid stuff, mostly Teddy, who was coming into town for Jack's graduation.

"Where's he staying?" I asked, handing Jack a steaming cup of tea.

"Probably some five-star penthouse suite somewhere," he said. "I'm sure he's just using this as an excuse to party his ass off on my dad's credit card. Bet you anything he doesn't even show up to the ceremony."

"Do you think he'll come to the party here tonight?"

"Never. I'm going to call it right now, Teddy'll take one look inside the house and won't set foot in it. Just watch."

Jack and Teddy had a strange relationship. When Jack first told me he had an identical twin, he described Teddy as his best friend in the whole world. But every time Jack talked about Teddy, the descriptions were sprinkled with jibes. His silly fashion choices, his terrible taste in music, how he didn't know the difference between "there," "they're," and "their." The stories he relayed from childhood all turned Teddy into the butt of the joke: the time he got his head stuck in a bucket, the time he set off fireworks and singed off his eyebrows. I assumed they just had that kind of relationship but then when Jack took me home to meet Teddy, I was surprised to see that the half-joking insults only seemed to go one way in the relationship. Teddy adored Jack. He took it in stride, as if he was used to laughing at himself. But I didn't ever see him fire back.

Jack's family lived in a Spanish-style mansion in Palo Alto. The first time he brought me there, I was alarmed at how well-off they were. They had more employees present than people: a landscaper working on the yard, someone cleaning their pool, a maid humming and washing the windows. It was classy, but cavernous and starkly silent. Clearly not a lot of living happened in the living room, nor much dining in the dining room, and the family room was cold and empty.

Jack's parents were friendly. They were one of those

couples who had been together so long they kind of resembled each other with their chestnut hair and bleached smiles and blue eyes. Their sharp wit and success intimidated me right away. We went out to dinner one night at a French restaurant and as I watched the family interact with each other, it was as if an entire two decades of context wordlessly unfurled before my eyes.

"Jack, did you have to wear a hoodie to the restaurant?" Teddy's dad asked with a dimpled smile. He raised his eyebrows at me. "Don't tell me this is how he dresses when he takes you out on dates."

I laughed. "He has a blazer I bought him that I make him wear when we go out. It's the date blazer."

"The Date Blazer," Teddy repeated, finishing his first glass of wine before everyone else. "You've got yourself a good one there, buddy."

Almost sullenly, Jack slipped his hoodie off. When he did, his mom gasped and grabbed his arm, rubbing his skull tattoo as if she thought it might come off. "Jack, what is this?"

"What does it look like, *Mom*?" Jack said, and I recoiled at the fact that this man I was building a future with could sound that way—like a petulant child. "Come on, I've had it for almost a year."

"Easy now, Jack," his dad said, and the table went silent.

"I'm going to order some snails and frog legs," Teddy said, finally breaking the silence. He helped himself to another generous glass of wine from the bottle. "Whatd'ya say?"

His mom and dad groaned, "Not the *escargots* again,"

and laughed at some inside joke.

"Seriously," muttered Jack as he continued his close reading of the menu.

"What about you, Leela?" Teddy smiled at me over the candlelight. The sight of him was still so peculiar to me— the man who was another version of the man I loved.

I returned the smile. "Sure, I'm down."

"Just ignore him," Jack said.

"What? I can handle a few snails and frog legs," I said.

"You want to have a contest?" Teddy asked. "See who can eat the most?"

I laughed and Jack cut in, snapping, "Why are you like this, Teddy? Just stop."

The table went silent again and suddenly I understood the dynamics at play. I saw how closely their father sat to Teddy, how Teddy styled his hair the same way as him, how their mother gazed at him with a special twinkle in her eye. But I also saw how Jack sat with his arms crossed and a scowl on his face as his family genuinely tried to engage with him. It was as if he had long ago designated himself the black sheep of the family and wouldn't have it any other way.

The night Jack died was the first day Teddy came and visited Jack in Berkeley. When Teddy showed up on Jack's doorstep that afternoon, Jack was wrong about his brother not setting foot in the house. Teddy strode inside with espresso energy, booming, "Wow! Look at this place! Lot of character in here."

Jack showed him his room and Teddy plopped on the bed, taking it in, picking up a dirty sock with two fingers and dropping it on the floor. "Cool, very cool."

"Just say what you're really thinking," Jack said.

Teddy put his hands up. "No! I think it's perfect for you, I really do."

"'Perfect for you.'" Jack frowned. "What does *that* mean?"

"It means what it means?" Teddy shrugged. "It's a great place."

He leaned over and grabbed the orange canister sitting on the night table next to him. They were the tranquilizers I'd been prescribed after I thought I maybe had a panic attack. He read the label. "This is some fun stuff," he said, shaking it.

"It really is," I agreed.

"Put it back, please," Jack said.

Teddy did as he was told. "Speaking of which, you know where I could get some powder?" Teddy addressed me directly with this one, as if he could tell I was the one to ask. He was right.

"I know a guy," I said.

Jack put a hand on my waist. "Kitten," is all he said.

"What? I was thinking of getting some anyway for the party tonight," I told him.

He gave me The Look, the one shadowed with grim disappointment. Jack hated hard drugs and had been harping on me whenever I did any ever since we got together. I mostly stayed away from them since I'd been with Jack, had tried to be a good girl and stuck to drinking myself silly and squeezing whatever fun I could out of prescription drugs I wheedled from the mental health clinic. But I couldn't help it, that little devil in me awoke at Teddy's suggestion and now I wanted some too.

"Baby, we're graduating," I reminded Jack. "It's a party. Lighten up."

"Sure, fine."

His voice was tight. His mouth a line. The tension in the silence of his room was stifling. I got up and opened a window, as if we could air it out. Then I texted the guy I knew named Casper who dealt coke out of his dorm room.

Teddy and I ended up walking across campus together to buy it because Jack refused to take part. It was fine. No big deal. Sure, underneath the surface, a storm was brewing, but I ignored it. Barely two weeks had passed since Jack's confession about kissing Lotus and my blowup in his living room where I threatened her. We hadn't discussed it since. My heart still ached but I didn't know how to talk about it—the best I could do was just take too many tranquilizers and guzzle bourbon to temporarily ease it. And now I was taking his twin brother to go buy coke.

"Jack okay?" Teddy asked me as we waited at a stoplight.

Teddy always looked to me like someone who was trying out for an ad in a men's magazine—tailored trousers, a button-up shirt, shiny shoes, the casual way he leaned against the traffic light pole.

"Great, yeah. Sure. What do you mean?" I asked.

"Well, if you've been with Jack a while you know how he gets," he said. "I say this with love, but … the moods, the impulsivity."

He wasn't wrong and I was surprised to hear him say

it so plainly, but I just smiled tightly and repeated, "He's great."

But that whole walk to Casper's through the long wide path and campus square where graduates were posing for photos, that word *impulsive* repeated in my head, a knife that seemed to bring with it the pain of our recent betrayal. Teddy moved on to talking my ear off about his job at Jolvix, which sounded incredibly boring, the whole explanation peppered with acronyms like *ROIs, KPIs,* and *MVPs* that I didn't even care to ask him to define.

Casper answered his door in a kimono and sunglasses. He had scraggly facial hair growing exclusively out of his chin.

"Hey, lookin' spiffy, Jack-o-lantern," Casper said.

"This isn't Jack," I said. "This is his twin brother."

"Whoa," Casper said as he let us inside. "Uncanny, brah."

Casper's dorm room was plastered with posters of greased-up, bikinied women on motorcycles but he also had a whiteboard with math problems scrawled onto it that made me wonder if he was secretly a genius. He plopped in a beanbag chair, pulled out a giant bag of white powder and a scale and asked what we wanted.

"Just an eight ball," Teddy said automatically.

Just? I raised my eyebrows. Even I'd never bought an eight-ball before. The most I'd bought was a gram to do some lines here or there, usually to prevent myself from blacking out and falling asleep after a night of hard drinking. Teddy looked so polished, so together, so fit—the kind of guy who ironed his pants, who got up early and hit the gym before my alarm clock was even ringing. And here he was, buying an eight-ball of coke as if it was nothing. And he paid for it with hundred-dollar bills.

When we got back to Jack's, I was in a sunny mood. We had drugs in tow and a raging party to look forward to that night. Best of all, we were graduating in a couple days and the future was golden and infinite. But Jack was clearly unhappy with both me and Teddy when we got back to his room. He didn't look up from his copy of *Infinite Jest*.

"Took a while there," he said. "You stop somewhere to snort some lines?"

"Of course not. It's for the party tonight, my man," Teddy said.

"Sure."

The rest of the day was like that, Jack sullen and bitter. Everything that came out of his mouth dripped with negativity. Teddy and I overcompensated by being as upbeat and sunny as we could. I couldn't tell who was caught in the middle here—was I caught in the middle of some off-kilter sibling dynamics? Or was Teddy caught in the middle of Jack and my tenuous relationship? Whatever it was, I started on a steady stream of Kentucky mules and ignored it the rest of the day.

That's where the edges of my memory start to blur.

The sun went down. People started to arrive at Hearst Castle and the reggae music bumped. Teddy and I hid in Jack's room and did a couple of lines together and when we went out, I couldn't find Jack again for the longest time. The house was thick with people and weed smoke. Teddy and I wandered everywhere looking for Jack and then finally, across the backyard, I spotted him as I stood on the back porch. He was sitting there next to a girl in glasses I didn't recognize and his arm was slung around her and he was whispering in her ear. He smelled her hair and she giggled. He wore a sly smile that I thought was only for me—the kiss-me smile. I'd never seen him flirt with someone like that. He drank from an open bottle of wine and handed it to her and she slugged some and handed it back to him. I remember the exact feeling, like a balloon losing air. Teddy saw it too and he turned to me.

"Everything okay?" he asked, rubbing under his nose.

"Yeah," I said, though my throat felt dry.

Right then, Jack glanced up and noticed me gaping at him from the porch. And what hurt most was the fact he didn't look guilty or caught. He didn't look sorry. He smiled right at me like this was a strange little revenge.

After that, I made a scene. It's both a bit of a horror and a relief that I can't remember it in complete detail, but I do remember trying to punch the girl in the face and Teddy holding me back. I remember sobbing on the porch in front of everybody like a girl back on stage again. I shouted that Jack was a piece of shit and he shouted, with his wine-stained lips, "You know what, Leela? You're not a kitten. You're a dog. Wave a bottle or a bag of powder and you'll follow anyone anywhere. You're a fucking dog."

Those were his last words to me. And mine?

"I wish you were dead."

I stumbled out of Hearst Castle, sobbing drunkenly. Teddy followed me out and tried to talk me down. The joyous scene of people dancing to bumping music on the lawn, the gorgeous full moon—it all seemed to be mocking me.

"It's over," I cried.

"It's just a bad night," he kept saying. "That's all."

He called us a self-driving taxi and took me back to his hotel suite in San Francisco, which was posh and had a full bar and a jacuzzi on a deck that overlooked the city. We drank, we snorted lines, we ordered room service we barely ate, we climbed in the hot tub and had long loud talks interrupting each other the whole time. I don't remember much of what we talked about, but I do know he helped me forget about Jack for a little while. And I remember at one point clinking glasses full of whiskey and Teddy murmuring in my ear, "Does it ever cross your mind that you picked the wrong twin?"

I laughed it off but shivered, electric.

Night turned to morning, the comedown started, and the dark cloud of what had happened at the party with Jack loomed over me. I was guilty for running off with Teddy and partying all night. I was scared I was going to return and find out Jack had been with another girl. I wasn't sure if our relationship survived the night. Teddy and I went back to Hearst Castle. The kegs were empty and the place was trashed. We walked upstairs and I knocked on Jack's door. I was shaky and sick, both from the comedown and from the mounting dread of what I'd find behind the door—hopefully not another girl in his bed with him.

"Jack," I said tentatively.

I pushed the door open. It was dark inside. It took a second for my eyes to adjust to what I was seeing. An alien-like figure with a human body and a peculiar-shaped head lying on his bed with Converse on.

"Jack?" I whispered.

I stepped inside and realized what I was seeing. It was Jack with a plastic bag on his head. I shook him as hard as I could and pulled the bag off his head and saw his wide-open eyes and violet lips and I screamed and screamed and screamed.

And I didn't stop screaming until Teddy pulled me off him.

I don't remember anything else. Like the entire long night, it's only shattered pieces after that, images that last a second like a traumatic slideshow. Talking to police. The coroner van. Throwing up all over myself and someone helping me get cleaned up. Being told he had taken all my tranquilizers that I had left on his bedside table. Repeating "why" over and over again as if it was the only word in the English language that I knew anymore.

His death was ruled suspicious because there was no note and no record of suicidal behavior and an investigation ensued. Witnesses from the party attested that I had threatened Jack's life and some housemates added that I'd threatened Lotus's life at one point too. Since Jack killed himself with my pills downed with a bottle of wine, I briefly became a person of interest until Teddy told the police I had been with him all night. Then the case was quickly closed. Jack's death was ruled a suicide. I drank whiskey for breakfast, lunch, and dinner to try to stave off the grief and the pain and I kept that up for a good year until I hit rock bottom out in DC and then Teddy saved my ass again.

This is why I can't help but feel like I owe him whatever he asks of me.

CHAPTER 29

"Oh my fucking God," I say as Teddy and I stand outside Dry, stunned and staring at the ambulance leaving and the police talking to the pigtailed bartender, who's in tears. Across the street, Esmerelda and Daisy's faces are pressed up against the picture window to get a load of the scene. My heart's beating so fast that for a moment, I swear I'm going to faint.

"That was ... that was a lot of drama for a bar with no alcohol," Teddy finally manages.

"I need to get out of here," I say.

"Sure, sure."

We walk up the street. I'm sure Daisy saw me and she's shitting her vintage granny panties because I was supposed to be working this afternoon but right now I don't care. About anything. All I can think about is that woman with a face that looked like raw meat, the way she cried the word *help*.

A sting intensifies behind my eyeballs. I blink to keep away the tears. It's my fault, isn't it? It's all my fault.

"I think that concrete block was meant for me," I say to Teddy.

"What?"

"The same thing happened at my work. Concrete block through the window."

"Yeah, well, someone lit a trash can on fire in front of my condo but that doesn't mean it was meant for me."

With a tug on my jacket sleeve, Teddy brings me to a stop. We're standing in front of a rock-climbing gym. Through the window, there are smiling, happy, fit people and they're a dozen feet away from me and a world away from me at the same time.

"Look at me," Teddy says.

Reluctantly, I meet his gaze.

"That wasn't for you," he says slowly, the way you might talk down a person standing on a ledge. "You have enough to worry about, forget about that. You're doing that paranoid thing where you think everything's about you."

"People are dying all around me," I say, clenching my fists, wishing there were a punching bag. "It's not crazy to think I could be next and don't you *dare*."

Teddy clenches his jaw so tight his facial muscles flex.

"I need to go somewhere and think," I say. "Alone."

He opens his mouth, surely to protest, but I cut him off before he can start.

"I'll be your alibi if it's just a phone call, Teddy, but I'm not doing more than that. I'm sorry about Genesis, I'm sorry, I …"

The volcano is about to erupt so I shake my head and wave at him and hurry up the street toward the BART station, a long jog that I hope will exhaust my anxiety. It doesn't. Pretty sure I could do a triathlon right now and it wouldn't make a difference.

The stress that has built, the things that are floating around in my head, are too much to bear. It takes every ounce of willpower for me to not go into *fuck it* mode and stop by the liquor store on the walk home. The concrete block, the injured woman, Genesis found dead in the hills, 3D-printed guns and the homicidal VixSpex and me on a livestream joking that someone should smite my enemies. I'm on the sudden verge of a nervous breakdown. When I get home I just crumple up on the couch like a woman with no bones. Even Nosferatu keeps a distance, judging me with yellow eyes. Lying here, I pull my phone out of my pocket and do a quick search to find the clip on YouVid—the one from my live debate with Eve.

There she is, Leela from fourteen months ago, that practiced plastic smile, too thin from the stress and misery of my Jolvix job. That day was such a shitshow, I was a hair away from running to the nearest bar and ordering five shots of bourbon.

In the video, I sit on a stool opposite Eve, who is radiant with her rage toward Jolvix. Her eyes are slits as she addresses me. "And I'm sorry—what do you do when some unhinged dude like Henry Leto decides he's going to hack into Barnett Briggs' novelty murder VixSpex and go on a killing spree?"

I laugh a very fake-sounding laugh, *ha ha ha*. "I'm sorry, are we writing science fiction stories right now or are we debating actual technology?"

"Do I have to remind you that you're talking to a

victim whose life was endangered by Jolvix technology ending up in the wrong hands?" Eve shoots back.

My face fixes itself into a serious expression. Sometimes I felt like an android when I was in PR—my mind pulling the strings of how I wanted my emotions to appear, even if there was absolute emptiness behind it all. Like one of Barnett's bots. Or like being a child actor, actually.

"Eve," I say in the video. "Our hearts go out to you at Jolvix. I can't tell you how devastated we are about what happened to you. I absolutely understand that, under the circumstances, you might be distrustful. But just like guns don't kill people, technology doesn't kill people either. *People* kill people. Instead of fearing technological advances and blaming them for violence and 'unhinged' individuals, we should be focusing on how to improve mental health—"

Eve waves her hand. "Oh my God, what's coming next? Thoughts and prayers? You're so full of shit you should become a politician."

The small audience laughed at that and I still remember the heat in my cheeks, the way I had to keep my smile fixed and keep breathing even though I hated every second. All I was thinking about was the clock on the wall and how much longer I had to sit there being annihilated by Eve.

"This is a silly conversation," I said. "There's one novelty VixSpex headset and it's hanging on the wall in a secure location—"

"Yeah, that one is. And what happens when someone

makes a copy? Makes a hundred copies? What happens then?"

"It's a patented and secret design that can't be replicated."

"Sure. Uh huh. And leaks don't happen. And bootleggers don't exist. Never have! Never will!"

I was fed up at that point, ready to end the debate early. Eve was relentless. I hadn't expected someone as traumatized as her to be so fiery. Why the fuck was I assigned this anyway? Where was the PR team for the Sunray that nearly killed Eve?

"Eve," I said through my teeth. "If there's someone out there smart enough to actually make a copy of the novelty VixSpex, bravo. Seriously. They can smite my enemies for me and I'll love them for it."

I said that.

I fucking said that.

Not a first by any means, but I wish I could jump back in time and strangle Past Leela. I close the tab with the clip in it, wait for the heart attack feeling to pass, and then make a call.

"Hey there," Eve says. "How goes it?"

"We need to talk."

"Sure. You okay?"

"No. A third person connected to me died. And the VixSpex? I went to see Barnett—"

"Hey! Ho! Hey! How about we talk about this in person?" she asks, cutting me off. "Because I'm a little careful these days about what's said on my *Jolvix-infested* device, if you know what I'm saying."

I sit up, dizzy. She's right. Our phones aren't safe. Even

if a phone isn't made by Jolvix, half the apps installed are. If Jolvix wants to, they can tap anyone's calls.

"All right then. Can we meet?" I ask.

"I'm in LA," Eve says. "Visiting my mom. Next week maybe?"

"No," I say.

I get up to find my suitcase.

"I'll meet you in LA," I say. "My mom lives there too."

"Seriously? Where?"

"Hollywood. You?"

"Boyle Heights."

"I'll grab a flight tonight and we can meet up tomorrow?"

"Sure, I guess. What the fuck is going on? This must be juicy."

"That's one way of putting it."

The train ride to the airport takes longer than the flight. I arrive at LAX right as the sun goes down and I'm knocking on Shasta's door not too long after that. At the sight of her, I dissolve into sobbing like a helpless child. She opens her arms, her many golden bracelets clattering, and she brings me in for a perfumed embrace.

"Honey, honey, honey," she repeats.

"Bad things keep happening," I say.

"I know. I know they do. Life's like that sometimes. It's okay. Shasta's here, babydoll."

And for a blink, I feel safe again.

CHAPTER 30

I can't crawl an inch in Los Angeles without associating everything everywhere with some tedious audition or meaningless role I had as a child. Oh look, there's the exit where my agent's office was, that slimeball who later got arrested for embezzlement. There's the warehouse where I tried out for an End Hunger Now charity commercial only to be told I was too fat to portray a starving child. And that there's the lot where I got to put on a bald cap and play a random kid in a cancer ward. Yes, I see the palm trees and the funky neighborhoods, the backdrop of the broad-shouldered mountains, but mostly I just see places I never wanted to go in the first place. If I mention this to Shasta, she tells me I'm being dramatic.

"You're the one who wanted to be an actress, I was supporting your dream!" she says, aghast.

Shasta's such a pro at revision she should have been an editor.

But I shouldn't think badly of her. She's driving me to Boyle Heights right now. I feel like a teenager again, my

mom driving me to see a friend for lunch. I'm glaring out
the window, a black stain in her puke-pink car with its
fuzzy puke-pink seats. As we speed down the 101 in the
fast lane, Shasta sings off-key to pop music she's way too
old for. Loudly. Like a woman belting it out to the back of
the room.

"Can you just …" I wince at her and point to my ear.

"What?" Shasta turns down the music with a *click-
click-click* of her acrylic nail. "Can I just what?"

"Your singing is deafening."

"Oh, I'm sorry. Am I bothering you? Does my *existence*
bother you?"

Lord. It's been sixteen hours since I got here and
already I'm counting down the minutes until I go home
again. I shake my head.

"If you don't want to *talk* to me, babydoll," she says
sharply, "I'm going to *sing*."

"I see," I say. "So it's punishment."

"That's very rude," she says, turning up the stereo and
resuming her shout-singing.

She's prickly because I won't delve into details about
why I'm so upset. I won't tell her why I'm here and what
the bad things are exactly that are happening. Shasta's a
nosy gossip. More importantly, she calls 9-1-1 at the
sound of a fart, and she's also my mom and thinks she
knows what's best for me, so she will call the police if she
knows about the "suicides" and the cinder blocks. And
though the police might be the right way to go in the
end, I'm not ready to open that Pandora's box quite yet. I
have been the target of heavy questioning in a murder
investigation and I'd do anything to avoid playing that

part again. First, I just want to talk to Eve and get her take.

Shasta drops me off at a trendy café with plant-covered walls inside. Eve's already nursing a mimosa when I get to the table. She's in a cute red romper that matches her lips, looking sunkissed and dewy as someone on vacation.

"Well, well, well," Eve says as I slide into my seat. "Never realized you were an Angeleno."

"Eh, I try not to be. What brings you down here?"

"Visiting my mom. Getting away from the Valley of the Androids." She folds her hands and leans in. "Call me crazy but I think Jolvix might be following me."

"What?"

"Yeah. That's why I didn't want to talk on the phone. No texts. Nothing." She holds her phone up in the air. "Turned mine off and you should turn yours off, too."

"Why would Jolvix follow you?" I ask, turning my phone off.

"Because I'm writing a book about them, for fuck's sake." Eve's expression cracks for only a split second, but long enough that I can tell she's capable of being nervous. She has a steely exterior—sometimes it's easy to forget she's human. "Anywho, I'm flattered you flew all the way down here for lil old me."

Usually I find Eve's smirkiness charming, but today I've got no time for it.

"I have so much to tell you," I say. "Can we talk off the record again?"

Eve lets out a frustrated noise somewhere between a whine and a sigh.

"Just … I want to get it out," I go on. "I know I said I'd give you details for your book, and I will, but first I want to just vomit it all out and then we can pick through it."

"Eloquent metaphor, Leela," she says, tilting more mimosa down her throat. "You should have been a poet."

My face must be as red as it's feeling right now because she puts up a hand and does a beckoning gesture.

"Okay, all right, vomit away."

It takes a moment for me to find my tongue, to know where to begin. My brain is such a tangled nightmare mess. I start with Genesis, about how her body was found in the San Jose hills. I tell Eve about the Peeps message and ask if she's ever heard that phrase: *You shine like a lone lighthouse on a dark sea.*

"I've searched for it online; nothing," I say.

Eve shakes her head. "I was a Journalism major. Ask an English major."

"I *was* an English major."

"Damn, those degrees are even more useless than I thought," she says. "Okay, so she's dead. She wrote you a note saying sorry, then she died. I'm trying to understand where this is going. By the way, I did a little digging into the other two women you asked me about—I didn't find much."

"Don't worry about that anymore," I say, waving my hand. "I think I've figured out how all this is connected to the VixSpex."

"Which would be …"

"Our debate, Eve. The livestream at the What the Tech?! conference." I lean forward and say, as quietly as I can, "I *jokingly—sarcastically—*suggested that the model

205

would be so hard to copy that if someone could, they should smite my enemies with one."

"Oh fuck," Eve says, sitting up straighter.

I let that sit a moment. Must land heavy because she downs her mimosa and flags the waiter to order another. It's noon on a Thursday morning but I guess when you've survived what Eve survived you earn the right to drink whenever you want.

"Fuck," Eve repeats when the waiter leaves. She drums her red painted fingernails on the table. They're manicured but short, fancy but practical. "Okay, can we just pause here and take a moment to acknowledge that I called this? I called this shit! During our debate!"

"Thanks, that's what's important right now, getting in your 'I told you so.'"

"Okay, okay," Eve says, putting her palms up. "Just making sure it was acknowledged. And again, I'm lost. Trying to connect the dots here. Where is the headset right now?"

"Barnett Briggs has it. I know this for a fact. But what I'm more concerned with are the copies that could be out there, like you said. The headset went missing, remember? And then it was returned."

The waiter comes with our salads and Eve and I abandon our intense, hushed conversation for sunny smiles and *thank you*s. Then the waiter disappears again and we're right back to it, ignoring our food.

"You think someone made a copy," Eve says. "Who do you know who is connected to these people, to you, and who would have the wherewithal to copy it?"

I'm at a loss, shaking my head. There were so many

people we worked with at Jolvix but no one who stands out in my mind. A lot of the time I was so consumed by ulcer-inducing crisis after ulcer-inducing crisis that I didn't schmooze with anyone around me. I worked closely with Teddy and sometimes other members of the executive team but no one else.

I can't help it, Teddy has crossed my mind. Teddy could have taken it and had a copy made. The headset reappeared in his office. He knows me, he knows my history, though I don't know if he knew anything about Madison. It wouldn't make sense. There's no motive for this madness. No motive for *anyone*, as far as I can tell.

"I can't think of anyone," I finally answer.

Eve stabs her salad with her fork. "I know a guy I might be able to ask to do me a favor with this."

"Yeah?" I ask, laying my napkin on my lap.

"He's an investigator and his whole area of expertise is the dark web," Eve says. "It's highly likely *if* replicas were made and sold, it happened there. That's where most Jolvix bootlegs and leaked information lives. He's been pulling all sorts of fun nuggets for me from there." She points her fork at me as she chews. "This, of course, lives here with us."

"Of course," I say. "You'll look into that for me?"

"Sure." She wipes her mouth with a napkin and leaves a kissy mark. "And what are you going to do for me?"

I glance out the window. A woman with impeccable champagne-blond hair that surely must be extensions walks by and I think of Genesis. I think of her dead in the dirt somewhere and a cold, skeletal hand closes over me. I think of the naked robot malfunctioning on the floor of Barnett's mancave and suck in a cold breath of air.

"Okay," I say, facing Eve again. "I have a story about Barnett Briggs. I'll tell it to you. And this time, I'll go on the record."

Eve raises a penciled eyebrow. "I'm listening."

CHAPTER 31

I spent a lot of time at Ricky's apartment in high school to escape Shasta's unbearable vicarious ambition and the flavor-of-the-week boyfriends who invaded our personal space. There's something comforting about coming back here now, a decade later. The scent of honeysuckle climbing the fences, the trimmed hedges with pink flowers, the sign that says *Paradise Canyon*—a real reach, if you ask me, for a four-plex apartment building the shape and color of a cardboard box. Ricky's got his own place on the bottom floor now and as I knock on his door, I'm hit with a wave of déjà vu accompanied by an ache. Oh, to be a teenager again with all the pain in life ahead of me.

I can't count the number of times in life I've pined for a time machine.

"Hey!" Ricky says, opening the door and stepping into a hug. He smells fresh, his hair wet and gelled like he got gussied up for me. "Surprise vacation?"

"Long weekend. I got two 'mental health days' off."

"How are we?" he asks, pulling back to look at me.

"We are mentally unhealthy." I point to his upper lip. "What the fuck is this?"

"What does it look like? I'm growing a mustache."

"Looks like you just forgot to finish your shaving job."

"Pencil 'stache," he says, beckoning me inside. "Fashion. You wouldn't know anything about that."

I collapse on his couch. "You're right, I wouldn't."

"Tea?" he asks, lingering near his kitchen doorway.

"Sure. Something fruity."

"Then fruity you shall have."

He disappears into the kitchen. I sit on his couch, jiggling my leg, imagining his mom's apartment that used to be directly above this when she was still alive—the enormous watercolor painting of the Virgin Mary, the floral couches covered in plastic, wall-to-wall shelves of knickknacks. Though the layouts are identical, the décor couldn't be any more different. Ricky's got an incredible eye. Turquoise shag rug, antique clock. Surreal art on the wall he picked up at a flea market and later found out was worth a fortune. He can draw and paint and he takes the most flattering pictures of me. I swear, some people are just born with it and Ricky was born with it.

"Lemon zinger?" Ricky calls from the other room.

"Zing me," I say.

Did I just say that? Teddy used to say that when we worked together and I made him tea at the office. Please tell me I'm not turning into a cornball like Teddy. Reflexively, I take my phone out and pull up our most recent texts that happened right after my plane touched down in LAX.

Can we talk, Leels? Please? I'm worried about you.

I left town. Need to get my head together.

Ok ... call me soon.

When I didn't respond, he sent another text about an hour later.

I feel like you and I could lean on each other right now. We don't have much else to lean on.

Then an hour after that, he sent one more.

You're not talking to anyone about anything are you?

Finally, I responded,

stop being a pushy mofo.

Nothing since then. Guiltily, rereading this, I send a quick text.

Hey. Sorry, been clearing my head down here. How are you?

"Okay, you have been zinged," Ricky says, floating back into the room with a steamy cup of tea and sitting next to me on the couch.

I pocket my phone again.

"So what is going on, Leelee?" Ricky asks. "Mental

health days? You didn't even take mental health days when you were a soggy hot mess, why now?"

I kick my boots up on his coffee table and Ricky winces as if I kicked him in the gut instead.

"What, this isn't allowed?" I ask.

"That coffee table is *custom built*."

I roll my eyes, taking my boots back to the floor. That's what I hate about nice things: people actually care about them. As I adjust my position to face him, I'm gathering my thoughts together, the mental equivalent of someone rerolling a runaway ball of yarn. I haven't told Ricky about Genesis. Since Lotus's funeral, our check-ins have been surface-level—him updating me on the disastrous zoo date with Huey's nephew Hugh where Hugh tried to feed the lions; me talking shit about Daisy and debating if I should quit my job and move back to LA.

Yes, Ricky's my best friend. But here's another thing: Ricky never met Genesis, but he despised her with a passion on my behalf. After that clip went viral, he tried to get me to seek revenge on her in some way. Along with replacing her shampoo with hair remover, his suggestions included hiring a hitwoman to beat her ass publicly and throwing a brick through her salon's window. I said what I said—*throwing a brick through a window.*

Jokingly, of course.

Right?

It's insane. It's proof of how unhinged I'm becoming. I've found myself wondering if *Ricky* could have had something to do with the darkness that follows me.

"Still upset about Lotus, is that what's going on?" Ricky says.

"Yeah," I say, snapping back to the room and sipping my tea. "How was your weekend?"

"My weekend?" he asks, a bit baffled. "This past weekend?"

Yes, Ricky. Where were you on Saturday morning? I have truly lost it.

"I went out to Temecula to visit my abuela. Why?"

"Just wondering how you are."

Ricky gives me a look. "You're acting weird."

"I told you I'm mentally unwell."

"What the hell is going on?" he asks, clearly irritated. "Why won't you let the Lotus thing go? Didn't we have closure at the funeral?"

I nod.

"Forget about her already. It's time to move on."

I meet Ricky's gaze, his deep, brown eyes wide as a doe and those sculpted eyebrows. "*Someone* is doing this to me," I say.

He lets out an exasperated sigh.

"They *are*."

Jiggling his leg, Ricky sips his mug. "All right, if we're going to play this crazy game ... what about that guy in theater in high school who used to stare at you all the time, the one in crew—John something?"

"Huh? I don't even know who you're talking about."

"With the shaggy hair?"

"Yeah, Ricky, I'm sure some guy I never even talked to back in high school is killing people on my behalf."

"Okay, well, Michael ever cross your mind?"

"Michael?" I ask, so taken aback I almost spill my tea. "Why?"

"Um, didn't you almost take a restraining order out on him?"

"Yes, but … not like that."

"Not like *what*? A restraining order is a restraining order."

"It was to protect him. I wanted to protect him."

Ricky swallows as he watches me. Usually, I can read Ricky like a press release. I've known him since before his voice changed. But right now, I have no idea what is going on in his head. He seems to be holding back from saying something. Finally, he reaches out and puts a hand on my knee.

"Have we been … you know." He makes a *glug-glug* gesture. Ever so tactful.

"We have not."

"Are we getting help?"

"Sure," I lie. "Yeah. Therapy. All that."

"Okay," he says, surprised. "Good, good." After a long pause, he adds. "Good then."

Ricky whisks us back to his favorite subject: himself. A hot barista girl he has a date with. How underappreciated he is at his job. What a jerk a reality TV "star" was to him at a company party, finger quotes included. An estate sale where he bought a vase that used to belong to a talk show host. Hollywood life. His movie, starring Ricky. I nod and smile and laugh appropriately. I play the part. But underneath it all, something has shifted. I lied to my friend. I said I was getting help and I'm not. Worst of all, I suspected my friend of something unthinkable, unsayable, and I'll never be able to shake the shame of questioning his loyalty in such a way. What is wrong with me that I would even *think* such a thing?

And meanwhile, the name *Michael* throbs like a headache.

CHAPTER 32

THE GAME

Leela, are you starting to understand?

Do you sense that there is a person out there willing to risk everything for you?

Who has been there all along, whose love for you is as deep and dark as death itself?

Who prays at night for your forgiveness?

Who is trying their best to make everything up to you?

Who is both your angel of death and your guardian angel?

When we finally meet, when I've finally proven to you how far I will go, when you have no one left in the world to hate, will you forgive me for what I did to you?

When I reveal myself—when you realize I've been here all along—will you love me back?

I'm sorry about what happened with Genesis.

I'm ashamed at how sloppy that ended up. There are news stories, an investigation; I've had panic attacks every time I hear footsteps outside my front door.

It was because I was hurrying. I didn't sit back and take my time.

I've replayed it over and over in my mind—I should have simply abandoned Genesis there and tried again another time.

It wasn't fun. It didn't feel like a game.

It felt like murder.

Murder leaves a bad taste in my mouth.

I need to re-center myself.

I'm biding my time with the next round.

I know who my opponent is—I've been following closely, though I've lost the trail several times, hours wasted on a street hunched in my car watching nothing but dark windows.

It's going to be the most challenging game yet.

But I'm sure this one will get your attention.

It was bold, wasn't it? Putting that line from the poem I wrote for you in Genesis's apology?

You shine like a lone lighthouse on a dark sea.

Do you remember when I recited that poem for you when we sat at that bar in DC?

What a night that was.

A sheer disappointment.

I'd fantasized about approaching you for years. You looked such a mess, like you'd aged ten years since I'd last seen you.

Lipstick smeared. Nodding off at the bar.

I could have taken you home. I could have done whatever I wanted to you—but no.

I was too disgusted with you to do that, though I blamed myself for the state you were in.

I was ultimately disgusted with myself.

Do you remember that night, do you remember me at all?

Do you remember telling me I looked familiar?

When we meet again, will you know me?

Or will you pass me by like you have so many times in your life?

CHAPTER 33

LEELA

It's nine in the morning a week later and I'm sitting in the "meeting room" at Feline Better, a blank nothing-space with a whiteboard on the wall and a single table and two chairs. Despite the cheerful orange paint job, it gives off interrogation room vibes. And Daisy, with her saleslady smile and the manila folder on the table with a tab that says CROWE, LEELA, is clearly playing the role of a bad cop playing the role of a good cop.

"Thank you for coming here on time today," she says like the passive-aggressive little wench she is.

I give her a wide, PR-worthy smile. "Sure, of course."

But I'm getting the nauseated inkling I'm about to get canned.

In about three seconds, I see my potential future in a quick array of snapshots. I could spin it, celebrate my firing as this position not being a fit for me. Let's be honest, I took this job excited to work with cats but it turns out there's far too much people interaction for my taste. Also, fuck you, Daisy. I'm ludicrously overqualified.

If I want to go another route, I could negotiate a hefty severance while gently threatening a lawsuit for discrimination because of something something mental health.

"How *are* you?" Daisy asks, performative concern in her gaze which is framed by dramatic fake lashes.

"I'll be better when this meeting is over," I can't help myself from saying. I clear my throat. "Um, is there a reason we're—" I gesture around the room. "—you know, instead of just talking in our office?"

"This conversation requires privacy."

"Okay. Sure."

Privacy. From whom? From Esmerelda seeing us through the glass wall, who's in her own world talking to herself most of the day? From twenty-three cats?

"So I'm going to be putting you on something called a PIP." Her smile says she's giving me a raise; her words say I should look for employment elsewhere. Once again, proof that the smilers that can't be trusted in life. "Do you know what a PIP is?"

Talking to me as if I'm five years old. "The protagonist of *Great Expectations*?" I ask, hoping a literature joke might break the ice. Alas, Daisy is too dense to appreciate it.

"It's a *performance improvement plan*," she says slowly. "As is covered in the employee manual on page fifty-three —maybe you never got around to reading it—if one of our staff members is underperforming, management will put that employee on one of these to ensure you can get you back on track. Listen." Daisy puts her hand on the table between us. It's a beautiful hand, petal-pink manicure filed into elegant ovals. I have the strange urge to put my hand on hers just to make everything worse.

"Yes, I read the manual," I say instead. "I know what a PIP is."

I cross my arms. I'm having a hard time faking it. My inner bitch is about to become my outer bitch and I consider getting up and leaving the room before I say something worse. Luckily Daisy seems to be immune to my attitude and breezes right over the comment and my angst, that invisible cloud polluting the room like a fart.

"I realize you've been going through some … *personal* things," Daisy says, offering a pitying nod.

I focus on the pinwheel cowlick she has in the front of her hair's center part. "Right."

"And I understand, I do."

Do ya, Daisy? Really? You understand what it's like to have your enemies hunted one by one? I keep my mouth in a straight line, a zipper zipped. "Mmm-hmm."

"My cat, Elvis Presley, was diagnosed with cancer last winter solstice. It was the most heartbreaking week of my life."

I can't even manage to emit a sound in response to that one.

"And … and you know," she continues, "we—we encourage time off for *mental health*. Our generous insurance package covers that. Through your insurance, you have access to amazing *substance abuse* programs. Just wanted to put that out there."

The pause swells and my ears ring with it. Suddenly, I realize what this is. It's been a while, but I can smell an intervention from a mile away.

"So this performance improvement plan is designed to

support you and your journey to wellness, whatever that looks like," she continues, opening her file.

"Wait—you think I've been drinking?"

Daisy puts a hand up. "It's not my business."

"Damn right it's not your business."

"No need to use foul language."

I'd like to show her what foul language really is.

"I'll just say I've noticed a change in you." She turns a page in the file. "I'm going to leave that there."

I blaze with humiliation. If I had more energy in my life, I would sue this woman for workplace discrimination. She's been treating me like a ticking time bomb ever since she found out I was a recovering alcoholic. But unfortunately there's no capacity for lawsuits in my life at the moment what with the whole, you know, murder thing.

"I've been tracking the coming and going from the office," Daisy says, pulling out some stapled papers scrawled with her signature hot-pink penmanship. "In the past month, you've been working an average of fifteen percent less per day. Over half the days you've been here, you're either coming in late or you're early to leave."

"This is a salaried position," I say, baffled. "I'm not an hourly employee."

"Right, but people are expected to work a certain number of hours—"

"Am I doing a good job, though, Daisy?" I ask, leaning my elbows on the desk. "Am I doing my duties? Are the volunteers happy? Are the cats doing just fine? Did I go above and beyond helping to raise thousands of dollars for this organization even though it's way outside my job description and my pay grade?"

"I'm getting a hostile feeling from you right now," Daisy says. "How about we take a moment to cool off?"

I sit back in my chair.

"Just breathe," Daisy says in her soothing voice, putting her beautiful hand-model hand on the table. "In and out."

I know how to breathe, bitch.

"You did go above and beyond doing media and fundraising," Daisy says. "And I *so* appreciate you. Did I tell you that the guy got caught, by the way? I'm going to be running an update on that soon. But don't feel like I don't see you and appreciate you, Leela. The reason I'm stepping in to give you this PIP is *because* I appreciate you so much that I want to see you *thrive* and I'm worried—"

"Wait," I say, her words catching up with me. "The guy got caught?"

"Yes. A couple days ago. The police came by to give me an update—unfortunately, you had left early—"

"Who is he?" I ask, grabbing the edge of the table. "What's his name?"

"Oh … I can't remember off the top of my head."

"I need to know what his name is," I say. "Like, now. Please."

Daisy's brow creases and she has a vaguely uncomfortable look on her face. Reluctantly, she pulls her phone out. "You think you might know this person?"

"Maybe."

She shakes her head, as if this is yet another disappointment in me to add to the list. "I have it in my notes."

She scrolls on her phone, her fingernail going *click click* on the screen. "His name is Reuben Cornwell."

"Reuben Cornwell," I repeat, getting to my feet, my pulse racing. "Reuben Cornwell."

Do I know that name? Is it familiar?

"Reuben Cornwell," I say again.

"Um … are you okay?" Daisy asks.

"No. I have to go. I'm sorry." I scoot the chair back with an excruciating scream of wood on linoleum.

"Leela, we're in the middle of your *PIP*!" Daisy says, astonished.

"Oh, yeah," I say, gesturing toward the paperwork. "I, um … I quit."

Feels so good coming out of my mouth. I get a rush. I can't believe I just said it.

She gasps.

"Yeah. Sorry, I can't with this idiocy," I say. "I'll come by to clear out my stuff soon. I have to run."

"Leela Crowe!" she yells after me, like she's my mother.

But I grab my purse and I'm in a taxi in under four minutes.

"Jolvix campus," I tell the self-driving taxi as I clip my belt.

I text Teddy.

> On my way. Need to talk.

He texts back,

> Why?

224

Then, a second later,

Never mind. Don't answer that.

I spend some time looking up Reuben Cornwells in this area and—bless his odd name—there's only one of them. There he is, the young Reuben, a red-faced guy with a butterball head whose vacant expression spells trouble. Does he look familiar? Do I know him? I'm so bad with faces and names. I try to learn anything I can about him but all his accounts are private, the bastard. It isn't until downtown Oakland that I look up at the flashing billboards and the brick warehouses and long strings of phone lines passing. It hits me like a bus—I quit my job. I just quit my job, like it was nothing.

What the fuck was I thinking?

CHAPTER 34

"Leela!" Teddy's voice booms as he walks into the Welcome Dome. "Great to see you! You ready to go on another hike?" He points to the receptionist. "Good afternoon, Louise!"

His voice is so loud it echoes off the floors. He's entered the building with the performative swagger of a man walking onstage and belting the first line of the play. I give him a look as I stand up and walk over to him. His arms are wide open, like he wants a hug.

"Um ... what?" I ask, walking into his hug to receive but not reciprocate it.

He claps my back. "Love these hikes we've been going on. Let's work those calves."

I don't even know how to respond, so I just follow him out the doors. Once we're out on the main path, passing a group of people on a tandem bike and a man yelling at a screen about algorithms, I put my sunglasses on and hurry my legs to keep up with Teddy's stride.

"What the hell is going on?" I finally ask. "What was *that*?"

"That was me strengthening my alibi," he leans over to yell-whisper. "SJPD reach out to you?"

"No," I say. "Thank God."

"Nobody has?" he asks.

I shake my head.

Teddy lets out a relieved moan. "I thought that's why you were coming here." He stops in the middle of the path, hands on hips, and eyes me while he catches his breath. He's in a seersucker jacket with rolled up sleeves. Yacht couture, I'd call his style. His aviators probably cost him a fortune. "Why are you here, then?"

A group is doing yoga on the lawn behind him, at least a dozen downward-dogging individuals with asses in the air. All at once, I don't know how to answer his question. It's dizzying—why *am* I here? Why did I immediately, reflexively come here as I crashed and burned my own life in Daisy's office?

Reuben Cornwell, my brain helpfully whispers.

"I found out who threw the cinder block," I say.

"Oh?" he asks, shielding his eyes from the sun.

"What if that's who did this, who, you know …" I put two fingers to my temple and pull an invisible trigger. "Genesis."

"Jesus," he says, his lip curling up.

"I'm sorry, I'm trying to be discreet."

"Well, you're terrible at it. Let's just … let's go on a hike."

"Seriously?"

"Seriously. I'll drive us there. To the same trail, you

know—" Here he raises the volume of his voice as we begin walking again and pass people chatting and eating sandwiches on benches. "—the one we walked the morning of Saturday, July 18."

"You are the guiltiest-looking innocent person I've ever known," I tell him.

He ignores me for the remainder of our walk to his car. Once we're in it—a self-driving Sunray, of course, the newest model—he finally turns to me.

"You need to be more careful," he says.

"Of what? We didn't *do* anything. I came here to tell you about the cinder block guy which is information that could get you off the hook."

Teddy takes his sunglasses off, along with his phony smile. Now he looks tired, sad, and generally beaten down by life. I've seen him like this, in the months after Jack died, but it's been a while.

"Oh, Teddy," I say, putting my hand between us on the seat. "You okay, bud?"

"I'm a fucking wreck," he says, pinching the area between his eyes. "Gen's funeral was yesterday."

"How was it?"

"Didn't go. Wasn't invited." He takes his hand away from his face. His eyes shine. "She hated my guts, remember?"

"The feeling kind of went both ways," I remind him gently.

"Yes, it did. But at one point … I loved her."

I nod.

"I mean, I loved her when I thought she was someone else," he adds. "Which is the most confusing part."

"It is confusing," I agree.

And I don't know why, but what he's saying is ringing a bell in me.

"The funeral looked beautiful," he says. "Just what she wanted. Everyone dressed in pink, the flash mob, all of it."

"How did you see it?" I ask, confused.

"It was livestreamed on her social media accounts. One of her wishes."

"Weird," I say.

"It is weird. It is." He swallows, his Adam's apple bobbing. "I haven't been sleeping. I keep having nightmares about the whole thing—dreams where Genesis is bloody, half her face hanging off—"

"Oh, Teddy," I say.

He leans in and says, much quieter, "Or dreams where I killed her. Where I actually realize that it was me, I did it. And then I'm caught and I go to jail."

"Teddy," I say, taken aback by his unraveled state. Teddy's a raging mess, but he's a mess who always keeps it together. "You need to get some help. See someone."

"Like a therapist?"

"Yeah. Something."

Teddy waves a hand, puts his sunglasses back on. "I don't have time for crap like that. Maybe my doctor can just write me a prescription." He takes his phone out. "So who is the guy?"

My head's spinning as I watch him straighten his posture and slip back into his Man With It Together persona. "Reuben Cornwell," I say.

"Reuben *Corn*well?"

I nod.

"You're shitting me," he says.

"You *know* him?"

"No, but that *name*."

"Made him easy to look up."

"Reuben *Corn*well," he repeats, typing into his phone.

"You're not going to find anything."

"Oh, I'm not looking into him. I'm tasking it to my Tasky detective. This guy's *good*."

"Same guy who found my cell number?"

"Yeah, he's amazing. Did that in twenty-seven seconds flat."

I watch Teddy as he tasks away, uncertain whether to feel creeped out or in awe of Teddy and his absolute disregard for people's privacy.

"He'll give us a full rundown of Reuben in less than two hours," he promises.

He puts his phone in his pocket and contemplates the scenery out the window. I join him. It's nice. My heart is a hammer in my chest and I feel like I'm drowning, but the tall trees and the blue sky sure are pretty.

"And how are you?" Teddy finally asks, as if he just remembered I exist.

"I quit my job today."

"What? Really? Why?"

"I—I don't know, honestly. She wanted to put me on a PIP? I don't know, I just cracked."

"You are so impulsive," he says, peering at me over his sunglasses. After a lengthy pause, he turns to the window. "I love that about you."

Something in me twists, hearing that.

"Oh, shut up," I say.

"You need a job?"

"No. Yes. But I mean … not at Jolvix."

"What about consulting? It's cushy, it's flexible, no commitment."

"Maybe," I can't believe I hear my own mouth saying.

The car parks itself like a good little car and Teddy and I jump out.

"Leave these babies in here," he says, tossing his phone on the seat.

I leave my "baby" next to his. We're near enough to Barnett's house that I recognize his driveway in the distance. There are two other cars parked on the shoulder with us here as well.

"Well, let's do it," Teddy says, slamming the car door shut.

And for just a fleeting second, as we walk onto the path, gravel crunching underneath the soles of our shoes, a faint wind making the leaves sing, I imagine another life, one where everything is okay. Where I'm safe. Where no one gets hurt. Where I've chosen to go on a hike for the sake of it and not because we live in a world where we fear being listened to and being watched and surveilled so much that nature is the only place where we are truly free.

CHAPTER 35

I jog city streets regularly and Teddy's a gym rat, but neither of us are hikers. After about ten minutes, both of us are muttering because the dust has stained our pants halfway up our legs. Then Teddy screams like a child at the sight of a lizard. I point to the first nice big rock under an oak tree I can find and he and I take a seat. Now this? This we're good at.

"Gen could be nice sometimes," he says. "You know? We paint her in black and white, but she could be charming. Sweet."

"Please don't ask me to agree with you," I say. "The only time I ever actually spoke a word to her was when she was punching me in the face."

"Yes," he says. "That's also true."

"Which I still don't understand," I say. "What the fuck set her off, I don't know."

"She was a highly suspicious woman."

"Delusional," I correct him.

Just talking about it is stoking a dormant rage in me.

Suddenly, I'm not just angry that she attacked me, that she was a terrible person or at least a person who did terrible things—I'm angry that I feel bad that she died. That I have expended sympathy on her behalf and felt weighed down by guilt, *guilt*, as if this is my fault.

"She thought you and I had a thing, you know," Teddy says. "Like everyone thought."

"Why the hell though, Teddy? Who even started that rumor?"

"Who knows."

"Also, it's so screwed, isn't it? That she was ultimately suspicious of you and then took it out on me." I think of Lotus, how the situations eerily rhyme. How women often turn against each other when their real enemy is the man they love. "Fuckin' patriarchy, man, I swear to God," I murmur.

"How did this become about patriarchy?" Teddy asks, his face crumpled in confusion.

I wave my hand. He wouldn't understand. Men usually don't. "Forget it. Anyway. You never ... said anything to anyone about us."

"Never."

"To Genesis. You know, when exchanging secrets. As lovers do."

"Leels," Teddy says. "Of course not. It's just—you and I worked together a lot. Long hours. Lot of days. We were close. We had a close working relationship. You know how it goes—sometimes you spend more time with co-workers than you do your own people."

I huff a little, my cheek still stinging from the memory of Genesis's fist.

"I think she knew you and I had a special bond," he says. "One that—you know. Because of Jack. Something that no one else can ever touch. You know?"

"What a stupid thing to be jealous of," I say flatly.

"I know. Gen didn't make sense. She also had serious issues—did I tell you she had like three personality disorders? Also this thing called orthorexia. She sobbed in her sleep. It broke my heart sleeping with her, I had to sleep on the sofa with earplugs." He shakes his head. "She wasn't all bad, though. She loved her pet rabbit Babette. And spa days. And nail art."

"I'm sorry, I'm not doing this," I say, standing up.

"Doing what?"

"Listening to you ramble about Genesis." My chest is so tight I put my fist to it, press it against the pressure. "Look, I know you almost married her, but she almost broke my face and I might be why she's dead and I just—I can't—I can't be the person processing this with you."

"Sorry," he says, getting up. "You're right. I just thought you might understand."

I give him a hug that he returns with intensity. "I do understand. I do. I know."

The pressure in my chest sharpens, changes from a vise to a knife.

"I know," I say again. "I don't want to talk about it, but I know."

I pull away, wiping under my eyes, feeling like the whole sky's going to shatter to pieces and fall down on me. Feeling like I'm going to implode, a person plunged to the bottom of the sea. But we keep walking, as we do. One foot in front of the other.

"Are you sure no one has reached out to you?" Teddy asks. "I went in for questioning and gave your information. I was sure they were going to ask."

"No one has."

"I wonder if there's another suspect. God, I hope so. What if they found the guy already?"

"Um, why do you assume it's a guy?"

"What, that's *sexist* now? To assume a serial killer is a man?"

"I'm just messing with you."

"Seriously, though. You know what? I'm going to ask my Tasky detective." Teddy touches his pants. "Fuck, phone's in the car. Let's go back." He stops in his tracks. "Good God in heaven, what is that in the middle of the path?"

"It's a bird nest."

"It's disgusting."

Then he proceeds to walk into a spider web and scream. It's like a slapstick routine, only no one's laughing and everything is terrible. It's decided: I dislike hiking and I especially dislike my hiking partner. As we continue hoofing it, the clouds part, the sun turns up the heat, and I break a sweat. Both of us are barely talking the entire way back to the car. Then, like idiots, we realize we actually have been walking in the wrong direction and turn back around, arguing the entire way about whose fault it was.

Back in the car, both of us are dirty and panting and pink-faced. Teddy grabs his phone like a drowning man reaching for a raft.

"That was actually fun," he says.

"No, it *wasn't*," I say in disbelief.

"So we're near Barnett's house, huh?" he asks, glancing out the window.

"I can see his driveway from here."

"I should give him a visit soon."

"If you do, prepare yourself for the uncanny valley."

"Do I even want to know what happened there?" he asks as he goes back to scrolling his phone expressionlessly. My phone's lit up with missed calls and texts from Daisy, which I ignore.

"Well, he murdered a robot in front of me. Did I tell you that?"

"Sounds like Barnett," he says.

"He's truly a repulsive person."

"He always had a thing for you."

I make a vomiting sound just as Teddy's phone dings.

"It's my Tasky guy," he says. "See? Told you he worked fast. He says he can meet in a church parking lot in twenty minutes."

"Why a church parking lot?"

"This guy is old school," Teddy says, fastening his seatbelt. "He only offers reports in person and on paper."

"Okay," I say.

Twenty minutes later we're in an empty parking lot of a steepled church when a Prius comes zooming in and parks beside us. A man who is literally dressed like a clown gets out of the driver's seat and knocks on the window, shouting, "Knock knock, ding dong, honk honk." It happens so fast I barely have time to register what is going on.

"This is your guy?" I ask.

"He moonlights," Teddy says, unlocking his doors with a button.

"As a *clown*?" I ask, just as the clown climbs into the back seat.

"I'm not a clown," the clown says, offended, as he closes the door. "I'm a Shakespearean actor."

I turn to behold this man—this bearded older man whose face is caked in white makeup, his balding hair dyed a strange shade of orange. He's also brought in a noxious cloud of cologne that makes my eyes water.

"Feste. *Twelfth Night*. I'm heading to dress rehearsal after this," he clarifies.

"Wow," I manage. "Okay then. *Twelfth Night*. I played Olivia once in high school."

"Fascinating," he says, pulling out some paperwork. "I charge by the second so let's get into it, shall we? Reuben Cornwell. Twenty-six years old, lives alone in a studio apartment in Berkeley, previous arrests include stalking a year ago but he never served time. Former employee of some place called Edwin's which used to be an electronics repair place that closed down about two years ago; same establishment where he was arrested for throwing a cinder block through a bar window recently. You know this? Your man of the hour is in jail."

"He is?" I ask. "For how long?"

"Undetermined. He's awaiting trial right now. Outcome doesn't look good for him. Woman he hit on the head was critically injured."

I wince and Teddy exhales sharply.

"Stalking," I repeat. "Who was he stalking?"

"A woman named Rihanna Perkins. Know her?"

I shake my head and look at Teddy, who shrugs.

"Don't have many details on that one except she has a restraining order against him," the clown or detective or whatever says.

"And … my thing? You get my message about my thing?" Teddy asks.

"I did and next time anything involving anything of that nature, as in anything involving the *po-pos,* needs to be in person. Speaking of which, you want a breath of fresh air?" the clown asks.

"Love one," Teddy says.

"I'll stay here," I say.

"Nice meeting you, lady," the clown says.

They climb outside. I watch them through the window, leaning in close and talking intently against the backdrop of the church sign with its giant cross. As I study the detective's clown outfit, I ask the air, "What the fuck?" Because sometimes in life, you need a good reality check and right now is one of those times. Not three minutes later, Teddy's back in the car and the Prius peels out of the lot faster than a spooked horse.

"Okay," Teddy says, rubbing his hands together. "Well, that was comforting." He leans over and says, in a voice just above a whisper, "Apparently the police are going in another direction at the moment. They found a footprint. At the, you know, crime scene or whatever."

"A footprint."

"Yeah. Phew. Okay. Maybe I can sleep tonight."

"And Cornwell's in jail."

"Yes, Cornboy's in jail." Teddy reaches over and rubs my arm. "Maybe you can sleep tonight, too?"

"Maybe," I say.

I lie back, closing my eyes, a wave of unbearable emotion drawing a shadow over me like a mounting tsunami.

"Leels?" Teddy asks, squeezing my arm. "You want a hug?"

I shake my head, keeping my eyes shut, willing the world away.

"It just feels like nothing is ever going to be okay," I croak. "I can never believe it's going to be okay."

"But it is," Teddy says. "You see? We just got proof." I feel his hand on my cheek, a comforting, cool feeling. "You've got to believe you're going to be okay."

"Even if Reuben was the guy—which, doubtful, Teddy, none of those details we just heard overlapped with my life or Madison's or Lotus's or Genesis's at all—or even if the police are on the trail of footprint man—"

"Why do you assume it's a man?" Teddy asks. "Ya sexist."

I open my eyes just to glare at him.

"Sorry," he says. "Trying to lighten the mood."

"Those people are still dead," I say through my teeth.

"Yes. They are. It's sad. Death is sad. But guess what, Leels? You hated them all. If anyone in the world has to get murdered, why not your enemies?"

So flippant. So unfeeling about other people's lives. Sometimes I can't tell if he's a sociopath or pathologically optimistic.

"You're really bad at comforting people," I say.

"You're really bad at accepting people's comfort."

He's not wrong. I would love a hug right now but

Teddy's hugs are too magnetic. If I get into his arms then I don't want to get out of them. It's a problem.

"Sometimes I feel like you've got this locked room inside of you," Teddy says to me, slinging his arm over my shoulder. "Ever since I met you I've been trying to find the key so I can look at what's really inside there." His fingers touch the back of my neck and play with my hair. "What have you got in there, Leela?"

I'm getting shivers being touched. It's been a long, long time since anybody touched my neck and played with my hair. Instantly, tears prickle my eyeballs—like underneath even the tiniest glimpse of pleasure, there's an infinite amount of pain.

"Every secret I've got, Teddy, you know," I say, without looking at him. "You're the only person I can say that to."

I shrug off his touch and inch away from him, wiping my eyes before anything escapes. I put my phone up in the air without looking at him. Don't look at him.

Instead, I say, "I'm going to call a cab home."

CHAPTER 36

The whole ride back to Berkeley, I'm grateful for the solitude and the quiet to process my shock from everything that happened today. Outside the window as traffic slugs along, a few weak city stars are haphazardly shining in the sky above the bay with its glitz of bridges and lit-up skyline. I can't exactly *relax* after learning what we learned from clown detective man, but it seems like I can at least give myself permission to forget about my dead enemies for just a little while. And even though there's so much to contemplate—like what the hell I'm going to do now that I quit my job like an idiot—the thought that keeps repeating is what Teddy said there at the end about me and my locked room.

Because he's right.

I've always been this way. Did it start when I was a kid, when my mom started dressing me up like a little doll and shuttling me to audition after audition so I could impress strangers? I carried with me a sense that there were things I couldn't show to those people—frowns, bad moods, the word *no*. Shasta insisted on the sunniest disposition and behavior along with ribbons in my hair and frills on my dresses when all I secretly wanted was unbrushed hair and pants. In school, I tried my hardest to be good, to turn in my homework, to never give in to the urge to procrastinate, to always "be my best self" as Shasta put it. Growing into the shape of a woman, I became an object of unwanted desire. Suddenly people stared at my body, catcalled me, said inappropriate things to me. I learned to walk the world avoiding the gaze of the public eye, knowing I was always watched but trying to forget it the way I could forget the audience when I was onstage. It was the secret of being an actress. The best performances are when you forget you're performing at all.

Deep down, though, I sensed an inner troubled underworld that had no words. A sadness, a loneliness, a feeling that there was something wrong with me. An urge to be rash and impulsive and act out. An urge to be my worst self. Maybe that's what's inside that locked room: my worst self, my deformed shadow I've hidden like a monster. I opened that door for Jack. I showed him all my selves—my most drunken, drug-addled, selfish self. The destructor. The self who yelled at him and said horrible things. The self who wished people dead sometimes. And now some of them *are* dead.

That locked room—it's almost like someone got the key.

Someone out there did these things because a part of me wanted them to.

CHAPTER 37

A week later I'm working on my resume in my robe and there's a knock on my door, which I ignore because I have no friends or acquaintances who would do such a thing. Once the knocking becomes more and more animated I begrudgingly get up, deeply offending Nosferatu who was in the midst of a long, lovely lap nap. Peeking through the peephole, I gasp when I see Michael's face and clamp a hand over my mouth.

"Oh my God, oh my God," I whisper, and then, louder, through the door. "Michael!?"

"Leela!" he says, looking at the peephole as if he can see me. "That you?"

"Just—wait, okay? I need you to wait."

My heart is pounding as I run to my room and get dressed, muttering nonsense the entire time because ... because how is Michael here? *Why* is Michael here? I don't want him in my apartment, I wasn't prepared to bring an ex-boyfriend into my apartment. I haven't seen the man in, what—three years? We've exchanged online messages. He's asked to see me. I've never said yes. Now he's giving me no choice. I hate that he's springing himself on me like this.

Goddamn it. I put on pants and answer the door.

"Hey!" I say as I see him.

Oh, Michael. Red-haired and dreamy and too sweet for my sour soul. He has this round, freckled face and a dimple in his chin and big brown eyes that make you want to sigh. And he hasn't changed a bit. I even recognize the HELLA BALLOTS T-shirt he's wearing for the voting org where he works. He leans in for a hard, muscle-clenched hug. The man still bench presses and I can feel it in his embrace. I melt into it for a split second before pulling back.

"What … are you doing here?" I ask.

"I'm in town for work! I tried to reach out to you but you didn't respond."

"You did?" I lie.

Yes, he did. I just kept kicking the can down the road. Now I know why he was so anxious to talk to me.

"How'd you get my address?" I ask.

"How'd …" His smile melts. "I send you Christmas cards and birthday cards, I have your address."

"Sure. Okay."

"Is this … not cool?" he asks, looking baffled. "I'm so sorry. Did I overstep?"

"No, it's fine. Just—my house is a mess. Maybe we can go get a cup of coffee?"

"Yeah, okay," Michael says.

He wanted to come inside. His face tells the story, darkened with hurt. I only dated Michael for a couple months but I noticed that about him right away, the way his bright demeanor could be erased in a second's time and replaced with an injured puppy expression. God, I hated staring at that expression when I called it off with him—and in the weeks after, when he wouldn't stop confronting me at my apartment, at my office, even at the bar, broken leg and all.

"How's your leg?" I ask him as I close the door and lock up behind me.

"Good as new," he says as we take the stairs to the sidewalk. He hits his thigh, as if to prove to me that those four surgeries to repair his shattered bones worked.

I shudder, getting that special sick feeling I only get with Michael.

"And how are you?" he asks.

"Um, good," I answer. "In between jobs. What are you doing out here for work?"

"I had a retreat out in Napa."

"Rough stuff."

"I know, right?" he laughs.

Michael's always been drawn to the gleam of my sarcastic armor. We had an opposites-attract thing going on when we knew each other—he's like a Red Bull and I'm like a double-shot of vodka. At the time I didn't know what he saw in me, why he pursued me so fervently when he moved into the apartment across the hall. There he was, a former rugby player who talked politics all day long and had the exuberance of a youth group leader. And there I was … a bitter, heartbroken drunk in a spiral of self-sabotage. It makes sense now. He wanted to save me. He saw a struggling woman whose fiancé had killed himself. He tried to get me to go to meetings. He tried to get me to see a therapist. He pumped me up and told me how amazing I was and he cuddled me and held me while I cried. Then, just months into us dating, a car struck him in a hit-and-run one night after he tried, in vain, to get me to leave a bar. His leg was shattered and his spleen was ruptured. I got completely spooked, feeling like it was my fault somehow—Jack had died only a year before. So I broke it off with Michael and he gave me puppy dog eyes at the hospital. I was a curse. I was a fucking curse and I wasn't going to wish myself on anyone, not ever again.

In the months afterward, as he healed, he was relentless. Flower deliveries at work. Constant texts. Love letters slipped under my door. It killed me to do it, but I threatened a restraining order against him. I did it to protect him from me, from the bad luck I apparently brought to the men who loved me. I had to cut him off. When I moved to California, we became friendly again, commenting on social media posts, holiday cards. But this is the first time I've seen him in a long time. And I can't say I'm glad about it. Instead, I'm flooded with a special shame, one for him and him only. On the walk over, Michael fills me in with small talk about DC life. I'm stiff, robotic, smiling when appropriate, offering titters of laughter when called for, but my guard is all the way up.

In line at the coffee shop, Michael and I study the hand-painted menu in silence as oldies play on the speakers. The coffee shop is very Berkeley. A man in a sharp suit works at one table, a lady in a rainbow knitted hat with no shoes on and a shopping cart full of recyclables occupies another. I order and then Michael does that thing he does where he gets whatever I'm having. The two of us sit down with black coffees near a window that looks out onto a bus stop and a busy Berkeley street.

"You're not happy I came, are you?" Michael asks me.

"Just surprised," I say, giving him a tight smile.

"How are you really doing?" he asks, leaning in.

"Well, still sober." I sip the coffee even though it singes my tongue. "Between jobs."

"Seeing anyone?"

It strikes me as strange, for the first time—that phrase. *Seeing someone.* As if to be seen means to be loved, possessed. I'm not seeing anyone. I'm not seen by anyone. If I were a superhero, I would want the power of invisibility.

"Nope," I say.

"I'm engaged," he says with a smile. "Did you see my post about it?"

"I didn't. Really?" I ask, sitting up a little straighter. "Wow, congratulations!"

It's like a muscle relaxing, to know this. Based on past experiences, I wasn't sure if he was going to try to reconcile anything. But Michael's sweet, a good man, one I never deserved in the first place. The kind of man who spends Thanksgivings volunteering at homeless shelters and goes to church on Sundays. The kind of man I would have ruined.

Michael pulls his phone out and shows me his engagement photos. His fiancé is stunning—wavy chestnut hair, freckles, bright eyes, in a flowery dress and cowgirl boots. They took professional engagement photos, of course. Staring into one another's eyes in a rustic barn, laughing while petting horses with a fat diamond on her hand, passionate kissing and haystacks.

"Good for you." I nod. "She's gorgeous. And geez, Michael, that ring's a *rock*."

"Cubic zirconia," he says. "We're actually getting Infinities."

"Wow." I raise my eyebrows. Call me cynical, but romance might be dead if getting an implant connected to your loved one is the ultimate gesture these days. But I shake the thought off. I shouldn't be judgmental. It's cute, it's sweet, it's meaningful for them.

"I met her when we were working the polls last election," he says, grinning as he pockets his phone.

"Well, that's perfect for you!" I say, warming up, unable to help smiling. "Seriously, congratulations."

The news of his engagement shifts the mood between us. The tension lifts and hey, look at me, here I am simply enjoying his company for the first time in years. We laugh about our old neighbors—the guy with the braid-beard obsessed with reptiles, the unit we thought someone was making meth in. We laugh about the crap weather in DC. We laugh so much that when I get home later, take my boots off, and sit in silence in my apartment, I ache with the memory of it. I ache with the thought of Leela in another universe—one smiling in her own engagement photos.

And I keep on aching.

CHAPTER 38

The next time I meet up with Eve, it's in Hayward for convenience's sake; Hayward is a city halfway between my Berkeley and Eve's Cupertino. I meet Eve out front of a random apartment building, which apparently thinks so much of itself it calls itself *The Hamptons*. It's not the Hamptons. It's an eight-unit stucco apartment building with a pool and a couple of cypress trees. Eve waves as she crosses the lawn to meet me, her hair blowing wildly, oversized sunglasses on her face.

"Hey you," she says. We give each other a half-hug. "Wanna go for a walk?"

"Sure. How's it going? How is it being back in Cupertino?"

"Oh, I fucking hate it," she says with a grin. "I can't wait to move back to LA when my research is over. And how are you?"

"Better than the last time I saw you."

"Yeah?"

"I think this all might be coming to an end," I say. "Sounds like either the police might have found a suspect, or the guy might be in jail."

"Well, what was it? The VixSpex?" she asks.

"I don't know yet. I have no real details. But it feels like everything might be on pause for now, thank God."

In the past ten days since Teddy and I met with the clown detective—yes, I counted—a slow creeping relief has blessed my life. I have dared to entertain the possibility that everything might turn out okay. That maybe the police are on it and I can live my life again. Teddy heard from the clown detective this week that SJPD found an eyewitness who thinks they passed the suspect on the trail where Genesis's body was found. Things are happening. It can go back to not being my business again.

"I almost didn't come today," I say. "I'm ready to just put it all out of my mind."

"Well, let's walk," she says, linking arms with me. "Maybe what I tell you will give you some closure or some shit."

I haven't walked arm-in-arm with someone in a long time. She's a bit shorter than me, but it works somehow. For a second. Then it's too cute for me and I unhook my arm. We stroll down a tree-lined suburban street that's pretty but unmemorable, a street like a million you've seen before. Houses with manicured lawns and long driveways and picture windows.

"Sorry to meet in this weird neck of the woods. I'm starting to think my apartment's bugged," Eve says.

"You're kidding."

"Jolvix doesn't mess around. Speaking of which, your phone's off?"

"Yeah."

"Thank you. I'd rather be over-paranoid than under, you know?"

"Sure."

"So let me unload what I found from my dark web guy," she says. "And I don't know, sounds like things are moving in the right direction. But maybe it'll clarify things somehow."

"Go ahead," I say, my throat tightening.

"It's like this," she says as we pass a house with sprinklers making rainbows over the yard. "In the months after that homicidal VixSpex headset went missing from your office, an *assload* of replicas showed up in a few sordid corners of the interwebs. I mean, there are likely hundreds out there. You'll never be able to chase their trails. I know this isn't helpful, but it is what it is."

"Okay," I say.

"Since then, there've also been numerous how-to's posted on how to adapt a regular VixSpex headset into a killer VixSpex headset. Which means this is completely untraceable at this point, I mean, anyone with a headset can buy some basic tools and parts from a hardware store and make their own ..."

I perform normalcy as best as I can, but inside, I'm choking at the thought of not just one or two but hundreds or perhaps *thousands* of these deadly weapons being out there—and this all maybe being my fault somehow, since I didn't alert the public that the master headset ever went missing. Jesus. What if I'm to blame for more murders, more suicides? This clinches what I've long suspected: I'm a bad person. I *must* be bad person, right? If we're sums of our deeds, my existence has led to the deaths of so many people already and now it's more? It could be *more* than this?

My vision goes spotty as Eve continues talking. I have to stop in my tracks and lean over. A cold sweat breaks on my forehead.

"Hey," Eve says. "You okay?"

"Fine," I mutter, squeezing my eyes shut and wishing I could leap into a black hole.

"Um," she puts her hand on my back. "Hey, buddy. What's going on?"

"I think I might be having a panic attack."

"Want some drugs? Xanax? Klonopin? I've got a fucking pharmacy here in my purse, you're talking to the *queen* of panic attacks, just say the word."

"No," I say. After a minute of collecting myself I stand up, the blood whooshing back into my face. "No, I'll be fine. Keep going. We can keep going."

"You're sure?"

"Yeah. Tell me the rest."

"The only other thing of interest," Eve picks back up, slowly, still watching me like she's concerned I might keel over, "is that due to the wonky sizing of the headset, the *only* guns that seem to fit the killer VixSpex are 3D-printed."

"Sure," I say.

I hear my voice saying it, but I'm in a tunnel of my own making right now. The vivid, colorful world around me, Eve's chic sunglasses and scarlet lipstick, the almost-mansions on a tree-lined street—I see them all like the light at the end of the dark place I'm in. I get quiet, receding into myself as the same thoughts repeat against the backdrop of my rapid heartbeat. There are countless replicas out there. They use 3D-printed guns, like the ones used to kill Madison, Lotus, and Genesis. So easy to get these days. Much easier to obtain illegally than a real gun. It's all just so out of control, so completely, utterly, unthinkably out of my control.

"You going to be okay, cupcake?" Eve asks me, pulling my sleeve.

"I just need—" I point to my temple. "I need some time to process it."

Eve nods.

"It's a lot to take in, all this."

"Oh, you have no idea the dark shit I've unearthed with this book I'm writing. This? Tip of the iceberg." Eve clears her throat. "Speaking of which, since you and I talked, I've been chasing some leads about Barnett's home life. Trying to figure out a way in there, to infiltrate—"

"I can't help you there," I say.

"Calm your tits," Eve says. "That's not what I'm asking."

We've circled the block at this point and have ended up back at The Hamptons. We both stop here, wiping sweat from our faces in the cool shade.

"I'm just feeling like since I started poking around …" Eve shakes her head at me and lets out a little laugh. "You ever feel like you're being watched?"

A man at a bus stop on the corner is watching us right now. I look up and see a woman in a window. A car passes, the driver slowing to leer at us. A doorbell camera on the front door of a nearby house. The passing faces that almost look familiar. The goosebumps on my skin that crawl sometimes when I feel eyes on me but don't look up to meet them. That creeping sensation that though I may be lonely, I am never, ever alone.

"Always," I tell Eve.

CHAPTER 39

Well, this might be the first time I've ever seen Teddy in jeans and sneakers. He's got a Giants baseball cap on, too. I almost didn't recognize him at first, waiting for me by the entrance to Redwood Regional Park against a back-drop of towering sequoias.

"You came ready this time," I say, unable to help myself from smirking at him.

"What?" he asks, hands on hips. "Look who's talking. Backpack. Water bottle. Your hair's up, have I ever even seen your neck before?"

I walk into his hug, half-returning it. He still smells slick and expensive, even if he looks like a dork. He really resembles Jack but I shake the thought.

"Are we outdoorsy now?" I joke as I pull away.

"No, just paranoid," he says. "A bug tried to fly in my ear when I was waiting for you. Let's get this over with."

The sunshine disappears as Teddy and I walk a path, passing a playground crawling with little ones. I feel like we're playing parts: Mr. and Ms. Normal People, in our comfortable clothes, going for a walk. After a minute, the trees get thicker and the shade darkens everything and cools the day off. With it, I can feel my smile disappearing, my heart growing heavy, and that horrible invisible hand coming back to squeeze my throat.

I've been carrying around what Eve told me now for three days. Three full days of ruminating over what has happened not only with the people I know who've been killed, but the many others I'll never even know about. That's how far the destruction has reached, I can't even see it anymore. My eyes blur and I wipe them as Teddy and I cross a bridge over a creek. I pull him into a clearing off the path, a place no one can overhear us, and stand near an embankment that leads down to the creek.

"Teddy, shit's bad," I say.

"Okay," he says, his brow creasing. "What now?"

"There are replicas out there of Barnett's fucking killer headset. Hundreds of them, probably."

"Uh-huh," he says, as if the meaning isn't sinking in.

"Not just replicas. It gets worse. There are directions on how to adapt a normal VixSpex headset with easy-to-find materials. Any asshole with basic tools can do it."

"Where did this info come from?"

"Someone I know who was able to dig into the dark web."

"Well, that's not our fault," he says indignantly. "What else?"

"What *else*? I ..." Exasperated, I look up at the trees, so tall I can't see their tops. I let out a breath. "Are you hearing me? It's our fucking *fault*. That headset went missing and we didn't tell anyone—"

"It's not our fault, Leels," he says, breezily, truly unbothered. "Blame Barnett. Did we make it?"

"No, but we had a responsibility to the public—"

"Did we take it?" he asks. "I know *I* didn't. Did you?"

"Of course not—"

"Did we leak the information? Did we replicate it? Put the replicas up for sale? Did we come up with the directions for how to create DIY murder VixSpex? Did we?"

"Teddy—"

"Leels. You're being silly. Of *course* it leaked. Of course some genius psychopaths out there figured out how to make their own. That's how technology works. You put something out there, you know soon it'll be corrupted. That's how humans work. They're corruptive little creatures."

"But—"

"You don't need to feel guilty." He pats my back. "It's not your fault and it's definitely not mine."

"With logic like yours, it's no one's fault."

"Exactly. Sometimes there's no blame. There's just misfortune, you know?"

"So you think nothing that we do ultimately matters?" I say, unable to help myself from raising my voice. The wind swishes my ponytail around and I straighten it back out. "We just do shit, people die, oopsie-doodle, who cares?"

Teddy removes his sunglasses so I can see the burn of his blue stare, the scar through his left eyebrow. Sometimes the smile on his lips doesn't match the despair in his eyes and this is one of those times. "If I was tallying my impact all the time—I mean, if I sat around counting all my fuck-ups and thinking of all the harms I've done in my short time on this earth ... I'd probably jump off a bridge."

I flinch at the thought.

"How were we supposed to know?" he asks, his voice catching. "How the *fuck* were we supposed to know?"

I nod and turn to the creek, needing a break from his stare.

"You didn't *do* anything," he says.

"Right," I say. "But this is one of those times in life maybe we *should*, you know ... do something."

A hawk cries above, interrupting us, and we both crane our necks to scour the branches for a glimpse. Neither of us seem to see it, though. In the silence, the rush of the creek roars in our ears.

"Do what?" Teddy finally says. "What exactly are you suggesting? Going to the police? Getting dragged all the way into this? Becoming part of the investigation for *murder*? And then—exposing what happened at Jolvix and how the VixSpex went missing, admitting we covered it up? What, you want to take responsibility for any replica that's out there, any disaster that happened because of our negligence? Get sued into oblivion?" He steps closer, lowers his voice like a person trying to convince someone else to put a pin back into a grenade. "Don't you think if these killer VixSpex were an actual, widespread problem where, you know, thousands of sad little VR-obsessed jerkoffs looking for a taste of Russian roulette were dropping off like flies and their corpses were found with *Jolvix headsets strapped to their fucking head* we would have heard about it?"

My nostrils flare as I consider what he's saying. About

twenty feet away on a path, two people pass by, arguing in another language. I wait for their voices to disappear before replying.

"What if we went to the press instead of the police?" I ask.

I'm thinking, of course, of Eve. She already has the information and the connection with the dark web guy. I've been feeding her details about Barnett's sexbot villa situation, but I could give her the go-ahead to sniff out a story about the VixSpex instead.

Teddy stamps his foot in frustration. "You're going to ruin me."

"What if we didn't even admit the part about the headset going missing?" I ask. "What if we just, you know, had someone look into the replicas that are out there? Break a story about them existing, maybe do some research to see if anyone out there has been injured or killed?"

"Who?" Teddy asks. "Who would you talk to?" His eyes twinkle knowingly. "You have someone in mind?" He pats my back. "Or have you already been talking to someone?"

I swallow, not wanting to admit the betrayal of talking to Eve. Teddy would flip out if he knew I've been getting cozy with a journalist hellbent on taking down Jolvix. But man, it also sickens me to keep secrets from Teddy.

Sometimes you need secrets to survive.

"Of course not," I say.

He sighs. "Look, can we ... can we let this goddamn investigation, Genesis's murder, can we let all that pass before we—we go down this road?"

"Talking to the press could lead to Genesis's murderer

though, you know?" I ask. "Whoever did this, they're using a replica."

"*Please*," Teddy says loudly, with a look like I'm giving him a headache. "This is about my sanity. I can't take this much, Leels, I can't."

I snicker bitterly at his selfishness.

"Your sanity too," he says. "You ever think that you're spending way too much time dwelling on your regrets?"

It stings, as the truth usually does. "Now you're going to therapize me."

"Yeah. You know what I'm talking about." He pulls my ponytail gently, just once. "Give yourself a break."

I shake my head.

"Stop punishing yourself. Stop looking backward. Aren't you supposed to be looking for a job?" He waves a hand over his shoulder. "Forget all that shit. Look at your two feet and where you're going next."

All at once, with a wave like a pill hitting, I am tired. Tired of chasing this horrible story, tired of the vague nightmare my life has become. Of spending my precious passion on caring deeply about dead people I'm only tangentially connected to, who are all people who suck and have hurt me. I'm sick of this ride and I want off.

"Walk a little?" Teddy asks.

I nod. And for the rest of the hike, for probably the first time in both of our lives, we shut the fuck up.

CHAPTER 40

THE GAME

When I was younger, I used to watch true crime shows with wild fascination.

The blood-flecked crime scene photos, images of naked corpses half-rotted in shallow graves—they didn't elicit fear in me.

I wanted to stare at those photos, study them.

Imagine myself as a detective on the case.

Imagine myself as the murderer.

I wondered again and again what it would take for me to ever reach that kind of breaking point and if I would be capable of it.

I would like to think I was smarter than most people, which would mean I was likely smarter than most murderers.

I would like to think I could quite easily get away with slaying someone.

Crimes of passion bored me. There's no intelligence behind killing one's lover in a blind rage.

In high school, when my stutter was debilitating and I

tried to live my life as a shadow, I would fantasize about someone giving me a mission to kill one of my fellow students and get away with it.

If my life depended on it, who would I pick?

I'm not a sociopath. I have feelings, deep dark feelings, and like anyone with those, the guilt would pose a problem.

I considered this fantasy often. Sometimes I entertained the idea of killing a teacher who gave me a poor grade or the jock who kicked the back of my chair throughout class just to subtly torture me.

But no.

I would have to find a victim who truly deserved it.

Then I heard about what Madison did to you.

That was my first true urge to kill.

I loved you, Leela.

You had no idea.

I called you sometimes from a blocked number and then hung up, unable to speak.

I wrote poems for you, talked to the mirror practicing what I would say to you.

Kissed my hand imagining your lips. Dreamt of you at night.

I couldn't bear to actually tell you this.

I wanted to grow up more, I wanted my skin to clear up, I wanted to turn into someone worth looking at and not looking over.

It was terrifying to imagine the violence of your rejection.

While you were onstage basking in the spotlight's

sunshine, I was one of the crew dressed in black, painting sets and working on costumes.

I knew you weren't my girlfriend, but in my mind, I created a world where you were. You were my girlfriend and I would do anything for you.

I would kill Madison for you if you asked me to.

After high school I forgot all about that for a while. Went to school, moved out and away.

My stutter faded, my style changed, I gained weight, grew into myself.

I still fantasized about getting a mission to murder someone.

Sometimes when I was bored my mind would go there and I would sit on a bench eating my lunch, imagining if I was a hunter, who would I hunt? Who would be the perfect prey?

It was just a game I played when my concentration wandered. It was just a game, until I saw you again, standing in my living room.

I'll never forget the way you looked in nothing but your boyfriend's T-shirt, like a raven-haired angel sent to me by a higher power.

"Shit," you said, covering your legs. "Um, hi. I'm Leela."

You didn't know me. I was new to you.

There was such an excitement in that newness, in meeting you here, both of us reincarnated in this new life.

That must be how an addict feels when they relapse.

I was smitten and I was doomed the moment I saw you again.

———

Murder has been a surprisingly humbling experience.

In my younger years, I was cocky, sure that I would easily get away with something those bumbling idiots in prison got caught for. Now look at me; I'm the bumbling idiot.

Yesterday I revisited the trailhead where I killed Genesis and out on the main road, on the trail sign along with the reminders to look out for snakes and wildcats, there was a sketch from SJPD of a murder suspect. I stood for a long time, studying it, my trembling hands in my pockets.

It didn't look like me. It didn't look human.

I had the strange urge to take the paper, crumple it up, and eat it.

I'm ashamed about how I handled Genesis. Amateur hour.

This time, I worked carefully.

I wasn't about to chase this one out of the house.

I have learned it's easiest to murder a person in the comfort of their own home.

This last one has been hard to nail down. Odd schedule. Gone for weeks at a time. Doesn't answer their door even when home. But her weakness?

DashDrone.

Food delivery—who knew it would be the death of her?

When the drone flies away and Eve Alexapoulis opens her door for her dinner tonight, I'm out of the shadows of her front porch so quickly the automatic light does no good.

I confront Eve, invade her personal space, nudge her backward into her doorway.

She's in a nightshirt, hair a strawberry mane, her lips a faded red.

"Easy," I say, showing her the gun. "Don't scream."

"Motherfucker," she says through her teeth. "Not this."

She inhales sharply, like maybe she's going to scream, but I push both of us into her apartment and kick the door shut behind me.

That was smooth. This is going well.

I rehearsed, and I'm getting a promising feeling right now, like I had at Madison's that first day when everything went according to plan. I'm holding the gun steady at Eve's head as I push her to a seated position on her couch.

The inside of her apartment is as bland as the outside, as devoid of personality as a vacation rental. It appears to be more a place to sleep than a home. There's a wooden sign on the wall that says *Live laugh love*, verbs I don't see Eve doing much of tonight, unfortunately.

"What the fuck do you want?" Eve demands, gun pressed to her temple. "Who the fuck sent you here? And what the fuck is that on your fucking face? You come here straight from Party City, asshole?"

Eve doesn't look as afraid as I expected her to be.

In fact, there's nothing but rage blazing in that expression. I have to take a second to center myself.

I remind myself, this is just a game.

I'm playing a game. This isn't real.

Eve seems to know what's good for her, is remaining

still, cooperating, but this is different than the others; they could barely stand to look at me, flinching at the sight of the mask, melting into an inhuman mess at the sight of a gun.

But Eve's looking into my eyes, without blinking, as if she wants to peel my layers off to see what I really am at the core.

It's horrific, that fearlessness.

"What, you too scared to speak? You too scared to show me who the fuck you are?" she asks.

This is much more confrontational than I expected.

Granted, I watched the video of Leela and Eve's livestream debate so many times I practically have it memorized. I expected Eve would be a handful.

But this? Right off the bat?

I consider shooting her through the head and leaving.

Job done. Hands clean. Might be wiser.

Would you know, Leela?

Would you care that I didn't fulfill what you asked for, that I didn't play the game again, that I wasn't clever enough?

"Your hand's shaking," Eve says, looking at the gun. "You're not used to doing this, are you? Is this your first time doing Jolvix's dirty work, or what?"

"Jolvix?" I repeat, confused.

"What did they send you for? Intimidation? To wreck my equipment? You want to torture me into telling you where my draft is stored so you can destroy it?"

My head is spinning. "What?"

"Don't you understand?" she asks, with a wide grin, looking deeply at my eyes. "You're never going to stop me. Go ahead, follow me everywhere. Bug my house. Send threatening letters to my publisher. You can't shut me up. You hear me, you fuckin' Jolvix goon?"

Her tone is grating on me.

It's getting underneath my skin and making me itch, making me sweat, making me want to run. It's ruining my plan and my mood.

My trigger finger trembles.

I enunciate every word like it's its own sentence. "I'm not here from Jolvix."

Eve's expression falters into confusion. Her brown gaze shifts around the room. Her breath becomes shallow. "Who—what?" A hint of desperation, of fear climbs into her voice. "Then why are you here?"

"I'm here to play a game," I whisper in her ear.

The air seems to swell between us. Carefully reaching behind me, I unzip my backpack and pull out the headset.

You'd think Eve became a mannequin, she goes so still and so pale.

"You're fucking kidding me," she says.

Her mind is at work, desperate thoughts flickering in her face. I'm close enough that I can smell her breath—both sour like stale coffee and sweet like cherry lip gloss.

"This is about Leela," Eve says in a shaky voice. "Right?" She gives me the side-eye and emits a nervous laugh, a fake laugh, the laugh of a bad actress. "I see. You—are you supposed to—is this mask supposed to look like her, or …?"

"You're smart," I say.

"So—so I'm … you're here because you think she hates me. That right? Put the VixSpex down, buddy, let's have a reasonable discussion about this."

I don't put the VixSpex down. I remain as statuesque as I can—though I'm trying to put together how Eve knows this.

"The thing is," Eve says, keeping her eyes on the headset. She shifts and I press the gun into her temple, harder, to still her again. "Look, I—I know about you." She swallows. "I know because Leela knows about you. Because Leela told me. Because Leela is my *friend*."

Her …?

I don't believe her.

"Shut up," I say.

"She's my friend, honest. Look in my contacts. Look in my phone," she begs. "Seriously." Her voice rises in pitch. "After the debate—you know the debate! At the, uh—the tech conference. You're here about to murder my ass because of it!" More maniacal, fake laughter. "She and I became friends. I just saw her last week. She's—she's talked to me about you."

I almost can't speak for a moment. "She has?"

"Yeah. The avenger. Real sweet of you."

Her voice has an edge to it I don't like.

I ask, "What—what has she said about me?"

"She, uh …" She swallows. "Look, take the gun off my face. We can't have a reasonable discussion with a gun pointing at my face."

Yeah, right. I keep the gun pointed right at her, not moving.

"Does she have any idea who I am?" I ask.

"I, uh. I don't know. Want to call her? You and I, we can call her together? Hell, let's send her a selfie so she can see how pretty you look in your Halloween mask—"

Holding my breath steady, feeling my gut tighten, I say, "You're making fun of me."

"No way, friend. No way," she says brightly. Too brightly.

I despise the way she's talking to me right now, the way she smiles at me, like I'm some kind of joke.

Reminds me of Madison in high school when I passed through the green room as the girls pinned their hair and powdered their faces. *Aw, so cute, a lil peeper. You gonna jerk off to this later?* she'd ask me in the mirror.

Or Lotus, the way she used to gush *Hey sweetie!* in a disgusting saccharine voice whenever she wanted something from me.

Or Genesis—one time when I was standing outside her driveway, scoping out her house. And there she came, behind me, out of nowhere. *Hi creep, something I can help you with?* she asked me, her voice so fake and sweet it was malicious. *If not, how about you move the fuck along before I call security?*

"Grab my phone," Eve says, snapping me back to the present. "I'll unlock it for you, you can look at my messages. Okay?"

My hand's quivering and something in me sinks, falters. Frozen. Not sure what to do next.

Eve's thrown me off, this wasn't what I expected. Friends with you, Leela?

No, no—that can't be right.

"Hello? Anyone home?" Eve asks loudly.

It's happening. It's sickening.

I'm shrinking into myself. I'm disappearing somewhere inside myself.

I'm a child again cowering under a table, a little rabbit, a cockroach scattering.

I hate Eve's eyes, the brightness of them, the force of their aim—and suddenly I don't want to be seen anymore.

Not by her, not ever again.

So I slip the headset over my wrist like a clumsy bracelet and reach around to my backpack again, this time to grab the duct tape.

Eve moans. "Come on, really?" she asks as I pull the tape with my mouth and rip it with a violent tug.

I don't respond, circling behind her while keeping the gun cocked to her head.

"Don't even have the guts to muster a fuckin' response, huh?" she asks, her pitch rising, a little tremble in her voice. "You realize I'm a human being? An actual living breathing person? You know what I survived to be here? What I lived through? Is this a fucking joke? And—and— you—you know Leela hates this. She hates what you're doing to her. You're ruining her fucking life. You love her so much, you're ruining her fucking life?"

Lies. She's lying.

I know you, Leela. I know you asked for this.

You sat on a stool opposite this woman and looked into the eye of the livestream camera and *you asked for this*.

I wrap the duct tape around Eve's hands, binding as tightly as I can.

Then, without a word, I come behind her and pull the headset over her face.

She's beginning to pant now, panic. "You're going to get caught. You know that, right? I'm pretty sure my house is bugged. Jolvix has been following my every move for weeks."

"That was me," I say in her ear.

She laughs tragically now, more sob than real laughter. "This is exactly what I said would happen," she whispers through clenched teeth. "Remember? In the debate?"

I flip the switch on the headset, heart racing, my whole body thrilled with pins and needles.

Game on.

"I'm so fucking sick of being right," she whispers.

With a gasp, she turns like a person in the dark, tentatively moving, headset blinding her.

She tries to run, stumbles around her living room. Her shin hits her coffee table and she screams with her entire lungs and then the gun *pops* like a firecracker and I watch her head explode.

She falls to the floor like a dropped marionette.

I stand, catching my breath and savoring the silence. Ears ringing loud as a bell.

The sight is ugly, yes.

But it's the most wonderful feeling, to know that it's over, to know that I've accomplished this.

Once again, I've gotten away with murder.

Not a dimwit. Never a dimwit.

Leela, you see how thoughtful I am, how well-planned each one has been?

You've never known someone who's pulled off anything like this.

The mess is horrid, but I pretend the blood and chunks of skull and hair drenching the once-cream carpet are just part of a game I'm playing.

I step around the gore with care. Stooping, I gently remove the headset from what's left of Eve's head, flinching when one of her eyeballs sags out of its socket.

I untangle her red hair from the head strap.

Slowly, slowly, I pull the duct tape from her wrists and insert the gun in Eve's slumped hand.

Her mouth hangs open, her face nothing but a sick violet-colored raw meat and splintered bone.

I unlock her phone with one of her fingers, still warm. Not for long.

Leela, you're in her contacts.

I open your messages, using Eve's limp finger to navigate the screen, frowning as I see your back and forth.

You *have* been meeting.

You've been talking.

No details in the messages—it doesn't sound warm and friendly.

Reads like business.

Why were you meeting? Something about Jolvix?

My mouth goes dry and a spider of worry creeps along my skin.

Have I made a mistake?

Did I do something bad again?

Leela, Leela, Leela—my lone lighthouse on a dark sea. These things I've done, I've done them all for you.

I've risked my life to play this game. This is the ultimate expression of love.

You know that, right?

I'm sorry I hurt you, I text from Eve's number, then drop her phone on the floor near a glistening wad of brain.

I swallow, flinching. I didn't do that.

The game did that. It's just a game.

This is what you asked for. This is good.

I know what's good for you, Leela, and if it hurts now, the hurt is only temporary.

Just like before. Just like the other times.

Your guardian angel of death knows what's best for you.

CHAPTER 41

LEELA

I'm out on a night run. There are a few half-assed stars in the blue-black sky and the air's a cool sting on my face. Berkeley's still alive in the dark, balcony barbecues and bicyclists and dinner smells wafting out of open windows. How I love zoning out to the rhythm of my rubber soles on the pavement, getting to that point where I've outrun my own thoughts and worries. Where I'm all body and no brain.

Waiting at a stoplight and catching my breath, I pull my phone from my pocket to check the time. But I don't even notice the time. All I see is the notification banner on my home screen with a text displayed from Eve.

I'm sorry I hurt you.

Sometimes all it takes is five words to stop the world's spinning.

"What?" I whisper to nothing, to no one. I open the text and, with a quivering fingertip, I text back,

Eve? Are you okay?

No three dots, no dancing ellipses, no *read* notification appearing. My text just sits in our open chat. And though I've now been standing on this corner where the light changes long enough that I should have caught my breath by now, my heart's hammering harder than it was when I had broken into a full-speed run. I call Eve but she doesn't pick up.

"Eve?" I say to her voicemail. "I'm worried. Can you call me back, please?"

This is different than the other times. I try to tell myself that. This didn't come through Peeps, it's pithy and not some paragraph-long message, it's not the same. But the sick pit in my stomach knows better. There's no logical reason that Eve would apologize to me right now, and besides, Eve doesn't strike me as the kind of gal who goes around handing out apologies to anyone.

My knees are jelly and the wind has been sucked right out of me. I hold my phone in my hand and turn one way, then another, suddenly lost in my own neighborhood. I—I don't know what to do, I don't know where to go. There's this nameless horror, this fear so insidious and intense, I don't know where to direct my body right now. I turn and head toward home again, feeling like fate kicked my chest in.

The panic isn't electric. It's crushing. I try Eve four more times, four more voicemails, walking slowly up the sidewalk, the sweat on my skin cold now and making me shiver. Cars pull in and out of the gas station. A dog walker passes me with seven panting poodles. A jazz trio plays inside a coffee shop window. But it's not real, none of it is real anymore, because all I can think is that Eve is dead.

She's not dead, the little hopeful idiot inside me says. *You don't know that for sure. It's just a text.*

But fuck you, hopeful little idiot. You're always wrong.

Okay, well, what if she can be saved? the hopeful little idiot tries. *What if she's not dead yet?*

"How am I supposed to save her?" I yell. "Why the fuck is this on me?"

The people enjoying one another's company at tables out front of the coffee shop turn to me with eyebrows raised. I guess I said the last part out loud. I look like a woman who is losing it, because I am a woman who is losing it. I bite my cheek and look at my phone again—nothing. I consider calling 9-1-1 but that fear of police, of being pulled into anything, it's got such a tight grip on me I shake my head and instead jog into the coffee shop. I don't want to use my phone for this.

The room's warmth, the sweet caramel smell, the sounds of laughter and jazz music all strike me as bizarre as I move through it in a rigid state of disbelief. Up at the front counter, I beg the rainbow-haired barista for the café's phone and keep stammering the word "emergency" until she hands me the cordless phone from beneath the counter. I crouch down and close my eyes, put a finger in my ear and call 9-1-1.

"I need you to perform a wellness check on someone," I say.

But as soon as the dispatcher hears I'm calling about someone in Cupertino, I get transferred. And as soon as another dispatcher picks up, I realize I don't know Eve's address. Just her first and last name. And as soon as they ask me why she needs a wellness check, I realize all I have is an apology sent via text and they won't get it, it's too deep, it's all too deep, so I just beg them to find her and hang up the phone and go back outside. I walk home in something like a trance, unable to imagine where I go from here. I can't go on like this, with people dying, with it being my fault but beyond my control.

For not the first time in my life, I succumb to a fantasy of escape. A bottle of pills, a plastic bag over the head. Instead, I walk straight into my neighborhood liquor store. I let that old *fuck it* feeling guide the way. I buy a bottle of my best friend and worst nemesis Jack Daniels. Inside my apartment, I collapse on my velvet chair while Nosferatu weaves between my legs, purring like a thunderstorm.

"Hey buddy," I say. "I'm going to put my brain on hiatus a little while."

He doesn't give a shit. Sober, drunk, emotionally healthy, falling all the way apart—cats love you just the same. It's part of their charm.

I gnaw the plastic wrapper off the top of the bottle and pop it open. The smell. Oh, that sweet familiar smell, the promise of forgetting. I don't care how many years it's been. I don't care how many meetings I've been to or what chip I've got. I gulp the fire down, thirsty for it, loving the way it hurts my throat on the way down. Do it. Hurt me. I sit back and catch my breath. I let it hit me, relaxing reflexively and immediately, and right as I'm having my first moment of bliss, my phone buzzes in my pocket. Teddy. My finger hovers over the green button a good long moment, so much flashing through me I'm not sure if I should answer it—but maybe he knows about Eve, maybe he has information.

"Hey," Teddy says. "How's it going?"

"Amazingly," I say, taking a long pull from the bottle.

"You sound weird."

"I said exactly one word to you, how can I sound weird?"

He doesn't answer.

"How are *you*, buddy?" I ask.

"Okay, what the hell is going on?" He sounds annoyed.

"Didn't *you* call *me*?"

He blows out a sigh that sounds like a rocket launch going off in my ear. "I wanted to tell you that my Tasky guy has an update."

"What is it?"

"I don't know yet. I was going to ask if I should go see him now or if you wanted to be there too, or …?"

I take another swig. "Sure. Both."

"You—now?"

Nosferatu jumps to my lap and gazes into me with his moon-yellow eyes. He flinches at my breath. "I think Eve might be dead," I say.

"Wait, what?" Teddy asks. "Come again?"

"I'm drinking right now," I say.

"You're—what the fuck, Leels?"

"I think she might be dead. So many dead people, Teddy. Too many."

"I don't know where to start with you. You're drinking? Since when?"

"Since … I don't know, ten minutes ago?"

"Where are you?"

"In my apartment."

"Are you drunk?"

"Will be soon."

"Look, can you—can you do me a favor?"

"Probably not."

"Stop drinking. Right now. Put it down. Okay? No matter what's going on, I promise, this won't help anything."

"It's already helping."

I take another pull from the bottle. Feels better than a kiss.

"I'm going to send a cab to your house right now," Teddy says. "You're going to get in it. You're going to come to my condo. Hear me? Whatever's going on, you're not alone. We can deal with this together."

"Have you ever considered that I don't want to be saved, Teddy?"

"Have you ever considered that you are a hundred percent full of shit?" he asks brightly. "Cab will be there in five."

Touché, Teddy. I pound as much whiskey as I can in five minutes, cap the bottle, and leave it on the counter next to my dirty dishes. Once I'm in the cab, I drift off a little as the booze fully hits me. The white noise of wheels on the road, the dim blue dash lights make it easy. Before I know it, the self-driving taxi is dinging an alarm and blinking its interior lights to wake me up and I'm sitting up wiping drool from my face. My tolerance sure has taken a hit. Teddy's out on the curb in front of his condo and when I emerge from the car, he's already shaking his head at me and shooting me a pitying look.

"Don't say anything," I say.

He doesn't. He helps me out of the cab. I push him away, thinking I'm fine, I'm not *that* drunk, when I wobble and almost roll my ankle and he catches my arm.

"It's these fuckin boots, man," I say.

"Mmm, of course," he says as he helps me up the stairs. "Is it your boots' fault you smell like a distillery and have your shirt buttoned wrong, too?"

"Everything is very bad right now," I say as he unlocks his front door.

"I'm sure breaking your sobriety made it a whole lot better, too, right?" He holds the door open for me and a little dog barks from inside. Teddy shouts, "All right, okay, she's cool, let's simmer down now, my girl."

"I forgot you have a dog," I say.

Teddy puts his hand on my back, leading me in. "Her name is Pickles and she's the best girl."

Pickles is tiny and gold and comes running up to Teddy with her tongue out. I'm drunk and I'm also not a dog person. For some reason, I salute Pickles—I don't know how to connect with a dog—and then collapse on his red leather couch. Pickles comes up and licks my hand, which I put away in my pocket.

"Why do dogs have to slobber all over everything?" I mutter.

"She's giving you kisses," he says, and then in a high voice. "You want some food, my lil gherkin?"

"Gherkin?" I repeat.

But he's left me here on the couch as he feeds Pickles

in the kitchen. I sit here like a pile of goo. His place is the same as it was years ago, the last time I saw it. Shelves of books he probably hasn't read, abstract art on the walls that he bought as investments. A picture of him and Jack up on the mantle, arms around each other at their high school graduation. You can hardly tell them apart except for Jack's glasses. Knife to the heart. Don't look at it. I didn't come here often when I worked with Teddy, tried to keep it professional between us, but he had me over a few times when I first moved to the area. Though last time it wasn't tipping the way it is now.

I fight the spins and open my phone, throw it toward Teddy. It lands on his hardwood floor with a clatter and Pickles runs to sniff it.

"Eve texted me," I say. "Apologizing. *Apologizing.*"

I begin to cry, unable to hold it in anymore. I try to keep telling him about what's happening, but mixed in with the sobbing, it just sounds like blubbering. Teddy sits next to me and puts his arm around me. I relax a little bit, closing my eyes, wiping my face with the edge of my shirt.

"I love your smell," I manage to say. "Like if campfire and cinnamon had a baby."

"Compliments? Really?" Teddy pats my back. "Now I know you're wasted."

"Why does everyone die?"

"I'm going to make you some coffee," he says, getting up and walking to the kitchen.

"Not like *die*, die. I mean—you know what I mean."

He doesn't answer. From this angle, tipped on my side on the couch, I can only see his bare feet on the tiled floor.

"You should wear slippers," I whisper.

I reach for my phone, still on the floor from where I threw it, and fall off the couch. Pickles runs over, her little toenails clicking on the floor.

"I'm okay," I tell her.

"Jesus, Leels," Jack says, coming in with a cup of coffee.

Jack—oops. I mean Teddy. *Teddy* crouches to give me a cup of coffee. The fact I just thought he was Jack for a second spooks me so badly that it truly hits me how drunk I am. That's bad. Very bad. Humbled by my own stupid decisions, I sit up into a cross-legged position and carefully exchange the phone in my hand for the steaming mug. Pickles pants at me and looks at me with beady eyes and her pink tongue hanging out. Fine, she's cute. I give her a single pet.

"Can we get off the floor?" Teddy says. "Come on, now."

I slither my way up to his couch and sit next to him.

"Who is this from?" he asks, peering at my phone in his hand.

"Eve Alexa—Alexopo …" I take a sip of coffee, wincing from the heat of it, and realize that even though she might be dead and I might be why, I don't know Eve well enough to remember how her last name is technically pronounced. On the phone with the dispatcher earlier, I spelled it instead of said it. "You know that woman who was almost killed by the Sunray? The one I debated in that techy whatchamacallit conference?"

"The journalist?" he asks, frowning at the phone. "The one writing the book about Jolvix?"

"Yeah."

He scrolls. "You were in contact with her?"

"A little," I admit.

Teddy's mouth drops. "Why?"

"Because … because, okay? It's complicated."

"Please tell me you weren't feeding her information protected by our NDAs."

I don't respond, gulping the coffee down. A wave of regret washes over me. I'm sure it will be the first of many.

"Christ almighty, Leela," Teddy says, getting up and stomping to the kitchen. He slams a cupboard shut and I wince. He comes back in with a steaming mug of coffee for himself and plops back down on the couch.

"The problem right now is I'm scared she's fucking dead, can we concentrate on that?" I ask.

Teddy takes out his phone. "How do you know she's dead?"

"I don't. But considering that every person who's reached out to say 'I'm sorry' lately has died …"

I hate it when Teddy's so mad at me he won't look at me, and right now he won't look at me. He's got a scowl on his normally sunshiney face.

"What are you doing?" I ask.

As if I'm not even here, he's typing on his phone.

"What's going on?" I try again.

"Well, you think she's dead? Then let's go meet up with my Tasky guy, get the update he has for me, and see if we can get him to find out about Eve."

This is what Teddy does. He's a good man to have by your side in a crisis—able to ignore the emotional weight of a situation and move full-speed ahead toward a solution. The night Jack died, he was the one who called the police. He was the one who broke the news to his parents. He was the one talking me down as I lost it on scene and Jack's roommates watched me melt all the way down. Act now, cry later.

"Pound that coffee," he tells me, getting up. "Wash your face and rebutton your shirt."

I nod, wiping my eyes and heaving my ass from the magnetic pull of his couch to stand up. I'm still fuzzy, but the tipping has stopped.

"What'd you drink?" he asks me.

"Whiskey," I say. "Straight from the bottle."

"How was it?"

I shake my head, already filled with regret. I can't even meet his stare, unable to bear the weight of his disappointment. He squeezes my shoulder. "It's not the end of the world. Just a stumble. You feel good right now?"

"Felt good for a few minutes," I murmur.

"Yeah. A lot of things feel good for a few minutes. Doesn't mean they're good ideas."

Now I can't help but look at him, because I'm twinging with a sting, unsure if that's a dig at me about something we don't ever talk about. God, I can't believe Teddy Lindmark, who was once the type of man who probably snorted cocaine off of strippers, is the responsible human being in my life. I bite the side of my tongue and head to his bathroom, correcting the buttons on my shirt and washing my face with soap that makes me smell like him.

CHAPTER 42

First meeting was in a church parking lot, the second takes place in a Mr. Droidburger parking lot. This Tasky detective guy's a trip. I hardly recognize the man who Teddy and I are walking toward. To begin with, he's not dressed as a clown. He's in sweats and eating a hamburger like a slob while sitting on the hood of his Prius. No one would ever guess he's a private detective. Teddy swears up and down that he's the best though, thousands of five-star ratings, even if he looks like someone in the "before" picture on a makeover show and is known only by his Tasky screen name which is, I am not kidding, TaskyDick.

TaskyDick waves at us as we join him in this dark corner of the parking lot where the dumpsters live. Shoving the last wad of burger in his mouth and hopping off the hood of his car, he approaches and shakes Teddy's hand.

"Hi lady," he says to me.

"Hey," I say.

I scan the nighttime scene, the busy section of the

parking lot in front of the cheerful, garish glow of the fast-food restaurant. A dozen palm trees line the parking lot with explosive silhouettes. The night air takes a bite out of the whiskey haze and sobers me up and all I can think of is Eve.

"Ready for the update?" TaskyDick asks.

"Hit me," Teddy says, like a dork in a casino.

There's a beep as TaskyDick pokes his wristwatch, an old-school plastic thing. "Wanted to give you a heads up: your man Reuben Cornwell's about to be released from county. It's happening tomorrow morning. Santa Rita."

"That early?" I ask, shocked to hear it. "I assumed that after, like, putting a woman in critical condition and endangering people's *lives* he'd be in longer than that."

"Not here to debate the merits and follies of our incarceration system," TaskyDick says, and shoots me a skeptical look over the frames of his reading glasses. "You want me to dig more into why?"

Teddy and I exchange a long look. He shrugs. I hesitate, still dumbed down by my earlier quickie with Jack Daniels, chewing my cheek.

"Tick-tock, tick-tock, I charge by the second," sings TaskyDick with Broadway gusto.

"No, don't worry about it," I say. "But—" I turn to Teddy. "Can we move on to Eve now?"

"Go ahead," Teddy says.

"I need to know—I'm afraid something bad's happened to a friend of mine," I say to TaskyDick, voice shaking. "I tried to get a wellness check on her earlier but—I don't know where she lives."

"Name," TaskyDick says.

"Eve Alexopoulos," I say, and spell it for him. He writes it in ballpoint pen on the palm of his hand. "She lives in Cupertino. Can you—is there any way—"

"Give me five minutes," he says.

I raise my eyebrows at Teddy. "I can pay you back."

"It's fine," he says.

TaskyDick walks a short distance from us and starts talking quietly into a phone while pacing the parking lot perimeter. I watch him, as if I can read his body language to find out the truth. My eyes are watering, my heart is a clenched fist. A breeze picks up and goosebumps prickle my skin. Teddy gives my arm a gentle pinch, bringing me back from my psychic pain and into the present.

"Didn't bring a jacket," he says.

"I was drunk."

"You not drunk anymore?"

I shake my head. "I hate my life," I whisper.

"Oh, come on, Leels," Teddy says, putting an arm around me. I'm in such a weakened state and so cold right now that I let him, even though I really don't want to. "It's just life, that's all."

"People die," I say. "Because of me. If I weren't here, these people would be alive."

"Are we whittling life down to simple arithmetic?" he asks. "If so, who knows. Maybe if you weren't here a bunch of other people would have died. Ever think of that? All that work you did at that suicide prevention place—" He snaps a finger. "Keep At It? Is that what it was called?"

"Keep Going," I remind him. "God, I can't even remember that part of my life, it was such a blur."

"Your existence isn't a math problem," he says.

I'm watching TaskyDick, the way he looks up at us right now while he's on the phone. A long look of concern.

"Eve's dead," I say.

"You don't know that," Teddy says.

But TaskyDick's pocketed his phone again and is striding toward us with his lips pursed and when he says the words, "I'm sorry," I know I'm right. I can't bear to meet his gaze. I can't even look at the world right now, it's too much, so I fold myself into Teddy's arms and just stay here, crying like a stupid child, while TaskyDick explains that Eve's body was found just a couple hours ago by a neighbor, a crime scene unit's on scene, and that it looks like suicide.

Suicide, suicide, suicide. A word that throbs through me with a violent, sickening force.

I'm so fucking tired of this déjà vu.

"All right, come on," Teddy says to me, pulling back and wiping my face.

TaskyDick's already peeling out of the parking lot in his Prius and it's just Teddy and me here in this dark dumpster corner.

"You've got to pull yourself together," Teddy says. "I know it feels impossible, but if anyone can do it, you can."

I'm in a state of shock as I catch my breath, staring up at the spinning Mr. Droidburger sign. Okay. I can feel it, the hardening, the sadness cooling into something practical and useful and full of fuel: rage. I swallow and try to think of this like a public relations crisis.

"I can't keep going like this," I say, my voice tight.

"We're going to figure this out," Teddy says, beeping his car to unlock it. "You and me. Tonight. We're going to sit down and we're going to tackle it together and we're going to come up with a solution."

He says it in the same tone he used when he was my boss, that chipper but firm way he used to order someone to build a slide presentation or to schedule a meeting or to send a press release. And I don't know why, but this puts me at ease. It brings me back to a role I fit into well, his partner in crime, his left hand, a rhythm I haven't heard in a long time but one that feels so familiar. A sigh of relief escapes me, as if someone stole a little air from my lungs. I nod at Teddy, grateful he's here but too inept to tell him.

He slides into the driver's seat and I get into the passenger's seat, a little turned around, uncertain for a moment which way time marches—whether I'm headed toward the past or toward the future.

CHAPTER 43

The shock of these "suicides" isn't comparable to Jack's. Madison, Lotus, Genesis, even Eve—along with the paralyzing shock of their deaths, it's not grief I experience so much as confused, sick guilt. I didn't know these people. In fact, I hated most of them. I can't exactly mourn. Sure, I had a couple drinks with Eve, but I don't know her personally. I knew her amazing survival story. I knew about the book she was writing and that she lived in Boyle Heights and wore red lipstick. I have no idea what she did for fun or who she was underneath these basic facts about her, facts anyone with a computer and a few minutes of research would know, too.

I'm realizing how superficially I know these people as Teddy and I set up camp in his dining room, multiple sheets of butcher paper taped to the wall, multicolored markers, laptop open. It's midnight and we're on our second round of coffee and we're infected with a familiar manic energy. We're brainstorming like it's back in the day and this is a solvable PR problem. One paper says

DEAD PEOPLE followed by four columns with every bit of information we can find or remember about each one of these people who've died. Another just says LEELA'S SHITLIST and nothing else. At a glance, it's so absurd it's laughable but no one, not even the man who is a master of cringeworthy puns, is laughing now.

"Your shitlist needs work," Teddy says, tapping the paper with a marker.

"I'm thinking," I say, petting Pickles.

Yes, Pickles is on my lap. I'm not a dog person, but she's small enough that if I close my eyes and pet her, I can imagine she's a cat.

"Don't be cautious, here," he says. "This shitlist could save lives." He contemplates the blank page. "The thing is, I'm trying to connect the dots between these people." A marker points to the DEAD PEOPLE page. "This starts with someone you knew back in high school. How many people knew about what Madison did to you?"

"I mean, everyone who was in the theater department with me, but I never saw most of those people again in my life after high school was over," I say. "And the obvious, you know, Ricky. Shasta."

Teddy scrawls their names on the paper.

"Really?" I ask, crossing my arms. "Ricky is such a wuss he can't get a shot at the doctor without taking a tranquilizer first. And you're adding my *mom* to the list of potential serial killers?"

"Let's just get it out on the table. Who else?"

"I wasn't shy about telling people about what Madison did to me. Over the years, I told the story to people I got close to."

"People you were close to," Teddy says. "Name names."

"I'm trying to think. I went on a few dates with this woman Anjelica when I first moved to DC, I remember telling her about it." Anjelica—that hypnotizing half-smile, that sexy haircut. She spotted what a mess I was from a mile away and let me down gently.

Teddy misspells her name, but she's such a far reach I don't bother correcting him.

"Who else knew about Madison?" he asks.

"Michael, of course."

"Michael," he says, squinting at me. "Who's Michael?"

"My boyfriend in DC."

Teddy's marker hovers over the page for a second before he writes Michael's name on the board. Teddy writes in all caps, the penmanship of a fifth grader. "Right. Him. Hit-and-run guy." Teddy rubs his jawline pensively. "And … he knew about Lotus, too? About Lotus kissing Jack and all that?"

"Yeah."

"Could he have known about Genesis and Eve, too?"

"That stuff happened way after we broke up, but … it was public. Both the video with Genesis freaking out on me and Eve's debate got a lot of play. I posted about both things on social media. Anyone who was following me would have known about it."

"Interesting." Teddy caps his pen and drums it on the paper as he gazes at it, deep in thought. "So far, I'm liking hit-and-run guy the most."

I gently put Pickles back on the floor and get up to refill my coffee mug from Teddy's absurdly expensive-looking machine on his kitchen counter. The little dog runs after me, like we're best friends now. I call to Teddy, "It's not him."

"How do you know?" he calls back.

"It's just not," I say. "I saw him recently. He's engaged."

"What does that have to do with anything?"

"He's committed, you know, he's moved on from me. He doesn't hold a flame for me anymore."

"You think he'd tell you if he did?"

"Him and his bride-to-be are getting Infinities. It's serious."

"Yikes."

Teddy picks Pickles up and lets her lick him all over his face. I repeat, he lets an animal who *licks its own butt* lick his face. Coming back from the kitchen, I sit down again and the disgust I'm experiencing must be obvious because Teddy asks me, "What's *that* look?"

"You and your dog, gross," I say.

"Sorry our love offends you," he says. "You don't have to *hound* me about it."

"Does the fact that people I know are being murdered one by one mean you could possibly put a moratorium on horrible puns for just a little while?"

"It does not," Teddy says gravely as he scratches Pickles behind her ears. "But come on, I've noticed you warming up to her." He looks deeply into her eyes. "She's irresistible, isn't she? Soon she'll be licking your face too."

"Never in a million years."

Teddy puts Pickles down and goes back to the paper on the wall. "Okay, besides hit-and-run guy, who else? Who else could have done this?" He points at me. "What about … what about that guy at Jack's house? The creepy guy in the room next to Jack's who you thought listened in on you two?"

"His roommate?" I ask. "The Yeti? How would he have known about Madison?"

"If he was listening to you?"

"It wasn't like I was walking around recounting the Madison story all the time, I was in college, I was over it by then."

"Try to think of anyone like that though. Anyone who might have creeped you out."

"Teddy, I'm a reasonably attractive woman in my twenties. There are far too many creepy encounters to list."

"Reasonably attractive?" he says, then shakes his head and moves on.

"I used to get calls in high school, a breather. They stopped for a while but then started again after I moved to DC. They don't happen often … once or twice a year, maybe."

"When's the last time you got one?"

"I don't know. Six months ago? I've learned to just hang up and forget about them."

"I wonder if we could trace them."

"Blocked number. Doubt it."

Teddy heaves a sigh and sits across from me, running a hand through his messy hair, tapping the marker on the tabletop.

"You're tired," I say.

"No, I'm fine."

After a minute of tapping, I reach across the table and put my hand on his to stop him.

"Sorry," he says.

I pull my hand back onto my lap and squeeze it into a fist. Both of us steep in a long silence as the AC kicks on with a low hum and the butcher paper on the wall wafts in the breeze of it. I steal a peek at my phone and see how late it is—how early it is. It's way past time for me to go home. But I don't want to go home to my apartment right now, where that stupid half-empty bottle of Jack still sits on my counter waiting for me to fuck up again. As exhausted as I am, as we both are, it feels like Teddy and I are close to some kind of breakthrough. This is how he and I work—in flurries of conversation and then long pauses where our brains percolate individually, together. And we almost always get somewhere. I hate to admit it, but we're a solid team.

"Well, we know who it *isn't*," Teddy says, sitting back in his chair.

"Who?"

"Corndog boy."

I squint at him. "What the hell are you talking about?"

"You know, the, uh …" Teddy snaps his finger. "The concrete block guy."

"Right. Because he's still in jail."

"Released tomorrow, though," Teddy says.

A yawn becomes too powerful for me to resist and I succumb.

"*You're* tired," he says, catching my yawn.

I shake my head and wipe my watering eyes.

"You never admit when you're tired," he says.

"Neither do you."

Teddy drinks from his coffee mug but it's clearly

empty because he puts it down with a disappointed look. A light bulb must have popped within him because his eyes brighten and he snaps a finger. "Okay, all right, I just thought of something. That guy, Corndog … didn't you do a public interview about the concrete block thrown at the cat place?"

"Yeah," I say slowly, not getting where he's headed.

"That guy better watch out," Teddy says, springing up and writing CORNDOG on the butcher paper that says SHITLIST. Under any other circumstances, such an entry would strike me as absurd, but here we are. "Am I right? If someone out there's following you and the things you say and do …"

I put my head on the table, overwhelmed by the thought of now having to worry about this asshole's life now being in my hands.

"Let's move to the shitlist," Teddy continues. "Maybe that's what we need to focus on. If we can figure out who's going to be next, then we could lure the killer in."

"Should we just call the fucking police already?" I ask, smacking the table. "I mean, what are you expecting you and me to do about this?"

"We could," he says, capping his pen. "Absolutely. And you know what'll happen? This will *explode*. Eve's high profile. Her 'suicide' is going to be news regardless, we know that. Now it becomes a murder—related to Jolvix?" Teddy pantomimes a bomb exploding. "The investigation would trace this entire thing back to the VixSpex going missing on our watch. On you and I pretending it never happened. Best case scenario, I lose my job, I'm black-balled by Jolvix and the rest of the tech sector by default.

You're professionally ruined. Our reputations are destroyed. But worst case? Civil suits up the ass by all the victims' families."

I make a sound somewhere between a moan and a scream that scares Pickles so badly she jumps off a chair and scampers out of the room.

"*And* you know by the time the police even catch on to what the hell is happening here, someone else is going to get—" Teddy puts an invisible gun to his head and pulls an invisible trigger. "They're going to need to call in the feds, get Jolvix in on the investigation, different jurisdictions, have the tech aspect explained to them over and over again, et cetera, et cetera. But you and me? We could figure this out. We could do it fast, too."

"How?" I ask, my voice breaking on the word.

Teddy comes behind me and puts his hands on my shoulders. He stoops and leans in to say into my ear, "You need to make a new enemy."

CHAPTER 44

A shiver runs through me like an electric current. Teddy squeezes my shoulders and then returns to his seat at the table.

"A *new* enemy?" I repeat.

"Yeah. Publicly. You need to put the bait out there."

"What bait?"

Teddy points to himself. His expression is slack, his blue eyes tired but twinkling.

"Huh?" I finally say.

"You put it out there. You say, 'I hate Teddy Lindmark. I wish he didn't exist.' I'm paraphrasing. You have a way with words, I'm sure you'll say it much better. A post on your social media pages. Or a video, whatever, you know what I'm talking about."

My heart's picking up speed imagining us doing something so stupid and dangerous. "I can't—I don't want to do that."

"I know, I know, it's scary to think about. But really. You want this to end? We've got to trap this person."

He's such a cocky asshole, he really makes it sound easy. The idea of *deliberately* putting a target on Teddy turns my stomach. It's far too risky. It's insanity, actually. Teddy has an affinity for action movies. I didn't realize he was so deluded he thought he was a hero in one.

"And *what*?" I finally ask. "What do we do with this psychopath when they sneak a surprise attack and try to kill you? Who do you think we are?"

Teddy doesn't answer my question. He gets up and paces the tiled floor, swept away by his idea. "I'll get a gun, hide it here in the apartment. Shit, multiple guns. A gun in every room. He breaks in, I run for it, *bam*."

"And let's say your hero schtick doesn't work out and he fucking kills you, Teddy? What if you're not fast enough to grab one of your many imaginary guns? My God."

"He won't," he says, waving a hand in the air.

I can't believe I'm not shutting this conversation down, that I'm sitting here imagining what we would need to do to make this happen.

"And where am I?" I ask. "Just sitting on my unemployed ass in my apartment while you save the day?"

Teddy shrugs. Because I guess he was imagining he was starring in his action movie solo.

"No," I say, a fire starting in me. "I don't need you to save me. If someone's going to kill this person, if someone's going to seek revenge on them, it had better be me."

"All right, so I figure out a way to call you when he gets there. Stall him 'til you arrive."

"Are you fucking serious right now? 'Oh, excuse me Murderer Man, could you kindly hold on one moment so

I can text someone before you kill me with your death goggles?'"

"We'd figure out some other way to communicate," Teddy says.

Pickles is now following Teddy as he paces back and forth across the room. Pickles is jazzed, tongue out, no idea we're plotting how to trap a murderer. Teddy stops, gazing out at his living room, scratching the back of his head. Slowly, he turns to me, eyebrows raised.

"Infinities," he says.

He might as well have just uttered gibberish. I don't even know how to respond.

"*Infinities*," he says again. "You know, we get them, we can track each other with GPS functions. We know where the other is at any moment in time."

"Phones can do that without us *implanting ourselves with computer chips*."

"But Infinities have that feature, you know, hold your breath ten seconds and it means 'I love you.' Only in this case, it would mean, 'he's here.' You could know the killer found me and see exactly where I'm at— which I'm guessing would be here in my apartment considering that Madison, Lotus, and Eve all died at home."

I swallow. "This idea is making me sick."

"Come on, though. Think about it."

"I am. Are *you* actually thinking about it? Teddy, I live over an hour away, I don't even see how this would logically work."

"You come back to work at Jolvix with me, just for a short period of time."

Did he really just suggest I go back to the job I rage-quit a year ago? I shake my head, but he keeps going.

"Complain about your jerk boss online." He points to himself with something resembling pride on his face. "Me, I'm the jerk boss."

"Yeah, I got it."

"You stay at Bliss Bay. You're a twelve-minute cab ride to my doorstep. I give you the code. All that means is I've got to stall this guy for twelve minutes. I can do that."

"You can stall a serial killer for twelve minutes."

"Yes," he says, with no hesitation whatsoever.

"How?"

"Because I know you. I know things about you no one else knows. And the killer won't be able to resist wanting to know them."

"Well, now I want to know what these salacious details are. Do tell."

"Come on, you know what I'm talking about. You really want me to name them out loud?"

I swallow, unsure whether I do. The thought of Teddy revealing my secrets to this person is a cherry on the shit sundae. He really thinks this will work, that we can pull this plan off. "Your arrogance is going to get you killed," I finally answer.

"We can do this, Leels," Teddy says, coming close to me, running his palm down my hair with such delicacy I can only barely feel it. "Don't you think?"

I take my time pondering this. "It's outrageous. Everything you outlined is assuming that nothing goes wrong. What if I don't get your alert? What if I'm late? What if I can't get into your place? What if—"

Teddy says, "What if everything goes right and we put an end to this person?"

I'm chewing a hole in my lip as I consider this absolutely bonkers idea. "If it backfired, though …" I can't even complete the thought. I look at Teddy, look deeply into him to drive the point home. "Teddy, if you got killed in this fucking crazy scheme, I'd kill myself."

We're at a standstill, he and I, and the only thing I can hear is his kitchen clock ticking on the wall, throbbing like an organ in the human body.

"I mean it," I say, my eyes watering, an internal ocean threatening me.

"We can do this," he whispers, pulling me into him for a hug. "I wouldn't do it if I wasn't absolutely sure we could pull it off."

"It's insane," I say, letting myself hug him back, closing my eyes and losing myself in him for just a little bit.

But here, in the darkness behind my eyelids, in the locked room inside me, something awakens. Life has proven itself to be precious, short, and mostly beyond my control. Time and time again, I've learned I'm not really the lead in my own life. I'm a player in someone else's game. And I'm so fucking tired of it all.

A new life?

A life of my own?

A life without fear?

Yes. I would die for such a thing.

I open my eyes and Teddy's watching me. Not just watching me—he's reading me. His eyes are searching for the meaning in my face.

"I can't believe the things you're willing to do for me," I say.

"You know what?" Teddy puts his head next to mine, holds me for an extra-long beat. "I can't believe it myself sometimes."

CHAPTER 45

Teddy makes us a witching-hour breakfast of eggs, bacon, and watermelon to settle my stomach. The combination of half a pot of coffee and a discussion about how we're going to murder a murderer hasn't exactly been pleasant on the gut. The silence of a few minutes of eating and ignoring the soul-crushing nightmare my life has become is greatly needed. For just a meal, I feel normal again.

"Thanks for this," I say, savoring my last bite of bacon. "I honestly wasn't aware you could cook."

"I can make breakfast. Or get me behind a grill, that's about it." Teddy puts down his watermelon rind and finishes chewing. He raises an eyebrow, the one with the scar. His sassy eyebrow. "Guess you've never given me a chance to make you breakfast, huh?"

"Mmm," is all I say, my breath hitching at the memory. "Yeah. Guess not."

I get up and clear the plates. There's a sick, nervous humming under my skin, a loop that won't stop repeating in my head. This crazy fucking plan. I can't imagine us pulling it off and yet I won't let myself imagine us *not* pulling it off—catch-22. Teddy's moved to the living room and I join him on the couch, a ghost-sized space between us. The exhaustion has paled him and painted his eyes a shocking shade of blue.

"There's a lot we still have to figure out," I say.

"Like what? I'll go to the office and get you set up as a consultant tomorrow. Or today, I guess, technically. Get you your pass, you check into Bliss Bay, put up your 'I hate Teddy' post on social media. Easy peasy, mac and cheesy."

"Don't say 'easy peasy, mac and cheesy' when we're discussing killing someone."

"Well, come on, shoot, what else do you need to know?"

"Um, to begin with, what—we're planning to kill this guy in your apartment once you lure him here? How?"

"Like I said before, I'll buy guns. Put them all over the house, one in every room."

"Right, your many hypothetical guns," I say, shaking my head. "And what do you do with his body after you shoot him?"

He yawns while he talks. "Buy a hacksaw, some tarp, scatter his body parts in dumpsters across the city. Look, I've watched a lot of mafia movies. I know how to get rid of a body."

"You're an idiot," I can't help saying. Immediately, I realize this man's risking his life for my ass and I follow up with, "Sorry, didn't mean that. I said 'idiot,' I meant 'optimist.' But this isn't a mob movie, Teddy, come on. You're a white bread tech bro. You really think you're capable of that?"

"Yep."

"You could sit there sawing through bone—" I pantomime this and make a creaking sound.

He shakes his head. "That's not what a saw sounds like."

"—and sopping up gallons of blood—"

"Hunters do it, why couldn't I?"

"You ever been hunting?"

Teddy sips his coffee and doesn't answer me, which reveals his answer.

"And even if it *was* that easy," I keep going, "follow that logically through. Let's say we do—" I swallow, hardly able to believe I'm uttering the words. "—hack the guy's body to pieces or whatever and we somehow manage to be geniuses and no one discovers what we've done. What then? That guy just disappears off the face of the earth. *Someone's* going to go looking for him. *Someone's* going to file a missing person report. What then? Cops will go through his stuff, his computer. Depending on how messy this guy is, that might lead them to figuring out he's been following Madison, Lotus, Genesis, Eve … and me. And who knows? Maybe they trace him to the murders that look like suicides and the murders that look like suicides to the VixSpex, which then leads the cops right back to us. Which means we get drawn into the investigation we've just *killed the guy* to avoid being part of. And now we get not only drawn into that investigation about the VixSpex, with our lives and reputations ruined and civil suits up the ass, but now we're suspects for *murder*."

I snap out of my soliloquy and am enraged to learn that Teddy is nodding off comfortably on his corner of the couch right now. I reach across the space between us and lightly punch him on the shoulder.

"What?" he says, annoyed, snapping to.

"We're planning a murder, can you please stay awake? Jesus."

"A murder of who?" he asks, looking genuinely confused.

"Drink your coffee before I start screaming," I say, gesturing to his cup on the coffee table. "Get up and do some jumping jacks. Whatever you need to do."

Teddy sighs, downs the rest of what's in his mug, and gets up. "All right, all right."

"Did you even hear any part of what I was saying?"

He begins doing jumping jacks, clapping hands and dancing feet. "Everything except the last part."

"What I was saying is that were he to disappear off the face of the earth, someone's going to look for this asshole. We really don't want that because who knows what's at his house, on his computers, what investigators might end up finding out. They could find out about the VixSpex, which leads them to the cover-up—"

"Yeah, yeah, I heard that part," he says breathlessly.

"Point being, your mafioso roleplay fantasy's not going to fly."

"Okay then, we make his death look like something else. We make it look like a suicide?" Teddy stops the jumping jacks. "Or an overdose!" he says, with way too much excitement. "So much less messy, too, get our hands on that super strength Oxy that's going around. No blood, no saws. We can drop him off at a place where newbs score drugs. You know how common it is, stories of newbs ODing off that shit."

I chew the side of my tongue. Teddy's not wrong, I read those stories every time I scroll local news. I can imagine that it would look pretty open-and-shut if we managed to pull it off without fucking up. But that's the issue … can we?

"All this is so complex. It depends on so much going right," I say.

Teddy watches me, like he thinks that I have more to say.

"I've never been able to depend on things going right," I finish.

Teddy waits, still catching his breath.

I say, "On this guy taking the bait. On our Infinities working. On me getting to your place in time, before you're done for, and us being able to stop this guy before he hurts one or both of us. On us being able to poison this guy and drop his body off somewhere and no one investigating his death."

My heart's sped up after rattling it all off so quickly. I burn, shaking my head, the impossibility of our reality crushing with such a weight I could disappear under it.

"You have to think positive," Teddy says simply, plopping down on the couch.

"Don't you dare come back at me with inspirational poster bullshit clichés."

"Hang in there, kitten."

My mouth is open, ready to fire back an insult, but I'm halted by the way he just said that. *Kitten.* Karate chop to the soul. He sounded just like Jack. It's like I'm in an alternate universe and I'm sitting here with Jack all these years later. And all at once, I break. I shatter like a glass figurine and begin sniveling into my hands, a human storm of snot and spit and tears.

"Christ, I'm sorry—what did I—what the hell?" Teddy says, sliding closer to me. "Leels, what is it?"

I sob, disgusted with myself for sobbing, hating this pain that still feels so raw even though I'm all scars. I ball up as if I can disappear myself, feeling his hand on my back.

"Was it the—was it the inspirational posters? That's what finally broke you?" Teddy asks, sounding genuinely baffled. "Is this a straw, camel's back situation?"

"It was his nickname," I say, my voice thick and wet.

The look on Teddy's face ... this must be how a car accident feels when people are looking at it.

"For me," I clarify, wiping my nose with my sleeve.

"I'm not understanding, I'm sorry," Teddy says carefully, slowly, with the care of a hostage negotiator. "What?"

"Jack!" I yell.

His name cuts through the air like a machete. I can feel Teddy deflating next to me on the couch.

"He used to call me 'kitten,'" I say.

"Oh." Teddy nods, his eyes glassy and focused now on something invisible to me, something in the air between us. "I didn't know that, I'm sorry." He gets up and mumbles, "I'll get you a tissue."

He gets me a whole box of tissues, one he's clearly never needed in his sunshiney life because it's covered in dust and the package is still sealed. While I sit and blow my nose, Teddy busies himself by tidying the dining room, gathering up the markers to put them away, straightening the throw pillows on his couch. I can tell he's bothered, that faraway scowl on his face.

"Did I upset you or something?" I ask.

"Not at all. I just sometimes forget I'm but a mere mirror image of a man you once loved." He says it all properly, like a theater actor. I'm not sure what he's going for.

"What? Don't be dumb, that's not all you are."

"I'm kidding," he says, like a big fat liar. I can recognize his brand of hurt when I see it. "I just think the night's caught up with me and I need to sleep it off." He stops and shoots me a weak smile, runs a hand through his hair. "Plus, work in the morning, all that. I'll go in late, but still. Better get some shuteye."

"I guess I should get a taxi home," I say, standing up.

"Oh no you don't. We've got work to do tomorrow."

I glance across the room, where Pickles sleeps in a dog bed shaped like a pickle, snoring cutely. "But my cat needs to be fed—"

"You can go home tomorrow afternoon and pack your bags for Bliss Bay and feed your cat. And don't worry, I can already see that worry wrinkle in the eyebrow you get, we'll find someone to catsit for you while you're temporarily relocated." He points to the couch. "It folds out. It's comfortable. Here, I'll open it up. There are sheets and blankets in the hall closet, go grab them."

In five minutes, the bed's made up. Five minutes later, I'm lying here in the dark listening to the tick-tocking clock while my brain's a carousel of waking nightmares. Despite how spent I am, how badly I want to sleep, there's too much to worry about. I can't believe Eve died last night. I can't believe I broke my sobriety. I can't believe Teddy's proposing we lure this murderer to us and I sure as hell can't believe that we're planning to murder the murderer. Every few minutes a car passes by on the street below, casting a long line of light across the ceiling that moves and then disappears. A faucet drips somewhere and Pickles is whimpering in her sleep. Even though I usually sleep in an apartment by myself every night, somehow I feel more lonely tonight under someone else's roof than I have in a long, long time. I keep thinking about what Teddy said about being a "mere mirror image" of Jack, how there was a detectable sting in his expression that makes me hurt for him.

I can't sleep with this merry-go-round in my brain. I get up and tiptoe to Teddy's bedroom, where the door is ajar.

"Teddy?" I say quietly from his doorway.

He sits up in the dark, his figure lit by the blue moonlight coming through his window. In just an hour or so, it'll be gold and sunny. "Everything okay?"

"Um, no," I say. "Not in any way, shape, or form." I swallow. "Could I sleep in your bed tonight?"

"Of course," he says, moving over for me.

"But no funny business," I say, crawling on top of his covers and pulling my blanket over me. "Got it?"

"I would never," he says in a mocking tone, lying back down.

We face opposite walls. There's no touching, no pillow talk. And yet I fall right asleep to the rhythm of his breathing, just knowing he's there behind me.

CHAPTER 46

Sometimes I feel like the older I get, the more my life's just a shitload of déjà vu.

After barely sleeping last night, tossing and turning and wondering if we're insane for hatching this plan to trap the killer ourselves, today Teddy and I go to the Jolvix campus to get paperwork filed and to onboard me as his new consultant. Luckily it's not as extensive as the first time I did this, because they've still got me in their employee files. No fingerprinting or picture-taking this time, they just print me a brand-new shiny lanyard that says CONSULTANT instead of DIR OF PR above VR SECTOR. Whole process takes a cool half hour, Teddy schmoozing with the onboarding receptionist the entire time and making her laugh. Meanwhile, I stand frowning as I stare out the one-way glass at the long stretch of lawn that spans from here to the Happy Days Pavilion where I spent many miserable nights at "recreational" work events. Mandatory fun's the worst kind of fun.

I can't believe I'm back here again, working for Teddy. What the hell am I getting myself into?

"Am I going to be forced to go to crappy work events?" I ask him when we step outside into the blazing hellfire of the late-summer sun.

"You're a consultant," he says. "You get to do whatever you want. You're a contractor, not an employee."

"Sweet."

I slip my lanyard on first, my sunglasses next, and follow Teddy up the path on our walk to the VR sector. An ice cream truck driven by a person in a horse mask passes us, the horse waving. I don't wave back. This place, I swear. In the distance, I can see a group of people testing out rocket packs on the lawn. The redwoods that offer us the cool relief of shade all have plaques nailed to them with poetry written by AI. Every time I come here, there's some new stupid shit.

In Teddy's office, he and I kick our shoes off and draw the shades. We knock out a few items on our mental to-do list, starting with what we're going to do with my cat while I'm parked at Bliss Bay.

"Just board her somewhere," he says, sitting back in his chair and popping a mint.

"I don't want to do that. And he's a him."

"Sorry I misgendered your cat. Do you think you can ever find it in your heart to forgive me?"

"If I weren't across the room, I'd kick you."

"Didn't you work at a cat shelter, for Christ's sake? Can't you put him there a while?"

"I didn't exactly end there on the best terms," I say. The thought of Daisy taking care of Nosferatu unleashes a silly amount of rage within me. Esmerelda floats to mind, though—she's got a big house and an even bigger heart. I know she'd do it in a second. "But actually, I do know someone."

"I think I'm going to board Pickles."

"Why?"

"Because if we're luring some homicidal maniac into my apartment, I don't want to put my dog in danger. Kill me? Fine. Kill my dog? You can rot in hell."

"I guess that's what a responsible pet owner would do," I say, staring at the ceiling, wondering if this is the first time in history that a dog has been boarded for such reasons.

There's a long silence, so long that both of us maybe fell asleep for a bit. I wake up with a jolt, the nightmare that is real life all coming back to me. Strangely, I keep expecting myself to want to back out of this bonkers plan, but it feels like the only option. Maybe the two of us have lost our minds together.

"Teddy, what if we die trying to pull this shit off?" I ask, sitting up.

He's swiveling in his chair like a child in his own world, tossing a stress ball back and forth between his hands. He comes to a stop and throws me the ball. I am shocked at my reflexes when I catch it.

"It's just life," he says with a shrug.

CHAPTER 47

Three days later, Teddy and I are in the waiting room of The Infinitorium, a glass building in downtown Cupertino where couples celebrate their union by getting computer chips implanted into their ring fingers. As if that weren't creepy enough, the receptionists are all identical bots that look a lot like Barnett's silicon army and there's a hologram floating in the middle of the room with the Infinities slogan: *And you thought diamonds were forever!*

One couple on the other side of the room are in full bride and groom garb and have a priest with them, apparently taking this process very seriously. Another couple can't keep their tongues out of each other's mouths and I imagine they'll be back here to remove these chips at some point in the not-so-distant future. I've caught myself eyeing the world through a new fogged glass lately, studying the strangers around me with a fresh edge of suspicion, counting the cameras on the ceiling. It's like I can feel the walls closing in on us. I can imagine the killer close by, watching every move. That old creepy-crawly sensation that all the world's a stage. Or that I'm a lone lighthouse on a dark sea. I don't even know how true it is, who this person is or what they want from me. But I have to wonder, everywhere I go, how near they are.

"Where'd you get your engagement ring?" Teddy asks.

I snap to, trying to register what the hell he's talking about. Then the memory of Jack and of the black diamond ring comes back. The ring that rests in a jewelry box buried in my dresser.

I clear my throat. "I don't know. Jack bought it for me."

Teddy stares at the shiny floor, as if trying to picture it in the linoleum's gleam.

"I don't think it's a real diamond," I admit. "Jack bragged that it was this expensive ten-karat custom-made fanciness but when I got it appraised once, the guy said that it was black cubic zirconia."

"Really?"

"Not that I care," I say. "Just seemed strange."

"Jack was weird about money," Teddy says, crossing his arms. "Stingy. He'd buy you a gift and tell you how expensive it was and he'd never let you forget it."

"True," I say.

Jack's absence suddenly blows in like a gust, like the oxygen's sucked out of the room. I feel we shouldn't be allowed to talk negatively of him, not when he's dead and can't defend himself.

"Mr. and Mrs. Lindmark?" a woman calls from a doorway.

"Oh, we're just—" I start to say.

"Yes, that's us," Teddy says, giving me a look. "You ready?"

I stand up and Teddy and I make our way across this bizarro lobby, walking through the hologram for a violet moment. "Is this just your sly way of getting a ring on my finger?" I joke quietly.

"Yep, everything up to this point has just been about getting to pretend you're my hateful little wife," he says.

Now we're where the woman stands. She's as young as us, but silver-haired—clearly a fashion choice and not a biological one. Her silver hair matches her slacks and blazer and her big hoop earrings.

"My name's Atria and I'll be taking care of you good people today," she says, her smile almost painful-looking.

"I'm Teddy Lindmark. This is my—my partner, Leela Crowe," Teddy says.

We all shake hands. *Partner*. Appreciate that he didn't try to pass me off as his wife. It occurs to me, as we follow Atria and her silver high heels clacking up the hallway, that Teddy is literally my partner in crime. Not sure a relationship can get any deeper than that.

Atria's office reminds me of my office at Feline Better, only instead of being surrounded by ten thousand pictures of cats, it's ten thousand happy couples showing off their ring fingers like they're flipping us the almost-bird. Atria gushes congratulations to us and then gets to work showing us the implants, registering them, and helping us download the apps to our phones.

"How many Invisible Love Letters would you like to register?" she asks, and then recites, as if to jog our memories, "Invisible Love Letters are the messages you can send to one another by holding your breath a certain way. For example, hold your breath for ten seconds to say 'I love you' and your partner will get a buzz in their finger and a notification on the app." She stage-whispers, "That's our most popular option."

"Sure, we'll take it," Teddy says.

Atria gets up, humming and smiling, and leaves the room to "retrieve the chipper." Chipper indeed. Kill me now. Teddy's scowling, looking around at the pictures on the wall.

"We should ask if I can burp three times and it can mean, 'go to hell,'" I say to Teddy, trying to cheer him up in my own way.

"Can you imagine thinking this is romantic?" he says, baffled.

"I mean, it's about as logical as wearing a rock on your hand and thinking it's romantic."

He sits back, as if I've plunged him down the hole of some kind of revelation. "I think I must not be a romantic person."

"You and me both."

The implanting process is as quick as it was when I got Nosferatu microchipped, only this time, Mendelssohn's "Wedding March" is playing and I feel the pinch.

"Ouch," I say, massaging the strange lump on the underside of my ring finger. Teddy's doing the same.

"Picture?" Atria asks with a gleeful expression, grabbing one of those old-fashioned cameras that spits out pictures right here and now.

"No," Teddy and I both say.

Atria looks as if we slapped her as she puts the camera

away. She seems confused by our lack of enthusiasm, but forges on cheerfully as she escorts us back to the waiting room. Despite the joyful pictures surrounding us, the glossy-eyed couples waiting in chairs, the hologram that sparkles in the center of the room, there's a cloud of gloom extending over Teddy and me as we wave goodbye to our lady in silver. And I swear, I know she doesn't mean to, but there's something so foreboding about the way she sends us off with a queenly little wave, exclaiming, "Enjoy infinity!"

Outside, under the speckled shade of a sidewalk maple, I scan the scene. The street where people bounce by with shopping bags, where shiny cars whoosh past us. I exchange a look with Teddy. The sleepless nights seem permanently stamped to our faces and we're both still rubbing the uncomfortable spots in our fingers where now we're united by silicon chip. I reach out and give his arm a squeeze.

"What are you thinking?" I ask.

He slips his sunglasses on and answers, "Guess it's time for you to make a video telling the world how much you wish I was dead."

CHAPTER 48

THE GAME

I've been in a dark place, Leela.

Since Eve played the game and lost—I didn't kill her, I'm not a killer—I've been spiraling.

Jolting awake in the middle of the night with visions of the dead arising like zombies.

Madison, a chunk of her face gone, asking, "Why?"

Lotus lurching toward me in her blood-spattered bathrobe.

Genesis screaming with her head blown to bits, jaw hanging loose.

And Eve most of all, that eye hanging from her skull and staring straight at me.

I'm not an unhinged person. Not a psychopath. I've felt everything I've done.

How heavy is the heart of a guardian angel of death.

I haven't left my apartment since Eve died, over a month ago.

It's not so strange for me. I've gone longer.

In Hearst Castle I barely left my room all summer long.

It was easy. Top Ramen, a hot stove, my own private bathroom.

Video games and notebooks upon notebooks of poetry.

And you and Jack to listen to through the wall.

I would lie there in bed and follow your conversations with a grin on my face.

When you made love, I closed my eyes and jerked off and I was there, Leela, making love to you, too.

That was the best summer of my life, spent in the dark of my room.

It's summer again and I'm hiding again.

I'm scared, Leela. I'm scared of what I've done and what will happen if I get caught.

News stories online about Eve and her "shocking suicide" say it's still an open investigation.

Genesis's father, State Senator Tiger McBride, has been posting videos begging the public for information about his daughter's death.

I fear that it's only a matter of time before they connect these cases.

Even bigger, I fear that I made a mistake with Eve, that she was a faulty target. That she was your friend.

All of this that I've done was an attempt to right wrongs. To make up for my past mistake, a festering guilt I've had to live with.

I ruined your life once, Leela. I can't bear the thought that I might have ruined it again.

There are so many options. Too many.

I could flee the country.

I could fake my own death.

Kill myself.

Kill you.

"Give me a sign," I keep telling the screen, where your picture beams back at me.

And then, one day, you do.

You post a video, the first you've posted in months.

My heart swells like an orchestra as I watch it.

"Welp, I'm back to work at Jolvix," you say, walking and talking to the camera, trees whipping by in the background and sunshine in your hair. "I must be a glutton for punishment. Once again, I'm working for Ted Lindmark, the most narcissistic asshole on the planet. He treats me like a glorified gofer, calling me at all hours, day or night, expecting me to drop everything to attend to his every need."

You stop walking and put the camera closer to your face and look straight into it.

It's like you're looking deeply into my eyes, into my soul, and then your red lips curl into a coy smile, one that holds our secret in it and makes me crack with thunder inside.

"I'd love it if he'd drop dead."

The video ends there.

The comments below it are a mix of confusion and concern.

Shasta says, *Hon??? U ok?? Call me* and Ricky says, *What in the what now?*

But I know exactly what it is.

It's a message for me.

You're talking to me, Leela.

My eyes sting with tears.

You understand what I'm doing and you're *asking for more.*

Which means you must not be angry with me about Eve.

Which means my efforts weren't in vain.

I'd love it if he dropped dead.

I hear you, Leela, loud and clear.

I get up. Wash my face. Get dressed. Find my binoculars, pack my bag.

Looks like I'll be spending the next few days tracking Ted Lindmark's every move.

This time, I do it with a lightness.

I leave behind the burden of my guilt, the zombie memories.

Because you've given me the sign, beamed it to me like a lighthouse.

You love me, don't you?

Don't you?

CHAPTER 49

LEELA

"Leelee, what in oversharing hell is that video?" Ricky asks me.

We're on a video call. I'm sitting on a bench outside Munchies, a snack shop near the VR sector at Jolvix, enjoying some garlic fries potent enough to keep the vampires away. Ricky looks like he's inside the dark hole of an office he has on the production lot where he works in LA. It's been a while since we talked face to face.

"Blond again?" I ask, changing the subject to his questionable choice of bleaching the tips of his hair.

"Don't skirt it with tantalizing fashion talk. What is going on? You're back at Jolvix? I thought you said never again in your life."

"Yeah, well, I quit Feline Better. I'm consulting now. It's temporary."

He pushes his face closer to the camera. "And why are putting out a call on social for your boss slash ex-fiance's twin brother's ass?"

"I was venting."

"You don't usually vent on social. You vent to *me*."

I pop a fry in my mouth and contemplate how to respond. After some thoughtful chewing, I decide I shouldn't tell Ricky anything. I'm too far down the hole now to explain myself to those whose feet are still firmly planted on the surface of the earth.

"I'm worried about you," he says. "Shasta's worried about you."

"Yes, I gathered from her fourteen missed calls this morning." I ball up my trash and throw it in the bin. "Listen, I have a meeting in ten. I've got to figure out where I'm pitching heartwarming feature stories about lonely seniors using VR to fill the existential void. I have to go."

"I can't believe you're back in the thick of it," Ricky says, studying me intently from hundreds of miles away. "I don't get it. I don't. There's more to this story and you're not telling me."

"It's just money, Ricky. Just a temporary way to pick up some cash."

"You're banging Teddy, aren't you?"

"I can't believe you would say that." I start back toward the building. "Friendship over."

"Something is up and you're going to tell me."

"I really do have to go."

"Rude. Bye."

We hang up and I hurry my pumps up the path. The rocks in the surrounding redwoods are playing jazz today and a janitor bot rolls over the manicured dirt, sucking up trash. I linger outside the building near the fountain, letting a brief peace settle over me. A breeze with a cool edge to it gives me goosebumps. Peering up at the VR sector, I think about how strange it is to be here again. How different it is this time around. Since I threw myself back into Jolvix a few weeks ago, since I unpacked my bags at Bliss Bay and called this manchild wonderland my temporary home, I feel an unexpected sense of safety here. You can't get onto this campus without a visitor's pass. You can't get a visitor's pass easily, and when you do, you're fingerprinted and they run you through a background check system. There are cameras almost everywhere and security is top-notch. Lookie here at these privacy-loving scruples of mine, chucked right out the window at the first whiff of danger.

I take the elevator upstairs. Inside the silver belly of the machine, I peel my lips back and practice my smile in my reflection.

"Good afternoon, everyone!" I say as I stroll into the meeting room, where a woman from the PR agency has a slideshow readied on the wall. It says *Alone But Never Lonely* and there's a picture of a smiling elderly woman with VR glasses on. "So excited to discuss these inspiring stories today."

Six Comms employees sit at a long glass table, eyes on me. But not really. Because this isn't the real Leela. This is the Leela in business casual and nude lipstick, the slick-talking, sharp-thinking communications expert. This is a role in a series of roles we call life. None of it is real.

The more I tell myself this, the more it numbs the pain and dulls the fear.

CHAPTER 50

This new chapter of life sneakily begins resembling a new dead-inside normal. Day by day, I relax into this solo, stripped-down routine of working my Jolvix job living on the Jolvix campus. I compartmentalize our preposterous plan, push it out of my mind, though I find myself absent-mindedly rubbing my ring finger in a newfound compulsion. In this temporary apartment, there's no Leela anywhere except what fits in my suitcase. No reminders of who I am, no furball to sleep with, no heavy metal records to spin on the player. I wear pantsuits to work and get home and change straight into my pajamas. No black shirts and black jeans anymore. I left that woman back in Berkeley.

Every time I think about our plan, I get a surreal jolt, mental electrocution. I can't believe we're doing this. If doubt creeps in, I reach out to Teddy, who shoots me down and tells me we're in too deep.

"We've committed," he says. "We're ready."

That term *committed* rings like a haunting verbal bell.

What a word, isn't it? People are committed to relationships, yes, but they're also committed to prison and mental hospitals. I'm not sure why people spend their lives chasing commitment. Yet here we are.

Days and nights go by where this plan we've hatched begins fading into the background of my mind. It's always there, similar to the hulking shadow-monster of grief I've spent years pretending to ignore. I can't look at it. I can't fall into a spiral of imagining everything that will go wrong. But as time passes, a little relief creeps in. A part of me begins to wonder if this isn't going to happen at all. If this guy isn't taking the bait. If we're not going to need to go through with any of this in the end. The internet tells me that Reuben Cornwell's still alive and well and I haven't received a Peeps message in months. I begin sleeping through the night again, comforted by the idea that maybe we've failed. Wondering when we pack it in and declare it over.

Then fate snaps its fingers.

One early evening weeks after the video drops, I'm eating leftover Chinese food from the Jolvix cafeteria in my Bliss Bay apartment, still stuffed into my work costume, when my ring finger starts buzzing.

My Infinity. Now my phone dings with notifications. The map shows Teddy's location, a blinking blue light at his home address.

"Shit," I almost yell.

I can't believe it. After Teddy and I conspiring for weeks, after waiting around for the mysterious killer to take the bait, the fishing line's finally jerking in the water with our catch.

The Infinity's continuous buzzing is the strangest and most unsettling feeling, like a bug crawling under my skin. An unscratchable itch. I'd like to rip my flesh open with a pin and dig it out. I spring to my feet repeating "Oh my fucking God" over and over again and fight the urge to vomit chow mein on the white floors. My ears ring as I slip my shoes on and go running out the apartment door, past a bunch of gleaming words on the common halls like *Restoration* and *Rejuvenation* that feel like the universe's joke on me. In the elevator, there's a fountain and a slideshow of people in Jolvix shirts and sleep masks—the universe's way of further rubbing my own panic in my face.

I fly down the sidewalk to the ride zone, choking on the air, everything becoming blurry. My fingers barely work as I summon a ride, which pulls to the curb in under a minute. It's all going according to plan. We discussed this, we went over it, we talked about it and planned it and walked it through a hundred times and so why is the dread threatening to crush me and why do I feel like I'm walking straight into the jaws of a beast?

Everything goes as it should. We accounted for stop lights, for traffic, when Teddy timed it at twelve minutes. On the ride over, I focus on counting my breaths and reminding myself where all the guns are stashed in Teddy's apartment—in a coat on his coat rack, and hidden under his coffee table, and tucked in his kitchen cabinet behind the dog food, and stashed in the medicine cabinet along with the pain pills, and in his bedside table underneath a Joan Didion book that Teddy's never read in his life. Easy. I'll grab one of the guns, I'll put it to the guy's head, and Teddy and I will get our answers and poison him with pills.

"Approaching your destination," the self-driving car says as it nears the condo.

"Go, go, go," I say, looking at my phone, the Infinity's notification dinging to say *Ted loves you!* "Shut up," I whisper to it. The second the car pulls in front of the condo, I'm out like a flash.

I'm up the stairs.

I'm typing the numbers into Teddy's front door lock, *beep-beep-beep-beep.*

I'm pushing the door open and diving for the closest gun, the one in the coat rack, and walking in with the gun cocked. I hear the door shut behind me. My hands tremble on the gun as I step, cautiously, into the living room. The terror I feel right now, the laser focus of it, is beyond anything I've even fathomed in my twenty-seven years. It's an out-of-body experience, as if I'm a ghost floating through the world, already dead, already cold from the shock of it. All I can think is, I'm too late. It's too quiet in here.

What the fuck am I going to find when I round the corner?

I tiptoe past the foyer into the living room, gun ready, holding my breath. But I'm not even sure how to process what I'm seeing in front of me: a set table with flowers and candlelight.

Teddy, smiling, freshly shaved, in a button-up shirt and trousers in his kitchen, like he's posing for a goddamn picture in a housekeeping magazine. Alone.

"Eleven minutes, twenty-eight seconds," Teddy says, pointing to his watch. "Impressive."

"Where is he?" I whisper.

"He?" Teddy asks, baffled.

"What the fuck is this?" I ask.

"You can put the gun down," Teddy says, as if I'm the crazy one. "It was a test."

I make a noise halfway between a cry and a scream and throw my gun behind me on the couch.

"Easy," Teddy says, hands up. "That thing's safety could be off."

"What the fuck—why would you—"

"To make sure you're ready, come on. You do know people have fire drills for a reason?"

I'm so dizzy with rage and relief that I have to squat to collect myself. "We didn't talk about drills."

"If you talk about drills, they aren't really drills."

"I thought you were dead!" I shriek, standing back up. I'm so pissed I don't know what to do, so I take my heel off and throw it at him. It misses his head by a couple of inches and something crashes to the floor behind him.

"Jesus, Leels!" he says. "I made you dinner."

"Oh that should make up for it!" I shout, coming over to him. "'Sorry about pranking you that our lives were over, here's some fucking tacos!'"

"Pasta," he corrects me, pointing to the pot.

"I hate you so much right now," I say, not moving. "I don't want to eat your fucking pasta."

Teddy's got a smirk on his face, like this is funny. It occurs to me that his levity, his constant happy-go-luckiness and upbeatedness, is perhaps pathological. Making pasta and cooking me some elegant-ass dinner while apparently conducting a drill for us to murder someone. How can I trust someone who takes it all this lightly?

"Leels," he says, opening his arms like he's going to hug me, like he senses the storm brewing behind my eyeballs. But I push him away.

"Give me my shoe," I mumble.

He bends down to retrieve it and comes back up with his scarred eyebrow raised. "You broke my cookie jar."

I won't apologize for throwing my heel at him and apparently breaking his cookie jar, even though I feel bad about it. Maybe later. Not now. I sniff and slip my shoe back on. Behind Teddy, in the dim kitchen, I can see the jagged shards of glass. I push past Teddy to bend down and start picking up the pieces, muttering, "I can't believe you own a cookie jar."

"Why wouldn't I own a cookie jar?" he asks.

I toss the pieces in the trash. "You don't bake cookies. You don't eat at home. I've seen the inside of your refrigerator, it's sad bachelor town, nothing but a bottle of ketchup and takeout leftovers." Standing up, I ask, "Where's your broom?"

He's got it in hand already and sweeps it all up and doesn't say anything except, "Sad bachelor town."

I collapse into a chair as he finishes the sweep. Watching him, his sad puppy expression, his quiet cleaning of my mess, turns the wheel in me. I heave a sigh and look at the ceiling as I utter the words, "I'm sorry, Teddy."

"It's okay," he says. "Want some pasta?"

"The adrenaline rush of the drill kind of killed my appetite."

We sit at the table together, empty plates and folded napkins. I reach out and touch one of the lilies in the flower arrangement. It looks so alive, yet it's already dead.

"I don't know about this plan," I say, meeting Teddy's gaze.

He's seated across from me, chin in his hand.

"I have the feeling we're going to get ourselves killed." I wipe the pollen on my finger on a napkin, leaving a streak of dandelion yellow. "Or we're going to kill this guy and it's going to be messy and we're going to get put in prison."

"You and I are an amazing team," he says. "Do you know how much seemingly impossible shit we tackle when we work together?"

"Yes, when reputations are on the line. But when our *lives* are on the line?"

"Do you know about the power of positive thinking?"

"I know it's a bunch of bullshit."

"You ever think that your negativity could be a gravitational force pulling negativity to you?"

"No, I don't."

"I believe in the power of positive thinking."

"Oh yeah?" I shoot back, my elbows on the table, chin on my balled-up fists. "Positive thinking save your brother when he decided to take the emergency exit from existence?"

Teddy's expression goes absolutely still, like I just sucked the man out of him and what's left is a mannequin.

"I'm sorry," I blurt.

After a still moment, the life returns to his face. "Positive thinking doesn't work miracles."

"I'm sorry," I repeat. I put my head in my hands, the guilt rising. Why am I so rude to this man who does everything for me? I can't stand myself sometimes.

"Just this once, can you do me a favor?" he asks, leaning in. "Can you just pretend everything's going to be okay? I know you're good at pretending."

His last sentence has a sharp edge to it, and it cuts me. He's right. I'm a professional pretender. I'm such a good pretender sometimes I don't know where pretending ends and reality begins.

"What exactly are you referring to?" I ask, sorry I'm even asking because I know I don't want to hear the answer but I've got to hear it anyway.

"You know what I'm referring to."

"I honestly don't," I lie.

Why am I goading him into saying it out loud? I don't want to think about it and I certainly don't want talk about it. Even the thought makes me so full of guilt I might explode.

"Never mind," I say. "Let's just—"

"We slept together and I told you I loved you and you pretended it never even happened."

And there it is. He just said it.

He just got the key and unlocked the door to my secret room and shone a light on what lies there inside.

CHAPTER 51

Back when I lived in DC, Teddy visited me just once. He was attending some virtual reality conference—ironically, an in-person event. The Friday night after the conference had wrapped up, we met in his hotel bar. He lit up when he saw me, waving from his cocktail table with one hand and holding a half-empty gin and tonic with the other. Though I'm sure Teddy would have said it was half-full.

He was dressed in a baby-blue dress shirt and Italian pants and looked so much more adult than I felt. Silly because I had come straight from work, clad in a pantsuit and heels. But I was playing a part when I rocked business attire, whereas with Teddy, it just seemed natural.

"Hello hello hello," he said gregariously, giving me a side hug. "Need a drinkypoo?"

"Yes, but don't say that," I said, putting my purse on the table.

"What's your poison?" he asked.

Already, two sentences in, he was too much. He was loud enough that people turned their heads. He spoke in clichés and said shit like *drinkypoo*. But he was Jack's twin brother and I couldn't help how I stood there, stunned by the slap of memory, at the sight of his face.

"Old-fashioned," I finally answered. "With a cherry."

"Be back in a jiff," he said.

I sat at the bar table on a high stool and steadied my heartbeat with some deep breaths as I watched Teddy laughing with the bartender. It was so surreal. The last time I had seen Teddy was a little over a year ago at Jack's funeral. Here we were, moving on with our lives, having drinkypoos while Jack lay under six feet of soil. It was so wrong. And yet I couldn't keep my eyes off Teddy, couldn't stop feeling like there was a little hummingbird in my chest. My stomach turned as I realized the last time I'd been in a hotel with this man, we'd partied our asses off while Jack killed himself.

"An old-fashioned with two cherries for the lady," Teddy said, handing me the glass.

"*Two* cherries," I repeated, taking a gulp, hoping it would settle me.

He took his seat and sipped his gin and tonic. His drink had sweat all over the table and he cleaned it up with a bar napkin. "Eh, you seem like you deserve extra."

"How are you?" I asked, eating a cherry. I eyed the contents of the glass, already calculating when I'd get my next drink.

"Great! Got promoted to COO. Running the whole VR sector now."

"That's quite the promotion. You must be good at your job."

"So I've been told," he said, with mock haughtiness. "What about you?"

"You know. Still miserable," I said, accompanying the harsh truth with a smile. "But what are you going to do?"

His smile vanished and he contemplated his glass for a moment. "I'm miserable too," he finally said, meeting my eyes.

"Yeah, I know."

"You've got to stay busy or it'll eat you alive."

"Busy or blitzed," I said.

"Either works," he agreed.

We clinked glasses and exchanged a special smile, a sad smile, one that held guilt and pain and hope, too. It came back to me with a rush how much I liked Teddy. How instantly he and I were familiar. There was never any awkwardness with him; he was so social and smooth, so agreeable. He made me feel like it was okay to be myself, my real self. I don't know what it was. A chemistry, a magic completely separate from his resemblance to Jack—I felt it the night we were in that hotel room. I felt it again now.

We chatted about surface-level shit, joked about our jobs. We made fun of the baseball game on TV. We got another drink. We whispered about the other bar patrons and made up silly backstories for each of them. We got another drink. I talked about how I felt like an alien in DC, the land of politicos, well-dressed schmoozers, and hyper-professionals. We got another drink. Teddy told me about a girl named Genesis he'd gone out on a date with, a state senator's daughter. It was set up by their parents, the modern equivalent of an arranged marriage. He told me he didn't care much for her but maybe he'd marry her anyway. We were drunk when we moved to the hotel restaurant for dinner. By the time Teddy paid the bill, we were smashed. But both of us were practiced drinkers at this point. Hell, we were alcoholics, but you couldn't tell us so that night. We bought another bottle of wine and went up to his hotel room on the top floor.

In true Teddy Lindmark fashion, his hotel room was ridiculous and over-the-top. There was a sitting room, two fireplaces, and a television in the bathroom, all of it a little fuzzy around the edges from the alcohol. I draped myself on the fainting couch as he filled my glass of wine at the bar.

"*Should* I marry a state senator's daughter?" he asked, almost more to himself.

I laughed, it seemed so out of nowhere. It was like he was picking the conversation back up that I thought we'd left behind in the restaurant.

"Didn't you go out on *one* date with her?" I asked. "Isn't it a bit early to be thinking about marriage?"

As if he hadn't heard my question, he just told me, "You know what she wants to do with her life? Be an influencer coach."

"An influencer coach," I repeated. "High achiever."

He crossed the room and sat in a stuffed chair next to me, handing me my glass of wine. With the push of a remote-control button, the fireplace blazed to life. I marveled at him, the way he made everything seem so easy.

"Sometimes I think it would be better to marry someone you didn't love," he said, gazing at the fire.

I waited, expecting some kind of joke, some lightness, but the statement just sat there instead. I sat up, my hair mussed, and finger-combed my bangs.

"Why would you say that?" I asked.

"You know, lower your expectations."

He swirled his wine, sniffed it, and then sipped it, like a refined person would. Not like me, who gulped it down like it was soda.

"No, Teddy, I don't think you should marry a woman who you went on one date with who you don't love."

Teddy glanced at me. There was something new, something deep, in his fixed expression. "What if the person you really want, you know you can't ever, ever have?"

I swallowed, a warmth blooming all through me. It was as if, just now, I became aware of my body. I felt my bones, my skin, my lips. I felt life coursing through me. What he said pierced me, made it hard to speak, because he said out loud something I already knew and had no words for. I put my glass of wine on the table and contemplated what I should do next. I was drunk. I knew this. I knew it would be best to breeze over what he just said, finish my glass of wine, and stumble downstairs for a cab. I stood up to do exactly that. I downed the glass, grabbed my coat. He watched me, slouched in his stuffed chair with his wine glass in hand, as if he already knew I was going to leave him. Then something inside me shifted —something that I still struggle to pinpoint or understand. Though is it that much of a mystery in the end? I simply changed my mind.

Stepping to the overstuffed chair, very gently, I

crawled onto him, straddling him. I raked my hands through his hair and pulled. He inhaled sharply and closed his eyes as if this were heaven. I shivered at the sight of his pleasure. I thought, I've never felt as wanted by anyone in my life as I know Teddy wants me right now. Running a fingertip from his hairline to his chin, I traced his profile, and then bent in to kiss him.

Drunk as I was, I still remember every second of that kiss.

Like a cool drink of water after a long, lost walk in the desert.

Even if he had Jack's mouth, he didn't kiss like Jack at all. He had a hunger, a magnetism to his kiss that was all his own. The way he put his hands on me and pulled me to him, hard, like he wouldn't let go of me—that wasn't like Jack, either. Teddy was his own man with his own grip and feel and push and soon I stopped comparing and it was Teddy, just Teddy, Teddy picking me up and laying me on the bed. Teddy pulling up my skirt and touching me and making me moan. Teddy's naked body on mine and Teddy whispering in my ear that he loved me and that I made him believe in soulmates and Teddy telling me he had never wanted anyone the way he wanted me and that he had come to the conference just for an excuse to be in DC and to see me again because he never stopped thinking about me. It was Teddy who I became one with for just a little while, the sex so unbelievably good it seemed impossible we'd never done it before. It was Teddy's name I cried out when I came and when I fell asleep in his arms, the room spinning like a merry-go-round, I thought that maybe there was a reason for all this. That maybe the dark, beautiful surprise I never asked for, the plot twist of my romantic life story, was that I met Jack to find Teddy. It all made sense.

Until the morning, anyway.

I woke up to the unwelcome sunshine, naked in bed in Teddy's arms. I sat up, shaky, nauseated, and absolutely rotten with shame. I peered down at his sleeping face in horror, remembering everything. Slipping out of bed, I hit the shower, where I sobbed and scrubbed myself a dozen times before realizing what I felt dirty with I could never wash away. All the things Teddy had said—that he loved me, that I was the only woman he'd ever really wanted— how could I ever forget? How could I move on from this? How could I ever look at myself in the mirror again? I had done something so awful, so forbidden, it was tattooed on my soul forever. But as I stepped out of the shower and toweled myself off, I dried my face and I did look in the mirror. I was the same Leela, same Leela I had always been. I decided right then that there was only one option moving forward, only one scenario possible.

"Hey," I said, coming into the room with a smile, seeing Teddy up and dressed again. His hair was a mess, his face looked bloated from last night's binge, and there was something in his eyes I didn't quite recognize—a nervousness, maybe.

He pushed a smile to his own lips. "Good morning, sunshine."

"Crazy night," I said in a chipper tone, slipping my shoes on. "A lot of fun. Too bad I can't remember anything past dinner."

Teddy's mouth dropped open. "You …?"

"I completely blacked out," I said, grimacing as I pulled my coat on. "I hate it when that happens. I'm sure we had a great time, though."

Teddy looked like someone had snatched the words right out of his throat. He wasn't usually one left speechless, but I'd done it to the poor guy. I came over and gave him a quick hug.

"So good to see you. Thanks for dinner. Call me next time you're in the DC area, okay?"

Finally, he managed a tight smile and the words, "Yeah. Sure." He gave me a long, sad, blue-eyed puppy look. "Take care."

I flounced out of the room with a faked confidence, wanting him to believe I didn't remember. I wanted him to believe it so bad that it would become infectious, the forgetting—and he might look back on that night and not remember it either.

CHAPTER 52

My cheeks flush at the way he looks at me now, years later, in his apartment. The memory comes with a temperature, undeniable suddenly because it's been said.

"I can't talk about that," I say.

"Why?" he asks. "Is it really so shameful that you have to fake like it didn't happen?"

"It's not shameful," I say. "It's horrible."

"Horrible," he repeats, his eyes narrowing like I just slugged him in the stomach.

"I was engaged to your brother, Teddy!" I almost yell. "You don't *do* shit like that."

"You weren't engaged when it happened. Jack was *dead*."

"It doesn't matter."

Teddy closes his eyes, collecting himself, I guess. His brow is knit and I wonder what's behind the curtain of his face. I realize for the first time that I think I hurt him badly and he's been walking around with a smile on his face being my buddy ever since. Great. I betrayed Jack and

I hurt Teddy, all in one drunken, lustful night. I wouldn't mind a black hole to jump into.

"You know what I think?" he asks finally, opening his eyes. "I think it does matter. I think it matters to you and that's why you can't talk about it."

I stare at Pickles' empty dog bed in the corner, unable to withstand the unflinching eye contact.

"Okay," I say flatly.

"I think you have feelings for me and I have feelings for you and if Jack wasn't a factor, we'd live happily ever after."

"Jack will never not be a factor," I remind him. "You'd never even know me if it weren't for Jack."

"Leels," he says, raising his voice. "I've known you and loved you way longer than you even knew Jack at this point. You got engaged in college after knowing each other for like two minutes. You really think if he were alive you'd still be together? Your relationship was rocky and he fucking kissed someone else and who knows what else happened that you didn't know about. He cheated on every girlfriend he ever had. He was my brother, and I love him, and I'll always love him, but … but I've been here for you now for years, willing to do anything, *anything* for you. And he's dead."

My soul's taking a beating right now as I do the math and realize that Teddy's right. That Jack's been dead now for over twice the amount of time I even knew him. That I've spent far more time with Teddy than I ever did with Jack. In a silent whisper I'd never voice aloud, I think that I might actually love Teddy as a human being more than I ever loved Jack. That I know him better, trust him more.

These revelations come with a river of pain that collects behind my eyes. I blink, controlling it, controlling it.

"Is that what this is about?" I ask, gesturing to the air. "This absurd scheme—is it about proving your love to me, winning me over?" I hold my finger in the air, the one that buzzed earlier. "Getting an Infinity in my finger? Because if so, that's just fucking stupid."

"No," he says. "That's not what this is about."

"Because this isn't going to happen, Teddy. You and me isn't going to happen, ever, no matter what silicon implant you get in my ring finger or what crimes we commit together. And I can't even believe you're springing this on me, like really? Of all times you could choose to talk about feelings, it has to be now?"

"Maybe I didn't want to end up fucking *dying* without saying something first," he says quietly.

With a dark expression, he gets up and puts the pasta pot in the fridge like a man who's never heard of Tupperware. He comes to the table and busies himself with cleaning up the settings we didn't use.

Lord. Is that what this is? Last words? Teddy's deathbed confession?

I can't. I can't do this with him.

"I think we should back out of the plan," I say, getting up. "Take the implants out. I'll delete the video and post another one saying I was kidding and I love the shit out of you."

"A little late for that," he mutters.

"I do love the shit out of you," I say, my throat tight. "You know that, right?"

"I don't know what I know anymore."

"I love the shit out of you," I repeat, but it's like he doesn't hear me anymore. He won't look at me. "I'm going to undo all this. In the morning, I'll go to the police. I'll take the fall for everything that happened at Jolvix, for the cover-up, everything. I'll take the civil suits and I'll take the media shaming and all of it. I'll take all the blame. The killer VixSpex, the copies on the dark web, it'll all be on me. I'll make sure you're untouchable."

Teddy's washing a fork in the sink, his back to me. "Sure, whatever you want."

Why do I get the sense, as I watch him there in his dim kitchen over a sink full of suds, that I've just slayed a man's spirit tonight? That I've shattered something special, something that is beyond repair? We were so naïve to think of this plan, to think we were some vigilante warriors who could lure a killer to us and get away with murder. To think we were some unstoppable team when we're just two broken people who, together, do not make a whole.

Absolutely not. Tomorrow this will end. Honestly, it's a relief to think of just going to the police and unloading the truth. Of getting whatever it is I deserve for the things I've covered up and pretended not to know.

I fight the urge to come up behind Teddy and give him a hug, but it hurts too much to imagine he wouldn't hug me back.

"Have a good night, Teddy," I say as I head for the door, putting the gun back in his coat pocket where it belongs.

He doesn't answer me.

CHAPTER 53

THE GAME

Edward "Ted" Lindmark. A familiar face.

I've had my eye on him before.

After I saw you in DC, Leela, witnessed the mess you had become, I backed off for a while.

I was guilty and confused and you were three thousand miles away from me.

The gap seemed unbridgeable.

I watched your social feeds to stay updated, but that was all.

Then, miraculously, you moved back to California.

It was like every time I tried to stay away from you, the world bounced you back to me.

Now you were working at Jolvix in Cupertino.

I started driving down, spending weekend afternoons hanging around your neighborhood.

One day I saw you with him in a café and my heart choked.

You were lunching with a ghost.

I followed him home that day instead of you.

Peeked at his mailbox. Recognized his name.

Edward "Ted" Lindmark.

Remembered Jack had a twin.

It made me ill.

I backed off after that.

Watched from afar but left you both alone.

And then one day, months later, I was riding my bike up a random street in Berkeley.

There you were, hair blowing, opening your apartment door.

You had moved back to Berkeley, just a mile from me.

Unbelievable.

Gravity always wins.

The world had rolled you back to me again.

You, Leela, are a habit I can't quit.

I catch a glimpse of you tonight through my tinted car window, scurrying away from Edward's place in your high heels and work clothes.

I hadn't expected to see you here.

It gives me pause.

For a heartbeat, I contemplate if there's something amiss.

A trick, a complication, a game you're playing.

Though you did say in the video that you've been at his beck and call …

I suppose it lines up, you leaving his condominium at this hour.

Perhaps Edward or Ted or whatever you call him had you run an errand after work hours.

You looked upset. Arms crossed like you were cold, despite the toasty air. Downturned red lips.

Upset, but stunning.

Upset, but unspeakably beautiful.

I scroll on my phone to your PicPost account and kiss your profile picture.

"You wanted this," I whisper, tracing the outline of your face. "You asked me for this."

I watch the deserted sidewalk and the streetlamp pops on, like it's telling me it's time.

I slip the mask on, pulling the rubber into place, a second skin.

A warm hug, your face all over my face.

I pull the wig on and brush it with my fingers.

Check my backpack: the VixSpex, the gun that fits into it, my gun, my duct tape, my stun gun, just in case.

Let the games begin.

CHAPTER 54

THE GAME

A piece of tape over the peephole of his door. A deep breath.

Knock-knock-knock.

It all happens in a blink.

The door opens and I show him the gun, stick it in his side as I push my way in.

Kick the door shut behind me, hear the automatic lock.

"Hey there," Ted says, putting his arms up. "Easy now."

I scan the room—tidy like a man with no life, soullessly classy, like a staged room in a catalog picture.

Ted is dressed like he's about to go out on a date, pressed slacks, woodsy cologne. He holds his breath until his face purples. All I can think of in this moment is Jack.

"You look just like him and nothing like him at the same time," I say.

Ted blows out a breath and his face washes of all color. "You knew Jack."

I nod, moving the gun up to Ted's temple.

"Ah." He swallows and stiffens at the gun to his head. His hands are still in the air like a hostage. I suppose he is a hostage. But there's no panic there. No frantic reaction.

Something is off.

I don't like it.

"Look, I know what you're here for," Ted says. "And sure, I'll play your game, I will. But I want to talk first, that's all."

"I don't care what you want."

I pull the duct tape out of my backpack, pulling the end to my mouth and using one hand to rip off a section. Smash the piece over Ted's lips. It's satisfying, like plugging an annoying leak.

"Sit down," I say.

I push him on the ridiculous red couch, like something you'd see in the VIP lounge of a tacky bar. Pull a long screech of duct tape from the roll and bind his hands so tightly they redden before my eyes.

"Don't move," I tell him.

While keeping the gun aimed at him, I do a quick sweep of the room, scanning for smart devices that could be recording this. That Maxine in Lotus's house spooked me. Edward "Ted" Lindmark is a Jolvix goon and probably has access to all kinds of tech. But surprisingly, I don't spot anything besides a blinking light on his TV screen that could be a camera. I smash it with the side of my gun, splintering the glass, and the light goes off.

I pull the headset out and squat so I can see eye to eye with the man slumped on the couch. Dangle it in front of Ted's face.

"You know what this is?" I ask.

A little panic lights up his eyes and a smile flutters to my lips at the sight of it.

"Of course you do," I say.

I stand up and pace a few steps, unable to stop staring at him. He remains perfectly still with a gaze that's trying to bore a hole into me. Trying to peel off my plastic skin. It won't work. I've got my armor, my costume. I'm your guardian angel of death, Leela, and I'm not going to let you down.

I wish you were dead, you said.

And your wish was granted.

"I'm feeling a wave of déjà vu," I say, unable to stop smiling, which bunches the mask up. I pull it tighter over my lips. "When I killed Jack, he looked as helpless as you. But he was so drunk. He didn't know what was happening. He just took the drink from my hand and pounded it. Didn't even taste all those crushed pills I'd swiped from his bedside table. I couldn't believe how easy it was. So easy. Passed out in his bed after that. I took a bag off his floor and tied it around his head and left him there. I slept well that night in my room, on the other side of the wall."

Ted's eyes widen and he squirms, tries to speak. When he moves to stand, I push the gun into his forehead so hard it leaves a mark like a peephole.

"She asked me to," I remind him, whispering in his ear. "Just like she asked for this."

Ted's expression has gone still, as if I've killed him already. A rabbit going limp in the trap. There is nothing more majestic in the world than watching surrender suck the spirit from the flesh.

He tries to speak again, *mmm-mmm-mmm.*

I shake my head and laugh. I crouch and dangle the VixSpex in front of his face, my limbs tingling with excitement.

I whisper, "It's playtime."

CHAPTER 55

LEELA

The taxi pulls in front of Teddy's place and I jump out, slamming my door. I'm hot and bothered, stomping back up his stairs that I just stomped down barely a half an hour ago. Teddy's playing games now. My finger's been buzzing since I got back to the plastic box in Bliss Bay that I temporarily call home and then I had to turn right back around again. This is some bullshit, even for Teddy. What are we doing, another drill? Is he going to try to talk me out of going to the police tomorrow? Does he want to keep rehashing the past? He didn't answer my texts on the way over. I'm beyond tired. I'm burned to a crisp. Oh, to get this plastic chip removed tomorrow and never feel the buzz of it again.

Punching the numbers into his door, *beep-beep-beep-beep*, I huff as I step inside, seeing the back of his head in the living room.

"What the fuck do you want from me, Teddy?" I ask, shutting the door behind me, hearing the mechanical whirr of the automatic lock. "I'm done. This is the last time I—"

As I step forward, I notice that Teddy has something on his head. Then it registers what it is.

Oh please God no.

He can't be. He can't.

He is, though. He is.

He's wearing the killer VixSpex.

Hands bound, mouth shut with a silver rectangle of duct tape.

He's moving around the room, ducking, jumping, panting through his nose, hiding from an invisible enemy. A captive in his own horrible world. Like those fools locked in the fun room at the Jolvix VR sector. And if it were possible for the human heart to turn inside out, this must be what it feels like. My knees get weak as I step forward, stumbling.

"Wait!" I yell. "No! No, Teddy, no, no!"

We had a plan but it's all scrambled now—I was supposed to grab the gun in the coatrack—but no, that's behind me near the door and Teddy's ahead and—and he wasn't supposed to have the VixSpex on—I have to get them off of him. I fly forward from the foyer to the living room and someone takes me from behind, a warm gloved hand over my mouth, holding me so tightly with their arms that I can barely breathe. I scream into the rough nylon material that covers my mouth.

"Don't scream, beautiful," a voice whispers in my ear.

I dissolve into sobs as I fight hard to be free, but this person's grip on me is a vise. I shake my head and beg them to stop, but they can't hear me.

"You weren't supposed to see this," the voice whispers in my ear. A low voice, a man's voice. He smells my hair, deeply, like he's trying to breathe in my bones. I can feel the inhalation on my neck. I can feel his muscles pressing against me. I can feel him growing hard against my ass and my stomach flips, sick goosebumps all over me. I try to pull away from him but he only squeezes me tighter, like he's trying to crush me into him. "It's you, it's really you."

I scream wetly into the glove. In the living room, not ten feet away from me, Teddy is running around his living room like a fool, oblivious to me even being here, bumping into furniture like a person fumbling in the dark. I can't believe this is real, that it's happening, I wasn't prepared. I wish it was me. I wish more than anything it was me.

"I don't usually like to watch," he whispers in my ear. "But do you want to watch?"

I scream again into the void of his thick glove.

"We can watch together," he says, the buzz of his low voice sending a shiver all through me. "I've never seen someone last this long. Usually they lose within a minute or so."

I can't do it. I can't watch Teddy's brains being blown out. I shut my eyes. I pray to a God I haven't spoken intimately to in years, since my fiancé died, since the earth's floor fell out from under me and grief stole my faith. I don't know what else to do. I pray that I can get Teddy out of this. I pray that this nightmare will end. Please, please, universe. You've taken enough from me. Let Teddy live.

My eyes fly open and suddenly my mind's focus is

sharp as a hunting knife. I calculate the distance between me and the guns Teddy stashed. The one under the coffee table is right where Teddy is right now and there's a couch between us. The one in the kitchen cabinet is beyond that, another eight feet away—too far, too hard to reach, what the fuck were we thinking. My best bet, my only bet with this goddamn beast holding me so tightly I can barely breathe, is to use all my force to push us both backward into the foyer where maybe, with enough force, I can knock this crazed jerk back straight into the wall where the front door is and startle him enough to let go of me. Maybe then I'll have a shot at grabbing the gun in the coat pocket on the coat rack.

It's a long shot. I'll have to take it.

With every conceivable bit of energy I can muster, I push myself backward, clenching my muscles and trying to break free and push this person off of me. Instead of us moving back toward the coat rack, though, we topple over like one clumsy thing and land on the floor. His arms go slack, hand slipping off my mouth, and I gasp in air that has never felt fresher. I hear the *oof* of the breath leaving the stranger's body and the room spins and now I'm staring at the ceiling. And somehow, all at once, I'm still listening to Teddy's every move, his every jump, his every step, his every breath, my body sick with waiting for the sound of a gunshot.

I scramble to my knees, thinking I'll turn and make a run for the gun before this guy grabs me again but then I notice a gun I don't recognize—a black revolver—that has fallen near my high-heeled foot and, in a flash of whip-fast adrenaline, I snatch it and point it at the person clad in black military gear who lies on the floor on his back.

His back … or her back?

This person, this figure, they look monstrous. Like something out of a black ops video game with a messy wig and grotesque plastic female face where dark eyes blink back at me.

"What the fuck is wrong with your face?" I ask, still on my knees, still catching my breath. Then it hits me with certainty like a landslide—it's a mask. "Who the fuck are you?"

He doesn't answer. He just puts his hands up in the air like he knows he's been caught. I realize, with my trembling hand pointing the gun at this horrible monster person, that even though I'm burning to know who's underneath the mask, I need to focus on Teddy right now. My eyes fall to the linen closet in the short hallway that leads to Teddy's bedroom and then to the dining room chair.

"Get in the closet now," I say, jumping to my feet and putting the gun to this person's head.

"As you wish," he says.

He gets up compliantly and walks to the closet. He's probably six feet, stocky, though I don't know if it's just the bulk of his military gear. I can see his dark eyes searing into me from behind the mask. Right now though, I'm all panic, I've got one job and that's to get that fucking thing off Teddy's head before it kills him. I push the man in the closet and close the door. I grab a chair and wedge it under the knob, locking him inside.

I'm turning to run to Teddy when I hear a bang and a crash. I scream so loud I could break glass as I run toward the living room and see Teddy's body sprawled over the coffee table.

I'm too fucking late.

CHAPTER 56

In life's most painful, horrible moments, time slows to a crawl, every heartbeat an eternity, every blink, every image stamped to the brain, never to be forgotten. The surreal nature of tragedy thickens the air into a suffocating silence. The only thing I can hear in this living room, as I stand over Teddy's body, is my own breath slicing that suffocating silence like a blade. Tears flood my face as I stoop down to look at him. I don't want to look, but I have to. He fell backward onto the coffee table hard enough to break it and he lies in a jagged pile of splintered wood.

"Teddy," I cry.

His mouth hangs open, his arms splayed. Still there in his tailored pants and dress shirt, he looks oddly beautiful and perfect, framed by the absolute mess of the demolished table. *Teddy is dead*, my mind whispers, and I can't believe it's true. I can't believe that this is how our story ends.

"You said we could pull this off, you asshole!" I say. "I believed you, Teddy!"

I push his leg with my finger and it doesn't move. Balling my fists up, I sob into them, closing my eyes, willing myself to disappear. When I open my eyes again the whole room is blurry and nothing has changed. Teddy's body still lies here, unmoving.

I crawl a foot to be near his head, which is tilted to its side so the gun attachment on the VixSpex isn't all the way visible. I'm afraid of what I'm going to see if I move him, afraid half of his skull will be gone. He's still warm. I run a hand through his hair, run my fingertips along his neck and Adam's apple. Gingerly as I can, I move his head to inspect the underside where the gun fixture is and I'm so shocked that the moment steals the breath from my lungs when I see that his skull is intact. It hits me that there isn't a drop of blood. There isn't any obvious injury.

An invisible hand that has been squeezing my heart relaxes just a little bit.

His mouth is still duct-taped. I run a finger under his nose and feel the tickle of hot air.

"Oh my God," I say, ripping off the VixSpex, the rubber seal slurping as I pull it off his eyes and ears. The device drops to the floor. His eyes are closed and there's an impression around them from the tightness of the headset. I slap his face lightly, to try to wake him. "Teddy!"

His eyes open. "Hey," he whispers.

"You're alive," I say, putting a hand on his cheek, leaving it there. The feeling—it's like my blood stopped in my veins and now it's started flowing again. I get an actual rush all through me, the relief hitting me like a stiff drink. "How the fuck are you alive?"

"I'm playing dead," he whispers. "Where is he?"

"I locked him in a closet," I say.

Teddy sits up, groaning, clutching his side. "I really messed up my back."

"I don't understand," I say, wiping my face. "This makes no sense. How did you not get shot?"

"I found the trap door." He says it to me like it's the most obvious thing in the world. "Barnett showed me the game when I visited him. He took the gun out and let me try out whatever it was he called it—'The Slaying Game'— in practice mode. I played it for a while. Prepared. So today I was able to find that trap door again. I jumped down it and when I fell over on this fucking table that almost broke my fucking back, I played dead."

"I thought you *were* dead, Teddy," I say, wrapping my arms around him and hugging him as tightly as I can. Inhaling his scent, his sweat mixed with his cologne, burying my face in his shoulder. I could sob, but I'm all sobbed out. All I want right now is to hold him and never let him go.

"Easy on my back," he says. "Something's wrong."

"Do I need to call an ambulance?"

"Are you kidding? There's a *murderer* locked in my *closet* right now. I'll be all right. I need to get up."

Reluctantly, I let him go and get to my feet, extending my hand. "Need help?"

"Yeah, that'd be swell."

Teddy Lindmark is the only person I know who would cheerfully say something like "That'd be swell" when he was just almost slaughtered. As I help him to his feet, I can't stop staring at the creases left by the headset on his face, the proof that this really happened. He did his homework and beat the game. I'm in awe of him. For the first time in my life, I think that maybe the swagger, the confidence that Teddy possesses, isn't faked. It's a hundred percent deserved.

"Why are you looking at me like that?" he asks, stretching his back with a wince.

"Because I'm still in shock that you're alive." I swallow. "Teddy, I don't know what I would have done. This whole plan is bonkers. We're in way over our heads, what we were thinking?"

"Leels," he says, locking his flame-blue gaze with mine. "That crazed prick in there killed Jack."

I experience my own personal sonic boom as I process that sentence. "Excuse me?" I manage.

"Maybe he was screwing with my head, I don't know. That's what he said. But he knew Jack. He knew who I was."

After an eternal couple of seconds processing this information and fighting the urge to hyperventilate, all I can manage is trying those horrible three words out for size. "He killed Jack." I swallow, the realization settling in with a chilling numbness. "He—he what—he forced him to eat the pills? He put the plastic bag over his head?"

Teddy clenches his jaw. "He crushed them up and put them in a drink."

I inhale sharply, beating back the pain, begging it to wait. We have a homicidal maniac locked in a closet. My trauma needs to sit on the back burner for now.

"Well then, I guess us feeding this piece of shit pills tonight and faking his overdose is poetic justice," I finally say.

Teddy's glassy eyes narrow as he glances in the general direction of where the monster is locked in the closet. "I want to slit his throat, Leels. I want to cut him to pieces."

"We can't do that."

"I want to beat the piss out of him before he goes, at least. He deserves to feel it."

I'm blazing inside with identical rage, so much so that my fists are trembling at my side. "I know," I say quietly. "But we can't. We have to make it look accidental or else all this is for nothing."

"He killed my twin brother."

"He killed my fiancé."

It's like we're both just trying out these statements for size. As much as I know this is true, I believe Teddy, another part of me just can't accept it yet. I've gone years now believing Jack took his own life. To imagine he didn't —to imagine he wanted to live and that life was robbed of him—it fills my heart and head with broken glass. It doesn't make sense.

"Who the fuck is he?" I ask.

Teddy raises his scarred eyebrow, which twitches. "Guess it's time we find out."

Teddy and I make our way around the coffee table. He's hunched a little, visibly in pain. He mutters, "I always knew that table was a piece of crap."

I pick the gun up off the floor, the one I stole from the killer, and show it to Teddy when we round to the foyer. "I took this from the guy."

"Swiped his gun *and* locked him in the closet with a chair under the doorknob trick," Teddy says. "Impressive."

"I've watched some action movies in my day."

"Had no idea you watched action movies."

"I contain multitudes."

"Here's what we're going to do," Teddy says, in a voice barely above a whisper. "You're going to hold the gun to his head. I'm going to tie him up so he can't move."

"Tie him up where?"

Teddy thrusts his chin in the direction of the closet. "To that chair that's under the doorknob."

"Okay. And what do we tie him up with?" I ask. "All that extra rope you have lying around?"

"The guy brought duct tape."

"Is duct tape strong enough?"

Teddy considers this. Once again, I get that sinking feeling that we're in over our heads.

"We're really bad at this," I say, hands on hips, eyeing the closet door.

"We trapped a murderer. I'd say we're rockin' it right now."

I roll my eyes. *Rockin' it.* To describe a kidnapping. This man, I swear. Stiffly, bracing his back with a hand, Teddy leans over to pick up the duct tape off the floor. He holds it up in the air. "I think it'll do."

"And if it doesn't?"

Teddy taps the gun in my hand with a single finger. "Plan B."

"Which is?"

"You blow his brains out and we cut him up with a hacksaw and get rid of the body."

A week or two ago, this sounded impossible, absurd. Teddy throwing this idea out there like we're a couple of hitmen in a mafia movie—come on. Look at us. But I'm now fueled with a fresh wrath I've never experienced before. It's beyond wrath. It's hatred. Pure, unadulterated hatred for this fucking sicko who has ruined my life again and again and again. Imagining tearing him apart limb by limb, I feel an upside-down sense of peace.

"Okay, boss," I say to Teddy.

He seems to like that. There's the first flicker of a smile I've seen since this horror fiasco started. It comes and goes so fast that if I blinked, I would have missed it. But it's just the boost I didn't know I needed, seeing that.

He points to the foyer. "We'll pull him out and put him in the chair right here, yes?"

"Sure. Faster we can tie him up, the less we have to move him, the better."

"He's oddly quiet in there," Teddy whispers, holding out the duct tape and picking it with his fingernail to ready it. "Maybe he suffocated."

"Would make our jobs easier." I swallow a lump, going over the next steps in my mind. *I am going to murder someone,* I think, and it doesn't feel real. "Should we get the pills ready right now?"

Teddy shakes his head. "Not yet. I want to get the story from him first."

"Yeah," I say. "Peel off that weird fucking mask and see who's under there."

We both stand side by side and observe the door in silence. We observe it so long that my ring finger starts buzzing and I realize Teddy's holding his breath. I nudge him and he releases it like a deflating balloon.

"You're making me buzz," I tell him, showing him my finger.

"Sorry."

"Or are you just trying to tell me you love me?"

"If I wanted to tell you, I would just use my words like a normal person and say 'I love you, Leela.'"

It hits me again, that invisible sledgehammer: I almost lost him. I came a millimeter away from losing him tonight.

"Love you too, Teddy." I take a deep breath and cock the gun. "Now let's kill this motherfucker."

CHAPTER 57

Teddy knocks the chair out from the door handle and I point the gun at the closet, a quivering fingertip hugging the trigger. Teddy flings open the door. I don't know what I was expecting—I had braced myself for this person to lunge out at us, for me to have to blow his head off. Instead, he's sitting on the floor of the closet under a bunch of hanging coats with his legs crossed and his hands resting on his knees like he's in a goddamn yoga class.

"Get up," Teddy says at the same time as I say, "Game over, dickhead."

We look at each other and Teddy nods at me like he's giving me the floor.

I clear my throat and try again. "Hands up," I bark, unable to shake the feeling that I'm playing a part. But that's life, isn't it? Part after part after part. "Get up off the ground, now."

"Okay, Leela," the voice behind the mask says, standing up with his gloved hands in the air.

"Sit in this chair," I say, gesturing toward the chair a few feet away from him.

Somehow the fact that this despicable demon obeys me this amiably is pissing me off even more than if he was trying to attack us. After getting him in the chair, Teddy pushes the guy's arms down and the guy folds his gloved hands in his lap. No resistance whatsoever. Total compliance. It's bizarre. The duct tape squeals as Teddy wraps it around the guy, over and over, dizzyingly, a spider wrapping up a fly. I can't stop staring at the horrid rubber mask, that fake female face. Teddy runs duct tape around the guy until the roll is done and then he stands back and we look at this serial killer we captured together. My breath steadies, relieved that we've made it this far.

"Want me to take the mask off?" Teddy asks.

I nod, keeping the gun pointed straight at the guy's skull. I hold my breath as Teddy pulls the wig off the man first, revealing a bald head underneath, shaved bald, I think, because I can see the bluish-black shade of stubble. He looks even more nightmarish with the mask on but no wig, the contrast of his pale skin color and the cartoonish peach tinge of the mask jarring and gross. Teddy peels the mask off with a slurping sound and I tense up, not knowing what to expect—afraid I'm going to recognize him. Afraid I won't recognize him. Teddy drops the mask and it lands with a plop on the hardwood, a disgusting puddle of fake skin. We stand back to survey this villain who's destroyed so many lives—including mine.

It's the oddest sensation, looking at him, making eye contact with this person. A creeping, spidery déjà vu crawls up my skin and gives me goosebumps. He's bald and pale and clean-shaven. He has a round face and a square jaw and he's smiling wide, *smiling*, like he's so happy to see me. It's like Teddy's disappeared from the room, the way this guy zeroes in on me with his unflinching, unblinking psychopathic stare, eyes the color of dirty dishwater.

"Who the hell are you?" Teddy asks him.

The man doesn't answer. He just keeps looking at me. "Hello Leela," he says. "You don't remember me, do you?"

I keep my eyes on him as a shiver snakes up my spine.

"Who the hell is he?" Teddy tries, asking me.

But I shake my head. I feel like I've seen him before, I swear I have, but I can't place him.

"I don't know," I finally answer.

The silence is oceanic. I'm breathing perfectly fine and yet I'm drowning.

"Who are you?" I ask.

The man's beady eyes never once move off my face, his thin lips cemented into that grin. There's something so reptilian about him, like a bleached lizard. My finger wants to pull the trigger now and end him but it would be a mess and I need answers. As much as I want to look away from him, break the eye contact, I don't.

"Who are you?" Teddy asks, overlapping with me asking, "Who the fuck are you?"

Teddy does an *after you* gesture to me and I ask again.

"Who the fuck are you?"

The guy chuckles to himself. In his chilling, terrible, unceasing eye contact, there's a nauseating affection as he stares at me. Like I'm missing out on a joke and I should know who he is. I want to beat him with the gun—would that be so wrong? Break his jaw? But it would be wrong, because we need to keep him intact enough to look unsuspicious when we dump his corpse somewhere. As he smiles at me and bites his lip as if we share some secret connection, I think, *I can't wait to dump your corpse somewhere.*

"Tell me who you are, motherfucker!" I explode, unable to help myself from brandishing the gun up in the air because the urge to clock his face is too much to bear.

Teddy puts a hand up to me and I bite my tongue, easing the gun back down and aiming it at the killer's temple. Like a patient dad whose toddler is having a tantrum, Teddy gets down on one knee and talks to the psychopath we have duct-taped to a dining room chair.

"Hey there, buddy," Teddy says, so cheerfully I could puke. "I know you must have a good reason for all this. We're just trying to understand. What's your name?"

But the dude doesn't even look at Teddy. It's like Teddy's not even here. He only has eyes for me. Teddy stands up and comes over to me and whispers in my ear, "Let's just kill him."

"I need to know who the fuck he is first," I say.

"You don't recognize me," the dead-eyed man duct-taped in the chair says.

"No. Who are you?"

"Who am I?" he parrots back with a ghoulish grin.

"Who *are* you?" I shout, full of dynamite, about to lose my shit.

"Come on, stop playing games," Teddy says to the guy, but I shake my head at him and let out a sigh to ease the pressure. What a silly thing to say. All this fucker *does* is play games.

The conversation ceases for about a minute as Teddy paces, his brow wrinkled. He makes it over to the window where he peeks out the curtains at the quiet night street below where no one is kidnapping murderers or interrogating them. Twenty feet and a whole wide world away. Meanwhile, I focus on the man's horrid face and try to remember who he is. Because I'm sure I've seen him before. I just can't place where or when. I've always been so bad with faces and names. Teddy crosses back over to me with a light bulb blazing behind his gaze.

"If we can't kill him," Teddy hisses in my ear. "How about we torture him a little bit, get him to talk?"

"We can't have any foul play suspected when his body is found," I whisper back.

"There are nonviolent ways to torture people," Teddy says. "I could search the internet."

Imagining Teddy typing *how to torture someone* into a search engine box, I close my eyes for a moment to let the stupid fade. "We're really bad at this," I whisper back finally.

"You're in on this together," the man says from the chair.

Teddy and I turn our attention back to him. My arm's burning from holding the gun up and I switch hands.

"I could never figure out what was going on with you two," the man says.

Yeah, champ, you and me both. This aggravating turd of a human being and his vague bullshit. Violence has never sounded more appealing.

"Who *are* you?" I say, drawing the words out.

"What about waterboarding?" Teddy comes and whispers in my ear.

"I don't know how to fucking waterboard someone!" I answer—realizing only after the words have left my mouth that I said them out loud.

The man laughs as if this is funny. His gaze has been glued on me since we strapped him to the chair. He's barely blinked. The way he looks at me, I feel like he sees underneath my clothes, underneath my skin, and it's stomach-turning. How the hell do we have this guy tied up and I'm holding a gun to his head and yet it feels like he still holds all the power?

"Fine," I say to Teddy. "Let's just kill him and hack him to pieces when we're done."

Okay, now this asshole's smile falters. It lifts my spirit to see his fall.

"You want to blow his brains out, or strangle him? I was thinking a cord around the neck might actually be less messy," Teddy says.

"I hadn't thought of that. I like that," I say, keeping my eyes on Teddy but watching our captive out of the corner of my eye. I can see his expression melt, like he's just now realizing the game has changed and we're the murderers now. "I had thought about slitting his throat, quieter than a gunshot, but I do like the idea of no blood to clean up."

"I mean, he'll probably shit his pants when he dies," Teddy says, also, I think, noticing that we're now beginning to actually frighten the nameless monster. "So there will be *some* cleanup. You know that happens when someone gets hanged or badly strangled? They poop?"

"I did not know that, Teddy, thank you," I say. "Maybe we can put a towel under him first then, make cleanup easier on ourselves."

"Doesn't the name ring a bell? 'Leela Lee,'" the man interrupts, louder than he's spoken yet, a hint of desperation in his voice. "'You shine like a lone lighthouse on a dark sea.'"

The outburst is so strange that Teddy and I exchange a look. But in the pause, the words land, they provoke meaning, and I remember those lines from the 'apology' note I was sent from Genesis.

"Great, he's a poet, too," Teddy says. "Now I *really* hate him."

"Shhhh," I say, putting a finger up, something on the tip of my tongue, on the edge of my brain. "Leela Lee. Why Leela Lee? That's not my name."

I turn and study the pale butterball face that belongs to the amateur executioner. He's not smiling, but he still watches me like I'm the only thing on earth and it still sends goosebumps all over me.

"Is your last name Lee?" I ask, puzzled, trying to put it together.

He brightens.

"Lee," I repeat. A common name. A name I've heard a million times. Then it hits me. I think I know where I know him from. It takes a moment to scan my brain for the rest of his name, but I can see it there, next to a black-and-white yearbook photo. He was in my high school class. He didn't look like this. He had side-parted brown hair that covered his eyes and wore hoodies so big they swallowed him. "Wait. John James Lee?"

"You remember me," John James Lee says, the smile returning.

CHAPTER 58

The thoughts are sticky and hard to shape. John James Lee, who was he? He was nobody to me. He was a boy who worked on sets in theater in high school, he was in crew backstage and I was an actor onstage. I'm not sure we ever said more than ten words to each other. I'm so confused.

"Who is he?" Teddy asks.

"Just—some guy," I finally answer. "From high school. I didn't even know him."

In fact, the only reason I even remember he exists is because Ricky mentioned him the last time we were together. I honestly would have probably lived the rest of my life and never thought about this guy again if it wasn't for that conversation.

John James Lee looks at me shyly, like this reveal makes him Cyrano de Bergerac and not a deranged stalker from hell. Though I know his name and it's clicking into place, I'm even more bewildered knowing more about him.

"He went to your high school?" Teddy asks. "In LA?"

I nod.

"So how does he know Jack?" Teddy asks me.

John James Lee chuckles.

"Shut the hell up," Teddy says, and in a flash he's charging toward John James with his fist raised.

"No, Teddy, no!" I yell, pulling him back by his arm. "You can't leave a mark."

"Okay," Teddy says, catching himself, breathing heavily and stepping backward. "You're right."

"Hearst Castle," John James says.

I've never seen eyes that look so excited and so soulless at the same time.

"Hearst Castle," I repeat, trying out the words. "You know Hearst Castle."

"I *lived* in Hearst Castle." John James cocks his head. "I looked different then, though. Grew a full beard, long hair. It was at least two years after we had graduated. You didn't recognize me."

Full beard. Long hair. The Yeti who lived next door, the one I thought spied on us and Jack thought I was nuts. Oh my God. I never made the connection, I didn't bother to study him hard enough. "JJ?"

He nods.

"You—you followed me to Berkeley?" I ask.

"No. The universe brought us together," he laughs. "That's the funny thing about it. I try to forget you, I try to get away from you, and Leela, the universe keeps bringing us together."

My hand with the gun quivers. I exchange a look with Teddy as the truth takes root in my mind. This guy's been in the background of my life and while I paid him no attention, he has some kind of obsession with me.

"Sorry about Jack," he says gravely. "I felt bad about that, I did. But you asked for it. I thought you wanted it. You wanted all of it. You asked me to smite your enemies. I worked so hard to find a copy of the lethal VixSpex, Leela, and to seek out the people who wronged you, to show you how much I cared. All I've ever wanted was to be your guardian angel, your guardian angel of death."

Teddy turns around and puts his hands over his face. His world's crashing down on him and so is mine. It can't be real. This guy really killed Jack, killed him, but he killed him because of my words and he killed him with my pills. I need a moment. I drop my aching arm with the gun in it. I squat on the floor, balling up, attempting to implode. I want to cry. I can feel a thousand tears, but it's like I'm emotionally constipated. The rage. I feel like it's turning me into a monster, too.

"I love you, Leela," the man who killed the man I love says, and that's what breaks me.

I shoot back up to a standing position. "Get the pills, Teddy. Shove them in his mouth and tape it shut."

Teddy's red in the face, unable to respond. He nods and leaves the room and John James Lee continues staring at me like I'm a whole world. I have so many questions, but I'm not sure I want the answers anymore. It doesn't matter. I know what he did and now I want him gone.

"I'm sorry if I hurt you," he says.

"Don't talk to me."

Teddy comes back in with an orange pill container,

shaking it so it rattles. I nod at him. He pops it open, pouring a dozen pills into his hand.

"Not too many," I say. "Put a couple back. It has to look accidental."

"Yeah, but what if he survives?"

"I guess this will be my final sacrifice," John James says to me. "I always knew I was willing to die for you, Leela."

"Shut the hell up," I say. I nod at Teddy. "Okay, just do it. Get it over with."

John James isn't grinning anymore. There's nothing in his face, nothing in his eyes as he watches me. It's weird—I've always felt watched. I didn't know why. Was it being a woman in this world, the inevitable gaze that follows like a spotlight? Was it my upbringing, hungry for the camera's approval? Was it this strange world where everything's documented and streamed online? But it was more than that; it was John James Lee. I tried so hard to ignore the always-watching world I didn't spot the danger.

I look at him. He looks like someone you'd pass on the street, someone whose name you'd forget right after they tell it to you. I pray that someday I can forget the sight of his grinning face.

As Teddy approaches with his fistful of pills, John James says one last thing. "I'll die happy knowing that you'll never forget me and what I did for you, Leela. Even in death, I'll always be with you. There won't be a day in your life you don't think about me."

Teddy tips John James's head back and shoves the pills his mouth. With a stifled scream, John James chokes on the pills and Teddy tapes his mouth shut, binding it all the way around his head multiple times to really seal the deal.

He stands back, at my side. We watch the monster struggle and choke and swallow, visibly in pain, gagging behind the duct tape, his eyes watering and snot coming out of his nose. It's horrifying. It's satisfying. I can't stop watching.

"We've got to dump him somewhere," Teddy says. "There's a neighborhood not too far from here. But who knows where he lives, maybe we should find somewhere around there."

"Check his pockets?" I ask.

Teddy nods and goes over to John James, who is red in the face and panting through his nose and writhing under the duct tape he's been mummified in. He must have swallowed all the pills by now. He's in such pain and discomfort he's in another world and no longer ogling. I can feel my heart thudding like a bass drum as I think through next steps, like how the hell we're going to transport this guy into Teddy's car without being seen. I chew my cheek and consider all we have to do.

"All he's got in his pockets is this," Teddy says, showing me a key fob.

"Oh," I say. "He drove here."

"Same model as mine," Teddy says. "We could conceivably just … put him in his car when he's passed out, send him to a parking lot in self-driving mode, make it look like he overdosed in his car."

"Teddy, if it's like yours, we could probably just get him in his car and say 'home' and it'll take him home. He'd be found in his parking lot or his driveway."

Teddy and I stand together steeping in thought, two mannequins.

"I could erase his last ride from his system, too," Teddy says. "Just in case anyone looks into it, there would be no connection to this neighborhood tonight. No connection to us."

I nod, hope flickering. I don't know what magic it is, but it's always been this way. Teddy makes me feel like anything's possible. We can get away with anything. Teddy goes out to wander the street with the key to try to locate the car with the button-beep, get it pulled up to the curb. While I wait in the apartment and listen to the sniveling sounds of John James panting out of his nose in the chair, I try my best to focus on other things. I stand at the window and watch the full moon, unblinking and pale blue, a single eye hanging in the night sky. I think of Jack. I think of the man slowly dying from an overdose behind me.

This is for you, Jack.

The fiercest love might be revenge.

By the time Teddy gets back to the apartment, he's a little winded. "He parked like six blocks away, took me forever to find it. Is he still conscious?"

I haven't given John James the satisfaction of even looking at him since Teddy left, but I glance at him now—hunched over, passed out, snoring.

"Barely," I say. "Can we just get him out of here?"

"Let's get the tape off him and see how he does." Teddy walks over and rips the tape off John James's face with an extra-long *snick*. John James's head has fallen forward. "Hey," Teddy says, pushing his head back, slapping his face lightly. The guy's drooling. "Anyone home?"

"He's out cold," I say.

Teddy puts his fingers to the guy's neck. "Pulse is slow."

"Let's get him out, I don't want to look at him anymore."

Teddy and I each get under one of John James's arms and lift him up like we're carrying a passed-out friend at a party. Teddy's sucking in air through his teeth like he's in pain and I'm struggling to keep him up, but we do it, dragging his boots across the hardwood floors. We have to wait a minute at the door for a neighbor to pass, and then we take him outside. The real challenge is the stairs, where both Teddy and I brace ourselves and grip the railing step by step until we reach the bottom. At the curb, the car awaits. Teddy opens the passenger door and we dump John James into the passenger seat. Teddy rounds to the other side, opens the door, and pulls John James into the driver's seat. Then Teddy gets in the car in the passenger's seat and I get in back. Thank God the windows are tinted. As we sit in silence, a woman walks by with a poodle, oblivious to the slow-burn murder underway three feet away from her.

"Prop up his head like this," Teddy says, positioning John James's skull properly on the headrest. "Think I should take his gloves off?"

"Yeah, take off his gloves. No one drives with those on."

Teddy pops open the glove compartment. "Burner smartphone."

"Pocket it and let's get rid of it."

"His registration's here. His address is in Berkeley."

"Where?"

"California Street."

"That's my neighborhood."

Teddy closes the glove compartment. "What a coinky-dink."

"Don't say coinky-dink."

"Ever the critic."

"Ever the dork."

Teddy starts the car with a cheerful little ding and navigates the computer screen, erasing today's trips. He wipes the screen for fingerprints, just in case, and turns to me. "I think we got everything."

I nod, eyeing the breathing corpse in the front seat. "Is he actually going to die, though?"

"Yeah. I gave him far beyond a lethal dose. He'll be long gone by the time he gets to Berkeley, that's a drive from here. You want to wait and make sure?"

"No," I say. "I trust you."

Teddy and I get out of the car. John James is pale, slumped. I stare at him, hard, one last time, and feel a steely contentment knowing he's dying. Fuck you, stranger. Fuck you for taking everything from me.

Teddy leans into the passenger side and says, "System: take me home."

He slams the door. The car takes off into the dark night with a dying man in the driver's seat. Teddy puts his arm around me and we stay there for a long time in silent disbelief. There's too much to process. It's throbbing like a headache. Everything hurts. I don't know how I'll ever move on from this. John James will be dead soon, but he was right: I'll never go a day in my life without thinking of him. I'll never think of Jack without thinking of him. He'll stick with me like a curse.

"You hungry?" Teddy finally asks. "I still have that pasta from earlier."

I snicker because it seems so absurd, to eat pasta after what we just went through.

"What?" Teddy says. "Revenge really works up an appetite, don't you think?"

"Is this what we're going to do?" I ask, turning to him. "Are we going to be breaking dark jokes about this traumatic shit for the rest of our lives?"

"What else can we do?" he asks.

Under the streetlamp with the shadows on his face, Teddy looks so tired, so worn down. Without his usual smile, I can see his suffering. I guess that's life, right? I guess that really is how we'll forge on, cracking jokes and playing pretend while the darkness lurks.

"Sure, I'll have some pasta," I say.

CHAPTER 59

It's no shocker that Teddy and I are messes after that—a miserable cocktail of PTSD, paranoia, and insomnia. Thanks to a meetup with TaskyDick in a big-box store parking lot, we learn within forty-eight hours that John James Lee did overdose, wherein I run to a nearby planter and vomit with a catastrophic sense of relief. Teddy just closes his eyes and leans on the side of his car, taking breaths deep enough to move mountains.

"Process this information however you want, kids, but remember I'm charging by the second," TaskyDick says, pointing to his watch.

"You can go now," Teddy says.

"Until next time," TaskyDick says with a bow, taking his bags of merchandise to his car.

I convince Teddy to take time off work and go on a trip to LA with me, get out of the south Bay. I tell him the sunshine and the change of scenery will do us good. Not that I'd say it out loud, but whenever I'm in despair, all I want is to see Shasta. Teddy picks up Pickles from the animal boarding house and we pack up the car and the three of us drive down there together. The sweet relief of seeing the metropolis in the rearview mirror, the silent, green stretch of central California farmland, is indescribable. And yet I know that it doesn't matter where we drive, how far we go. Everything still rings with tragedy. The signs for Fresno remind me of Madison La Rosa, a billboard for Lotus Vineyards offers wine tastings, and I keep noticing *Re-Elect Tiger McBride* bumper stickers. As Teddy's self-driving car speeds down the freeway at a solid sixty-five miles per hour, the memory of Eve and all she went through just to die at the hands of my fucking stalker prickles my eyeballs with tears. I turn on a heavy metal album to drown out my feelings.

"Pickles hates this music," Teddy tells me, pointing to Pickles sitting on his lap, who looks perfectly content because she's pretty much always perfectly content.

"Don't blame your terrible taste in music on Pickles." I reach over and scratch under her chin. "I miss my cat."

"You should have brought her on the trip with us."

"Well, first, Shasta's allergic to cats. Second, you can't bring cats places like that without them getting all wigged out."

"One of the many reasons dogs are superior."

"Shut up," I say, but I keep petting Pickles, because I have to admit she's grown on me.

When we get to LA, Shasta is immediately mortifying. She's wearing her pink robe with a feather boa and introduces her cockatoo Sugarkins to Pickles using a weird baby voice she uses to talk for her bird.

"Wookie here, a big fuwwy fuwball fwend!" she says.

"I'm so sorry," I whisper to Teddy, whose face has lit up with amusement.

"Teddy, I've heard so much about you," Shasta says.

What? No, she hasn't. But whatever. I can tell she's just fascinated by Teddy's existence because she remembers Jack. She's also a thirsty-ass crone, telling Teddy how "handsome" he looks and asking weird mom shit like if he's financially stable and whether he wants children someday. By a half hour into our trip, I am already seriously contemplating getting back in the car and driving home. But maybe that's the upside-down positive effect this trip is meant to have—because when I'm busy being irritated by my mother, John James Lee stops knocking at my memory.

And then there's Huey, my mom's beau who apparently lives with her now. I'm polite to him, even though he's closer to my age and spends most of his time vaping fruity-smelling clouds on the balcony while gabbing on the phone.

"He's a businessman," Shasta explains proudly.

"What business?" Teddy asks as he studies the wall, where every childhood headshot of mine still hangs. Me in tutus, me in tap outfits, me with my hair teased and lipstick looking like a pageant child from hell.

"Birdseed," Shasta says, casting a dreamy glance at Huey who is currently picking his nose and practically shouting into his phone outside. "We have so much in common."

Lord, love makes people stupid.

Shasta orders a nice dinner though and invites Ricky

over. After Huey leaves early to go line dancing, Teddy passes out in the guest room, spooning Pickles. I stay up with Ricky and Shasta eating diet ice cream sandwiches that taste as disappointing as they sound. We sit at the dining room table watching Shasta's floating feather duster dance around the apartment like it's entertainment and laugh about old times. The time Shasta caught me and Ricky smoking weed in my room in high school and demanded to get high with us, resulting in my mom getting so paranoid she became convinced she was having a heart attack and then called an ambulance. The time when Ricky painted a covert penis on the backdrop of the set for *Our Town*. The guy with amazing long hair who Ricky and I both had a crush on junior year who became a record producer and just won a Grammy.

"Oh, since we're gossiping about high school," Ricky says, licking his fingers. "Remember that guy John who was in crew with me? John James Lee?"

I'm so stunned by the mention of his name that I have no reaction. I am a woman made of ice.

"We talked about him last time you were down here. The one who had such a thing for you?" Ricky clarifies.

The relaxed smile that has been on my face since this kitchen table stroll down memory lane began melts. "Um, yeah. I think so."

"I heard he OD'ed," Ricky whispered.

"No!" Shasta exclaims, even though she probably has no clue who we're talking about.

"Yeah. Apparently he lived up near you now, LeeLee. You know that? Up in Berkeley. You ever see him?"

"Nope, never." I wad up the ice cream sandwich

wrapper in my hand, crush it so tiny and so compact it's like a paper bullet in my palm.

"He had *such* a thing for you," Ricky reminds me, really twisting that knife in.

"I think I remember him," Shasta says, snapping her pink-manicured fingertips. "Wasn't his mom really weird? I feel like I met his mom once."

"His mom was *bizarre*."

The mention of John James Lee has blown out the flame in me. I need to leave the room, say goodbye, end this conversation. I start to get up but Ricky pulls my sleeve. He's searing me with his gorgeous brown gaze, like he knows I'm holding back something, like he can see I'm lying to his face. Like he can see I'm forever marked, scarred by what I've done, that I'm a murderer.

"LeeLee," Ricky says. "We know you're keeping something from us."

The feeling—like a trap door opening under my legs.

"We know, honey," Shasta says gently. "We know. We can tell."

I look from one to the other, uncertain how to respond. The potent mix of being called out unexpectedly and of disgusting diet ice cream makes my gut ache.

"Tell what?" I finally manage, faking a half-smile.

Shasta and Ricky exchange a look and all I can think is, how? How would they know something? Am I that transparent? Oh God, did the police reach out to them? Are they looking for me?

"You and Teddy," Ricky says. "Don't pretend like you don't know what we're talking about."

I breathe in sharply, trying to remain calm when the

relief I'm experiencing is a goddamn tsunami. Of course they don't know about what I've done. I let out a little laugh, a little pressure release. "Oh, we're just hanging out a lot."

"*Hanging out*," Ricky says skeptically.

"He's *so* good-looking, honey," Shasta tells me.

"What is going on?" Ricky asks. "Details. Now."

"We're just friends," I tell them with a shrug.

Sometimes the truth is bigger than words.

I crawl into bed with Teddy after that, Pickles in the middle. I lie there looking at the window, the glow of streetlight, the curtain moving. I think of ghosts. I wonder if John James Lee is one. But I guess it doesn't matter—either way, he'll always haunt me.

"You okay?" Teddy whispers, reaching across the sleeping pup to touch my hand.

"Yeah. You?"

"I was just lying here thinking about Jack," Teddy whispers. "Remembering the first time he called me and told me about you."

"What'd he say?"

"He said, 'I met a real-life femme fatale.'"

I choke on a little laugh, it's so perfectly nerdy and Jack.

"He was right," Teddy says, squeezing my hand.

I guess he was, wasn't he?

CHAPTER 60

Silicon Valley is at its most beautiful from a distance. Up here, on the top of the hill, Teddy and I catch our breath and behold the valley. A violet haze of smog blurs the view of the bay. The flatland is polka-dotted with trees and neat rows of buildings. And in the middle of the suburban spread of neighborhoods, the enormous eye-shaped Jolvix campus stares back at us.

"Sit?" I ask, pointing to a flat rock.

"Sitting is my favorite part about hiking," Teddy says.

We take a seat, sharing sips of water from a bottle. This has become our spot. It's where Teddy and I can meet and feel fully free to talk about anything we want, where we don't have to pretend anymore. It's been six weeks since we killed John James, six weeks of being nervous wrecks and faking like life is normal. Six weeks of waiting for a hard knock on the door that never comes. Every time I think the anxiety's faded, I wake up choking from a nightmare remembering the relentless stare of his spiritless eyes.

"I don't know where to go from here," I say, my chest tight. "I don't know how to keep going after what we've gone through."

He shrugs, putting the water bottle down. "You just keep going."

"Very deep. Must have taken you a while to come up with that one."

"Life's not that complicated, Leels."

"I think it's incredibly complicated." I kick up some dirt, just to see a cloud. "I'm tired of how fucking complicated it is."

"Then simplify it."

"Can I just complain without you trying to tell me how to fix it?" I ask sharply.

He's quiet, shaking his head at me like I'm the annoying one. The sound of footsteps behind us makes both Teddy and I whip around, though it's only another hiker passing. We're still twitchy ever since the whole murder thing. After the silence settles again, we turn back to the valley, that depressing unblinking eye of Jolvix upstaging everything else within view.

"I think I might want to move somewhere else," I say. "Far away from this mess. Somewhere full of trees, where I can have a garden and grow flowers and see deer in my backyard." I swallow a lump. "I want to start over."

Teddy smiles, but it's a bittersweet one. "If that's what you want, do it."

"Maybe I will," I say, like I've accepted a challenge.

And all at once the future gleams with promise. I can imagine a quiet world that exists somewhere without the rushing sound of traffic in my ears. A place where I can see the stars at night, where I can hear crickets, where my cat could chase birds and butterflies. Where there are no people to watch me. No people—just a single person.

"Would you come with me?" I ask Teddy.

He holds his breath for a few beats as he thinks about it. I clench up, afraid he's going to tell me no. He has an important job here. He has a car and a condo and a life. Suddenly, my ring finger buzzes and he lets out a breath.

"That answer your question?" he asks.

My finger itches madly and I scratch it, muttering, "You know I hate it when you do that."

"That's why I do it," he says, grinning. "I love irritating you."

"You're so good at it, too," I say.

I lean my head on his shoulder anyway.

I've done some terrible things. I've kept secrets I shouldn't have, secrets that resulted in widespread danger somewhere in the dark web that I can't even fully comprehend. I've wished people dead who then died because of me. I killed a man. I don't know how I can keep living with myself sometimes. But this is the truth I will wrestle with and reckon with all my life. These are the things I've done that I'll keep locked up. This is who I truly am: the raw, flawed creature forever hiding behind my mask.

Just like everyone else, I guess.

ONE MORE THING ...

Want to read a bonus epilogue for *The Slaying Game* from Teddy's point of view? Sign up for my newsletter and download it for free!

If you enjoyed *The Slaying Game*, good news: there are five other books set in the same universe. I call them **The Jolvix Episodes,** and you can **grab the first three books in this discounted box set** or read them one by one.

NOTE: These standalone novels can be read in whatever order you want, but *Eve in Overdrive* is technically a prequel to *The Slaying Game*.

- **AMEN MAXINE:** A newlywed woman's smart device begins offering chilling predictions about her husband.

- **VIOLET IS NOWHERE:** A kidnapped woman and a stranger on the end of a phone line have one week to figure out how they're connected or their lives are over.

- **WHAT JANUARY REMEMBERS:** A dysfunctional family and their sentient companion bot gather for the holidays for the first time since their last Christmas together—which ended in attempted murder.

- **PEARL IN DEEP:** The love of one woman's life turns out to be a psychopath with a disturbing talent for deepfake video.

- **EVE IN OVERDRIVE:** An outspoken journalist buys a cutting-edge car only to find herself at the mercy of a vengeful internet troll.

- **THE SLAYING GAME:** A former Jolvix employee ends up at the center of a serial killer's deadly game.

- Or you can grab the first three Jolvix Episodes in this box set.

A NOTE FROM THE AUTHOR

Hey you! Yeah, you! Thank you for giving my book a chance. As an indie author, I put a *lot* of time and sweat into each book—not just writing, but editing, marketing, and everything else it takes to guide a book through the whole process from a glimmer in the brain to a real, actual thing you can hold in your hands. And I appreciate every single reader who takes a chance on me and my weird, dark little books.

If you enjoyed this one, please consider leaving a review. Reviews truly make an author's world go round. If you're interested in keeping up with book news, please join my newsletter or follow me on social media. And I love to hear from readers anytime at faith@faithgardner.com.

As always, I tried my damndest to fix every typo, but alas, I am only human. If you spot an error, please let me know! I appreciate every reader who makes me look smarter.

ALSO BY FAITH GARDNER

THE JOLVIX EPISODES

Amen Maxine

Violet Is Nowhere

What January Remembers

Pearl in Deep

Eve in Overdrive

The Slaying Game

OTHER BOOKS

The Second Life of Ava Rivers

Perdita

How We Ricochet

Girl on the Line

ABOUT THE AUTHOR

Faith Gardner is the author of ten books, mostly thrillers. When she's not writing, she's probably playing music with her band Plot 66, cooking up a storm, or reading books in a bubble bath. She's also a huge fan of true crime, documentaries, and classic movies—with a special place in her dark little heart for melodrama and anything Hitchcock. She lives in the Bay Area with her family and you can find her at faithgardner.com.

Printed in the USA
CPSIA information can be obtained
at www.ICGtesting.com
LVHW091105261223
767447LV00031B/417